OLYMPUS BOUND

She grabbed the shafts in the thief's hands and stood above him, her feet braced on either side of his hips.

"Tell me where the rest of your friends are, *mortal*."

He stared up at her, pale eyes narrowed with pain, but said nothing.

The Huntress shook her head with a frown. "Is that how you want to play this? Do you know who I am?"

His lips twisted. "Do you?"

She barked a laugh in his face. "Right now, I'm She Who Leads the Chase. And you're my prey." She levered the shafts wider, tearing at the holes in his hands. "Don't forget—some predators like to play with their food. So start talking while you still have a few fingers left."

By Jordanna Max Brodsky

Olympus Bound

The Immortals
Winter of the Gods
Olympus Bound

OLYMPUS BOUND

OLYMPUS BOUND: BOOK 3

JORDANNA MAX BRODSKY

www.orbitbooks.net

ORBIT

First published in Great Britain in 2017 by Orbit

1 3 5 7 9 10 8 6 4 2

Copyright © 2017 by Jordanna Max Brodsky

Excerpt from *Strange Practice* by Vivian Shaw
Copyright © 2017 by Vivian Shaw

The moral right of the author has been asserted.

A CIP catalogue record for this book
is available from the British Library.

ISBN 978-0-356-50730-9

Papers used by Orbit are from well-managed forests
and other responsible sources.

MIX
Paper from
responsible sources
FSC® C104740

Orbit
An imprint of
Little, Brown Book Group
Carmelite House
50 Victoria Embankment
London EC4Y 0DZ

An Hachette UK Company
www.hachette.co.uk

www.orbitbooks.net

For Tegan, my beloved sister in storytelling

CONTENTS

THE GODS' FAMILY TREE

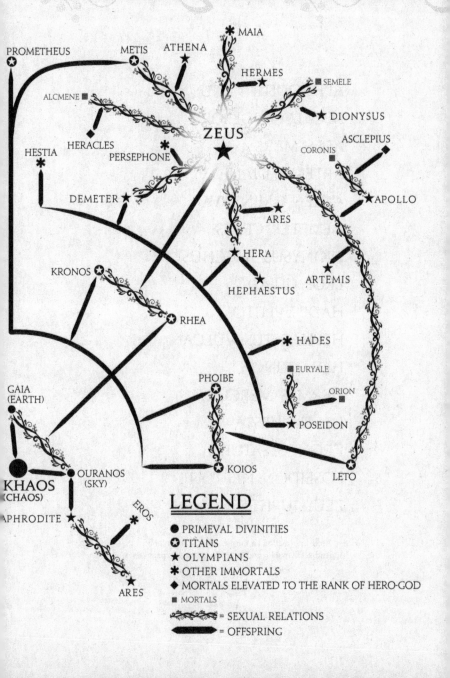

THE GODS' ROMAN NAMES

APHRODITE: VENUS

APOLLO: APOLLO

ARES: MARS

ARTEMIS: DIANA

ATHENA: MINERVA

DEMETER: CERES

DIONYSUS: BACCHUS

EROS: CUPID

HADES: PLUTO

HEPHAESTUS: VULCAN

HERA: JUNO

HERMES: MERCURY

HESTIA: VESTA

KRONOS: SATURN

POSEIDON: NEPTUNE

ZEUS: JUPITER

For more information on the gods, please consult the
Appendix: Olympians and Other Immortals on page 489.

When Morning in her saffron robe had cast her light across
    the earth,
Zeus, lover of lightning, called the gods in council
on the topmost crest of serrated Olympus.
Then he spoke and all the other gods gave ear.
"Hear me," said he, "gods and goddesses too,
that I may speak as my heart urges.
Let none of you, neither goddess nor god,
try to cross my laws,
but obey me every one of you that I may quickly
bring this matter to an end."

Homer, *The Iliad*,
CIRCA EIGHTH CENTURY BC

Chapter 1

SHE WHO LOVES
THE CHASE

Just outside the city walls of ancient Ostia, on the banks of the River Tiber, the Huntress stalked her prey down the street of the dead with only the moon to light her way.

She walked with silent tread on wide basalt paving stones still warm from the unrelenting summer heat. Her stealth was superfluous: Even if her boots scuffed the street, the piercing drone of cicadas would drown out any sound, and the man she hunted seemed oblivious to everything but the mausoleums around him.

Yet she studied him with a hawk's keen gaze. He was young, clean-shaven, his weak chin and protruding nose accented by blond hair shorn mercilessly close to the scalp. His haircut and muscled physique proclaimed him a soldier. Another foolish mortal recruit in an ancient battle between gods.

The Huntress felt no sympathy. He might be a mere foot soldier, but his army had destroyed her life. They had ripped her from the world she knew, and now they threatened what little family she had left. Somewhere, they held her father captive. Somewhere, they tortured him and prepared him for sacrifice.

Perhaps right here in Ostia.

Either this young man would lead her to her father or he would die. Simple as that.

She followed his gaze to the necropolis's older buildings, each pockmarked with niches just big enough to hold an urn brimming with ashes. The more recent mausoleums, she saw, housed grand sarcophagi instead. Even the passage of centuries wouldn't erase the scenes of myth and history so deeply carved into their marble sides.

The young man paused before one of the stone coffins that flanked the mausoleum's entrance. With a reverent finger, he traced its sculpted depictions of Sun and Moon, Birth and Death.

Then he quickly crossed himself.

The Huntress shuddered: In this pagan city, a mere twenty miles from the Empire's seat in Rome, the Christian gesture seemed a harbinger of things to come.

Once, she'd watched with pleasure as pious Romans sent their loved ones skyward on the plumes of funeral pyres. The smoke would reach the very summit of Mount Olympus and swirl about the feet of the gods themselves. But more and more, the Romans chose to bury their dead within these marble tombs, where the corpses could await bodily resurrection. A sign, she knew, that soon the Empire's citizens would abandon the Olympians entirely, praying only for their promised reunion with the Christ.

The Huntress imagined the richly bedecked corpses in their cold tombs. *Meat turned to rot turned to dust,* she thought with disgust. The Christians waited in vain for a resurrection that would never occur and a god who did not exist. A bitter smirk lifted the corner of her mouth. *It serves them right.*

At least for now, the Olympian Goddess of War and Wisdom still guarded Ostia's main gate with her stern gaze: Minerva, whom the Greeks called Athena, carved in stone with upswept wings and a regal helmet. The sight gave the Huntress a measure of comfort. *We're not completely forgotten. Not yet.*

She hid in Minerva's moonshadow and watched her prey

leave the necropolis behind as he ventured into the city itself. He strode down the wide avenue of the Decumanus Maximus, past empty taverns and shops, guildhalls and warehouses. The man wore all black as camouflage in the darkened town, but he took few other precautions, walking boldly down the middle of the deserted thoroughfare.

He clearly hadn't counted on Minerva's vengeful half sister following in his wake.

He passed the public baths, bedecked with mosaics of Neptune, and the amphitheater, adorned with grotesque marble masks, before finally turning off the avenue to wander deeper into the sleeping city. Only then did the Huntress emerge from behind her marble sibling like a statue come to life—as tall and imperious as Minerva herself, moving with such grace and speed she seemed to float on wings of her own.

She darted silently from shadow to shadow. With her black hair and clothes, the Huntress melted into the night. Only her silver eyes gave her away, reflecting the moonlight like deep forest pools.

As she passed the darkened buildings, she could imagine how they'd appear when full of life. Vendors and merchants would clamor for attention, the perfume of their leeks and lemons fighting the stench of the human urine that produced such brilliant blues and reds in the nearby dye vats. The warehouses would bulge with foreign grain and local salt. Shopkeepers would hawk elephant ivory from the colonies in Africa, fish from the nearby Mare Nostrum, and purple-veined marble from Phrygia in the east, all destined to sate the appetites of the wealthy Romans a day's journey up the river. Great crowds of toga-clad men and modestly veiled women would bustle down the Decumanus Maximus, pushing their way past ragged children begging for scraps. While some headed for the amphitheater's worldly pleasures, others processed to the grand temples to offer sacrifices to Vulcan or Venus—or even to the Huntress herself.

But as she followed her prey down an alley bordered by tall brick tenements, she knew this man sought a very different sanctuary. Of the dozens of temples in Ostia, a full fifteen housed a cult dedicated to a single god: a deity not numbered among the Olympians, one who would never claim as many followers as the Christ. Yet one who held the power to destroy her.

Mithras.

Her heart picked up speed. This could be the end of her search. The most famous of Mithras's sanctuaries lay at the end of the alley: the Mithraeum of the Seven Spheres. Unlike the Olympians' temples, graceful public edifices with open colonnades and wide entrances, Mithras's shrines lay tucked into caves or small buildings, where his rites were kept secret from all but the cult's initiates. Harmless rites honoring a harmless god—or so the Olympians had once thought. Now the Huntress knew better.

Fire scorching my flesh. Water flooding my lungs. Torture of both body and soul. The memories cracked across her brain like a whip. She forced them aside, turning her attention to the temple before her.

From the outside, the mithraeum seemed no more than an unadorned shed of layered brick. Locked iron grates sealed off the single small window and narrow doorway. The Huntress had searched the mithraeum before and found no evidence of her father's prison. Then again, the cult's leader—the Pater Patrum—was notoriously wily. *The entrance to their lair might be here after all,* she hoped, taking a careful step closer to her quarry.

The young man in black fished a pair of lock picks out of his pack. The gate squealed open. He strode forward slowly with a gasp of reverence.

The Huntress repressed a disappointed groan. He didn't look like a man returning to his cult's headquarters: He looked like a worshiper entering the Holy of Holies for the first time. *This is a pilgrimage. A holy errand. The rest of his army waits elsewhere with their Pater Patrum. And that means my father is elsewhere, too.*

She'd hoped to simply follow her prey to his cult's base, reconnoiter, then devise a plan to rescue her father. Now she'd need to force the correct location out of him instead. Unfortunately, initiates into this cult never broke, even under torture.

At least so far.

She slipped to the side of the barred window and peered inside the cramped shrine. Low platforms bordered a central aisle so the cult's members could recline during their ceremonial feasts. Black-and-white mosaics covered the platforms and floor, their designs faded and chipped; though her night vision rivaled a wolf's, she couldn't decipher the images in the dark. But when the man pulled a small lamp from his bag, she saw the signs of the zodiac adorning the feasting platforms: a fish for Pisces, balanced scales for Libra, two men for Gemini.

Along the length of the aisle, seven black mosaic arcs on the floor symbolized the seven celestial spheres that gave the mithraeum its name. On the platforms' sides, the tiles formed crude representations of the Olympians—or rather, of the heavenly bodies named for them. A woman holding an arching veil above her head for the planet Venus, a man with a spear and helmet for Mars. The Huntress saw herself there, too: a woman bearing an arrow and a crescent. Fitting symbols for the one called Diana, Goddess of the Moon, by the men who usually worshiped in this sanctuary. Across the Aegean, the Greeks named her Huntress, Mistress of Beasts, Goddess of the Wild, and above all—Artemis.

What name would this man use if he turned around and saw me? she wondered. *Pretender? Pagan? Likely, he'd dispense with such niceties and just slice out my heart.*

At the far end of the aisle hung an oval relief that encompassed the cult's entire religion in a single carven image: the "tauroctony"—the bull killing. Mithras, handsome in his pointed Phrygian cap, perched on the bull's back, one knee bent and his other foot resting on a rear hoof. He plunged his knife into the beast's neck, completing the sacrifice. A dog, a snake, a scorpion, and a crow encircled the bull. Like everything else in Mithraism, the image contained several layers of meaning. To a woman like the Huntress, who preferred a world of starkly defined categories— night and day, female and male, immortal and mortal—such complexities provided yet another reason to despise the cult.

The animals in the tauroctony symbolized the constellations that rotated across the sky on the celestial spheres. Mithras, or so his followers believed, controlled those spheres. To some who feasted atop the sanctuary's platforms and offered sacrifices upon its altar, Mithras was only that: a god of stars, one more deity among the dozens worshiped by Ostia's citizens. But not to the young man gazing upon the tauroctony with a fanatic's fervor. To him, Mithraism was no mere Roman mystery cult; it was the truest form of the one religion that terrified the usually fearless Huntress: Christianity.

According to the cult's pseudo-Christian doctrine, the shifting of the celestial spheres would usher in the "Last Age," a twisted version of the biblical End of Days. Mithras-as-Jesus would walk the earth once more, bestowing salvation and eternal life upon his followers. Only one thing stood in the way of that promised resurrection: the existence of the Olympians. Thus, to make way for their savior's return, the Mithraists had sworn to destroy the gods.

And now, finally, the Huntress thought, imagining the pain she would inflict on the man before her, *the gods are fighting back.*

She watched him crouch before one of the black mosaic arcs; he pressed a finger against the tiles, tracing the seam as if he— not his god—could shift the celestial sphere it represented and move the world into the Last Age.

He reached inside his pack for a pouch of tools. A line of sweat trickled down his smooth jaw as he placed the blade of a chisel against the floor and raised a hammer.

The Huntress wasn't about to let him steal the mosaic. She

didn't care about preserving some other god's holy artifact, but she didn't intend to let the thief get what he'd come for. As an authentic sacred symbol, the arc might hold some unknown power. More than one Olympian had died at the hands of a Mithraist wielding a divine weapon—she couldn't let the cult acquire any additions to their arsenal.

Very slowly, the woman once known as Artemis, the Far Shooter, turned away from the window and slid her pack off her shoulders. Soundlessly, she withdrew two gleaming lengths of metal and screwed them together at the handgrip to construct a divine weapon of her own: a golden bow forged by Hephaestus the Smith.

She slipped two arrows between the knuckles of her right hand and aimed their razor-sharp tips at the back of the thief's neck. *This would be much easier if I could just kill him right now,* she thought. But that wasn't part of the plan. She needed him to talk first. And she couldn't simply shoot him in the leg and tie him up—she'd tried that with the last Mithraist she'd stalked. He'd been about to haul off an altar from a mithraeum in Rome. When she'd charged toward him, her arrow at the ready, he'd simply used his own dagger to stab himself in the heart before she could elicit more than a terrified moan. Clearly, the Mithraists were under strict instructions to avoid capture at all costs.

She spread her knuckles a little wider. With a nearly inaudible thrum, both arrows flew between the window bars and into the sanctuary. The young man grunted in astonished pain and dropped his tools as the shafts simultaneously pierced the backs of both his hands. He tried to rise, but she tore through the doorway, moving nearly as fast as the arrows, and smashed him to the ground; the back of his skull thwacked against the tiles. The lamp rocked, its beam spotlighting the impassive face of the carven Mithras watching the chaos below.

She grabbed the shafts in the thief's hands and stood above him, her feet braced on either side of his hips.

"Tell me where the rest of your friends are, *mortal*."

He stared up at her, pale eyes narrowed with pain, but said nothing.

The Huntress shook her head with a frown. "Is that how you want to play this? Do you know who I am?"

His lips twisted. "Do you?"

She barked a laugh in his face. "Right now, I'm She Who Leads the Chase. And you're my prey." She levered the shafts wider, tearing at the holes in his hands. "Don't forget—some predators like to play with their food. So start talking while you still have a few fingers left."

Chapter 2

THE PHILOSOPHER

Professor Theodore Schultz usually spent Columbia's summer session teaching small seminars to an eclectic mix of the university's overeager and underachieving. On days as nice as this one, when the sunlight burned hot and the breeze blew cool, he liked to bring his classes onto the quad. Surrounded by youthful faces—enthusiastic and bored and everything in between—he imparted his love for myth and history in much the same way he imagined Plato or Aristotle might have in ancient Athens's outdoor agora.

But today Theo sat on the quad with only books and notes to surround him. He barely noticed the smell of new-cut grass or the laughter of a nearby circle of students playing Frisbee. Despite the sun beating on his shoulders, his mind kept tumbling back to the previous December. He could still feel the wind's bite, the snow's sting. It all came back in an instant: the desperate flight over New York Harbor in Hermes' winged cap, the weight of Selene's limp body, her sad *"I love you, you know"* as she pushed away his grip and slipped through the clouds. He'd been spared the sight of his lover's body slamming into the water and splintering apart. That didn't stop him from imagining it every time he closed his eyes.

When he'd first met Selene, he'd thought her odd. A private investigator who kept the world at bay with an icy stare and a bitter laugh. Her reticence made sense once he learned—after a week of terror and elation—that she was actually the Greek goddess Artemis. As with all the Olympians, her powers had faded after millennia bereft of worship but, unlike her avaricious kin, Selene had never stooped to brutality to restore her strength.

Nonetheless, she'd been unable to prevent the series of human sacrifices that had restored many of her abilities. With Theo at her side, she'd become an avenging goddess once more, her senses keen as a hawk's, her strength beyond mortal imagining. He'd thought her invincible. He was wrong.

After her death at the hands of the Mithraic cult, he'd been broken in both body and spirit, unable to eat, barely able to speak. For the first time in his thirty-three years, he'd thought death would be easier than living. With his friends' help, he'd finally moved out of that darkness, but he'd still spent the spring semester too devastated by grief to do more than sleepwalk through the classes he supposedly taught. The university administration readily agreed he should take the summer off. They probably imagined he'd spend it recuperating on a beach. Instead, he'd barely left the library, and when he did, on a day like today, he took the books with him.

He adjusted his glasses and rolled his neck. *You're a Makarites,* he reminded himself. *A "Blessed One." You can find the answers you seek, just like Jason found the Golden Fleece.* In antiquity, epic heroes such as Jason and Perseus had won the title of Makarites by feats of arms. Theo, on the other hand, had earned the epithet through his studies of the gods and their stories. His status as a Makarites attracted the Olympians; it even allowed him to use the divine weapons most of the gods were too faded to wield themselves. But so far, it hadn't helped him on his current—and most vital—quest.

He put aside a treatise on Platonic solids and pulled a narrow wooden sounding board from his satchel. Hunching over it, he plucked the single string.

"Didn't know you were the hippie sing-along type."

He looked up to see Ruth Willever standing before him, her face alight with gentle teasing.

"To what do I owe this honor?" He managed an answering smile for his friend.

"I saw you working outside, and I was done at the lab, so I thought I'd pick you up and walk you home."

"I feel like a fifties schoolgirl. You want to carry my books?"

She laughed too heartily for his lame joke, no doubt thrilled that he'd attempted any humor at all.

"I've got plenty of books of my own, thank you." She lifted her capacious tote bag, probably full of tomes on kidney function or enzyme structure or something else Theo found impressive and soporific in equal measure. He didn't ask why she was coming over to his house; since he'd lost Selene, Ruth had become his unofficial housemate and perennial dinner guest. If it weren't for her, he wouldn't eat at all. "It's six o'clock," she reminded him.

"I thought I still had half an hour before my daily force-feeding."

She plopped down beside him, hiking her skirt to her knees so she could stretch her bare legs across the cushion of grass. "I'm early. Too nice a day to stay at a lab bench." She glanced at the sounding board on his lap. "Do I even want to know what that is?"

"It's a monochord." He plucked the single string again.

"Seems like you'd play some pretty crappy songs with only one string."

"It's more than a musical instrument. It's an ancient experimental apparatus."

Ruth's eyes lit. No skepticism, no doubt, just complete fascination. "Explain."

So he did. He'd spent so long alone with his research that sharing his findings—even the limited portion he could allow Ruth to know—felt like kindling a long-dormant spark. In the grief of the last six months, he'd lost sight of his lifelong passion for learning. Now Ruth's excitement fed his own, and he found himself actually enjoying his discoveries for the first time since he'd made them.

He lifted the monochord with a hint of his old flair for theatrics. "I'm about to demonstrate the discovery that fundamentally altered mankind's perception of the universe."

Ruth put a hand to her heart in a suitably dramatic gasp. "My goodness. Please go on."

The gesture made him pause. Teasing, play, fun...they still felt awkward to Theo. He felt like a stroke victim deprived of speech, laboriously relearning the words he'd known since childhood. Ruth was his therapist, coaxing and prodding him toward recovery even when she pretended not to. Now she sat staring at him hopefully. Waiting.

"The Greeks once sought the answers to life's mysteries in myth," he said finally.

Her smile froze, dimmed. Theo, too, had once sought answers in the ancient stories. In a woman who'd stepped out of myth itself to take over his life. A woman light-years away from everything Ruth represented.

"But eventually," he went on, ignoring her obvious discomfort, "as their civilization progressed, Plato and Socrates and the other philosophers began to look for new ways to understand the world."

"They turned to science?" The sudden insistence in Ruth's tone pulled him up short. It was the closest she'd ever come to outright begging him to finally move past Selene and turn to her instead.

"Yes, *they* did," he said with careful emphasis. He looked away from her flash of disappointment and down to his instrument once more. "Not all at once, not very quickly, but yeah. Greek philosophers walked along a bridge between worlds, trying to reconcile their religious beliefs with their new understanding of logic and reason. It all started with Pythagoras."

Ruth crossed her legs and leaned her chin on a fist in a pose of determined interest. "*A* squared plus *b* squared equals *c* squared," she said with forced cheer.

I don't deserve her, Theo thought, not for the first time. *Another woman would've gotten fed up with my depression months ago.* "I see you haven't forgotten ninth-grade geometry," he said, offering a small smile. "But the truth is, Pythagoras probably didn't discover his right-triangle theorem; the Babylonians knew about it long before the Greeks. His real contribution"—Theo lifted the monochord—"was this."

He plucked the string once more. Then he placed a finger exactly halfway along it and plucked it again, the note considerably higher. "See, I make the string half as long, and the new note is exactly one octave above the first." He slid his finger down the string. "If I stop the string two-thirds of the way down, it produces a perfect fifth. Make it three-quarters instead, and we get a perfect fourth." He demonstrated each interval in turn, then repeated the pattern as he kept talking. "Those three ratios—one to two, two to three, three to four—produce three intervals that just happen to be the most pleasing to the ear, at least in Western music."

Seeing Ruth's foot tapping, he couldn't resist altering the rhythm of the notes just slightly and launching into the guitar riff from "Wild Thing." Ruth's eyebrows shot upward and soon she was crooning, *"You make my heart sing!"* in her sweet contralto, twitching her fists in a series of highly restrained dance moves.

Theo couldn't help grinning and singing along. *I haven't smiled this much in months,* he realized. It was almost enough to make him forget the real purpose behind his research into Pythagoras. Almost.

He finished the song with the closest approximation to a trill he could coax from the single string and then gave Ruth a round of applause. She bowed shyly and lay back on the grass with a laugh, her head only a few inches from his lap. She squinted against the sun, then shaded her eyes and tilted her face toward him.

"So what do your harmonic ratios have to do with Mithraism?" she asked carefully.

Ruth had learned the truth about the Athanatoi—Those Who Do Not Die—the night he lost Selene. Sometimes he thought she didn't totally believe it all—his semi-immortal girlfriend and her Olympian family, the ancient Mithras cult out to kill them led by Saturn, Selene's own grandfather—but she pretended for his sake. She knew Saturn had escaped after causing Selene's death, and she believed that Theo's research aimed at finding him again. A hundred times, she'd told him revenge wouldn't bring him happiness. He'd managed to convince her that he just needed to stop the Mithraists before they hurt anyone else. She didn't like his explanation, but she'd finally accepted it.

Too bad it wasn't true.

"Mithraism is a syncretic religion," he told her now. "It combines elements from all sorts of sources. And some of their beliefs about astronomy and salvation may have been inspired by Pythagoras." That much was true, although it was far from the real reason for his interest.

"Huh. And I thought Pythagoras was just a mathematician," Ruth said a little wistfully, as if nostalgic for a time before the gods had waltzed into her life. Yet she'd stuck by Theo for the last six months, nursing him through the injuries—both physical and otherwise—that he'd received the night he and Selene drove the Mithraists from New York.

"Nope, definitely more than a mathematician." Theo reclined on his elbows so she wouldn't have to crane her neck. "His discovery—that mathematical ratios produce real-world harmonies—changed the Greeks' entire understanding of the world. It was like they'd uncovered a secret language that held the keys to existence. After all, if mathematics and numbers underlay something as fundamental as music—as *harmony*—then maybe they underlay the rest of the world, too."

"They do," she offered. "I mean, that's what scientists believe." She blinked at him, her face only a foot from his own. "That math and algorithms and quantifiable evidence can explain everything."

"So says Dr. Ruth Willever, the microbiologist," he teased. "A poet might disagree." *A classicist might disagree,* he amended silently. *Math can't explain why even as I'm staring at Ruth's smile, I'm thinking of Selene's. Only the ancient elegies can do that.* A snippet of the Roman poet Meleager floated across his brain.

Where am I drifting?
Swept on by Love's relentless tide,
Helpless in my steering,
Once more to doom I ride.

"Theo?" Ruth laid a gentle hand on his shoulder and didn't let go.

"Hmm? Sorry. I was…" *With Selene,* he was about to say, but Ruth cut him off.

"You were about to tell me what you're doing with the monochord," she prompted, heading off his melancholy. "I still don't see why you're researching harmonic ratios in the first place."

Theo pulled away from her touch and plucked the string again thoughtfully. "The Pythagoreans didn't understand the physics behind the note's frequency, but they understood that the ratios of the lengths of the string related to the pitch of the sound. And they decided that those same digits that make up the harmonic ratios—one, two, three, four—must be the fundamental numbers in the universe."

He put the monochord aside and grabbed one of his notebooks, flipping to a page of his more innocuous scribblings. He showed Ruth a sketched figure: four dots in a row, then three above it, then two, then one, creating an equilateral triangle consisting of ten total dots.

"The Pythagoreans called this triangle a *tetractys*," he explained. "A 'fourness' that represented the perfect number. They thought its unity, its symmetry—four lines, four numbers, three equal sides of four dots each—must be magical."

Ruth looked skeptical for the first time. "Magical? More like basic geometry."

"They thought the tetractys might be part of a larger pattern." He searched for the right way to explain the ancient mysticism to Ruth's logical brain. He couldn't tell her too much—she'd probably have him committed if she knew the whole truth—but he always thought better aloud. It was why he'd liked having a partner.

Before thoughts of Selene could derail him again, he pressed forward with his explanation. "Remember how the Mithraists believed in shifting the celestial spheres to bring about the Last Age, so they could achieve salvation with their resurrected god?" Ruth nodded. "Well, the Pythagoreans believed something similar: that the ultimate goal of existence was to achieve unity with the divine."

"And they did that...how?"

"By being a *philosophos*. A 'lover of knowledge.'"

"A philosopher?" She rolled her eyes.

"Yeah, but not Kant or Nietzsche or some nineteenth-century effete sitting around pondering the meaning of morality. More like a *natural* philosopher." She still looked dubious. "The word 'scientist' comes from the Latin for 'knowledge,' you know. So that makes you basically just a philosopher in a lab coat."

She looked mildly affronted but gestured for him to go on.

"The philosophers studied nature to uncover the pattern that unifies creation. That pattern, they believed, embodied the wisdom of the gods. The divine will that created the world. And once they found that pattern, *if* they found it, they could reach the ultimate purity of the soul. They could become gods themselves."

Ruth laughed, her patience for mysticism clearly running thin. "Sounds like unified field theory, if you ask me." When Theo looked at her curiously, she went on with a shrug. "You know, how quantum mechanics and general relativity don't play by the same rules. Einstein spent an inordinate amount of time trying to come up with a theory that worked for both."

"A pattern that unifies creation, huh?"

"Yup. But he didn't find it. No one has." She rose to her feet, looking down at Theo pointedly. "And something tells me, despite all the library books you've got spread across the quad, you won't either."

He shrugged, trying to look appropriately sheepish.

"Theo..." she began, a suspicious frown tugging at her lips. "How is all this going to help you figure out where the Mithraists' leader is hiding?"

Saturn...Every time Theo thought of the old man with his curved sickle he had to fight back a tide of rage. Selene's grandfather was both the God of Time and the Pater, or "Father," of the Holy Order of the Soldiers of Theodosius, also known as the Host. A secret cult dedicated to destroying the Olympians in order to allow the rebirth of Mithras-as-Jesus. The Host's initiates had killed four Athanatoi before Selene and Theo finally confronted Saturn himself on the Statue of Liberty's torch last Christmas Eve. In the end, his men had unleashed a lightning bolt to chase them from the sky.

Theo saw it again: Selene falling through the clouds like a needle piercing the fabric of the world.

"You said that's what you were working toward, right?" Ruth pressed, dragging him back to the present. "You're going to help find the Pater so he doesn't hurt anyone else?"

"Yeah," he lied. After fleeing New York, Saturn might have gone after Selene's father, Zeus, like he'd threatened to. He might be holed up in some dingy mithraeum, scheming with other members of the Host. Maybe he was just enjoying life back in the Old World, reveling in past glories among the ruins of the Roman Forum. Theo didn't care.

There was only one person he wanted to find.

Selene's body lies at the bottom of the harbor. He knew that. He hadn't completely lost his mind, not yet anyway. But in his time with Selene, Theo had learned that *nothing* was impossible.

The tetractys was more than a pretty triangle. It was a code. A clue. The key to the pattern that defined the universe.

Ruth kept talking as Theo gathered his books. He nodded vaguely at her words as they walked off campus and into the tumult of Broadway, but he heard only the insistent whisper in his own mind:

If the Pythagoreans were right, the tetractys reveals the divine pattern that created life in the first place.

Which means it can create it again.

And I can bring Selene back from the dead.

Chapter 3

WILY ONE

"Do you understand who you're dealing with?" the Huntress demanded again of the man pinned beneath her arrows on the mithraeum floor.

His lips twisted. "Miss Selene DiSilva, I presume." His voice carried a faint Germanic accent.

She leaned on the arrows in his hands again, enjoying his gasp of pain. "Wrong. I gave up that name when you and your precious Pater attacked my city."

The American passport safely stored in her apartment in Rome identified her as Selene Neomenia, born in New York, New York, in 1986. But she wasn't about to tell that to the Mithraist.

"Now stop resisting and tell me where you're holding my father."

His thin lips remained firmly shut, his pale eyes unblinking.

"Do you have him in one of the other temples in Ostia?" she demanded, watching his reaction.

One corner of his mouth twitched into a fleeting smile.

"I'll take that as a no." She leaned closer to him, her words a low growl. "You think you're doing the right thing, don't you? Protecting your leader? Preserving his plans for your Holy Order?

But do you know what your precious Pater Patrum has done? *He killed my twin brother before my eyes.*"

The memory sliced like a blade even now. Apollo, Bright One, God of Music, Healing, and Prophecy. God of everything civilized and beautiful in the world. Her glorious twin. The Host's initiates had lashed his back with their whips, striping his tunic with red lines as brilliant as the clouds at sunset. Selene had offered to sacrifice her own life for her twin's—the Pater killed him anyway.

"Apollo looked at me while he died," she hissed at the man beneath her feet. "'I can't see the sun'—that's what he said to me. The god who once drove the sun across the sky in his golden chariot was reduced to a bloody corpse, his heart sliced from his body with a sickle."

The man's gaze flicked away from her. His jaw tightened.

"You can't look me in the eye, can you?" she seethed. "You know what you've done is wrong." She eased the pressure on the arrows in his hands. "I don't want to hurt you," she lied. "Just tell me where to find my father, before your army kills him, too."

He shook his head.

"Is that why your Pater cuts the hearts from his victims?" she snarled, losing patience. "Because his men have no hearts of their own?" She wrenched the arrows wider. "Talk to me, and I might not punch two more arrows through your feet."

His eyes rolled back in his head. She thought he might pass out—not an ideal conclusion to their fight, but something she could work with. Instead, with the strength and speed of a trained soldier, he jackknifed his knees into her gut. Her grip loosened.

One palm swung toward her face, her own arrowhead his weapon. She dodged. Her weight off balance, he hooked a leg over her hip and threw her.

They both scrambled from the ground and hopped onto opposite platforms. The man faced her with bleeding hands outspread—a crucified Christ. Selene held her bow before her like a staff.

He vaulted onto her platform, slapping his hands together as if to impale her on the arrow points like a bear in a trap. Instincts just faster than a mortal's sent her bow flashing, kicking one arrow aside but only diverting the other. The point sliced into a tendon in her hip. Her left leg went dead—she buckled to the floor once more.

He paused, his smooth face flushed and glistening with sweat, a rosy-cheeked child with arrows in his bloody palms.

She stared up at him, defiant. "Not sure whether to kill me, take me captive, or run away, are you?" She pressed a hand against the wound in her side. "They don't call me One Who Does Not Die for nothing. You may *try* to kill me, but you won't succeed. And in case you're wondering, I didn't come alone. My backup will be here any second. And his rage will be *volcanic*."

The man whipped his head around with obvious trepidation. Taking advantage of his distraction, she jammed her heel into his ankle. He stayed on his feet but staggered off balance. She surged up, ready to knock her prey out with a well-placed fist. The man in black ducked the blow, but her words clearly had an effect. He ran.

On any other night, she would've had him. But her hip gave out, her leg collapsed, and her quarry dashed away into the night.

Selene cursed roundly and grabbed hold of the platform edge to lurch back to her feet. Limping, she gave chase. Back down the alley, past the crumbling brick tenements. The entire city was a necropolis, its crumbled columns lying like toppled funerary urns, its roofless ruins as empty as desecrated sarcophagi.

Instead of a hundred Roman legionaries protecting its gate, a single night watchman, currently fast asleep at his post, guarded the archeological site. The Huntress and her prey had the city to themselves. Nearly.

Flint Hamernik—whom the fifty thousand residents of ancient Ostia had worshiped as Vulcan, God of Volcanoes, and the Greeks had called Hephaestus, the crippled Smith—lay in wait at the opposite end of the city. She spared a second to fumble out her cell phone and call him.

"No good," she panted. "They're not holding my father in Ostia, and the Mithraist got away, but I'm sending him toward you. If you trap him, we can still get some answers."

"Wait," came the rumbled response. "There's—"

"Just be ready!" Catching a glimpse of her prey up ahead, she hung up.

Arrow-speared arms pumping, the man in black veered left at the Decumanus Maximus. Selene sent an arrow skimming just past his cheek, forcing him to turn right instead. A moment later, he made for the western border of the city—another arrow steered him to the south. A third shaft stopped him from ducking into a ruined home. A fourth forced him past a round temple to a forgotten god. All the while, Selene kept him just within sight, each arrow a hungry wolf in her pack, herding her quarry toward capture.

One arrow left. She sent it sailing over his shoulder, driving him into a triangular field at the very edge of Ostia.

The wound in her hip shot blinding sparks of pain through her leg like fire from Zeus's thunderbolt. Wincing, she rounded the corner into the Campus of the Magna Mater, the field where the Romans had paid homage to the Great Mother in an age long past. The chase was almost over, Selene's part in it complete. She'd once cherished her role as a solitary huntress, but now she was glad she had backup. She staggered forward and waited for Flint to spring his trap.

Except Flint was nowhere to be found.

Her enemy awaited instead.

The man in black stumbled to a halt, the arrows still protruding from his palms. He gave a breathless laugh and said something in German, clearly relieved to have found his comrades. Another man—also clean-shaven, his close-cropped hair dark against pale skin—crouched before a soaring stone sculpture of a pine tree, chiseling it from its foundation. But it was the old man standing nearby who drew Selene's gaze.

Saturn. The Titan God of Time. The Wily One. Pater Patrum of the Host, murderer of so many. The man Selene had been hunting ever since he escaped her clutches in New York six months before.

Her grandfather.

His lined face bore a branching scar down one cheek that disappeared beneath a neat white beard. His hair had burned away from half his head, leaving only shiny scalp behind. Despite his scars, he towered over his mortal acolytes, his skin glowing faintly in the darkness with a divine aura he should no longer possess. Like so many of her kin, Selene's grandfather had been willing to do anything to regain his old powers—he'd just been more successful than most. Rather than kill humans, the millennia-old Mithraic cult he'd created had murdered four members of his own family. The sacrifice of so many Athanatoi had granted him power that Selene could never match.

He held his divine sickle with a firm grip, the curved blade reflecting the light that emanated from his flesh. Even now, Selene could hear the bloody ripping sound it had made as it cut the heart from her twin brother's chest. Apollo. Hades. Mars. Prometheus. All sacrificed to Saturn's cult.

She wanted to laugh. Or sob. After all this time, all the complicated schemes and fruitless interrogations, Saturn had walked into her reach of his own volition. She would finally have her revenge.

She reached instinctively for her quiver.

Empty.

At her gasp of dismay, the old man looked up.

His scowl only deepened the creases on his ravaged face.

"Not happy to see me?" she called out to him.

He turned back to the man chiseling at the pine tree with a hissed *"Hurry."*

She wanted more than anything to send a golden arrow straight through his traitorous heart. But she'd come to Ostia without her divine shafts, hoping merely to find the Mithraists' lair—not to confront her grandfather directly. Even if she'd had any wooden arrows left, they'd do no permanent damage to Saturn's immortal flesh. And his sickle would slice her apart if she attacked him hand to hand.

That didn't mean she was helpless.

She reached under the collar of her shirt for the gold necklace Flint had given her months before. The moment she snapped open the clasp, it unfurled into a long, gleaming whip. She ignored her grandfather and sent the lash whistling toward her original quarry instead. It snaked around the young man's leg and toppled him to the ground.

Ignoring the searing pain in her hip, she lunged. A twist of the whip's handle and it hardened, straightened, metamorphosed into a javelin.

She jammed its sharp tip against the soft flesh of the young man's throat while stomping the arrows in his hands deep into the dirt, anchoring him in place. This time, she stood above his head so he couldn't knock her loose. He kicked with both legs anyway, succeeding only in tearing larger holes in his palms.

She ignored his agonized groans and called to her grandfather instead. "Tell me where you've taken my father!"

"Or?" Saturn asked calmly.

"Or I kill your man."

"What makes you think I would bother to save him?"

"I killed all your acolytes in New York. You don't have many more to spare." She hoped that was true.

"My followers know what future awaits them when the Last Age arrives. Resurrection. Eternal life. Salvation. Why fear death?"

"But perhaps they fear pain." Selene spun the javelin so its tip drilled a shallow hole beneath the man's spasming Adam's apple. She glared down at her young captive. "If your Pater won't do what I ask, maybe you will. Last chance: Tell me where my father is."

"I don't——" he gasped.

"Yes, you do." She whipped her javelin around to slam it against his jaw. "My *father*. Don't pretend you don't know who he is. Jupiter. Lightning Bringer." She smacked him again with each title. "Leader of the Fates ... King of the Gods ... *ZEUS*."

"It won't work," Saturn said, sounding mildly amused. "He won't tell you anything. Have you forgotten that I'm his Pater Patrum?"

"And have you forgotten who *I* am?" She jabbed the weapon's point into the man's right shoulder, then his left, twisting it with each shallow cut. "The Arrow-Showering One. The Punisher. The Huntress."

A grinding of stone interrupted her tirade. She'd nearly forgotten the dark-haired man sawing away at the stone pine tree in the center of the field. He put down his tools and began tying a series of ropes and pulleys around the statue. "Almost there, Pater."

"Good," Saturn replied. "Finish quickly. We must take our treasures and leave." The wary glance he cast at his granddaughter proved he hadn't forgotten she was the Punisher after all. He'd been fleeing her clutches for months; even now, with his soldiers around him, he'd rather run than attempt to add her to his pantheon of sacrifices.

"Stop!" Selene cried, pressing her javelin once more against her captive's throat. "I don't care if this kid is just one more innocent deluded by your lies, dreaming of a Last Age that will never occur. I *will* kill him if you try to leave."

"No," Saturn said, "you won't." He gave a brief nod to the wounded man lying beneath her javelin.

With a strength of will she'd rarely seen in a mortal since the battlefields of Troy, the young man ripped his right hand free of her arrow, leaving his pinky and ring finger behind. He tore out the shaft piercing his other palm.

Then plunged it into his own eye.

Furious at the waste, the stupidity, Selene kicked the body aside and raised her javelin. She knew Saturn was fast enough to dodge the throw. She was counting on it. *One more step to his left,* she prayed, *and he'll trip Flint's booby trap.* The steel net lay buried in the grass, ready to spring around its captive and inject him with a neurotoxin powerful enough to paralyze even an Athanatos.

Her grandfather took one look at her raised javelin and *tsk*ed mildly, as if reading her thoughts. "Put that down, child. You may be too hard to hold captive, but not all the Olympians are quite so fierce." He took a deliberate step to the side. No steel net rose up around him. Instead, she finally saw what had lain behind him the whole time:

The trap was already sprung. And Flint lay writhing in its grip.

Chapter 4

THE LAME GOD

Selene stood frozen, javelin raised, staring at her captive friend. Flint's broad shoulders strained against the metal threads of the net, but his massive arms only twitched weakly. She saw no sign of his crutches, and his withered legs lay trapped beneath him, motionless. His head jerked—she could make out the whites of his rolling eyes. With his usual uncanny skill at inventing weapons, Flint had embedded multiple needles inside the net, each one ready to administer a shot of paralytic neurotoxin in case their Mithraist proved recalcitrant. One dose would prevent the captive from either escaping or killing himself. Two doses would knock him completely unconscious so they could transport him. Three would kill him outright.

Saturn raised his hand. He held a button affixed to a long cord stretching from the net. His thumb hovered over it. "I've already used one dose to keep the Lame One quiet. If you threaten me further, granddaughter, I'll have no choice but to use two more." He moved his thumb a centimeter closer to the button, then another, until Selene finally lowered her javelin.

"That's right," he said. "You know I can't be beaten by your feeble plans. You know who I am."

"Oh, I know, Grandfather. But does *he*?" She looked to Saturn's remaining acolyte. The dark-haired man dropped the complicated harness he'd been securing around the pine tree statue. His eyes darted to his Pater, questioning, while his hand moved toward the gun at his hip. A spatter of moles marred his otherwise smooth cheek like a dark constellation of stars.

"Do you know this man is Saturn?" she asked him. "A *pagan* god?"

"Saturn, yes," he replied, his German accent echoing his dead compatriot's. "But he is no pagan. The Pater is the Father."

"Foolish child," Saturn chided her. "He knows more of my story than you do."

Selene pointed an accusatory finger at the mole-spattered man. "You're a Christian, aren't you? I've seen the crosses you wear, the way you genuflect before your god. You think Mithras and Jesus are the same. You think Saturn will bring you closer to them both. You're *wrong*. He doesn't give a crap about your messiah. He only works for his own power."

"My syndexioi know the truth," Saturn said, using the Mithraic term for an initiate into their secret cult. "I *can* bring them closer to Jesus. I brought the *world* closer to Jesus. Without me, no one would even remember his name."

Selene gripped the javelin hard, running out of patience. But the longer her grandfather spoke, the more chance Flint had of recovering. Saturn wouldn't know that the neurotoxin lasted only ten minutes. If she could keep him talking, they might have a shot.

"You have nothing to do with Jesus." She turned to the dark-haired syndexios. "You claim your messiah is all about love and mercy. Turn the other cheek. I ask you, do you think your Pater believes in such compassion? What kind of Christian would murder his own family?" The young man looked at her blankly. Her voice rose in frustration. "Any 'Last Age' he ushers in won't be a time of salvation and peace. The lion won't lie down with the lamb. Don't you see? It will be an age of greed and bloodshed and mayhem—the same horrors Saturn has always wrought on those around him. And if you let him kill my father and make himself all-powerful, it won't just be my family that suffers. It will be the whole damn Christian world."

"Since when do you care about Christians?" Saturn asked.

"I don't," she spat. "But I do care about innocent mortals. And since a lot of them happen to be Christians, I don't have much of a choice. Protector of the Innocent, they called me. That's a title I'm still proud to claim."

"You think you have me all figured out." Again, that cold, confident smile on his burnt face. "But I told you months ago that you didn't."

Arrogance is so embedded in his withered soul that he can't imagine I'm a threat, she realized. *He's the Wily One—I'm just a dumb goddess. I can work with that.* She curled her lip in disdain. "Why don't you enlighten me?"

The mole-spattered syndexios frowned at her, his hand resting on the butt of his gun. "A Pretender should not question the Pater."

"No, it's fine, my son." Saturn jerked his chin toward the pine tree statue. "Keep working while I tell my ignorant granddaughter the truth."

Selene had no idea why Saturn wanted the sculpture, but it was important enough that he'd come in person to the Campus of the Magna Mater to claim it while sending a lowly syndexios for the mosaic arc. *He'll keep talking, thinking he's distracting me so his henchman can complete the theft,* she realized. *Meanwhile, I egg him on, waiting for Flint to recover. We both want to drag this out: For once, we share the same aim—with very different consequences.*

She kept one eye on Flint, only half listening to Saturn's tale.

"Our Lord Jesus died upon the cross," her grandfather began. Selene gritted her teeth and prepared for a recitation of the entire New Testament. One of her own medieval witchcraft trials had begun much the same way.

"His followers in Jerusalem mourned him, loved him, but

even they did not know the truth—that Jesus was no mere prophet, but the true and only son of the true and only God. Then a Pharisee, an unbeliever, set out on the road to Damascus—Are you listening to me, *Diana*?"

Selene's attention flew back to her grandfather. He raised his remaining eyebrow and waggled his thumb above the injector button. When he spoke again, his voice resonated with power. "Listen closely as I tell you of another Time."

He continued his story, and Selene suddenly saw it unfold before her. Months earlier, Saturn had sent her visions by using the God of Dreams' divine poppy wreath. This was different, as if Saturn's status as the God of Time had somehow given him the power to control history itself. Walking through the ruins of Ostia, she'd remembered only snatches of the ancient past. Now his words dragged her deeper with an inexorable force. They filled her eyes, her ears. She drowned within their pull.

A man rides a mule down a dusty road. He wears the robes of a Jew, his head veiled, his beard long. A trio of servants plods beside him. They look like they've traveled far and have farther yet to go.

Suddenly, the bearded man gasps and reins his mule to a halt. The servants turn to ask their master what's the matter, but he has already slid from his animal. He kneels now in the dust, his face so full of wonder that the servants look around, convinced there must be an angel crossing his path. They see nothing.

But the bearded man sees clearly who stands before him. A god, twelve feet tall, with a snowy white beard and eyes of midnight blue. He wears a Phrygian cap and a star-spangled cloak. He holds a sickle in one hand.

The god's voice blares like a shofar, although only the bearded man can see its source.

"SAUL OF TARSUS . . ."

"Yes," the man replies, awestruck. "Who speaks to me?"

"It is I, your Father. The Host. I come to tell you of Mithras."

Saul looks bewildered. "The Roman god? An idol worshiped by pagans?"

"Mithras has many names. You call him Jesus."

"The rebel? The one they killed in—"

"Jesus can never die, though you hang his body upon a cross. He is my only son. He alone contains the Holy Spirit. He alone moves the heavens on their axes. He alone forges the path to salvation. That is the good news you must spread throughout the world. Not just to Jews, but to the gentiles as well. That is your task. Now rise, for you are Saul no longer. You are Paul. And you will be my greatest servant."

Selene ripped herself free of a memory so vivid it felt as if she'd witnessed it herself. Something about the bearded man tugged at a remembrance buried deep beneath the accumulated weight of millennia, but she shrugged it off.

She interrupted her grandfather before he could complete his tale. "So you came down to Saint Paul while you were still an omnipotent god," she accused him. "You told him a Jewish rebel was a Mithraic god—one who, conveniently, already presided over rituals that granted his followers salvation. And you did it all knowing that if your plan worked, your own family would fade and die. You weren't a victim of Christianity's rise— you were its cause."

The syndexios, she saw now, had finally knocked the pine tree loose and lowered it onto a large dolly, ready to transport it out of Ostia. He looked up from his task to gaze at his Pater reverently. "Saturn has been here since the world began," he said. "He is no Pretender—he is the *true* Father. He helps Mithras shift the stars. The heavens move at his command: The sun passes through Taurus, Aries, Pisces. Each constellation a new Age, until now, finally, the Last Age begins."

Selene wanted to scream. This acolyte recited the ancient Mithraic version of astronomy as if he actually believed it, despite a thousand years of science that proved him wrong. The sun wasn't moving at all, nor were the constellations. It only looked that way from the perspective of the ever-spinning, ever-orbiting, ever-wobbling earth. Unaware of the mechanics of the heliocentric solar system, the Romans had credited the god Mithras with the heavenly shifts instead. These modern followers of the god still clung to that explanation, and Saturn fed on their stubborn faith.

He flicked a quick, covetous glance at the pine tree before turning once more to Selene. "I do not need the Lame One to bring on the Last Age, you know, not when your father lies chained in the dark, ready to be sacrificed. Flint Hamernik is just an insurance policy. A very *useful* insurance policy who can craft weapons to strike down even the strongest Pretender. But if you come after me, I will kill him. Just like I killed your twin."

Selene only clutched her javelin tighter at the reminder of Apollo's murder. She had no intention of letting Saturn kill Flint, much less her father; the sacrifice of the King of the Gods would give her grandfather unimaginable power. Power he would use against her, the scattered remnants of her family, and the world itself. Humans and gods alike were mere pawns to the Wily One. She didn't doubt he would knock them all off the board if it suited his purposes.

She glanced at the steel net—Flint stared back, his expression calm, determined. He made a fist with one hand, the muscles of his bicep swelling like a basketball. The drug had worn off. He was ready. Jerking his chin toward the side, he raised his grizzled eyebrows in a silent reminder.

On a pile of dry grass only a yard away from the marble pine tree lay his duffel bag. A duffel bag full of contingency measures.

"Please, Grandfather." Selene twisted her javelin back into a necklace. She raised her palms, forcing them to tremble. "Don't hurt Flint. I beg you." She walked to the corpse of the young Mithraist, crouching beside his arrow-studded eye in a show of penitence. "No one else should die today."

"I'm glad you finally understand." Saturn turned to his molespattered syndexios. "Get the tree—"

Selene ripped the bloody arrow from the young man's eye

with one hand as she retrieved her bow with the other. The wooden shaft streaked across the clearing and into Flint's duffel.

The bomb inside exploded in a fountain of flame.

The grass beneath caught fire, threatening to engulf the pine tree, the syndexios, and the Pater himself.

Saturn dropped the injection cord and scuttled away from the flames, shouting for backup. In the distance, barely visible beyond the billowing smoke, three more black-clad men hopped over the city wall. Their drawn guns glinted blue in the moonlight.

Already Flint's clever fingers had untangled the net.

Selene lunged forward, threw an arm under his broad shoulders, and half dragged, half carried him from the field. She could hear the Mithraists pounding closer and worried Flint wouldn't move fast enough to escape them. Risking a backward glance, she saw that the explosion's sparks had set Saturn's sleeve ablaze. Two of the syndexioi rushed toward their leader to douse the flames; a third ran toward the pine tree and began to roll it away from the fire.

Urging Flint to move faster, Selene led the way into the ruins. She tried to ignore the flaring pain in her hip while tracing a circuitous path through the narrow alleys and crumbled buildings. The crackle of flames grew fainter in the distance, but sirens wailed in their stead. Soon Ostia's fire brigade would arrive to save the archeological site. Saturn and his men would have to take their pine tree and run.

"You should've just killed Saturn when you had the chance," Flint panted.

"With what? A wooden arrow? And you know I can't lose my only shot at finding where he's holding my father."

Flint grunted, clearly in too much pain to rehash their old argument.

"Besides," she snapped, "with all those soldiers, if we'd stayed another second, we'd be riddled with bullet holes. I might survive, but you wouldn't."

Flint's craggy cheeks burned red above his thick beard. He looked enraged and embarrassed all at once. He'd fallen victim to his own trap. And without his crutches, he was no match for his enemies.

Selene had little desire to salve his bruised pride. Saving his life was more important.

She veered toward the old city wall and clambered over it, hauling Flint up behind her.

By the time she made it to his parked motorcycle on the far side of Ostia, she'd gained a new respect for the Smith. He'd lived for over three thousand years with both legs withered and near useless, barely able to support his broad blacksmith's torso. She'd had one bum leg for thirty minutes, and she wanted to scream with frustration—or cry from pain. Now they were both limping, two Lame Gods instead of one.

"We need to get you to the river water," Flint said, maneuvering himself onto the motorcycle's seat while she climbed on behind, lifting her wounded leg with her hands.

"I'll make it back to Rome. I can go into the Tiber there." As the Goddess of the Wilderness, she could use running water from a natural source to heal any injury inflicted by a mortal weapon. *I'll bathe in the river and come out as good as new,* she thought with a pang of guilt. *Flint lives this way all the time. He'll never be healed, never be whole.*

Unlike Selene, who'd regained some of her preternatural strength and senses, Flint lived a mostly mortal existence. Even before the fading that had affected all the Athanatoi, he'd been lame, crooked, his coarse features a pitiable contrast to the other gods' beauty. Yet his frailties had made him the most humble of the gods, the one best able to deal with their slow descent toward mortality. "He of Many Arts and Skills," the ancient Greeks called him. That epithet, at least, he still deserved. His inventions might no longer be supernatural, but they still seemed magical to Selene, blends of mechanics and electronics, both elegant and functional, that granted him power beyond his own faded strength—except when someone else used them first.

She wrapped her arms around Flint's waist as he took hold of the adaptive hand controls and revved the motorcycle. Normally, she laid her hands only lightly on his hips to steady herself; tonight, she grabbed on tight.

I need the support—with this leg, I may slip off the damn machine, she told herself. But in truth, there was something comforting in the nearness of him. It had been many months since she'd been so close to another person—except to tackle them to the ground.

His hand moved to hers, pulling it even tighter across his wide rib cage. The gesture reminded her of Theo Schultz—the memory of him a sharp, guilty stab that dwarfed the pain in her hip. *I'm glad you're somewhere safe tonight, far from murderous cults and wrathful gods.* She often spoke to Theo like this—a silent, one-sided conversation that did little to soothe the ache of his absence.

Theo's frame was narrow where Flint's was broad, his smile easy where Flint's—well, Flint rarely smiled at all. But they'd both been willing to die for her. The thunderbolt's scar on her chest proved Theo's devotion; the gold chain hanging around her throat proved Flint's. Yet since the day he'd given her the necklace, despite living and working together with her in Rome for the past six months, Flint had never mentioned his feelings.

Perhaps tonight he'll finally break his silence.

Her first instinct was to loosen her grip on his torso, afraid of what he might read into the gesture. *But I'm tired,* she decided. *Tired of constantly worrying if Saturn will catch us or we'll catch him, if my father will survive, if I made the right choice with Theo. Maybe I don't have to worry about Flint, too.*

So she didn't let go; she pressed herself more firmly against his back instead, grateful for the roar of the engine as they skidded away from Ostia and onto the road to Rome. Even if Flint wanted to say something, she wouldn't hear it. And right now, his silence was exactly what she needed.

Chapter 5

HE WHO SOOTHES

A brownstone on West Eighty-eighth Street, just steps from Riverside Park on Manhattan's Upper West Side. Half as wide as its neighbors, rust pitting its iron railing, peeling paint feathering the windowsills. A house that begged to be ignored—just like its previous owner. Selene's house.

Her half brother Scooter Joveson had given Theo the deed when she died, so it was technically his now, although he still didn't think of it that way.

Two women sat hand in hand on the stoop, waiting for Theo and Ruth with three shopping bags from Zabar's.

Gabriela Jimenez stood, holding aloft a bottle of wine. "I come bearing gifts."

Minh Loi hefted a cake box in turn. "Heavy gifts, full of chocolate."

"I never turn down chocolate, but what are we celebrating?" Theo asked, pulling out his keys.

"Minh just got a paper accepted into the *Annual Review of Astronomy and Astrophysics*," Gabi said, fairly beaming with pride as she kissed her girlfriend on the cheek.

"Congratulations!"

Minh gave a self-deprecating shrug. "They were looking for female contributors."

Gabi rounded on Minh. "Your article's not being published because you're a woman. It's being published because it's awesome."

"Thanks, babe." Minh rolled her eyes with a wry smile, managing to discourage Gabi's effusiveness and bask in it all at the same time.

"And, Theo-dorable," Gabi went on, "since your house has more space than all of our apartments put together, we decided to have Minh's party here."

"Party?" Theo asked with a raised brow, grabbing the shopping bags.

"Just a few friends from the museum," she assured him breezily as she stepped inside and headed confidently toward the kitchen, pulling Minh by the hand. "Bring the groceries in here, will you?"

Minh looked over her shoulder at Theo with a grimace. Clearly, none of this was her idea, but Gabi was just about the most stubborn person Theo knew. If she wanted a party, she got a party.

With the other women out of sight, Theo looked to Ruth, whose cheeks burned a suspicious shade of crimson. "You knew about this, didn't you?"

"They needed a place that could host a dinner party for ten."

"Selene's table only holds two." He lugged the grocery bags into the foyer. "Four if you squeeze." He tried not to sound pissed. His whole life, he'd tempered confrontation with humor. But sometime in the last six months he'd lost much of his talent for levity.

Ruth's flush darkened. "I ordered a folding table from Costco."

"Why didn't you just ask me first?"

"We knew you'd say no. You'd come up with some excuse so you wouldn't hurt Gabriela's feelings, but you'd still refuse."

"That's not true. I'm happy for Minh."

"I'm sure you are. But you *always* say no." Ruth's voice slowed, as if she hesitated to admit the truth. But for all her shyness, Ruth never lied. When he asked a direct question, she answered it. Theo wished he could say the same about himself.

"You just want to work, Theo. You know I support your research, but the way you're going about it isn't healthy. It's bringing you more pain than joy. You keep looking into the past and ignoring what's going on around you. Pythagoras, Mithras, Saturn—they mean more to you than your own friends. You're sublimating all your grief into your work, rather than reaching out to those who want to help."

"You're right. *Sublimating* is exactly what I'm doing," he snapped, more harshly than he'd intended. "The sick and suffering of ancient Greece used to go to the shrines of Asclepius, He Who Soothes, and offer themselves to his snakes for healing. The snakes knew the secrets of the Underworld. They could cure sickness by bringing men right up to the border between life and death, between god and mortal. That's what 'sublime' means, Ruth—to come 'up to the threshold' between worlds. There's nothing wrong with trying to do that. I've been broken apart, and that's the only way I know how to heal."

"Well, in chemistry, 'sublimate' means to turn a solid directly into a gas," she shot back. Finally, his loyal friend had lost her patience. Theo was almost relieved. If she was angry at him, it made it that much easier to push her away. "That's what you've become, Theo. Ether. Air. Floating above it all in a cloud of theories, living with dreams of a goddess. That's not healing! Come back to the solid world! Come back to your very real, very human friends. Gabriela and Minh have been dating for three months now, and it's the best thing that's ever happened to either of them. They want to share that with you, but they barely ever see you."

"I won't see them tonight either, not with ten people in the house."

"I know you don't like guests, because she never wanted people over, but you're not her." Ruth reached for his hand. "You're your own man, and you've always liked having friends around. Retreating from the world isn't good for you. We all thought it'd be nice for you to socialize."

Nice? How about if all my friends stop telling me how to live my life? That *would be nice,* he thought angrily. *Ruth wants me to stop researching. Gabi wants me to throw a dinner party. Selene—if she were alive to want anything anymore—would want me to live on without her.*

"Screw this," he muttered, pulling away. He turned toward the stairs, intending to spend the rest of the day up in his bedroom with his research notes, not wasting time on frivolity. Then he heard the clatter of claws on the kitchen floor and the unmistakable sound of Hippo's tail thwacking against someone's legs. The huge dog barreled down the hall, bumped him happily in the groin with her head, and gave Ruth's hand a lick before hurtling back into the kitchen to greet Gabi and Minh once more, her paws slipping and skittering on the hardwood.

Selene might not have liked guests, but her dog sure did— female ones, at least.

As always, the sight of the massive, brindled dog with her floppy ears and wagging tongue softened the edges of his grief. Hippo was the only other creature in the world who'd been as devastated as Theo by Selene's death. If she was finding a way to heal, maybe he could too.

All right, Hippo, he conceded silently. *I'll be a gracious host—but only for you.* "I'm going to change," he said more calmly. "I'll be down in a minute."

Upstairs, he closed the door to the bedroom—the one he'd shared with Selene for a few short and glorious months—and yanked off his tie like a man reprieved from hanging. He was free of his button-down and rifling for a T-shirt when a faint knock sounded on the door.

Ruth stood awkwardly, her eyes darting to his bare chest

and then back to his face. "I want to apologize. You're right. I should've asked you first. This isn't my house."

Somehow, Ruth's speed at making amends only annoyed Theo more. "It's fine, really." He tried to banish all evidence of impatience from his voice but could tell from the hurt in her eyes that he'd failed.

She took a tentative step closer, and for the first time all day, he noticed that she'd abandoned her usual sensible biologist's outfit. A soft blue skirt swung around her knees, tanned shoulders peeked from a sleeveless white blouse, and an enamel pendant in the shape of an amoeba hung at her collarbone—a gift Theo had bought her years ago, more as a joke than anything else. At the sight of the pendant, his annoyance dissipated, transformed into something closer to guilt. Ruth had spent the last hour—the last half a *year*—trying to help him, and this was how he repaid her?

"I didn't mean to be an ass," he said.

Ruth's eyes, large behind her glasses, flitted back to his chest. He lifted a self-conscious hand to the pale Mercury symbol on his flesh, evidence of his run-in with Saturn's branding iron.

"Sorry. I wasn't staring at it," she said quickly.

"Just at my pecs?" he asked, surprising himself with the joke, then immediately regretting it when Ruth looked away, abashed. He knew full well that she had feelings for him, feelings he had no right to encourage—at least not until he knew his own heart better. He pulled on his shirt hastily. *I never should've let her claim the room down the hall as her own, or leave her toothbrush beside mine.* But as isolated as he'd become, he could never completely divorce himself from the extrovert he'd been. Having someone to talk to, or even just to sit in silence with, had eased some of the throbbing loneliness he felt every time he saw something that reminded him of Selene. In Manhattan, that was just about everything.

That spring, the cherry trees had bloomed early in Central Park, their branches heavy with pink puffballs. When the wind blew, the petals drifted down like blushing snow. He'd sat beneath the trees, their drooping limbs forming a secret, wondrous bower, unable to believe that he'd never share such beauty with the woman he loved. *Surely,* he'd thought, *she'll show up, pushing aside the branches and scowling at the excessive pinkness. She'll laugh when I say I thought she was dead. "I found a way to be reborn, of course. I'm an Athanatos! One Who Does Not Die. Or did you forget that?"* But after two weeks of riotous glory, the petals had turned to brown mush, the trees leafed out and looked like any other trees—and Selene never appeared.

Theo sat heavily on the bed, one hand pressed against the still-tender skin that surrounded the Mercury brand, a constant reminder of Selene's death. He could smell the burning flesh, the acrid tang of electricity as the lightning bolt struck them both.

Ruth sat beside him. After a moment, she laid a hesitant arm around his back, her fingers curving lightly around his shoulder. Her breast brushed his elbow. She smelled like soap and summer grass. When she'd lain beside him on the quad, the bustling students and open air had tempered the intimacy. Now his body responded involuntarily—but he didn't move. She rested her head against his arm. Her sun-warmed hair was pulled back in a loose ponytail, a few unruly wisps tickling his skin.

"Ruth," he said finally, quietly, not sure what to say, knowing he had to say something.

"I know," she replied in a whisper, stopping him from having to figure it out. "You're still thinking about her, and you can't promise me anything, and you don't want to hurt me. You don't know how you feel, you don't know what you want." He didn't bother trying to deny it. She knew him well, this friend of his. "It's okay," she went on. "You don't have to do anything." She rested her other hand on his thigh, and he could feel its warmth through the fabric of his pants. He sat like a statue, wondering if she'd move her fingers. Wondering if he wanted her to.

Eventually, she turned her head so her mouth pressed against the flesh of his arm. She didn't kiss him, just rested her lips there.

Instinctively, he turned his head in response, his chin just touching the crown of her head. He felt her fingers curl a centimeter tighter on his shoulder, the crescents of her nails pressing into his flesh as her breath quickened. He inhaled sharply, formulating the right way to tell her to stop.

The doorbell saved him. Hippo barked, Gabi laughed, Minh's footsteps pattered into the foyer.

"More guests to drag me from my work, kicking and screaming," he murmured before gently pulling away. She looked up at him with a smile so trusting, so warm, that he almost told her the truth about his Pythagoras research right then. But he didn't.

This was one quest the hero had to undertake alone.

Chapter 6

CHTHONIC ONE

Rome is not Manhattan.

Selene sent the silent thought to Theo and imagined him laughing at the understatement. Classicist that he was, he probably preferred Rome. But as she stood on a bridge over the Tiber after returning from her adventures in Ostia, the former Roman goddess Diana found the city's famous river, for all its languid beauty, a creek compared to the mighty Hudson. The dome of Saint Peter's looked like a squat dwarf beside the graceful spire of the Chrysler Building. And the public transportation—from the rattling, barely air-conditioned buses to the paltry metro—paled beside the intricate web of New York's immense subway. Yet at night, when the city's heat lifted and the floodlights set the Coliseum aglow, she had to admit that Rome felt, just a little, like home.

She looked down the river's length. Walkways crowded with pop-up restaurants and boutiques ran along either side of the water, part of the city's summer market. In the predawn hours, the tents stood dark, the sidewalks empty. The only movement came from the treetops that bordered the nearby roadway, their leaves rustling in the faint wind like whispers from a long-forgotten past. More than the broken pediments of the city's Roman ruins, it was the trees that reminded her of her time as a goddess. Great flat umbrella pines, soaring columnar cypresses, gracefully drooping plane trees. *They, at least,* she thought, still carrying on her silent conversation, *haven't changed.*

But she had. She glanced at the bloody stain at her hip, where the Mithras-worshiping syndexios had stabbed her with her own wooden arrow. When the Romans had called her Diana, Selene couldn't have been harmed by a mortal weapon. Now her leg had stiffened so badly she could barely walk.

She limped down the bridge and onto the riverside walkway, grateful to still retain at least one supernatural ability: The Tiber's waters would heal her as no mortal medicine could.

Beneath the arch of the bridge, deep in the shadows, Selene lowered herself gingerly into the gritty water. Compared to the night's clinging heat, the tepid Tiber felt deliciously cool. She hung from her elbows, submerged only chest deep.

"I call upon you, mighty Tiber," she prayed. "Remember your birth from a mountain spring. Do not forget the Goddess of the Wilderness. She Who Dwells on the Heights. Lend her your aid."

Power flooded through her, stronger than the river's sluggish current. Her hip itched where the skin knit closed, and she felt a sharp shock through the length of her leg as the tendons and nerves healed. After a few minutes, she knew she should haul herself from the water and return to her apartment to discuss the night's events with Flint. They needed to plan their next move, to comb through any new clues that might help them track Saturn or find Zeus.

Yet still she clung to the riverbank, her legs floating motionless in the water. On the back of Flint's motorcycle, clutching his broad chest, she'd been content to take comfort in his nearness and avoid any difficult conversations. *If I go back to the apartment now,* she mused, *will he finally admit how he feels about me?* She still wasn't sure what she'd say if he did. She valued him, depended on him—loved him, even. But the thought of kissing him—she released the ledge, dunking her head quickly beneath the water as if to wash the image from her brain.

When they'd gotten back to Rome, she'd used her injury as an excuse to leave him in their apartment and go to the river alone. Flint hadn't objected. In fact, he'd remained silent the entire trip from Ostia, as if he, too, wasn't sure what to say.

Selene propped herself once more on the ledge. She rolled the thick necklace he'd forged for her between her fingers. A simple gold chain when clasped around her neck, but when it unfurled into a whip or telescoped into a javelin, the carvings along its surface burst into view. Flint had engraved the entire length with images from her past: her carefree youth dancing on the shores of Delos with her twin; her centuries of power, wreaking supernatural vengeance on the men who dared to defy her; her wanderings through Europe after the Diaspora; her lonely attempts to build a life in New York. Flint had cared for her all that time, and she'd never known.

Despite his feelings, often the whole night would pass before they exchanged ten words. *Maybe we're too much alike.* Selene couldn't repress a small sigh. For most of her existence, she'd thought a silent man the best kind. She wasn't so sure anymore.

If you were here, Theo, you'd already have offered your opinions on everything from the hunt for my father to the plotline of the latest Star Wars *movie.* For months, she'd been plagued by guilt, worried that Theo would never get over her. Now, despite knowing it was for the best, she worried that he had. The warm breeze on her cheeks reminded her that they'd never shared a summer's day. *In our one frigid winter together, the only warmth came from your body pressed against—* She stopped herself from imagining it any further. It would only hurt more.

With a groan more of weariness than pain, she climbed back onto the walkway. Clothes wet and clinging, hair dripping streams of water down her back, she headed to the apartment she and Flint shared. She couldn't help thinking of the path from the Hudson River to her brownstone in Manhattan, a walk she'd taken with Theo countless times in the few months they'd known each other. *Stop dreaming about someone you'll never see again,* she told herself. *Start imagining a reunion with someone you will.* Yet thoughts of Zeus made her feel equally guilty.

She'd gone to find her father six months earlier to warn him that Saturn's Host would try to capture him. After faking her death in New York, she'd flown to Athens, then Crete. In the dark hours of the morning, she'd reached the Lassithi Plateau high up in the mountains. The bells of goats tocked in the distance—the herds in the village of Psychro searching for fodder among the patchy snow. Above her loomed the legendary Dictaean Cave, a black slash in the pale, moonlit cliffside.

Selene had pulled her leather jacket closer and climbed carefully toward the cave on steps made slick by the chill January rains.

The cave looked utterly deserted—a fitting home for the mad hermit her father had become. She hadn't seen him in over fifteen hundred years—not since he'd commanded all the gods to wander forth from Olympus, unloved and forgotten, into the mortal realm. Zeus had been imposing, black-haired, with eyes of stormy gray and a beard as twisted as the lightning bolt that symbolized his rule. Yet Selene's memories of him were not of the fearsome King, but of the doting Father. He'd taken her on his lap when she was little more than a babe. She could still remember the feel of his wiry beard as she twirled it between her fingers.

And now? As the King of the Gods, surely Zeus still retained much of his physical vigor. But his mind—she'd been told that was a different story. Once the ultimate Sky God, he'd devolved from celestial to chthonic—a creature of secrets and darkness and earth—and much of his sanity had fled at the same time.

Before her, the wide entrance to the cave yawned dark and foreboding. She could just pick out the glint of a metal staircase descending into blackness. This was the path the summer tourists took—it couldn't be the way to Zeus's home. Nonetheless, she stood at the top of the stairs and called softly into the night.

"Father?"

Better to give an Athanatos of Zeus's strength fair warning of her approach.

Hearing nothing in response, she pulled a penlight from her pocket and peered into the depths. Stalactites hung like dragon's teeth from the ceiling, black and dripping and covered in icy moss. She padded down the stairs to the first landing, then hopped over the railing and onto the cave floor, slipping a little on the slimy rock. She steadied herself and called out for her father again.

"Zeus? Jupiter? Jove?" So many names for the Father of the Gods. The King of Olympus. Yet tonight, he answered to none of them.

What will he say when he sees me again? she wondered as she moved deeper into the cave. On the frenzied journey from New York, she'd been too preoccupied with thoughts of Theo's grief and Saturn's escape to worry about her relationship with Zeus. That day thousands of years before, when she'd sat upon his lap, she'd asked him to grant her six wishes: a golden bow, matching arrows, and a tunic short enough to run in. A band of nymphs to be her companions and wide-antlered stags to draw her chariot. He'd given her everything, even her final wish, the one that defied every tradition of their patriarchal society: eternal chastity, her most important attribute of all. In that moment, her father's love had felt like a rainbow meant just for her. Something beautiful and scintillating that seemed to stretch on forever. Now she wondered if that rainbow had long ago faded back into the storm clouds from which it had sprung. She still loved her father—but would he feel the same?

He'll probably ask me where the hell I've been for the last fifteen centuries, she realized. *Why I knew he was holed up here, slowly going mad, and did nothing to help him.* She didn't have an answer besides the honest one: *I thought we'd have time. I thought we were immortal. I didn't realize how quickly those we love can be ripped away from us.* The thought of her twin's murder at Saturn's hand firmed her resolve.

"I'm here now, Father," she whispered into the dark. "And I'm not going to leave you again."

With one hand on the dripping wall for balance, she threaded her way through the forest of stone protrusions, searching for a hidden entrance to some deeper recess. It wasn't unusual for gods to hide in plain sight like this. Perhaps deceiving mankind made them feel more powerful, or maybe they simply couldn't resist haunting the places they'd once made sacred. Such a tendency seemed pitiful to her now, like rats scurrying gleefully toward a trash heap, happily wallowing in mankind's unwanted leavings.

She stopped before a particularly bulbous stalagmite, its veins of rock twisting into a braided column. In the beam of her penlight, quartz flakes sparked. The stalagmite narrowed at the center, then widened again, forming the hourglass shape of Zeus's thunderbolt, so different from the sawtoothed lightning in modern depictions.

Peering around the column, she felt a moment of triumph. Her instincts proved right: Behind it, a narrow crevice stretched to the ceiling.

Her shoulders scraped against the jagged walls as she slipped inside. Beyond the crack, the cave widened into a larger chamber, empty but for the sudden storm of bats rushing past her ears. The pings of their sonar, inaudible to humans, pierced her more acute senses like knife blades. She plugged her ears with her fingers and thought seriously about trying to shoot them down. Unfortunately, the dozen arrows in her quiver wouldn't make a dent in the colony's hundreds. Ducking low, she scooted forward to search the cave for signs of non-bat occupation.

White guano covered the floor like thick paint. Between the stench and the sonar, Selene nearly gave up and turned around. She saw no painted symbols or hidden messages, none of the usual clues Athanatoi left to signal their whereabouts to other divinities. The thunderbolt-shaped stalagmite might have been pure coincidence. If Zeus was truly as mad as she'd been told, maybe he didn't want visitors. Even if he did, he might not have the resources to construct the sort of elaborate hidden lair other immortals enjoyed.

Only then, when she stopped searching the walls for some secret clue, did she notice the footprints pressed into the guano— long, bare, male footprints, the toes spread wide like those of a man used to going without shoes. Beside them were several partial bootprints from a smaller foot.

I'm not Father's first visitor, she realized with a tremor of foreboding.

The footprints led to a mossy wall. When she placed a hand on the ice-crusted green, it opened before her, nothing but hanging vegetation disguising another crevice. She passed through to a small chamber.

A filthy pallet lay against the far wall, the blanket twisted. A bucket sat beneath a dripping finger of rock, filling with milky water. A pile of bones—bats and mice and the occasional goat— lay strewn in the corner.

Her Huntress's nose led her to a stain barely visible against the rocky ground. She knelt, touching a fingertip to the congealed surface, and took a closer sniff. Only a day or two old. And not animal blood from one of the carcasses. Not human either. At least not entirely. An Athanatos was injured. Maybe dead.

She'd come too late.

"No..." she said aloud, anger coursing through her veins, hot and bitter. She ran to the pallet, ripping back the blankets as if to discover her father's corpse underneath. Spinning in a circle, she looked for further clues. With a deep breath, she forced away the rage. *I must stay calm,* she knew. *I was a cop once. I just have to follow the clues.*

Walking more deliberately around the chamber, she tried to think rationally. *I would know if Father were already dead. I would see his passing's effect on the world, just as I did with my other kin.* When her gentle mother had died, the infants in the hospital's nursery had wailed with grief. When Saturn murdered Apollo, the nearby mortals couldn't restrain the funeral dirge that ripped from their lungs for the God of Music. *If Zeus Lightning Bringer died, the sky itself would sing lamentations,* she thought desperately. *Storms would lash the earth. The stars would fall from the heavens.*

Not far from the puddle of blood, she noticed white guano scuffed into the ground. She followed the trail back to the chamber's entrance and squatted down to examine the bootprints more closely. They weren't made by one man, she saw now, but several. And the prints that pointed toward Zeus's chamber were shallower than those headed back out. *Many men went in empty-handed,* she decided. *They came out carrying my father.*

The thought infuriated her—but it also gave her a modicum of hope. It meant that Saturn hadn't come alone, desperate to enact his final vengeance upon his son. Instead, he'd brought his syndexioi. And since she and Theo had personally killed all the known members of the Host's Manhattan sect, that meant Saturn had another group of acolytes somewhere in Europe. As much as she dreaded having to face another army of Mithraists, their presence would ensure that Zeus would be sacrificed in a formal ceremony, not murdered hastily in his cave.

They may have taken Father, she knew, *but they won't kill him until their ritual is in place. There's still time to save him.*

She pounded up the metal staircase and stood in the cave's mouth, looking out over the fields and pastures, where only a scant smattering of farmhouse lights punctured the darkness.

"Hark to my words, Wily One," she said aloud. "Wherever you've taken my father, I will find him. And wherever you've hidden yourself, I will hunt you down. You will die at my hands." She raised her voice, shouting into the silent air, offering up the Olympians' most solemn oath: "I swear this upon the relentless waters of the River Styx!"

At the time, she'd felt confident of her vow. She and Flint had left Crete and headed to Italy, Mithraism's birthplace, thinking it the most likely place to find Saturn. At the cult's height, Ancient Rome had housed hundreds of mithraea. She'd been sure one of them would serve as the Host's modern headquarters.

Standing now before the door to her Roman apartment with her keys in her hand, water still dripping from her hair and clothes, she felt a wave of helplessness. For months, she and Flint had scanned the mithraea open to the public—and a few others besides—but had found no signs of recent occupation. Possibly, as in New York, the Host had built an entirely new sanctuary rather than repurposing an original one. Either way, tonight in Ostia she'd glimpsed Saturn for the first time since she'd fought him in New York. And he'd gotten away. Again.

Her anger made her throw open the door with no thought of her magnified strength. It crashed against the inside wall of the apartment. From the far bedroom, Selene's preternatural hearing picked up the rustle of sheets. She'd awoken Flint.

He'd better not go back to sleep, she decided, marching across the small apartment to pound on his door.

"Get up," she called to him sharply. "We have work to do." She heard his weary groan, followed by the scrape of a crutch on the floor.

She was taking out her frustration on Flint, and she didn't care. Until she had Saturn before her and her arrow at his throat, someone would have to bear the brunt of her ire.

It's a good thing you're not here, Theo, she decided. *You wouldn't have put up with such treatment.* Flint, on the other hand, never complained. He accepted her ill temper and impatience with the same surly reserve he accepted the other hardships in his life.

Listening to his shuffling gait through the bedroom door, she smothered a wave of guilt. *If he doesn't like my bossing him around, he can leave,* she assured herself.

But she knew he wouldn't.

And somehow, rather than making her grateful, that just made her angrier.

Chapter 7

DAUGHTER OF ZEUS

Without a word, Flint emerged from his bedroom. Shirtless.

He smelled like sleep and sweat and smoke.

Selene followed his hooded gaze, belatedly aware of the way her wet clothes clung to her body. She fought the urge to cover herself—she'd done that for far too long. *Let him look,* she decided. *His appetites aren't my problem.*

After so many millennia of avoiding men, she still wasn't sure how to deal with them. Sometimes she felt like she was thirteen years old instead of three thousand, first exploring her effect on men and theirs on her, behaving erratically, even cruelly, in her attempts to navigate her own feelings. Flint, on the other hand, had many lifetimes' worth of experience with women. He had, after all, once been married to Aphrodite, the Goddess of Love.

His bloodshot eyes flicked away from Selene; he limped into the kitchen on a simple aluminum crutch. She heard the clatter of the moka pot against the gas burner and retreated to her own bedroom to change into dry clothes, telling herself it was only because she didn't want to drip on the furniture.

A few minutes later, she returned to find Flint hobbling to the table with a cup of coffee in one hand. He lowered himself into a chair half as wide as his frame required.

I see he hasn't bothered to put on a shirt, she noted with annoyance.

She sat across the table from him anyway, trying to keep her eyes from wandering to the broad planes of his chest or the bulging muscles of his arms.

"We need a new plan," she began without preamble. "Killing members of the Host may be thinning their numbers, but it's not getting us any closer to finding my father."

Flint stared pensively at his coffee, his lips a flat line. He'd never been fully on board with rescuing Zeus in the first place—she knew that. He wanted her to focus solely on killing Saturn, both as revenge for the deaths of so many Athanatoi and to prevent any future murders.

"We *have* to rescue the King of the Gods," she repeated now in reply to his unspoken remonstrance. "When Saturn finally sacrifices him, there's no telling how powerful he'll become. You saw how quick he was to discard one of his own loyal syndexioi. How do you think he'll treat the millions of humans who've forgotten all about him for the past two thousand years?" She shook her head angrily. "We've seen what gods do to the mortal world when they're trying to regain their power. Innocents die, Flint. How much worse will it be once one actually gets the power he seeks?" She shuddered. "Even the strongest Athanatos won't be able to stand against our grandfather once his Last Age begins. The mortals will have no one to protect them."

Flint nodded slowly. "All the more reason to kill him without delay."

"And leave my father to rot in some Mithraic cell that we'll never find? Or let the syndexioi kill him as revenge for the murder of their Pater? No. We find Zeus first. We save him and prevent Saturn's rise at the same time. Then we go for the kill."

Flint grunted noncommittally. Over and over, those first few weeks after Crete, he'd reminded her of all her father's failings.

Zeus had been a shameless womanizer, a negligent parent, and a wrathful god.

"He's my *father*," Selene insisted heatedly. "He may be imperfect, he may have done unforgivable things—but so have we all. I punished women I should've protected; I cared only for my own glory; I killed innocents. I've tried to make up for those crimes by helping the mortals I once disdained. If I can forgive myself, don't I owe my father at least that much?" Flint didn't respond. "I can't abandon him," she went on. "I just can't. You wouldn't understand. You never *had* a father."

She watched the muscles of Flint's forearms pop as he squeezed his cup, wondering if the ceramic would shatter. *Not the best time to remind Flint of his unusual parentage,* she realized belatedly.

"My stepfather could've been a father to me," he growled. "But he was too busy throwing me off Olympus." He glanced up at her, his eyes flashing beneath his thick brows. "Or did you forget that part? The part where my mother birthed me without the help of her husband's seed, the smallest payback for the dozens of children he'd sired on other women, and in revenge, Zeus tossed me from the mountaintop like a sack of trash. *Trash*, Selene, not a child."

"I know," she said quietly.

She'd watched as her once cheerful young stepbrother had disappeared through the clouds, hurled from Olympus by her own father. Weeks later, when Zeus's temper had cooled, she watched Hephaestus return, untrusting, bitter, closed. His legs crippled beyond repair, his face creased in a frown that would become his hallmark.

"I was there. I saw it happen," she said now. "And...like all the rest...I did nothing."

Flint, always so stoic, winced as if slapped.

"You didn't remember that part, did you?" she murmured. "You thought I was off hunting, dancing. You didn't know I witnessed your fall. You didn't remember I could be so cruel."

He shook his head, not meeting her eyes.

"And if you had known... would it have changed how you—"

"No," he said quickly. But he didn't look at her. And he didn't explain.

Finally, she began a story of her own, the only way she knew to make him understand why, despite all Zeus's failings, she still felt such loyalty to him. "When I was merely a child, they say I sat on my father's lap and asked him to make me a huntress. To give me nymphs for my playmates and a bow to wield and everything else my heart desired. And he said yes. Yes to all of it. That's the story the poets tell, and I remember it well. But there's another story, one so faint I see it only in snatches. One never recited by Ovid or Homer or Callimachus." She turned her gaze to the rustling plane tree outside her window, as if its shuddering green would help her remember.

"I was on the slopes of Olympus, where the wildflowers glowed like flame in the sunlight, but the forest was cool and dark. I'd run away from the summit that day. Probably to escape my stepmother's hounding."

Flint snorted, not bothering to defend his mother. Hera was Zeus's queen. Birthing her fatherless son was one of her less violent attempts to punish her husband for his infidelity. Usually, she took out her rage on Zeus's consorts and bastards—Artemis, Apollo, and their mother, Leto, among them.

"I found a place where the Queen wouldn't find me," Selene went on. "Beneath trees so old and twisted that their branches bent into dryads' thrones. I had the bow my father had granted me... the one *you* made for me. But I didn't know how to shoot it. Arrow after golden arrow went flying through the trees. Those beautiful arrows you'd crafted, with leaf-shaped blades and..." She hesitated, trying to remember.

"Hawk-feather fletching," Flint whispered hoarsely.

"Yes." Her face softened at the memory. "Black feathers,

while Apollo's were white. I'd forgotten that. Well, all those arrows went disappearing into the woods, and the woods were growing darker, the sun setting, and then..." Her voice caught at the memory, as if she were a child again, suddenly scared and alone and knowing she'd made a terrible mistake. "I saw two points of light in the shadows. The glowing eyes of a wild boar. Its tusks as long as an elephant's. Or at least...they seemed that way to me. It snorted, pawed the earth. Then it galloped toward me, and I froze." She felt Flint's eyes on her, questioning.

"I was a child still, not a huntress, despite my father's promise. I was about to be gored. That tusk was an inch away, and I didn't even have the breath to scream, and then...then my father was there." A smile tugged on her lips. "Eighteen feet tall, at least. Hair shadow-black and those eyes like a summer sky and arms as wide and strong as tree limbs. The boar skidded to a stop, its sharp hooves digging into the soft earth, its nostrils pumping steamy air into the night. Then it *bowed*. First to Father. Then to me." She gave a small laugh. "Then the fearsome King of the Gods taught me how to shoot. Stayed there all night with me, arrow after arrow, showing me how to aim, how to watch the arrow's flight, how to find the shafts again in the dark. I was never scared of wild animals again. Or the forest. Or the night. He made me who I am. He gave me that gift."

Her hand strayed to the necklace at her throat. Flint's gift. "My father loved me," she said. "He still does. I have to believe that. That sort of love doesn't just disappear, no matter how many thousands of years have passed. My twin loved me like that. And my mother. They're both gone. I won't lose my father, too."

Flint allowed a small, pained nod. Selene held her breath, waiting for him to say something, to acknowledge that Apollo and Leto and Zeus weren't the only ones to love her. But when he turned to her, his eyes dark and simmering with millennia of unspoken emotion, her heart seized with fear. She was back in that forest again, facing a long-tusked boar. If she didn't do something, fast, she'd be run through. Gored. And all her immortal powers would never close the gaping wound.

So she broke his gaze and said brusquely, "We still don't know why the Wily One hasn't already sacrificed my father. Or why he's accumulating new artifacts."

Flint's face instantly shuttered. He looked away, granting her no more than a shrug.

Selene felt a stab of loneliness, guilt. *How much of his brooding silence is because I won't let him speak?* Theo's face flashed before her. Open, honest. *You'd never let me shut you up. You'd insist I listen to what you had to say, even if I wasn't ready to hear it. You'd talk it all through with me. Your feelings, my feelings, and Saturn's whereabouts, too. Together, we'd find Zeus.*

She'd longed for Theo's help since she first got to Rome. Her half brother Scooter Joveson—once known as Dash Mercer, and before that as Hermes, the Messenger God—still kept in contact with her former lover. So far, Scooter had kept her secret—Theo still thought she was dead.

Scooter had admitted that he'd requested the professor's assistance on their hunt for Saturn—against her express wishes. *"I faked my own death to keep Theo safe,"* she'd shouted at him over the phone. *"I want to remove him from this battle between gods—not thrust him right back into danger, you bastard."*

Thankfully, Theo had refused to help Scooter—which was exactly as it should be. *I want him to forget about me,* she reminded herself now. If he'd agreed to join the hunt, not only would his life be threatened, but she risked running into him on the streets of Rome. The thought made her throat clench. *His rage at my lies would break me in half. And I barely feel whole as it is.*

The last time she'd allowed herself to spy on her former lover, only a week after her supposed death, she'd had Philippe—aka Eros, the God of Love—shoot a dart into Theo's arm. Just enough, Philippe had promised, to smooth the jagged edges of Theo's grief. To make it possible for him, someday, to love someone else.

I should've asked Philippe to shoot me too, she thought with a surreptitious glance at the man sitting across from her. *Instead, Flint and I just hurtle forward, slamming into dead end after dead end. Unable to find my father. Unable to find each other.*

She pressed on, seeking distraction in the hunt that had driven her for so long. "We know that Saturn's plan in New York was to perform a series of Mithraic rituals paired with the sacrifice of Athanatoi. Hades, Mars, Apollo—all killed as steps along the way to the Host's final goal." Her old training as a cop taught her that reviewing the facts could help her predict her target's next moves. "The cult chose Prometheus as the final offering. His murder would've completed the ritual and ushered in the Last Age, complete with the resurrection of Saturn's own omnipotent power. Instead, Prometheus refused to become a willing sacrifice. He died in a lightning blast, rather than at Saturn's hand—the ritual was left incomplete. So now Saturn and his acolytes have to start over."

"Except they're running out of Olympians to kill," Flint interjected grimly.

"Right. Now that we know he's after us, we're not so easy to catch. But he already has my father—the most powerful sacrifice the cult can make. Killing the King of the Gods is the only way to finally complete the ritual and return our grandfather to power."

"But Zeus is still alive." Flint didn't look particularly heartened by that fact.

"Which is a *good* thing," Selene snapped. "The problem is, we don't know what Saturn's waiting for." The Host must have an elaborate rite planned. She knew from recent experience that restoring supernatural power required more than just murdering a god. You had to do it right: collect authentic artifacts, find the perfect location, pick the most auspicious time, assemble the most dedicated worshipers. Otherwise the ritual didn't work.

She took a deep breath as she considered the information they'd just uncovered. "I assume Saturn wanted the black arc from the mithraeum floor as a representation of the celestial spheres that Mithras controls. But we still don't know why he was so obsessed with the marble pine tree. It's an attribute of the Great Mother, but Mithraism's an all-male cult. It doesn't make sense. How could *she* help them bring about the Last Age?"

Flint scowled. "From what I remember, she wasn't exactly... pro-male."

"That's an understatement." In her godhood, Selene had rarely paid much attention to cults beside her own, and the Great Mother, whom the Greeks called Cybele and the Romans called the Magna Mater, wasn't even an Olympian. Just an eastern goddess who eventually joined their pantheon. Still, Selene had always admired her proto-feminist bent. "From what I remember, her Roman priests dedicated themselves through a sword dance in front of her statue. Cymbals crashing, drums pounding, hair flying. Eventually, they threw their offerings onto the statue's lap."

"What kind of offerings?"

"Their testicles, of course."

Flint shifted in his chair, looking ill, but the thought of castrating a few syndexioi made Selene feel considerably better.

"I was thinking," she went on eagerly, "that next time, we need to have a tracking device ready. If we'd managed to get one into a syndexios last night, we'd be hunting Saturn down right now and finding whatever mithraeum he's hiding in, instead of sitting here like useless idiots, hoping he doesn't track *us* down first."

"A tracking device might work," Flint agreed. She waited for him to go on, but he didn't.

She heaved an exasperated breath. Holding up a one-sided conversation was utterly exhausting. *How did you ever stand talking to me, Theo?*

"If you show the device to me," she urged, "I can try to attach it to an arrow."

He mumbled something that sounded like assent, then fell mute.

Five minutes of awkward silence passed before Selene slammed her fist on the table. "If you want to say something, just *say* it."

Hurt flashed across Flint's face. He reached for the pocket of his sweatpants, resting his hand there as if unsure whether to withdraw whatever was inside.

"What?" Selene pressed. "Are you being surly for no reason? Or do you just not care about finding Saturn anymore?"

Flint's jaw twitched beneath his bushy beard. "He killed my brother, too. Of course I care."

"So then why the silence? Do you want to talk this through, or should I just go back to the river and talk to myself? Because honestly, it'd be just about as useful."

His fingers curled around his pocket. Something in his hesitation, in the tension that rippled across his wide forearms, made her worry that she'd pressed him too far. That he'd lash out. Or perhaps just walk away. She braced herself for either, unsure which would be worse.

Instead, he pulled out a piece of card stock, gilt-edged and embossed with a mass of curlicues and flowers. A wedding invitation.

She couldn't see the names on the paper. Didn't *want* to see them. She could feel the boar's hot breath on her face.

Flint shifted in his seat to face her and braced his hands on the arms of the chair, as if to rise. *He had that invitation printed up as a proposal,* she knew suddenly. *He's going to kneel down on those withered legs and ask me to marry him.*

"I have an idea," he said finally. "You're just not going to like it."

It was Selene's turn to be speechless. *No, please no,* she begged silently.

He sighed, a slow exhale like a volcano venting steam. "I know this is the last place you want to go, and the last person you want to see, but she might help us understand the Magna Mater connection."

"She?" Selene stammered. "Wait...who?"

He passed her the invitation. "My mother's getting married right here in Rome. Tomorrow morning."

Selene could breathe again.

Flint's lips twisted into a grim smirk that she suspected was his attempt at a smile. "So, Selene Neomenia, I'm officially asking...do you want to be my date?"

Chapter 8

THE LION-HEADED GOD

Artemis watched him.

At least that's how it felt to Theo every time he walked through the Greek and Roman collection at the Metropolitan Museum of Art. He avoided the far end of the gallery entirely, where an ancient bronze of the young Huntress, her arms flung wide after just releasing her arrow, stared over the tourists' heads with silvered eyes.

But the goddess was everywhere. Her sharp profile painted on vases, her lithe body sculpted in metal or clay or marble. Each image reminded Theo of the woman he'd loved and lost, yet none of them were his Selene. The short tunic and knee-high sandals were nothing like the baggy clothes and heavy boots she favored. The youthful archer in the bronze statue had none of the cares that had creased his lover's brow. The simple terra-cotta figurines could not move with her grace. The flat vase paintings forgot her smile—and her more frequent glare.

Apollo watched, too, of course. Artemis's twin brother with his sculpted lyre and laurel wreath. And Mars. Hades. Prometheus. All those Theo had been unable to save when the Host began to hunt down the city's immortals. He felt the reproach in their eyes and walked faster. Today, he had a different god to meet.

A long line stretched before the entrance to the special exhibit, nearly blocking the banner: MITHRAS AND MAYHEM.

"The sensationalist alliteration was your idea, I take it," he said to the man waiting for him beside the crowd.

"You know it." In a faded *Wrath of Khan* T-shirt, Steve Atwood looked more like the head of a college sci-fi club than of the Met's Onassis Library for Hellenic and Roman Art. He'd proudly refused to conform to the museum's unofficial male dress code: glasses, balding, white. Instead, with the dreadlocks gathered on top of his otherwise shorn head and the perennial gleam in his eye, he looked like a mischievous black samurai—an impression he proudly admitted to cultivating.

Despite the doubts of many an Upper East Side dowager, Steve had managed to pull together the Met's most popular exhibit ever in the span of only six months. The existence of the Olympians—and Mithras's direct connection to Jesus—remained a secret. But the final battle atop the Statue of Liberty, when Selene and Theo had defeated the Host, had been impossible to hide completely. The bodies of the dead syndexioi had led to the discovery of the hidden mithraeum beneath Saint Patrick's Cathedral, full of ancient artifacts and high-tech torture devices. The existence of a secret temple practicing human sacrifice in the middle of Midtown had sent the city into a frenzy of conspiracy-theorizing and ignited a passionate interest in Roman cults.

Theo eyed the crowd skeptically. "All those years I spent trying to make classics cool through compelling lectures and witty essays—I should've just killed a few people instead." He barked an angry laugh. "Works like a charm."

Steve, oblivious to his misery, flashed his museum ID to cut the line. "If people keep reviving ancient mystery cults, we're going to have to make this a permanent exhibit. I'm thinking *Classical Crazies: Making Sacrifices for All of Us.*" He winced before Theo could. "Sorry, man. I keep forgetting about—you know."

"It's okay." But it wasn't. As Steve well knew, the first cult to terrorize Manhattan had claimed Helen Emerson, Theo's ex-girlfriend, as its victim. Less than three months later, the Mithraists had killed Selene. He'd trade every minute of renewed interest in classics for one more second with the women he'd loved.

"By the way, thanks for the dinner invite last night," Steve said, clearly trying to change the subject. He didn't know Selene was a goddess—but he knew Theo had loved her. Even more than Ruth, Steve tried to avoid the "dead girlfriend" subject whenever possible.

"Wish I could claim credit, but the invitation was the ladies' idea," Theo admitted. "I think they wanted to make sure I had a friend to talk to when Minh's coworkers started rattling on about quasars."

Steve laughed. "Yeah, even Ruth Willever looked bored when that came up, and I thought she was incapable of expressing any emotion besides polite engagement."

"No, she definitely has plenty of other emotions." Theo thought of her hand settling on his thigh.

"Yeah, I'm starting to get that impression."

On another day, Steve's admiring tone would've invited closer scrutiny. But as they walked past the various artifacts on loan from museums around the world, Theo could think of nothing but his research. Most of the pieces in the gallery were tauroctonies: statues, reliefs, and frescoes of Mithras standing astride a bull with his knife at its throat, surrounded by a scorpion, crow, snake, and dog.

"I'm afraid I never want to see another tauroctony," he grumbled. "I've spent way too much time with them already."

"Don't worry," Steve assured him. "What I've got to show you

is much cooler than the same old Mithras-kills-the-bull crap."
He led the way through the throng and into a darkened gallery.

A three-foot-tall statue of a creature with a man's body and a
feline face stood in a pool of light.

"Say hello to the Lion-Headed God."

"Holy Roman Empire," Theo cursed, taking a step closer.

"Yeah. Except not exactly *holy*. He looks more like a demon,
doesn't he?" Steve sounded like a kid gleefully shivering over his
first horror film. "Or a fallen angel, you know, with the wings."

"I didn't even notice the wings, there's so much else going
on." Four small feathered appendages grew from the lion-
headed creature's body, two from his shoulders and two from
his hips, like a grotesque butterfly. A thick snake twined its way
up his naked form, leaving just enough space between its coils to
display the lion-headed creature's very human penis. The snake's
head rested atop the lion's mane like a diadem. In each hand, the
creature held a strange, L-shaped implement.

"You recognize him?" Steve prodded.

"I've never seen anything like him. With the animal head and
his posture, he looks almost Egyptian. Where did you—"

"Archeologists found similar statues in several Mithraic temples around the world, side by side with the tauroctonies. This
particular beauty was originally found in the ruins in Ostia, but
the Vatican Museum owns it now. You know those Catholics—
nothing they love more than collecting pagan art, hypocrites
that they are. My bosses got it on loan because it's so freaking
bizarre that it gets more press for the exhibit. They didn't think
our own version was dramatic enough."

"Your own version? I've never noticed anything like this in
the Met."

"Turn around, buddy, and meet our newest acquisition." He
gestured to a small display case on the opposite wall. "We found
this little guy down under Saint Patrick's."

Theo pulled himself away from the larger statue and peered

into the case. A crude terra-cotta figurine, no more than six inches tall. It had the same lion's head and twisting snake, the same L-shaped tools and four wings. But this creature balanced atop a sphere like a clown at the circus.

"We think the ball he's standing on could be a celestial sphere," Steve offered. "Especially since you explained that our local cult members believed Mithras controlled the movement of the heavens."

"Mm-hm," Theo murmured. He'd walked a fine line for months, sharing most of his Mithras knowledge first with the police and then with Steve, while withholding the ultimate secret of the cult leader's identity. Not for the first time, Theo wished he could explain to his friend that Saturn—the ancient Greco-Roman god who just happened to be his dead girlfriend's grandfather—was the cult's true focus. *Steve would shit himself if he knew.* But having Gabriela and Ruth in on the secret of the Olympians' existence was dangerous enough. *Steve would never be able to resist mounting a whole exhibition about it. "Gods-zilla" or "Gods-smacked" or some other nonsense.*

"I haven't even gotten to the good stuff yet," continued Steve. "You asked me to keep an eye out for anything related to Pythagoras or the tetractys figure, right?"

"Yeah..."

"Well, I got nothing on number theory. *But* you also said to look out for anything about rebirth or reincarnation." Steve gestured Theo toward the next gallery and led him to a marble relief of a young man emerging from a broken eggshell. A thick snake wrapped his naked body, and feathered wings hung from his shoulders. The animals of the zodiac surrounded him in a perfect oval border. His face was human rather than leonine, and he carried a torch instead of L-shaped tools, but otherwise the resemblance to the Mithraic lion-god was undeniable.

"You know what that eggshell means." Steve looked immensely proud of himself.

"Creation, life cycle, and—"

"*Resurrection*. You're welcome, by the way."

"But the lion-headed god was on a sphere," Theo began.

"Yeah, I know, but come on! They're obviously just different versions of the same god. Like Zeus and Jupiter—or Artemis and Diana."

Theo tried not to flinch at the reference. "But *what* god?"

"I didn't recognize him at first either," Steve said with only a hint of condescension, "but I did a little digging and found several similar figures depicted on mosaics and frescoes in a few European museums. Young man. Snake. Wings. He's not an Olympian—not part of the standard classical pantheon at all. But he shows up in a couple different sources as the 'Protogonos.'"

"Like … a proto-god?"

"*Ding ding ding!* And not just *any* old proto-god. This one's specifically worshiped by initiates into the Orphic Mysteries." He held up a hand. "I know what you're going to say … there's never been a connection between followers of Mithras and followers of Orpheus. But check it out." Steve pointed to the faint Latin words inscribed at the base of the relief. "This beauty was once owned by an ancient initiate into the Mithraic cult. And look at the zodiac border! You're the one who told me the bull and scorpion on the tauroctony were constellation references. So the symbolism is definitely both Orphic and Mithraic."

Theo couldn't even protest. He'd seen how cults combined—and stole—rituals and deities from each other. Saturn had inserted Mithraism into Christianity, after all. But was it really possible that he'd injected *Orphism* into Mithraism as well?

"I only know the usual Orpheus myth." He'd found the story of the legendary musician's journey to the Underworld especially poignant since Selene's death, although he didn't need to admit that to Steve. "I don't know anything about his cult or his followers."

"Of course not," Steve said with a grin. "No one does. It's one of the most mysterious of all mystery cults! They left behind no temples—only a few of the gold leaves they put around the necks of their dead. But we do know the Orphics were big into hymns, and we've still got a bunch of the texts, each dedicated to a different god—including one to our friend the Protogonos. They thought he was the first god. A primordial deity who cracked open an egg to create the world. Then the Mithraists popped a lion's head on him and turned his egg into a celestial sphere." He finally paused for breath. "Now as to *why* they did that?" He pointed a finger at Theo. "I was hoping you could tell me. You're the Mithras expert."

Because Saturn was trying to regain his omnipotence—and he'd steal power from any number of gods to do it, Theo almost blurted. He settled for, "Because the cult initiates thought they could resurrect Mithras. They couldn't resist any god associated with rebirth and reincarnation."

Steve laughed aloud. "I get that the *ancients* thought that. But the dudes hanging out under Saint Patrick's? They really believed they could resurrect their god? Totally looney tunes."

Theo forced an answering smile. *Except they weren't crazy at all. Saturn* did *get more powerful through his ritual sacrifices. Everything he did had a purpose. Which means if the Mithraists believed the lion-headed creature could help resurrect a god . . . then he can help* me *do the same thing.* He sucked in a breath. *The key to reincarnation lies not in some divine numerical pattern—but in the Protogonos. He can bring back Selene.*

He felt as if an abyss had suddenly opened in what he'd thought was solid ground. He teetered there on the edge, arms pinwheeling to remain upright. Was he really about to abandon his research into Pythagoras and start down the path of a far more esoteric cult instead? And would this Orphic-Mithraic deity even hold the answers he sought?

The Protogonos should be the farthest back I can reach—the very first god, he thought desperately. *But I know better. If I look beyond his myths, I'll find someone else. And someone else again. And when there are finally no gods left to study, I'll fall tumbling into* Khaos, *the chasm of nothingness from which the world was born. And I may never climb out again.*

"You look a little green, my man." Steve cocked his head.

"No, just putting it all together," Theo lied.

"I thought you'd be psyched." Steve rubbed his hands gleefully. "Now that we know about the Mithras connection, I'm going to bust open the whole Orphism mystery like the Protogonos cracking the World Egg. You should go check out the Rodin sculpture on the second floor. I put a little extra Orphic something up there that I think you'll appreciate."

Theo nodded distractedly and turned to go.

"Hold up! I didn't mean right this second. Don't you want to see the collection of zodiac-symbol branding irons we found in the Saint Patrick's mithraeum? They'll blow your mind."

"No, trust me, I've seen them." He scratched self-consciously at the Mercury symbol hidden beneath his shirt. At Steve's bewildered stare, he added hurriedly, "I'm fine. I just—this is a lot to take in. I'll go look at the sculpture. I just…" He wasn't even sure how to finish the sentence. *Just wasted six months of my life on Pythagorean number theory for no reason?*

His feet carried him out of the gallery and up a flight of stairs to the Nineteenth-Century European Sculpture wing. He stood before a white marble Rodin. A naked man in polished stone raised a hand to cover his eyes. Behind him stood a woman, her lips parted as if in exhaustion or pain, her half-carved hair emerging from the rough-hewn stone that loomed behind them.

"Who's that guy?" a voice piped from beside him, interrupting his reverie.

The little boy's head barely cleared the statue's base. Theo looked around for a parent and saw a woman in sweatpants sitting cross-legged on a bench, staring at her cell phone.

"Is that your mom?"

"Nanny," the boy said, not bothering to look. "She doesn't know anything about statues. Do you?"

Theo cleared his throat. "I know about this one."

"I like it," the boy said, pointing a chubby finger at the marble man. "I just want to know why he's covering his eyes."

"He's Orpheus," Theo began. He remembered the first time he'd read the myth. He'd been only a little older than this boy, but it had stuck with him for the rest of his life. "He had a lyre. That's like a—"

"Like a harp," the boy interrupted.

"Yeah," Theo said, surprised. He liked young children; he just wasn't sure whether to treat them like puppies or colleagues. "Well, they say Orpheus played music so sweet that the animals would gather at his feet to listen. Even the rocks rolled close to hear his song."

The boy nodded. "Cool."

"He fell in love with a girl named Eurydice. But they were only happy for a few short months before a viper rose up and bit her on the foot. She died." He stopped, wondering suddenly if this story was too scary for a kid. But the boy just stared up at him expectantly. Theo went on. "Orpheus traveled all the way to the Underworld to get her back. Hades, Lord of the Dead, and his wife, Persephone, laughed at him. No one who dies can be resurrected. But then Orpheus began to play a dirge. A song of mourning so bittersweet, so beautiful, that Persephone, cold Queen of the Dead, dissolved into sobs. 'Make him stop,' she begged her husband, 'or I'll drown in my own tears.' So Hades relented. He let Orpheus lead his love out from death, on one condition." Theo paused for effect. The boy was still listening. "On the journey from the Underworld, Orpheus must never look back to check that Eurydice followed him. True love requires trust.

"So, lyre clutched in his hands, Orpheus began the long trek back to the world of the living." *Perhaps, if Steve is right,* Theo thought, *Orpheus wasn't alone.* A snake-twined, four-winged, lion-headed god might have flown before him, leading the way. But for now, Theo stuck to the myth he knew.

"Orpheus couldn't hear Eurydice's footsteps behind him, but he trusted that she followed—at least at first. Then a cold dread gripped him, and he grew convinced that she'd turned back or fallen behind or had never chosen to come in the first place. Just steps from freedom, from life, from happiness...Orpheus looked back."

The boy's mouth gaped open.

"He caught one glimpse of his love's horror-stricken face before the hand of death swirled forward and snatched her away once more."

Sudden tears sprang to the boy's eyes. He gave a tiny, hiccupping sob.

"Oh shit," Theo began. "I mean, *darn,* I didn't mean—"

The nanny jumped up from the bench, finally attentive, and grabbed the boy by the arm. "Come on, Ben." Theo was convinced he was about to be arrested, but the woman seemed angrier with the boy. "Stop bothering the gentleman." She dragged the kid off to the next gallery, leaving Theo alone with Orpheus.

I know how you must have felt, he thought, staring at the marble man with his covered eyes. *To have love ripped away just as you thought it'd be yours forever.* There was only one difference.

I trusted, he reminded himself. *I wouldn't have looked back, I didn't* look back. *I trusted her with my heart and she broke it in half.* His last memory of Selene returned: her silver eyes full of tears as she pried herself free of his arms and plummeted through the night. Snatched away by the hand of death.

Orpheus himself, if he'd ever existed, was no Athanatos. He was long dead. Yet Theo couldn't resist offering a prayer to his shade. *You found a way. You almost brought back your love.*

"Please," he whispered aloud. "Teach me the secret of resurrection. Tell me if it's you or your religion or your lion-headed god. And I swear, upon the dark waters of the Styx, that I will succeed where you failed."

Beside the statue hung a set of headphones. The nearby placard explained that scholars had recently uncovered the musical notation for the *Orphic Hymn to Protogonos*.

Listen to a musician play the melody on a re-created ancient lyre, it invited, *and imagine Orpheus himself playing it to escape the Underworld.*

A bit fanciful for the Met, Theo thought, *but the patrons will love it. Typical Steve.*

He put on the headphones. The lyre twanged percussively, more like an Indian sitar than a modern harp, each new note reverberating into a chord that resonated somewhere deep in his mind. He thought of his paltry Pythagorean instrument with its single string. He'd wanted to simplify his impossible quest to its purest essence—mathematical ratios, numbers on a page. Comprehensible, rational, straightforward. But the mysteries of death and life were not so clear—and neither, for all its grounding in math, was music. The ancient Orphic hymn that pulsed through the headphones was heart and soul and memory.

I remember this tune, he realized suddenly. He looked again at the placard. Archeologists had only recently discovered the musical notation carved into a marble grave marker, so why did he feel he could sing along with the melody? Why did it conjure such a vivid image of a naked man standing in front of an open fridge, humming the song as he twirled his copious chest hair with one hand and pawed through moldy leftovers with the other?

Theo ripped off the headphones with a groan. *I knew that if I looked beyond the Orphic Protogonos, I'd find another god. I just really hoped it wouldn't be this one.*

A decade earlier, this particular Athanatos had spent four years as Theo's grad school roommate, luring him into drunken revelries that usually ended with him feeling both physically ill and morally compromised—when he could remember them at all.

This time, Theo resolved, *when Dennis Boivin offers me a cup of wine, I'm going to refuse.* But he'd sworn the same thing many times when facing the God of the Grape. It had never worked. Then again, a little immoral hedonism would be a small price to pay for his ultimate goal.

To resurrect Selene, I'll go wherever I have to, he knew. *And unlike Orpheus, I'll never look back.*

Chapter 9

GODDESS OF MARRIAGE

Tight leather pants despite the heat, boots laced to her knees, a sleeveless shirt that showed the corded muscles of her arms. Selene had chosen the outfit with care.

It wasn't every day she met her ancient nemesis for the first time in fifteen hundred years.

Normally she preferred clothes that concealed her figure from men's prying eyes, but she needed to make a statement. She wished she could hide the streak of white in her black hair; she was no fading goddess, resigned to death. She was the Huntress still, modern and fierce. From the hungry look on Flint's face when she left her bedroom, she might've succeeded too well.

His gaze traveled appreciatively up her body to the gold necklace at her throat.

"You do realize this is a wedding—not a fight club?" He wore a summer suit that strained across his biceps and shoulders. She could just make out the lines of his titanium leg braces beneath the fabric of his pants. She'd never seen him in anything so formal. He'd left the collar of his shirt open—it barely fit around his neck anyway.

"This whole wedding is ridiculous. Hera's already married."

"Not sure she sees it that way."

"Oh?" Selene demanded. She didn't fundamentally care about her stepmother's fidelity, but she found herself defending her father's honor nonetheless. "How does *Zeus* see it?" She couldn't resist using her father's real name for emphasis.

Flint shrugged. "I'm sure my mother hasn't asked. And doesn't care. But trust me, she *will* care if you show up to her party wearing that. And don't protest," he said, before she could do exactly that. "If she's offended, she's liable to throw us out before she answers any of our questions about the Magna Mater. She's always been touchy."

You want to see touchy? Selene thought. *Try forcing me into a dress.* She grabbed a long, gauzy green shawl spangled with mirrored sequins from above the kitchen doorway—one of the apartment manager's misguided attempts at interior decoration—and draped it around her neck and shoulders. "Better?"

"Yes. But you don't need to bring your bow," he said, gesturing to the large bag slung over her arm.

"You clearly don't remember the Trojan War," Selene snapped back.

"Oh no, I remember." A rare glimmer of humor danced in his eyes.

"What's so funny? You *liked* watching me get my ass kicked by your mother?"

"I'd always thought you were..." He paused. "Heartless. Invincible. Then I saw you weren't. That's all." He shrugged and turned away, leaving her both curious and annoyed.

Selene's pique turned to outright rage when they arrived at the steps of the Church of the Most Holy Name of Mary.

"A *church*? You're kidding, right? I won't step foot in there."

"Where else did you think she'd get married?"

"Since when has your mother gone over to the enemy?"

"Wait here," Flint said, not bothering to answer. He walked stiffly up the stairs and into the church.

A short time later, the voice of a priest floated through the open doors. Despite her fluent Latin, Selene had a very shaky grasp of modern Italian. She caught something about Christ and God and love, then just tuned the whole thing out. She sat on the steps, staring across the street at Trajan's Column instead. The ancient monument towered a hundred feet above the sunken plaza on which it stood, dwarfing the surrounding ruins. The plaza hadn't originally been below street level, of course, but over the centuries, Rome built upward, covering much of its past beneath avenues and piazzas. Selene felt a shiver run up her spine as she realized that even now, on the steps of this church, she sat atop unknown layers of her own history. Perhaps a temple to Diana once stood on this very spot—a fitting site for a church dedicated to another holy virgin in another age.

Man is fickle, she mused, *turning from one god to another. Bad enough they abandoned me for Mary. What happens if Saturn gains such power that they abandon Jesus for him?* The thought brought her to her feet. The sooner she could speak to Hera, the sooner she could continue her quest to find her father before it was too late.

She moved to the threshold of the church, peering down the main aisle toward the altar. She knew her refusal to enter was a little silly—it was just a building, after all. She wouldn't melt or burst into flame just because her foot touched sanctified marble. *I'm not a vampire,* she told herself sternly. She caught sight of the icon of the Virgin Mary hanging in a massive, gold-encrusted frame above the altar and forced herself to meet her replacement's mild gaze.

Beneath the painting of Mary stood Selene's stepmother—Hera, Queen of Olympus, Goddess of Marriage and Families. She looked like a middle-aged housewife from the flyover states. Her famous white arms were rounder than before; the hair that had once crowned her head in inky coils now flopped around her ears in a curly gray mop. She wore a calf-length dress of ivory lace, with no waist to speak of. The only hint of her former status as the Queen of the Gods was a curving diadem made of dozens of tiny gold willow leaves. It looked out of place—a tiara for a youthful bride. Hera should've stuck with a sensible hat.

The groom clasping her hands stood a full head shorter than she—not surprising, considering the goddess retained much of her divine height—and looked half his bride's age. Handsome, stylish, his narrow jaw shadowed with stubble. He wore a neat white suit with an overlarge lotus bud in his lapel, and he stared up at his bride with all the adoration of an acolyte at a shrine. She looked down at him with equal fervor, her cow eyes large and dark and full of love.

Selene grimaced and stepped back from the entrance.

It wasn't long before the bride and groom appeared on the church steps—Hera holding a water lily bouquet in one hand and her young husband in the other. Selene moved forward to intercept them, but three dozen grinning Italians in rainbow hues blocked her way. Flint emerged next, a dark cloud floating in their wake.

"What are you scowling about?" Selene asked him as the couple pulled away in their waiting limousine and headed toward the reception site. "This was your idea."

He glared at her from beneath his grizzled brows, and she was taken aback by the anger she saw there. *I should've remembered that weddings would put him in a foul mood.* His own marriage to Aphrodite, Goddess of Erotic Love, had soured early on. She remembered the wedding only vaguely. Even then, the bride had eyes only for Hephaestus's handsome brother Mars, God of War.

As they followed the crowd down the street toward the reception, she couldn't stop herself from asking, "So your mother clearly thinks she's free of her first husband. Do you still consider yourself married?"

"*Hephaestus* is still married to the Goddess of Love," he said. "That's what the stories say, and nothing I do can change that. But as for *Flint*...no."

"That's a bizarre way to look at it."

"It's the only way I know how."

"But Hephaestus..." She paused. One did not bring up a god's fading, or speak his real name aloud, without good reason. "He doesn't really exist anymore, does he? I mean," she said quickly, "Artemis feels very far away to me."

Flint said nothing at first, and a sudden tension thickened between them. She watched his powerful hands clench when he finally spoke. "I see her every time I look at you."

He means more than the fact that Artemis and I share the same face, the same body, Selene knew. *He's always managed to see the divine in me—and the human, too.* It was a rare gift. One she wasn't sure she deserved...or even wanted.

In the reception hall, an accordion and a mandolin played American seventies pop standards. The dance floor already brimmed with frolicking guests by the time Selene and Flint arrived. A large placard in curling letters read, *"Tanti Auguri a June e Mauricio!"*

The bride herself came to greet them at the door, throwing her arms around her son. He hugged her back a little gingerly. *And I thought my relationship with my mother was complicated,* Selene thought. Hera was the only parent he'd ever had, and she'd risked Zeus's wrath to bring Hephaestus into the world. In return, he'd always shown her loyalty, even though she'd rarely returned the favor.

When the woman turned to her, Selene stiffened, expecting her to be as arrogant and hateful as always. Hera had chased Artemis's pregnant mother across the world, full of jealous rage and determined to prevent her husband's latest consort from giving birth. Years later, she'd met Artemis on the fields of Troy and smacked her into submission like she would a recalcitrant child. Yet when the bride reached to take Selene's hand, she no longer appeared as jealous Hera, nor her Roman incarnation, imperious Juno. She was just *June*. A woman with a broad Midwestern accent and a smile to match.

"My niece! Thank you for coming, dear."

Niece? Selene thought. True, Hera was Zeus's sister (and, in the usual incestuous morass of Olympian genealogy, his wife), but she'd never been much of an aunt to Artemis, Apollo, or any of Zeus's many other out-of-wedlock children.

"We're not here for the party," Selene insisted, taking June's hand cautiously. "We came to ask questions. Did Flint tell you—"

"Plenty of time for that!" June laughed and brushed a lavender fingernail against Selene's necklace before turning back to her son. "I see you finally worked up the courage to give it to her. Now you two get out there on the dance floor!"

"I don't dance, Mother." Flint's cheeks flushed above his beard.

June swatted him playfully on one of his bulging biceps. "Don't be absurd. This isn't the nineteenth century, hon. You don't have to waltz! Just get up there and sway. It would do you both good."

"June—" Selene began.

"*Aunt* June, please. Although don't say it too loud—the family relationships are a bit hard to explain, aren't they? And I don't want to hear another word. If you want to talk to me, you'll have to wait. I'm a little busy!"

At that, her handsome husband appeared, his arm around the shoulders of an even younger man with the same narrow jaw—probably his brother. Without preamble, Mauricio grabbed Flint's face and pressed a hearty kiss on each cheek. The God of Volcanoes looked about to erupt.

"This is Flint Hamernik, an old family friend," June explained in English to her groom.

She hasn't told Mauricio she's an Olympian, Selene realized. *Otherwise, she'd introduce Flint as her son.* With his graying hair and furrowed face, the Smith looked nearly the same age as his own mother, something June couldn't justify without a complicated lie—or the even more complicated truth.

Mauricio made for Selene next, but she held out a hand to stop him. He grabbed it and pressed a wet kiss on the back. The young man at his side, clearly more attuned to her obvious discomfort, merely gave her a courtly bow. His black hair drifted across his forehead in a Superman curl.

"E questa bella donna?" the brother asked.

"Flint's date," said June quickly. Selene didn't miss the wink she threw in her son's direction, nor the answering glower he sent back.

The band began an old Italian folk song, one not nearly old enough for Selene to remember. With a joyous cry, the guests made for the dance floor.

"Come!" Mauricio declared in English. "You will join!" He took June by the hand, and the couple jogged off toward the center of the room.

With a brilliant white smile, the groom's brother reached for Selene. She was about to wrench away when she caught the look on Flint's face. He was jealous of this young, handsome Italian. *Good,* Selene decided. *Let this remind him that he has no hold over me.* She placed her hand in the young man's.

As they made their way to the dance floor, he patted his chest. "Stefano," he said by way of introduction. He was easily ten years younger than Theo, and had ten times his fashion sense, but something about his guileless smile reminded her of the man she'd loved.

I hope you're somewhere dancing today, she prayed. Then she realized she didn't even know if Theo liked to dance. She'd never gotten the chance to find out. Stefano, however, was clearly enjoying himself. His shining eyes locked on hers as he led her through the unfamiliar steps.

The guests around her clapped and shouted, encouraging the stranger in their midst. If anyone minded her leather pants, they certainly didn't say so. Normally a paragon of grace, Selene found herself discomfited by her own awkwardness as she tried to match the rhythm.

"Relax," Stefano said, his hand warm in her own. "Enjoy, yes?" He beamed at her and, for once, she listened to a mortal's advice.

Millennia ago, her worshipers had named her She Who Leads the Dance. She hadn't had much use for the epithet in recent centuries. Dancing involved people and music and crowds—all things she studiously avoided. But in a different age, her feet had pounded out the rhythm that her twin, Apollo, coaxed from the strings of his lyre. The girls who worshiped at her ancient sanctuary at Brauron had followed her lead, the youngest children dressed as bear cubs, covered in robes of yellow fur. The teenagers had shed their clothes entirely and danced with wild abandon among the sacred groves, reveling in their last days of freedom before returning to Athens for marriage and motherhood.

Selene closed her eyes and let herself fall back into that ancient rhythm, not so different from the one currently filling the hall. She released Stefano's hand and found herself in the center of the circle. She pulled the green shawl from around her neck and danced with it as she would a partner, twining it around her hands, her body, letting it swing through the air. The crowd around her stopped to watch. They stamped their feet, urging her on. Stefano stood with parted lips, panting softly with exertion—or perhaps desire.

Sweat pricked her temples and the hollow between her breasts; the band picked up speed and spurred her feet to fly. She now wished she hadn't worn her boots. She longed to feel earth between her toes, moonlight on her upturned face, the cypress-scented wind on her bare skin. She barely noticed the faces around her, but if she had, she would've seen their delight transform to something akin to awe.

Unaware of her own body, she felt the music course through her like a rushing brook. Leaping now, twisting in midair, then landing to trace intricate patterns on the floor while her hands spun the shawl into ever more fantastical shapes. She danced not for joy—but for release. All the emotions she'd kept bottled up since she'd left New York poured forth: fear for her father, rage against Saturn, longing for Theo. But most of all, she danced for Apollo, whose death had ripped the music from her life. She danced to honor her twin, to bring his melody back to the world, to prove to his shade that she had not forgotten the lessons he'd taught her: how to dance, how to love.

The music crescendoed, slowed, stopped. The guests broke into wild applause. Panting, Selene closed her eyes, clinging to the image of her twin, his fingers dancing across his lyre, his honeyed voice wrapping her sacred grove in its warmth.

After a beat, the band launched into a cheesy popular love ballad, dragging Selene back to the present, where the soaring cypress trees were merely plaster pillars and the soft earth thin parquet.

The sweating guests paired off. She felt someone approaching and knew Stefano would ask her to dance again. She could smell his cologne, too strong for her liking, but not entirely unpleasant. How would it feel to have a man's arms around her?

But Flint got to her first.

"What are you doing?" she murmured as he swept her away from the young mortal and into his embrace.

"Listening to my mother." He moved without grace, swaying just a beat behind the music. The callouses on his hand tickled her palm. His barrel chest brushed against her own as they moved. He wore no cologne, but the odor of sweat and embers washed over her. He stood only an inch shorter than she; she had to turn her face to avoid his simmering gaze. He'd never once held her like this. On any other day, she wouldn't have allowed it. But Apollo had told her to open herself to love. She'd spent months keeping Flint at a distance, and he'd spent months respecting her wishes. Now, with her heart still pounding from the dance, and the memory of Apollo's music still thrumming through her heart, she wasn't yet ready to return to her life of solitude.

Months before, lying wounded in Ruth Willever's apartment, Flint had kissed her. She still remembered the taste—smoke and sparks.

His hand tightened just a bit on her waist, as if he, too, remembered that kiss. His fingers splayed wider, feeling more of her body through the fabric of her shirt. His scent changed, too, so subtly only the Huntress would notice. She stiffened in response.

"You can't own me," she said next to his ear.

"I'm not trying to own you," he rumbled back. "I just like the . . ." He didn't finish the thought. He didn't need to.

I like it too, Selene admitted silently, surprising herself, although she wasn't ready to say the words aloud. For once, it was Flint who kept talking.

"That day on the battlefields of Troy, when you faced my mother—"

"Are you going to make me relive that?"

"Shh," he chided. "Let me finish for once." His breath was hot in her ear as he continued. "I watched as Mother grabbed your wrists and called you a hussy and ripped the bow from your grasp. And you ran in tears."

Selene snorted in annoyance but allowed him to go on.

"I'd never seen you brought low. I took your bow from my mother and sought you out."

"But you were fighting for the opposite side. I defended the Trojans—you and your mother protected the Greeks."

"I went to you anyway." He paused for a moment. "Do you remember?"

"It's not in the epics…"

"It's okay. I didn't think you would." But she felt his shoulder tense beneath her hand and knew he was hurt. "You were hiding in the forest beyond the city. Sitting by a pond, watching the ducks. I handed you your bow. I thought you'd shoot one of the birds, but instead you just looked at me and said, 'I've seen enough blood today.' And there was such…softness in you. I hadn't known you cared for the fates of the thanatoi. I'd thought that, like all our kin, you fought only for your own pride, while I alone, who saw my imperfections reflected in the faces of mortal men, truly felt their pain."

Did I really care? Selene couldn't help wondering. The Trojan War was a distant, half-formed memory to her now, the only clear moments those recorded by Homer or Virgil, but she knew the goddess she'd been. She may have wearied of war, but that didn't mean she empathized with those who fought it. Yet the Selene she'd become did care about the mortal world. She'd risked her own life many times to protect it. *Perhaps in that moment outside Troy, Hephaestus saw me not as I was, but as I would be. He knew me better than I knew myself.*

"I wanted to take you in my arms and wipe away your tears," Flint went on quietly. "But you wiped them away yourself and disappeared into the woods. You ran too fast for me to follow." He took a breath before he said, "I've been chasing you ever since."

His hand moved from her waist, his fingers brushing her ribs with the same delicacy he showed toward one of his intricate inventions. He pulled away, just far enough to meet her eyes. He stopped dancing. The song, Selene realized belatedly, had ended long before.

He looked at her expectantly, his lips tight, defensive, but his dark eyes hopeful. *You would've smiled at me, Theo,* she couldn't help thinking. *But I'll never see you again. I made sure of that. So why can't I let Flint into my heart instead?*

She stared at him, roiled with uncertainty, her right hand still clasped in his left as if they might start dancing again at any moment. He pulled it gently between them and laid it on his chest. She felt the swell of his muscle, the pounding rhythm of his heart, fast and urgent as he waited for her reply.

I'm not ready, she wanted to say. *I know you've already waited for millennia, and I know you don't have millennia left to wait.* His hair was more gray than brown, the lines beside his eyes scored deep. Athanatoi weakened in proportion to mankind's disdain for their names and attributes. No one worshiped blacksmithing or fire anymore. Another fifty years, a hundred perhaps, and Hephaestus the Smith would fade away entirely. But she couldn't give him what he wanted. Not yet. She opened her mouth to tell him so when June trotted into view, her gold diadem bouncing.

"Don't let me interrupt," she called cheerily. "But if you want to chat, let's do it before I have to cut the cake."

Flint turned to glare at her. "This isn't a good time."

"Oh, I think it is." June looped her arm through Selene's and walked her quickly off the dance floor. In the sudden tightening of her grip, Selene felt a reminder of the goddess's old strength. June leaned close and whispered in her ear, "My son is the best thing that ever happened to you. I may look like a weak old woman to you, niece, but if you play with his heart, I'll find a way to kick your ass one more time. Understand?"

Before Selene could respond, June gave her a motherly pat on the cheek and pulled away, a bride's ecstatic smile plastered once more across her face.

Chapter 10

RELEASER

Theo wasn't sure when he'd lost his clothes. Sometime after the mushrooms and before the drum circle. *Mushrooms I did* not *realize I was eating,* he insisted woozily to himself. He'd been in such a hurry to rent a car and get on the road that he hadn't stopped to eat. By the time he reached the compound outside Woodstock, he'd wolfed down the offered shroom-laced chocolate chip cookie without question.

He tried to remember how he'd wound up sitting in the dirt in the middle of an orgy in upstate New York. *If I had half a brain, I would've waited for Dennis to return to the city.* But when the man once known as Dionysus had texted back the address of his upstate compound, with an invitation to join in one of his monthly bacchanals, Theo's impatience had gotten the better of him. The sooner he discovered how Orpheus had rescued his love from the Underworld, the sooner he could do the same for his own.

Now, between the initiates gyrating ecstatically around the bonfire and the ceremonial wine making the rounds—or, knowing Dennis Boivin, something more than wine—Theo felt like he'd unknowingly joined yet another cult. The bacchants all wore gold leaf-shaped pendants around their necks—and not much else.

He sat in the circle of revelers with his hands resting over his nakedness, although the mushrooms made it hard to care about modesty—especially while the two men and one woman next to him engaged in a dizzying variety of oral-anal permutations that had Theo alternately wincing and aroused. At least four other initiates had approached him with blissful grins on their faces and asked him to join in. So far, he'd managed to politely refuse.

Finally, the host himself appeared.

Theo had expected Dennis to show up as naked as everyone else, but instead he wore a pair of skintight, groin-high cutoffs and a stained tank top that did little to conceal his potbelly, his copious chest hair, or his bulging crotch. Like his followers, he wore a gold pendant on a leather cord.

"Why do you get clothes?" Theo asked, peering up at him blearily.

"Benefits of godhood," Dennis said, settling himself on the ground and taking a swig from a plastic cup of purple liquid. "Also, keeps off the mosquitoes," he added as Theo swatted at an insect gorging on his thigh.

"So is this how you keep your power?" Theo gestured to a woman standing a few feet away, pouring wine over her hair. "God of Frenzy, right?"

Dennis laughed. "You know it. But real power would mean some human-sacrifice shit, and you know I gave that up back in the good old days. This is just for fun."

"Fun? Honestly, I've got leaves up my ass and insect bites on my balls and my brain's so fried I can barely remember why I'm here."

"That's the whole idea, dude." Dennis stretched his arms overhead. "Let it go. Let it all go."

"I can't. I need to know about..." Theo fumbled through his mind and finally came up with, "Orifice? I mean *Orpheus*."

"I miss that little motherfucker with the lyre," Dennis said with a lopsided grin. "Man spread my rites over the earth faster than chlamydia in a whorehouse."

Theo's balls shrank as he imagined just how many viruses were currently joyriding inside the bodily fluids streaming nearby. "*Your* rites? I thought they were Orpheus's."

Dennis shrugged. "Both, dude. The whole Orphic cult was inspired by me."

"*Why?* Tell me. Why do you know the Orphic hymns? What do you have to do with reincarnation and resurrection?"

"Whoa now! The fancypants scholar needs my help. Finally coming down from that Ivory Tower of yours to play in the mud with me, huh?"

Theo tried to sound angry, but his words emerged slurred and confused. "I'm not playing, Dennis."

"Uh-huh. That's your problem." He rose and dragged Theo to his feet. "Tell you what—if you want to know more about Orpheus, then you gotta dance, bro." He stamped his flip-flopped feet against the earth, then ground his hips like an over-the-hill Elvis impersonator.

"No thanks." Theo blinked heavily, but Dennis's figure remained before his closed eyelids. Impossibly, he no longer wore his shorts and tank top but rather his full regalia as the God of Wine: a leopard skin draped across his hips, his hair twined with ivy, his lips grape-stained. When Theo opened his eyes again, the hallucination didn't disappear. He moaned softly.

"Hitting you now, is it?" Dennis—Dionysus now—asked, a wicked smile on his purple mouth. "Dance with me. It's not a request, Professor Schultz. It's an order."

The god started to dance again, his figure blurring into psychedelic colors. He turned away, hips swaying. The leopard skin lay across his shoulder now, the feline head staring at Theo with glowing yellow eyes. It blinked at him slowly, then licked its wine-stained jaws with a long pink tongue. It looked more sensuous than threatening, as if it'd rather be licking something else.

Theo felt his own feet move in response to the pounding rhythm of the drums. The others around the circle swung their hair like hippies at a love-in. The gold pendants bounced against their chests. He tried to copy them, flinging his head from side to side, hands raised high, as if to catch the starlight in his palms.

Not all the dancers are human anymore, he noted offhandedly. One had cloven hooves for feet. Another sported small horns on the crown of his head.

Theo turned back to Dionysus, desperate to ask if the satyrs were real or merely another hallucination, but the Athanatos had moved to the other side of the circle and now stood with his hands raised for silence. All the drums quieted but one: a steady, tripping heartbeat.

"You would know what Orpheus taught," the god proclaimed in a clear voice devoid of his usual indolence. He spoke to the crowd, but Theo knew this lesson was for him. He took a step closer, willing his sluggish brain to focus.

"Orpheus tells us that the only path to resurrection is to follow the God of the Grape." He lifted his cup of wine in a toast to himself, chugged the contents, and tossed the cup into the flames. His bacchants cheered.

He leered at a young maenad beside him, one of the few still wearing clothes. "The God of the Grape is He Who Unties! The Releaser!" She loosed the belt of her robe and let it drop to the ground as if to illustrate the power of the god's epithet. Her blond hair brushed against the rise of her buttocks. Her gold leaf pendant nestled between ruby-tipped breasts. Wine and firelight flushed her face. Dionysus cast a lingering gaze on her before turning back to the circle of revelers.

"The Releaser frees us from more than our inhibitions. He can release us from *death itself.* You want to know how?"

"Yes!" Theo's shout merged with the crowd's.

Dionysus thrust a hand toward the night sky. "Look for the eagle!" His followers' heads shot up in unison. Even Theo found himself squinting into the darkness, searching in vain for a bird.

"God comes with wide wings and wicked talons." The

alliteration shaped Dionysus's mouth into a lascivious kiss with each word. "He looks down with eagle eyes and seeks his perfect mate. A woman who has no fear. A woman who wears her hair loose and runs with the beasts upon the mountain slopes! Whose veins pump wine and whose feet never cease to dance. And when he finds her, he dives down in eagle's guise to take her for himself."

He held out his hand to the blond maenad beside him. The last shred of Theo's lucidity started with alarm, afraid Dionysus would reenact his ritual on this unsuspecting woman, but she walked toward him willingly, and when the god placed his hands on her stomach, it was an act more of benediction than possession. Theo was surprised to see something akin to love shining from his eyes.

Dionysus is telling his own birth story, he realized. *To him, this woman is Semele, his mortal mother, impregnated by Zeus in the form of an eagle.*

"The woman is ripe and full and ready to burst," the Athanatos went on. "She has God's love." He traced the curve of her flat stomach, and it seemed to swell and round beneath his touch. "She should be content with that. But *no!*" He turned from her with a feline snarl. "A demon convinces her to beg God for a final favor."

Dionysus didn't describe this so-called demon, but Theo knew her name: Hera, Zeus's jealous wife, who'd made a career of torturing her husband's mistresses.

"God the Father is a loving god, a generous god," Dionysus continued. "He swears to give his lover whatever she wants. So when she asks to see his true form, he can't say no." His voice darkened. The crowd grew silent, afraid. As if they knew what was coming.

"God appears not as an eagle, not as an angel, not as a burning bush—but as glory unleashed. So brilliant that mortal eyes can't bear the sight." Dionysus was shouting now, foam flecking his lips. "The Father comes like a lightning bolt. The woman turns to ash. Only her heart remains unburnt."

Dionysus gestured to one of the naked men beside him. No muscled youth, but an over-the-hill satyr with gnarled horns on his head and breasts as saggy as an old woman's. The satyr reached into a cooler at his feet and pulled out a tupperware full of raw meat. Not the shrink-wrapped kind from the supermarket, but dripping and bloody organs, red and brown and floppy like the flesh ripped from an animal. The old satyr handed the heart, all swollen lobes and protruding arteries, to Dionysus, then passed the container to the next initiate.

With the blood from the raw heart dripping down his wrist, Dionysus reached into the bonfire with his other hand and grabbed a fistful of embers. They tumbled through his fingers, red-sparked gray; if the coals burned him, he showed no sign. "Does God let the child burn within her womb?" he asked the crowd.

"No!" they shouted in response.

"He snatches the unborn babe from the flames and plants him in his own thigh. He pulls the mother's heart from the ashes and keeps it safe. And when the boy-child is born from the Father's thigh, he carries his mother's burning embers in his own soul. His feet dance to the same tune, his veins flow with the same sweet wine, he knows no fear."

The crowd shuffled toward the fire, close enough for sparks to land on their rapt faces, their bare limbs. Theo found himself doing the same, a moth drawn to the flames. The sparks sent pinpricks of hot pain across his skin. The blood from the meat in his hand dripped cold across his knuckles. He had never felt so alive.

"The Releaser will find his mother!" Dionysus cried. "He will journey across the River Styx and the River Lethe to bring her back from the dead. But to do so he must rip apart Time. Tear through Time's boundaries, release the serpent coils that hold him in place. Let Unbounded Time burst from his sphere! Let him fly on his many wings!"

The crowd's groans oscillated between despair and arousal. Theo closed his eyes, seeing the image before him. The lion-headed creature hiding in the depths of the mithraeum, a winged proto-god made of snake and man coiled one within the other, holding their secrets close.

"The Releaser travels into Death itself and grabs his mother by the wrist." Dionysus's gesture echoed his words, seizing the blond maenad's arm with his soot-stained hand. "His mother crumbles at his touch, for she is only ash. But he has her heart!" Dionysus held aloft the raw organ, the blood running down his arm. "Holy Spirit and mortal flesh! Join them into one! Bring the woman back from the Underworld. Bring her back to life!"

Each reveler raised the bloody meat to his or her mouth simultaneously.

"This is the blood and the body!" Dionysus cried. "Whosoever believes in me, though he dies, yet shall he live!"

They bit with gusto, blood streaming over their chins. Dionysus opened his own mouth wide and dropped the fist-sized heart inside, swallowing it in one inconceivable gulp.

Theo remembered the last time he'd seen men eat raw flesh— the syndexioi had made it part of their feast the night they'd sacrificed Mars. *I'm on the right track,* he assured himself, staring at the meat in his own hand. *Mithraism and Orphism combined into one.* Yet his stomach revolted as he raised his portion to his lips. Chewy and spongy at the same time. Blood gushing against his tongue. Arteries sticking between his teeth. But then, suddenly, it wasn't raw organ meat anymore. It felt hot and golden in his mouth. It tasted like electricity—like the spark of life itself. Without thinking, he swallowed, wondering at the sudden feeling of warmth and energy that filled his veins.

Dionysus looked pointedly at Theo as he went on. "We can be Releasers!" He pounded a bloody fist against his chest. "Release from Death! Release from Time! Release from all the rules this fucking world binds us with." He ended his tale with a bastardized quote from Plato. "We are dead, and the body is a tomb. But our souls are immortal, divine—"

"And full of wine!" the crowd roared in unison, finishing his sentence.

Then, as if on cue, the drummers threw themselves back into action and the dancing resumed, wilder than ever.

Dionysus gyrated his way back toward Theo. "Does that answer your question?"

"What did I just eat?" Theo asked, swiping at the blood already congealing on his stubbled chin.

"The woman. The god. The Holy Spirit. Whatever you *thought* you ate—that's what you ate."

"But the Holy Spirit is—"

Dionysus laughed. "Let your scholarly mind go, Theodore. *Believe*, and your heart's desire will appear before you."

And then he was gone again, and in his place stood a tall woman with eyes like the moon, a single streak of white shining in her black hair. The firelight tattooed each sculpted curve of muscle with flickering shadows and played across the shallow rise of her breasts, the sharp corner of her jaw. Theo took a step forward, eyes stinging with sudden tears.

"Selene..." His breath caught in his throat.

She slipped into his arms, her breasts pressing against his chest, her thighs hard against his own. Her mouth was on his, tasting of wine and blood and wonder. He had a million questions, yet for the first time in his life he feared the answers.

She wrapped one long leg around his hips, and the moment he'd relived every night for half a year came rushing back to him. He clutched at her as if she could disappear at any moment. He drew her down onto the ground, or she drew him, and then she was on top of him, head thrown back, her pulse thrumming visibly in the long column of her neck.

She pressed her hands against his chest and ground her hips against him. He reached upward to bury himself in the sweaty valley between her breasts, but she pushed him backward and then fell onto all fours, crawling over him until her groin hung above his face. He grabbed her thighs and pulled her downward, a moan rising in his throat. She stayed there, perched above him like a she-wolf birthing her cubs, until she cried aloud with pleasure, then squatted backward and pressed her face against his cheek, panting softly.

"How?" he whispered in her ear. "How did you come back?"

She said nothing, just raised her head and smiled at him, gentle and warm and sweet. That's when he knew it wasn't her. The real Selene was never sweet.

And just like that, he ceased to believe.

The woman was blond, not black-haired, her cheeks too round, her body too soft. She smelled wrong, tasted wrong. She wore a gold leaf pendant around a neck too short, too thick.

She must've seen the horror in his eyes, because she rolled off him.

Theo lurched to his feet, anger chasing the arousal from his veins.

The dancers weren't satyrs after all. Just middle-aged men with paunches, young men with bony hips, old women with sagging flesh. The woman beside him wasn't Selene—she was no maenad either. Just another drunken actress in Dennis's little play. She darted into the woods, giggling maniacally. Dennis, in a tank top and shorts once more, danced nearby with his eyes closed, a stoned hippie believing his own nonsense.

His mind suddenly clear, Theo grabbed his old roommate by the arm. "I came here for answers! Not to be tricked into your damn orgy."

Dennis's eyes flew open, but he seemed more amused than angry. "You're the only man I've ever met who has to be *tricked* into an orgy. Get it together, dude."

"You're saying you really brought your mother back from the dead?" Theo demanded.

Dennis shrugged in time to the beat. "That's how the myth goes. The truth? I don't even remember. But that's the story Orpheus told to his followers, so I'm sticking with it."

"Your mother returned from the dead because you ate her flesh."

"Mm-hm. The Christians stole that from me, yeah? Fuckin' Eucharist. So I decided to put a few Christian touches into my little liturgy here. What'd you think? Saturn did it with Mithras—I figured why not give it a go? Makes the crowd go wild."

"Right, but it doesn't actually bring back the dead, does it? I thought maybe Pythagoras—"

"That nerd? You can't bring anyone back with just numbers, although I'm sure you'd like that," Dennis scoffed. "You keep trying to avoid the obvious: If it doesn't involve *death*, it can't create *life*."

"Then how did Orpheus bring Eurydice back from the dead?" Theo begged. "How does *anyone* return?"

Dennis stopped dancing, looking at Theo with eyes instantly hard. "You're not thinking what I think you're thinking, are you?"

Theo didn't reply, just met his stare and refused to back down.

Dennis threw back his head and laughed so hard he choked. "I know you're a Makarites." Theo's ancient title sounded like a joke on Dennis's lips. "And because of your oh-so-special status, you can use the gods' divine weapons better than the gods themselves. But that doesn't mean you're *actually* an ancient hero, man! You sure you haven't been eating too many of my shroom cookies? This is all just touchy-feely shit. A little wine and revelry to pass the time. You think Selene's actually hanging out in the Underworld, waiting for you to show up and lead her out?"

"I know it's a long shot," Theo answered tightly. "But I have to try, don't I?"

"So that's why you came all the way up here." Dennis clucked. "And I thought you'd finally loosened up."

"You're my last hope," Theo said. "If Pythagoras's numbers don't hold the key to her reincarnation—"

"Enough. This is fuckin' pitiful. You want to know my connection with Orpheus? Fine. When he went to get his chick out of the Underworld, he figured I'd know the way because I'd gotten my mom. He asked for instructions—I gave them to him. Told him how to get in and how to get past Aion on the way back out."

"Aion?" The Greek name wasn't familiar to Theo, though his whirring brain immediately connected it to the English word "eon."

"You heard me. Aion. The name means 'Unbounded Time.' Weren't you listening, dude? That was the best part of the story: 'Release the serpent coils that hold him in place. Let Unbounded Time burst from his sphere! Let him fly on his many wings!' You've got to release him to release death."

"The lion-headed god! The one who looks like the Orphic proto-god. You used to sing his hymn all the time when you were especially wasted."

"Yeah. Protogonos. Aion. Same thing. But he didn't have a lion's head last time I checked. That sounds like some Magna Mater shit—the Great Mother was the one with the lions sitting next to her throne like some dominatrix in a bestiality porno. The point, Theo-bore, is that my instructions to Orpheus *didn't work*. Or has the classics genius forgotten how the myth ends? Orpheus failed, even with my help."

"You gave him instructions," Theo said, pouncing on the one part of the story that mattered. "Now give them to me."

Dennis snorted. "Go get them yourself. Everyone's wearing them around their necks."

"The pendants! Followers of Orpheus wore them, right? They're found in burial plots all over the Hellenistic world."

Dennis rolled his eyes. "Too school for cool. As usual."

Theo looked around the clearing with new eyes. "You had

that many authentic gold leaves left over? Or did you make precise copies?"

"Yeah, precise copies, sure." Dennis's hand drifted to the leather cord he wore around his own neck.

A gray-haired woman with dirt on her breasts and leaves in her hair broke from the revelers and grabbed Dennis's hand. "Dance with me," she panted, blood staining her teeth.

Dennis grinned at her and made to follow.

"Hey, wait!" Theo lunged forward and wrapped his arms around Dennis's neck in a crushing hug. "Thanks, man," he gushed, "for your help."

"Finally I get a little love." Dennis squeezed Theo's ass in both hands. "Anytime, fucker."

The God of Revelry jigged his way back toward the fire.

Theo looked down at the necklace in his palm. The snapped leather cord was still damp with Dennis's sweat. The gold pendant was paper-thin, shaped like an ivy leaf. He could hardly see the Greek characters etched on its surface, but he could tell from their shape that this was no cheap modern re-creation. As he suspected, Dennis had kept the authentic artifact for himself.

Theo closed his fingers over the pendant, then shouted after Dennis, "But how do I *get* to the Underworld in the first place?"

Selene had once told him that Hades lived in an abandoned downtown subway station, but he knew that couldn't be the actual entrance to the realm of death. In the myths, heroes like Orpheus entered through a natural cleft in the earth. But which one?

Dennis glanced over his shoulder with a drunken leer. "We're not in the Age of Heroes anymore—you really think you can just saunter into the Land of the Dead like some lamer version of Odysseus?" He waggled a finger. "You're a shitty student, Professor. You forgot what I said: If it doesn't involve *death*, it can't create *life*."

"So to enter the Underworld"—Theo choked—"I have to kill someone?"

"Don't worry, dude." Dennis began to laugh. "Only yourself."

Chapter 11

INTERMISSIO: THE TETRACTYS

The man who called himself the Tetractys watched from the forest as Theodore Schultz hunted for his clothes. The professor didn't look much like a Makarites at the moment, not with his glasses askew and the irritated look on his face. Then again, the ancient heroes had usually performed their greatest deeds in the nude, and Schultz looked surprisingly buff for a classicist—likely because he hadn't been eating much since that whole unfortunate episode with the Huntress. His grief had burned away any softness he'd possessed; he looked lean and strong, ready for anything.

The Tetractys didn't resemble his title either. He looked nothing like the perfect equilateral triangle for which he'd been named. *I'm full of flaws,* he admitted to himself with a shrug. *Foremost among them that I can't keep my mind off that blonde.*

The woman who'd spread her legs for the professor had run right by the Tetractys's hiding place, cheeks flushed. He'd marked her route, sure she'd be up for more action later on. *If she thinks Schultz can make her come, just wait until she meets me.* It took every ounce of his self-control—and he didn't have much to begin with—not to take off after her right then. He could use some release. Someone to ease the knot of worry in his stomach.

Six months ago, his life had unraveled. The tune he'd danced to for so long had grown too faint to hear, and the man who'd written the music in the first place—the man he called Father and who'd first granted him his secret title—was lost to him. The Tetractys had escaped the brutal battle atop the Statue of Liberty to find himself alone, no brothers to help, searching in vain for the missing Father, trying to remember the notes to a melody he'd never fully understood.

He remembered their last hurried conversation. *You are the only one left to me,* the Father had told him, although the Tetractys doubted that was true. How could he trust a man who had schemed for so long? Wiles ran in his blood.

So many gods dead, the old man had said, nodding his white head sorrowfully. *Yet I had no choice. We sacrifice a few for the good of the many.* Though so many of the Father's family lay dead, he spoke with nothing more than weary resignation. *It will all be worth it when the symphony plays.* And that, at least, the Tetractys believed.

But sometimes, just before he drifted off to sleep, he'd jerk back into wakefulness, heart racing, skin chilled, stomach clenching with an unfamiliar emotion it had taken him months to name: *Guilt.*

He caught a buzzing mosquito between his fingers, wondering whether the blood smearing his fingers was his own. *One little libation, sacrificed for a higher being,* he thought. *How much more blood will be spilt before this is over?*

He watched as the man who would inevitably become the next sacrifice shoved on a pair of sneakers and headed out of the meadow at a jog, clearly eager to leave the orgy behind. The Tetractys stepped back a little farther into the shadows, unwilling to be seen as the classicist passed his hiding place.

The Tetractys hadn't heard Schultz's conversation with Dionysus, but he worried about what might've been said. Schultz's dogged-ness, he felt sure, would eventually lead him to the Father, but he was taking his own sweet time about it—following paths of his own making, swerving away from the ultimate goal—and the Tetractys's patience was wearing thin. Whether through force or cunning, he needed to keep Schultz on track.

There's that guilt again, he noted, watching the professor go. Despite the summer heat, the familiar chill prickled across his skin. *He's a good man. I've watched him long enough to know that. But even good men must sometimes die for the sake of the greater good.* The knowledge gave him little comfort.

And me? Am I a good man? It was a question he'd never asked before.

Perhaps because he already knew the answer.

The Tetractys caught a glimpse of Schultz's blonde seduc-tress meandering from the forest into the clearing and back, her pale skin flashing through the trees like a beacon. He stood, brushed the leaves from his pants, and ran a hand through his hair. Schultz would be in his rental car by now, heading back to the city. The Tetractys would have plenty of time to track him before he made any further moves.

At this point, he decided, *one more sin won't make a difference.*

He donned his most charming smile and headed toward the glimmer of flesh, determined to enjoy himself while he still could. Soon enough, he'd have to start leading Schultz, rather than following. The Father had made his wishes clear:

You, my Tetractys, may play the harmony that makes my sym-phony soar—but the Makarites is the note to which we all must tune our instruments.

Chapter 12

WHITE-ARMED

The corridor behind the ballroom smelled like garlic and lilies and talcum powder. Trailing her own discordant scent of vanilla perfume, June led Selene and Flint through the crowds of well-wishers—exchanging kisses and congratulations in fluent Italian as she went—and into a small lounge reserved for the bridal party. Two older women in matching lilac dresses sat in the corner, dabbing on makeup.

June collapsed onto a couch, pulled off her high heels, and began to rub her toes like any other fiftyish woman grateful to get off her feet. She looked like a blissful bride, happy to be exhausted.

Selene joined Flint on a love seat opposite, careful to sit as far away from him as the narrow sofa allowed, unwilling to give either him, June, or herself the wrong idea. Yet despite the space between them, she could still feel Flint's smoldering heat—and she was pretty sure it had nothing to do with his erstwhile God of Fire status.

As soon as the other guests left, June's smile vanished. She grabbed Flint's hands in her own. "Tell me what happened to my son."

She's talking about Mars, Selene realized after a moment of confusion. Hephaestus's brother, the God of War, had fallen victim to the Mithraic cult six months before, just like Apollo.

As Flint related the story of Saturn's betrayal, all trace of the good-natured Midwesterner vanished. Suddenly, despite the wrinkles and the eye shadow, June became Juno once more.

She pulled her hands from her son's and sat straight on the couch like a queen on her throne, as stern and imperious as she'd been in her godhood, when brilliant peacocks had strutted at her feet. The diadem no longer looked foolish wobbling on her brow. "Zeus should've destroyed our father long ago," she seethed. "We should've known better than to let the Titan loose in the world."

"The Wily One's been playing a very long game," Selene interjected. "Tying himself to Christianity for the last two thousand years. He's proud of it—he's the one who took a crucified prophet and merged him with Mithraic ideas of salvation. If it wasn't for him, it's possible Jesus would've faded away, and *we'd* still be ruling from Olympus." But even as she said it, Selene knew that wasn't true. Saturn's plan wouldn't have worked if mankind hadn't already been desperate for something new. They *wanted* a personal savior; they were tired of appeasing vengeful Olympians. If Jesus hadn't come along, someone else would have.

"Our father was always clever," June admitted, her shoulders slumping again, as if she lacked the energy to maintain even her most violent maternal rage for more than a few minutes. "Someone was bound to latch on to Christianity. I would've, if I could, but there's no room for a Goddess of Marriage in a religion based on a celibate messiah. They worship some prudish virgin instead." She slid a curious glance at Selene, who wasn't about to mention that she no longer fit that description. That was a secret that would stay between her and Theo.

"If things were different," June went on, "if Christianity were a matriarchal religion instead, and I garnered strength from it . . . well . . ." She didn't need to continue. *Maybe her feet wouldn't be sore after half an hour of dancing,* Selene thought. *Maybe she wouldn't look decades older than her new husband. Maybe* all *the goddesses of Olympus would still retain their ancient powers.*

"If you're so disdainful of the Church," Selene asked, "then why get married in one?" She couldn't help the sharpness that crept into her tone. She was still smarting from June's threat moments earlier.

June just smiled, as if she'd already forgotten that she'd promised to kick Selene's ass. "Because Mauricio, the sweet boy, is Italian. We met when he was on business in Indianapolis. He wanted a Catholic wedding back home, and what do I care? I've had dozens of weddings. I'll have dozens more."

"Doesn't it make you mad, seeing their idols everywhere? Their cathedrals?"

"You still holding grudges against the Christians, dear? Not much point in that. It'll drive you crazy faster than a spittlebug in alfalfa. Nope. The key to enjoying this half-mortal life of ours is accepting the things you can't change. Like your father, for example." She chuckled as if genuinely amused. "Think of all the time I wasted chasing him and his lovers across the earth. At the Diaspora, I didn't just leave Olympus, I left *him*. And let me tell you, that was the best decision I ever made. Now I love who I want, when I want. Husbands, you see, are replaceable. Children, on the other hand…" Her smile collapsed in a spasm of grief, and she looked at her son with a new softness. "I only have one of those left."

"All these years," Selene ventured. "And you've never had any more?"

June looked surprised. "We can't. Didn't you know that?"

Selene shrugged. In truth, as the proverbial Chaste One, she'd never bothered to find out, although she'd always assumed such a thing was possible. After she and Theo had made love for the first and only time, she'd assumed her lack of pregnancy was due either to luck or her body's long hold on virginity. She'd never once had a period—perhaps she was just sterile. It had never occurred to her that the same might be true of all the Athanatoi.

"When your father proclaimed the Age of Heroes over, that was it," June explained. "No more procreating with mortals."

"I thought you didn't bother obeying him anymore."

"Oh, I didn't say anyone *obeyed* him. But the goddesses just never got pregnant. And the gods started shooting blanks. I don't know if your father's command had anything to do with it, or if it was just a side effect of our decline. I thought about adopting..." Tears pooled in her lower lids, quickly blinked away. "Not fair to the kids, is it? To have a mother who ages so slowly. Eventually, I'd have to either abandon them or explain who I am. And that's too much for mortal children to bear. So I marry men young enough that we'll have plenty of years together. When they finally wonder about me, I either tell them—or I don't. Either way, I'm a *fantastic* wife. Turns out, it's my speciality. No jealousy any longer, just commitment." Her eyes flicked knowingly from Selene to Flint and back. "Speaking of which, Mauricio's waiting." She reached for her high heels.

"Before you go," Selene said, "how about you help us catch the Wily One and bring him to justice?"

"I told you, I don't fight what I can't change." June stood up, wincing at the pain in her pinching shoes. "Don't get me wrong: Vengeance is sweet. I remember its taste. But I've given it up, along with so much else. What's done is done. My Mars isn't coming back."

"Forget Mars," Selene said harshly. "What about everyone else who's still in danger?"

"Like who?" she asked with a hint of fear. Despite her famous boxing match with Artemis, Hera had never been a goddess of war. She had no weapons beyond her own white arms. "Me? Flint?"

"All of us. Grandfather had Flint in his clutches two nights ago. And with each murder, the God of Time gets stronger. If we let him continue his sacrifices, he'll become something all-powerful, monstrous. Who knows what that could mean for mortals like your new husband?"

June looked alarmed, but Flint grunted dismissively. "Grandfather's clever—but arrogant. He's so focused on his upcoming sacrifice that we got away from him."

"Upcoming—" June began.

Selene jumped in. "My father."

"And would that be such a loss?" June pursed her lips, as if tasting once more the vengeance she'd foresworn. "My former husband is not to be trusted. I know that better than anyone. If he's gone, the world is a safer place. I'm warning you both, leave Zeus to his just deserts."

"Mother—"

"No, Flint. He's beyond redemption. Why would you help him after what he did to you?"

"After what *he* did?" Flint asked softly. "Look at yourself, Mother, then answer that question. Selene wants to help her father—who am I to disagree? We love our parents even when they hurt us. We help them even when they've failed to help us."

I finally convinced him, Selene marveled. But her gratification evaporated when she considered the alternative: *Or he just loves me so much he can't refuse me.*

To her surprise, June knelt arthritically at her son's feet.

"Zeus threw you off Olympus," she said softly, placing her hands on his narrow knees. "But yes...I stood by and let it happen. And your legs, your beautiful legs..." She ran her hands down his shins, the tears falling now without cease. "This is my fault."

"Mother," Flint said hoarsely, reaching for her shoulders to raise her up.

"No, let me say my piece," she commanded, mascara striping her cheeks. "I was scared of Zeus, scared of losing my place in his heart, even though I should've known I'd lost it long before.

When he tossed you off the mountain, I did nothing to stop him. I chose my husband over my son. I will never do that again." She rested her cheek on his lap. "I will help if I can. Forgive me, Hephaestus."

"I forgive you," he said hastily. "Please, Mother, get up." He lifted her bodily to her feet, his voice gruff but his eyes overbright.

"If you want to help us," Selene said, eager to save Flint from emotions he clearly wasn't ready to confront, "tell us what a Mithraist would want with a pine tree sculpture from the Campus of the Magna Mater."

"I don't know anything about Mithras," June said, reaching for a tissue to wipe the blackened tears from her face.

"But the Magna Mater?"

She sighed a little wistfully and lowered herself once more to the couch. "You know I always chafed at my husband's rule. Well, I thought for a while there I was finally going to get my shot at power when the Greeks brought the Great Mother from the east." She paused. "*That* part's like Mithras, isn't it? An eastern deity."

"Go on," Selene urged. "I remember her priests castrating themselves, but that's about it."

June winced. "Yes, that explains why I never succeeded in merging her worship with my own. I'm a goddess of fertility, not of *eunuchs*. Besides, my mother beat me to it."

"You mean—"

"Rhea. Titan wife of Kronos. Your grandmother. By the end, you couldn't tell where the Magna Mater began and my mother ended." She linked her fingers together. "One and the same, just like Kronos and Saturn."

Selene felt a rush of adrenaline. The desire to share her findings with Theo was a physical ache. She imagined how his eyes would light up as they slotted another clue into place. "No wonder he wanted the Magna Mater's pine tree. She's the only one ever to outsmart him. He's hated his wife ever since she plotted to save her youngest son from being swallowed like the rest of her children. If it weren't for her, Zeus would still be inside Saturn's stomach—and Saturn would still rule the world. Now he must be stealing her attributes as some form of revenge. Maybe her artifacts let him take her power for himself."

"What power?" June said sadly. "Mother died long ago."

"You sure?" Selene had once thought Saturn dead, too. Instead, he'd been secretly scheming for millennia to kill everyone she loved.

"I sat by her bedside and held her hand." The wrinkles in June's face deepened. She looked old, haggard, all the joy of her wedding day subsumed in the memory of grief. "A cruel irony, isn't it? We've forgotten so much of our godhood, so many glorious moments of power and strength. Yet our mortal histories are seared into our minds, as much as we might want to forget them."

Selene felt an unaccustomed empathy for her old nemesis. "I, too, sat with my mother while she died. As much as it broke my heart, she died peacefully with her children beside her."

"Rhea did not go easily." June shook her head. "She lived in a hovel, deep in a forest in Prussia. It was the early Middle Ages. Not an easy time to be poor. Not an easy time to be a woman living alone, possessed of strange memories and stranger powers. I didn't know what had happened to her until my sisters brought me word. I was still strong, living off the importance of my attributes. Marriage, the family—they still formed the foundation of the world in the Middle Ages. But Rhea, Cybele, Ops, the Magna Mater—for all her names, Mother had been forgotten by everyone but the people of the nearby village. When the Black Death came, they blamed the witch in their midst. They hanged her. And when she didn't die, they killed her again. And again. A stronger Athanatos might have survived it all, but there was no place for a Great Mother in a Christian world dominated by

God the Father. Finally, they burned her at the stake. Her body was black, charred, and still she clung to life until her daughters arrived to say good-bye. She died an hour after we got there."

Selene's stomach roiled. She hadn't known her grandmother well, but she, too, had been accused of witchcraft in the Middle Ages. She'd survived her own experience with the pyre, but that had been centuries ago. If it happened again, she doubted her fading body could withstand the flames.

Flint took his mother's hand. Despite the pity in his eyes, he remained focused on the task at hand. "So if Rhea is gone—and her husband surely doesn't want to bring her back—why did he want the pine tree?"

Selene felt like she knew the answer already. "Remember how many of our divine weapons he stole for himself? The Sea God's trident? My father's lightning bolt?"

"But the pine tree's not a weapon," Flint insisted. "Why steal it if it represents a goddess with no power?"

With her right hand, June traced the creases that scored her left. Despite the elegant gold wedding band and a delicate diamond engagement ring, her hands were those of an old woman. "No power indeed..." she mused. "And yet Mother was once the most worshiped goddess in Rome. From inside her sanctuary, you could hear the chariot races in the circus next door. When the crowd roared, their thunder put Zeus's to shame. Then, as soon as her priests brought out the bull for the climactic ritual...well"—she laughed shortly—"you didn't notice the crowd noise anymore."

"What bull?" Selene asked, sitting forward.

"The supplicant would stand in a pit. The priests walked a bull onto a grate overhead and slit its throat. And then—let's just say the result was dramatic."

Selene looked at Flint. If Mithras and Rhea both centered their worship on bull sacrifices, that could explain Saturn's interest in his wife's cult.

June went on. "The taurobolium—the bull sacrifice—allowed the supplicant to become one with the divinity, able to transcend death itself. Like the pine tree, each man holds the seeds of his own rebirth. He just needs to be watered correctly."

A tauroctony and a taurobolium, both symbolizing salvation and resurrection. The parallel was striking. "This temple to the Magna Mater—" Selene began.

"They called it the Phrygianum," June interrupted, "since the Mater came from Phrygia—that's Turkey today, I guess."

Selene thought of the conical Phrygian cap Mithras always wore. "Which circus was it near?" she asked eagerly. In New York, the Host had chosen a major city landmark—Saint Patrick's Cathedral—as the location of their sanctuary, but the extant mithraea in Rome were mostly situated beneath relatively minor churches. If Rhea's Phrygianum lay in a more significant site, Saturn might not be able to resist adapting it for his own use.

"The Circus of Nero," June replied. "But don't get too excited, dear. Her Phrygianum's not there anymore, not even the ruins. It's all buried under Vatican City." She smiled apologetically. "So that can't be what you're looking for, can it?"

This time, Selene laughed aloud. "Actually, Aunt June"—she kissed the woman on the top of her gray curls—"it's perfect."

Chapter 13

THE HOLDER OF KEYS

"I've told you before. It *won't* work. Hades is dead, his wife is off getting high on coca leaves with her mom in Peru, and if you think some hocus-pocus will magically make Selene reappear at your front door, you're as deluded as a blue-collar Republican." Scooter Joveson's disembodied voice echoed so loudly through Theo's cramped rental car that he had to lower the volume on his cell's speakerphone.

Months before, he'd contacted Selene's younger half brother and asked for his help reincarnating her. As the god Hermes, Scooter had once overseen more domains than nearly any other Athanatos, serving as both divine Messenger and Psychopompos, the Conductor of Souls to—and from—the Underworld. Yet Scooter, who'd returned to Los Angeles shortly after the final battle on the Statue of Liberty, had flatly refused to help.

Now, on the ride back to the city from his upstate bacchanal, Theo had called from the car to beg the Athanatos's assistance once more. Unsurprisingly, Scooter picked up his cell, clearly wide-awake—it was only ten o'clock on the West Coast, and despite his recent incarnation as a cybersecurity expert, he still kept his old movie mogul's hours.

"It's not *hocus-pocus*," Theo insisted. "I'm going all the way to the Underworld to bring her back."

For once, Scooter fell silent. Theo listened patiently to the hiss of his breathing over the speakerphone, waiting for him to state the obvious. Finally, "You know what that means?"

"Yeah, I'm not crazy, Scooter—I don't *want* to die. The plan is just to die temporarily." The words made Theo grip the steering wheel like a life preserver. He could barely believe he'd even said them. "I find Selene in the afterlife, then bring her back out with me." He barreled on, knowing that if he stopped to think, he'd lose his nerve. "But I'm going to need help, and you're the only one I can ask. So get on your private jet and meet me at Selene's house tomorrow."

"Have you lost your mind?"

"I don't have time to debate this." Theo fought the impulse to slam his foot on the gas for emphasis. "Archeologists found cherry pits at many mithraea sites—that means the original Mithraists held their most important rituals in summertime. And knowing their penchant for astronomical connections, probably at the summer solstice. That's *two days* from now. And if the Mithraists chose propitious times to imbue their rites with the most power, I should do the same."

"Kronos's gullet," Scooter cursed. "Selene died so *you* could live, remember? I'm not going to let you kill yourself! If you want to honor her memory, you'll help me track down Saturn instead. Trust me, if the old bastard had killed *you*, she wouldn't have rested until he was just as dead."

For months, despite Scooter's begging, Theo had refused to help find Saturn. He'd insisted he was simply too grief-stricken to bother with revenge. In truth, he'd had a far more important task to focus on. He drummed his fingers on the steering wheel, impatient with the old argument. "Selene wasn't the same vengeful goddess anymore. She would've rather had me back than see Saturn punished. I believe that."

"I'm warning you, Theo. Don't even think about doing this. It's stupid. It won't work." Scooter sounded deadly serious. He sounded *scared*.

"I didn't know you cared."

"Damn you," Scooter hissed. "You're all I have left of my sister. Of course I care."

Theo fell silent, stunned to hear such emotion from the usually blithe god. "If you loved Selene so much, then you'd want to get her back."

"I won't—"

"You're in Los Angeles! Even with all your money and your private jet and your computer hacking skills and whatever else you're amusing yourself with out there, you can't stop me. I'll do it with or without you."

"No!" the God of Eloquence spluttered, seemingly at a loss for a more convincing argument.

"Then get on a plane to New York and come help make sure this isn't all for nothing."

Scooter gave an agonized groan. "Don't do anything until I get there."

"Then you better hurry."

"Wait. Wait. Forget New York, Theo." He took a sharp intake of breath, as if struck by an idea. "If you really want this whole ridiculous resurrection plan to work—and may I just stress again that it won't—you shouldn't off yourself in some Manhattan brownstone."

"Why not? I don't have to go to some physical entrance to the Underworld. I just have to die."

"Sure, but location matters, my friend. Remember how the Mithraists always performed their rites at landmarks in the city? They not only chose times with astrological significance—they picked significant *sites*, too. You want to bring Selene back, you need a location scout to find someplace with serious ties to the afterlife and resurrection cults."

"Then maybe we can both get what we want," Theo said, his eyes still on the dark highway before him but his mind thousands of miles away.

"Now you're talking. What did you have in mind?"

"Our Mithraists, it turns out, were equal-opportunity worshipers. They also prayed to a lion-headed god—a version of Aion, the Orphic Protogonos. His statue was right there in the mithraeum under Saint Patrick's. He's a crucial element in their understanding of reincarnation. So if I find Saturn's current mithraeum, I also find the best possible place to perform my own rite of resurrection."

"*Now* you want to help us find Saturn?" Scooter sounded more satisfied than surprised.

"I want to find the mithraeum—an active site of worship with the power to make my own quest succeed. If we find Saturn, too, well, that's extra credit."

"Uh-huh. You're talking about the mithraeum somewhere in Rome that Flint's spent half a year looking for? The one I've been begging for your help in finding and you've refused to bother with. That one?" he asked pointedly.

"Yeah."

"What about 'we've been searching for six months' didn't you understand? Looks like you're going to have to delay the suicide pact. Who knows how long it will take us to find it?"

"You're only stumped because I haven't been helping."

"Hah! What happened to the humble professor, awed by the presence of the immortals?"

"He died about when Selene did."

Scooter fell silent. *That's twice in one conversation that he's been speechless.*

"I'm close, I can feel it," Theo went on. "I even have instructions." That was technically true, although the illegible Greek on the stolen gold pendant wasn't providing much help so far. "If we can just find this Aion, we can get Selene out. At least that's what Dennis said."

"You talked to Dennis? You really are desperate."

"Yeah, I wound up both enlightened and morally compromised. As usual."

"You're probably still high. That explains a lot."

Theo ignored him, even though Scooter had a point. He probably shouldn't be driving, much less contemplating suicide. Yet he felt surprisingly clearheaded. When his hallucination of Selene had vanished, he felt he'd lost her all over again. He'd do anything to bring her back—for real, this time.

"Did you know Aion?" he pressed. "I think I'd trust your recollections of him more than Dennis's."

"Man with a lion's head? Sounds like if I had, I'd remember."

"He's twined with snakes, he's holding two L-shaped tools in his hands— Here, let me just show you." He risked taking his eyes off the road long enough to send a photo he'd taken of the lion-headed statue in the Met to Scooter's phone. A moment later, Scooter's disembodied laughter rang through the car.

"I hate to admit it, but you may be onto something. I don't recognize the god, but those tools are *keys*, Theo. Roman keys."

The words of a Pythagorean prayer came back to Theo: *Bless us, divine number, you who generated gods and men. O holy, holy Tetractys that contains the root and source of the eternally flowing creation. The never-swerving, the never-tiring holy Ten, the key holder of all.* But if the lion-headed god held keys as well, all the more reason he could open the doors to the afterlife.

"So Aion holds the keys to reincarnation..." he pondered aloud. "Keys to heaven..." He nearly swerved off the road as he made the connection. "Who else holds two keys to heaven?" he nearly shouted.

"Uh—"

"*Peter*, for God's sake! *Saint* Peter. As in Saint Peter's Basilica.

Where the pope lives! Saturn's been inserting Mithraic ideas into Christianity since the very beginning. He even put them into the Vatican itself! We know where our mithraeum is, Scooter!"

"*Styx*. You *are* good. You think the mithraeum's actually inside Vatican City?"

"Under the biggest church in the whole damn world. Yeah, I think that's *exactly* where it is." Theo's mind spun, already judging how quickly he could get home, pack, and book a flight to Rome. "I can get there by tomorrow evening. You?"

"So you're putting off the whole suicide thing for a day." Scooter let out a long breath. "Good. That gives me time to change your mind."

"If we don't find the mithraeum before the solstice," Theo said sharply, "I'll kill myself anyway. I'll slit my wrists in the damn Trevi Fountain if need be. Going to Rome is not procrastination. I'm just giving myself—and Selene—the best chance I can."

Scooter sighed. "You sure you can find Saturn?"

"Of course not!" Theo took a deep breath to steady himself and added more calmly, "But it's worth a shot."

"And all I have to do in return is promise to help you die."

"Nope. Pretty sure I can manage that on my own. I need you to help me live again."

"There's no guarantee—"

"I don't need a guarantee. I just need a chance. Worst case, at least my misery is over. But if I'm right about the mithraeum, you still get Saturn."

Scooter sighed again. "I'll meet you in Saint Peter's. But Theo, since we're about to face an army of angry syndexioi— don't forget to bring the... *you know whats*."

"Hey, what kind of Makarites would I be if I showed up without my magic weapons?"

"A dead one," Scooter answered unnecessarily.

"Oh, I think that's a given at this point." Theo forced a laugh, then hung up before Scooter could say another word.

Chapter 14

BRAZEN-ARMED

Theo had died before.

Soon after he'd met Selene, he'd stood in a cave in Central Park, surrounded by cult initiates who believed his death would grant them immortality. One raised a knife. Then everything had gone black. The next thing he knew, he'd awoken in Selene's arms, gasping back into life.

So why, oh why, do I think there's an afterlife now if there wasn't one last time? he asked himself as he reached for another T-shirt to shove into his suitcase. Yet he remembered what Dennis had said—the raw meat at the bacchanal had transformed into something more because he *thought* it did. Belief itself could create reality. Weren't the gods themselves proof of that? They had come into being because they were worshiped—because mankind *believed* in them. Before learning Selene's true identity, Theo had considered himself a confirmed atheist. Nine months later, he still didn't believe in God, but he sure as hell believed in the *gods*.

Even if the Underworld didn't exist for me before, he reasoned, *maybe it does now.*

From the top shelf of his closet, he pulled down a large

cardboard box. He hadn't opened it since Scooter gave it to him in December. Now, raising the lid, he found his gaze caught by the empty holes in the dark bronze helmet. With its flared nosepiece and long cheek guards, it looked like the face of Death. When he lifted it from the box, frost stuck to his fingers, sapping the warmth from his body as surely as any wind blown from the Underworld.

This is my inheritance: Hades' helm. Emblem of the Lord of the Dead, he thought grimly. *Who knew it would be so fitting?*

"Theo? You finally home?"

He quickly wrapped a shirt around the helmet before turning to Ruth with studied casualness. She stood blinking at him in her pajamas. "It's four in the morning." Her eyes flicked to the half-packed suitcase, and a hint of fear tightened her voice. "Are you going somewhere?"

"Rome," he answered shortly, placing the wrapped helmet into his suitcase. "Flight leaves in two hours."

She didn't say anything for a long moment, just stared at him. "Please tell me that means Scooter and Flint have found Saturn, and you're just going along as a . . . consultant?"

"Not exactly." He returned to the cardboard box and, with his back to her, pulled out a second divinely forged item. He shoved it into his satchel before she could see it, making a mental note to transfer it to his checked baggage before he got to the airport. Otherwise, he'd be spending the summer solstice trying to get out of TSA security rather than the Underworld.

"You're going by yourself."

"Not exactly."

"Theo, you *can't*," she said, sitting down heavily on the bed.

"That's what everyone says." He tried to sound cheerful as he tossed a flashlight into his bag. "But I defeated Saturn once before, remember? Tracking him down again shouldn't be too hard. I have a lead."

He tried to sound confident, but he'd only gotten as far as:

Get to Vatican City. Miraculously find hidden mithraeum. Kill myself. The whole "come back from the dead and bring Selene, too" part was still pretty fuzzy. His last-minute plane ticket included a layover in Iceland and another in Geneva before he finally made it to Rome, giving him a total of sixteen hours to figure out how to defeat Death itself. *No problem.*

Ruth brought him back to the present with a small groan. "And when you find Saturn..." She didn't finish the thought.

Theo didn't like lying to Ruth, but he'd been doing it for months now. It was getting easier. "I'll make sure he doesn't hurt anyone else again."

"But Selene's gone," she said softly. It was the first time he'd heard her speak Selene's name in a very long time. "Revenge won't bring her back."

He felt her eyes on him and this time said nothing. He just kept packing, moving a pile of underwear to hide the crown of the dark bronze helm—it had slipped from its wrappings like a corpse rising from the grave.

"Theo? It *can't* bring her back. You know that, don't you? Please, tell me you know that." He heard the tears in her voice a moment before they streaked her cheeks.

Crouching beside the bed, he took her hands in his. "I have to try, Ruth. There's a chance she might not be—out of reach."

She clenched her jaw tight, as if to hold back her words, but he read the accusation in her eyes: *I'm not enough. You'd rather go after a dead woman than be alive with me.* Then her nostrils twitched, her eyes widened, and she blurted, "You smell like..." She jerked away from him with a dismayed gasp. Theo hadn't yet changed out of the clothes he'd worn upstate.

His first instinct was to explain. To apologize. To tell her about the drugs and the dancing and the hallucinations, then laugh it off with a joke about Dennis's jean shorts, all so she wouldn't feel worse than she already did. So many months living in the same house and he'd never done more than hold her. How must it feel to think he'd chosen to have sex with someone else while she waited desperately for him to make up his mind?

But he didn't say a word. *If Ruth thinks I love someone else more than her—she's right. And I owe her the truth, even if it hurts.*

He stood, threw his toiletries into the suitcase, and zipped it shut. He picked up his satchel, heavy with its divine burden, and slung it over his shoulder. He paused in the doorway, resisting the urge to embrace her one last time.

"I'm not going to follow you," Ruth said slowly, talking more to herself than to him. "I'll want to. I'll want to chase you to the airport and smuggle myself aboard that plane and help keep you safe as you face these...whatever they are. And when you fail, I'll want to be there to hold you when you feel the hurt all over again. But I can't do that, Theo. I can't bear knowing I'm your second choice. I've been doing that for months. I won't do it anymore."

"I know," he said. "And I'm sorry. For everything." He turned to go.

"Theo—" Her voice was thick with desperation.

"Yeah?"

"Be careful. You're not a superhero, you know."

She was right. He wouldn't heal quickly like the gods. His arms weren't as strong as Flint's, nor his feet as swift as Scooter's. But he had three things they didn't: a god-forged bronze sword, Hades' Helm of Invisibility, and the magic to wield them both.

With such weapons, I might just make a convincing hero after all, he thought, jogging down the stairs. His satchel banged against his chest; he could feel the sword's razor edge resting against his ribs in silent remonstrance.

That is, if the damn things don't kill me before I make it out my own front door.

Chapter 15

HE OF MANY ARTS AND SKILLS

Standing in the vast elliptical plaza before Saint Peter's Basilica later that day, Selene felt like a grasshopper trapped in the web of a great hairy spider, chirping out her protests in vain while the silk bindings grew tighter and the numbing toxin sapped her strength. Hordes of tourists meandered around her like flies thrumming their wings, unaware of their own captivity. Bernini's colonnade hemmed them in, embracing the plaza in two sweeping arcs and drawing the eye to the obelisk in the center of the web.

Carved four thousand years ago to proclaim the glory of ancient Egypt long before a wandering tribe of Hebrews dreamed of a single god, the obelisk rose seven stories into the air. No longer did it remind its viewers of Ra and Isis: The copper cross parked atop the stone tip demanded homage to Christ, instead. But even that soaring emblem paled before the building beyond it: the grandest church in Christendom. The great domed basilica loomed over the plaza, a tangible symbol of the immense wealth and far-reaching power of the vast hairy spider itself—the Vatican.

Selene squinted up angrily at the row of colossal statues perched on the basilica's roof.

"I count twelve," she said to Flint.

"Twelve what?"

"Twelve statues. Twelve holy figures. Remind you of anything?"

He peered upward, shading his face with his hand. "That's Jesus and his eleven apostles."

"Hah. Or Zeus with the other eleven Olympians."

"Selene..."

"I'm just saying." She waved a hand at the colonnade that surrounded Saint Peter's Square. A full complement of one hundred and forty smaller saints watched over the faithful from atop the Doric columns. "That looks to me like a host of lesser gods—male and female, warrior and virgin and you name it." She pointed back to the basilica itself. "And those are like the Olympians looking down from on high."

"Just because our grandfather mixed Mithraism with his own brand of Christianity doesn't mean the whole Catholic Church is secretly worshiping us."

"Maybe not." She shrugged. "But at this point, anything's possible."

For so long, a bright dividing line had existed in her mind between the time before the Holy Roman Emperor Theodosius had outlawed worship of the Olympians and the time after. Unlike the earlier eastern cults that had come to Rome, which had coexisted peacefully with—or even integrated into—classical religion, Christianity insisted that its single "God" not be polluted by the sin of polytheism. Or at least, that's what Selene had always thought. Now, between the twelve "divinities" on the church's facade and the towering Egyptian obelisk at the plaza's center, she was beginning to think the Church had even more in common with Saturn than she'd thought—both had no compunction about stealing other people's sacred objects and using them to demonstrate their own power.

Flint ignored her musings and glanced down at his large tablet phone. He hadn't said a word about his feelings since the wedding that morning. No doubt he was waiting for her to finally respond to his confession. But even without June's warning, Selene would've kept her mouth shut: Until she was absolutely sure what she wanted to say to Flint, she wasn't going to say anything at all. She'd spent the afternoon focused on the chase, instead, and Flint, as always, had followed along.

He swiped his screen, the images flashing. "I found a map of the current Vatican overlaid onto the structures that existed in the Imperial Age."

She moved to peer over his shoulder. "Where's Rhea's Phrygianum, exactly?"

"No one knows, unfortunately."

"Your mother said it was right near the Circus of Nero."

"Yes, but look." He pointed to an enormous elongated oval track on the map. "The racetrack was longer than two football fields end to end. It stretched from about where we're standing in Saint Peter's Square all the way past the current basilica. The Phrygianum could've been anywhere around here." He scowled down at his phone, as if angry at the Internet for not providing more specific information.

"We know it's underground, just like the mithraeum in New York. So how're we going to find it?"

Flint cocked a bushy eyebrow at her, then turned back to his phone, swiping and tapping with renewed vigor.

"What? You see something?"

"No," he answered shortly. "But I might *hear* something." He pulled a steel cylinder about the size of a soda can out of his bag, plugged its long cord into his tablet, and rested the can on the ground. "You know I monitor seismic vibrations."

"Yeah. Although I'm not sure why."

"God of Volcanoes. Means I like to know when they're about to erupt."

"In the *Vatican*?" She looked around pointedly.

"I also power my forge through geothermal activity," he said gruffly, walking a few steps and resting the can in a new location. "It means I'm really good at hearing any vibrations or sounds emanating from underground. And from what we know of their mithraeum in New York, the Host is quite technologically advanced. They'll have all sorts of high-tech equipment, power generators, climate-control systems—"

"And futuristic torture devices," she added, thinking of the shooting flames and glass prisons she and Theo had suffered through beneath Saint Patrick's Cathedral.

"All those machines produce vibrations. And their communications apparatus will also be sending out wireless signals. If they're underground somewhere nearby, I'll hear them."

"And you think the Swiss Guard hasn't?" Selene asked doubtfully as she followed him around the circumference of the elliptical plaza. She could see a pair of the guards even now, standing under an arch in the colonnade like Renaissance statues, mildly ridiculous in their parti-colored hose and velvet tunics. "Aren't they trained to defend the Vatican against all dangers?"

"No one bothers monitoring seismic waves as deep as I do." He kept walking his can around the plaza, his face intent.

After a few minutes, Selene grew impatient and headed in the other direction, looking for more clues. As absurd as it seemed that the Host would put an entrance to its ultrasecret hideout in a place as public as Saint Peter's Square, she'd bet her entire stash of gold arrows that it had. After all, in New York, the syndexioi stuck a hidden door right into the base of the famous Atlas statue in the middle of Rockefeller Center. They seemed unable to resist displaying their influence in plain sight—at least to the initiated. They also had a tendency to connect their ceremonial locations with landmarks, believing the sites' greater importance added power to their rituals. What greater place of power could there be than the seat of the Catholic Church itself?

At least, that's what the Christians think, she mused, looking at the Vatican City flag snapping overhead. Its coat of arms featured two crossed keys below a pope's miter. *They think Saint Peter holds the keys to heaven itself. That's not so different from Mithras, who grants his followers salvation by shifting the celestial spheres to bring about the Last Age.* Saturn had admitted to manipulating Saint Paul on the road to Damascus—why not co-opt Saint Peter as well? She felt more certain than ever that her grandfather would choose this place for his sanctuary.

Zeus is probably chained somewhere right beneath me, she thought, clenching her fists with frustration. She closed her eyes as if that might help her sense him. *If he begs for help, will I hear his pleas?* she wondered, before admitting to herself that such a thing would never happen. Not because she couldn't hear—but because her imperious father never begged. *If he'd ever asked for my help before, I would've gone to him,* she decided. *Instead, he was content to live alone in his cave, and I was content to let him.*

She opened her eyes at the sound of a child's giggle. The scene before her seemed placed by the Fates as a reminder of her failings as a daughter. A gangly brown man in a Denver Broncos T-shirt and baggy cargo shorts carried a little girl on his shoulders. She couldn't have been more than five years old, her skinny arms wrapping his bald head like a victor's wreath. Selene heard him patiently attempting to explain the major tenets of Catholicism as he pointed out the saints above the colonnade.

Did Father ever carry me like that? she wondered. A memory flooded back to her, so sharp and quick her eyes burned with sudden tears. *Yes. The first time I saw my sacred city of Ephesus,* she remembered, *it was from my father's shoulders. He brought me down from Olympus and across the wide Aegean Sea to Asia Minor. "Your worship will spread beyond Greece,"* he told me. *"Your glory has no bounds—and neither does my love for you."* It hadn't mattered how many other gods and heroes Zeus sired—in his presence, she'd always felt like a beloved only child.

Selene watched as the little girl on her father's shoulders rested her cheek against his shining skull. Her eyes drifted shut, but she was still alert enough to ask, "What's the pope?"

Then, after his muddled response about a man ordained to carry out God's will, she demanded, "Are there ever any girl popes?"

"Not yet," the dad replied.

"Not ever," Selene grumbled under her breath.

The dad caught her eye. She expected him to scold her. Instead, he winked, his smile more friendly than flirtatious. "Never say never." He patted his daughter's tiny leg affectionately, as if he really believed that the little girl could grow up to change the world.

That's what my father believed about me, Selene thought, turning away from the man before he could engage her further. *And now I'm so powerless I can't even free him from a prison right under my feet.*

Her cheeks burned, the unrelenting Mediterranean sun exacerbating the heat of her shame. She passed by one of the round fountains at the end of the plaza, letting the cool spray brush her face, but it provided little relief. She could feel the warmth of the sunbaked black cobblestones through her boot soles—until she couldn't anymore. She looked down, curious.

She stood on a large circular slab of white marble. Inscribed around its circumference: SAGITTARIO25NOV and ACQVARIO-21GENN. From either side of the plaque, a thin granite line emerged. She traced its course to the Egyptian obelisk in the center of the plaza. A total of seven marble circles sat along the line. Selene walked from one to the next.

The middle circles each bore the names of two constellations of the zodiac, along with two dates. The circle farthest from the center contained only the Latin inscription for Capricorn and 22DEC. The circle closest to the towering obelisk listed only Cancer and 21JUN. The winter and summer solstices. *But why?*

Selene took a step back, then another—only then did she notice that the obelisk's shadow lay across the plaza like a black finger, pointing directly along the granite line. The shadow's tip rested just above the summer solstice marker.

She peered upward at the sun—it hung almost directly overhead. *Noon,* she thought, looking down once more at the obelisk's shadow.

The granite line, she saw now, was a meridian: As the sun moved from east to west every day, the shadow would trace a semicircle within the plaza. Only at midday would it align with the granite meridian, allowing church officials to identify the right time for their noon prayers. The zodiac markers, on the other hand, indicated the sun's progression throughout the course of an entire year.

"Hey," she called across the plaza to Flint. "What's today's date?"

"June nineteenth," he shouted back, already walking toward her. "Why?"

In two days, at the summer solstice, the sun would rise to its highest point in the sky, and the 130-foot obelisk would cast a shadow only a few yards long, its tip resting squarely on the Cancer marker.

Selene felt her heart lurch. *I finally know why Father is still alive.*

Flint joined her beside the meridian line.

"The summer solstice," she told him. "That must be what they're waiting for. Two days. That's all the time we have before they kill him."

Flint nodded gravely. "Then we'll find him. The clues have to be here somewhere. But it doesn't make sense."

"Of course it does! The Host sacrificed the other Athanatoi on the days surrounding the winter solstice. They're obsessed with astrology, solstices, and equinoxes. So the summer solstice is the obvious choice for their next rite."

"I agree. I meant the meridian line doesn't make sense." He pointed at the marble plaque before them. "At the summer solstice, the sun doesn't rise in front of the constellation Cancer."

"Maybe it did when they built the plaza," she offered.

Much of the original religion of Mithraism, according to Theo's research, centered on the fact that the position of the sun and constellations during the solstices and equinoxes moved over time due to the earth's wobble. The ancients, who knew nothing about the wobble, had credited the god Mithras with this shift of the "celestial spheres." They believed that each time the heavens moved, the world entered a new Age named for the position of the sun at the spring equinox. Some modern astrologers believed something similar, crediting major changes in society to the turning of the Ages that occurred approximately every two thousand years.

Although the lack of distinct borders on the constellations made definitive pronouncements impossible, most observers claimed the world was currently at the very end of the Age of Pisces—about to move into the Age of Aquarius. Saturn's cult believed that if they performed the correct rituals and murdered the correct gods, the next Age would be the Last Age, when Mithras-as-Jesus would once again walk the earth, bringing ultimate salvation to mankind.

Flint brought up something on his phone, shaking his head all the while. "The meridian line is newer than the plaza. 'The Vatican built it in the early 1800s,'" he read aloud before looking down at the zodiac markers again. "Since the position of the spring equinox shifts every two thousand years or so, what was true when the meridian was built in the nineteenth century would still be true today—we're in the Age of Pisces, so at the summer solstice, the sun rises in front of Gemini."

"So by saying the summer solstice is in Cancer instead..." Selene paced the length of the meridian again, stopping at the middle circle of the seven. "It's like turning the clock back two thousand years."

A small voice piped, "I'm a Cancer!"

The man and his daughter were back.

Arms outstretched, the little girl ran tight circles around one of the marble plaques like a crazed seagull. "Cancer the Crab! Snap snap! That's the sound a crab makes."

Her father laughed. "That's right, Lily!"

"No, it's not," Selene couldn't help retorting.

The father threw her a startled glance that warmed into friendly interest when he recognized her from their previous conversation. "Crabs don't go snap?"

"She's not a Cancer."

"Selene..." Flint warned under his breath. "Leave it."

But Selene was tired of suffering the consequences of mortal stupidity. The Mithraists' blind acceptance of Saturn's lies had gotten her twin killed and her father kidnapped. *Theo would've seen it as his duty to enlighten this idiot,* she decided with a pang. *And since Theo isn't here ...*

"When the Babylonians defined the zodiac three thousand years ago," she began, crossing her arms and glaring at the dad, "the sun rose in front of the constellation Cancer at the end of June. That's why your kid thinks she's a Cancer. But the earth *wobbles*, and our view of the stars keeps shifting over time, so if you actually watched the sun rise this morning, you'd see it pass through the previous constellation instead—Gemini."

Little Lily had stopped her circling. "Gemini like the Twins?"

Selene hadn't realized the girl was listening. "Yeah, the twins."

The constellation had nothing to do with her and Apollo— the "twins" were Castor and Pollux, two ancient heroes—but the words stuck in her throat nonetheless. She felt her brother's absence like a missing limb.

Lily stared up at Selene, lips pursed as if noticing her distress. "Don't worry. I'd rather be a twin than a crab anyway."

"Huh. Me too."

The dad offered Selene an indulgent smile. "The Vatican has an astronomical observatory and everything." He cocked his head like a schoolteacher patiently explaining something to a particularly dense student. "They wouldn't get the zodiac wrong."

Cheeks flaring red, Flint took half a step toward him. "Are you saying she's lying?"

The man raised both hands as if to fend off an angry bear, all trace of condescension vanishing. "No, no. It's cool. I'll Google it." He swung Lily onto his shoulders. "Nice meeting you all. Have a good time in Rome," he offered before hurrying away.

Selene stared after the pair thoughtfully, repressing her urge to chastise Flint for needlessly defending her from a dad in cargo shorts. "He has a point, you know. If, like the meridian says, the summer solstice is in Cancer, then at the *spring* equinox, the sun rises in *Aries*. Which would mean we're currently living in the Age of Aries."

"But we're *not*," Flint grumbled. "We moved from the Age of Aries the Ram into the Age of Pisces the Fish sometime between 1 AD and 300 AD—around the time Mithraism flourished in Rome."

"Exactly. But remember how the Atlas statue in Rockefeller Center holds a celestial sphere above his head? It shows the spring equinox in Aries, too. That's how Theo knew the Mithraists had planted the symbol there to mark the entrance to their mithraeum beneath Saint Patrick's Cathedral—they love referencing the era when Mithraism was at its peak." She pointed at the granite line accusingly. "This meridian is doing the same thing. The astronomers at the Vatican know the real science perfectly well. So whoever put the solstice in the wrong place didn't do it by mistake—this is our entrance."

"You're still convinced the Vatican is in on the plot?"

"I'm not saying the pope himself is a syndexios," she admitted. "But the Host has been around for almost two thousand years. If they had time to infiltrate the police force in New York, why not parts of the Vatican, too?"

Flint didn't look convinced, but he dropped his steel cylinder onto the marble Cancer plaque nonetheless. "I'm not picking up any vibrations." He walked up the meridian, testing each circle in turn. "Nothing."

Selene scowled and paced back over the circles, stopping at the Mithraists' other favorite constellation—Taurus the Bull, the central animal in the tauroctony. *I must be missing something,* she thought. *If Theo were here . . .* She stomped her foot in frustration. Then she stomped again, her preternatural hearing noting the slight variation in tone between this circle and the others. A grin spread slowly across her face.

"There may not be any seismic waves, but there sure as hell's a big hole right underneath my boots."

Chapter 16

SHE WHO WORKS IN SECRET

"I still think we need a better plan," Flint grumbled when they returned to Saint Peter's Square that night.

"We don't have that luxury," Selene insisted.

They'd debated it all day. They had fewer than forty-eight hours before the solstice. If they tried to break in tonight and it didn't work, at least they'd get another shot tomorrow.

"I still think we should wait for Scooter," Flint insisted. "He's a smarmy little bastard, but we could use his help."

As the God of Thieves, Scooter Joveson had a talent for breaking into locked places.

"You tried to call him, right?"

"Voice mail every time."

"So he's either taking one of his spa days, stuck somewhere on a plane, or locked away in bed with his latest starlet."

"He's not a movie producer anymore."

"You think tech moguls don't sleep with hot celebrities?" she scoffed. "Regardless, we don't have time to wait for him to get here from Los Angeles. It's got to be tonight."

"Then I should go in with you." He gave her that look again.

The same one he'd been casting her way all day when he thought she wasn't looking. The "maybe I should trap her inside one of my famous nets and make sure she can't get away" look. But the Smith was nothing if not smart. *He knows that the minute he allows his love for me to devolve into overprotectiveness, I'll run.*

"I'll be fine," she said, a remonstrance more than an assurance. "I'm not planning on any fighting. I'm just going to sneak in, find where they're holding Father, and get him out. It'll all be over before sunrise."

She patted the bulge in her pocket, where she'd stored the modified two-way radio Flint had given her. Unlike a cell phone, it transmitted super-low-frequency waves that could travel underground. "I'll signal when I've got Father, and you just make sure you're back here in the plaza to create another distraction so we can get back out without being seen by the guards." She found strength in saying the words aloud. After so many futile months, she would finally rescue Zeus. She felt, for the first time since she'd left New York, like herself again. Like She Who Helps One Climb Out.

"Once Father's safe," she went on, "*then* we can deal with Saturn."

Flint just frowned beneath his beard.

"Hey, they also call me She Who Works in Secret, right?" She tried for a cocky smile.

"And Lady of Clamors, don't forget. What if you set off an alarm?"

She waved aside his concerns. "I'll be in and out before they even notice I'm there."

But Flint was right. No matter her many relevant epithets, their plan was weak. Usually, he cooked up intricate strategies involving ingenious mechanical inventions and a thorough understanding of probabilities—that's how they'd traced their last Mithraist to the ancient town of Ostia. For Flint, He of Many Arts and Skills, such tactics were second nature. But

Selene had always been the Goddess of the Wild; on the hunt, she relied on reflexes alone to avoid the boar's tusk and drive her javelin home. Tonight, they'd do things her way.

She gestured for Flint to head toward the southern end of the plaza, where the Swiss Guards stood watch at a broad archway leading to the rest of Vatican City. The two men on duty in their long velvet tunics and purple-and-yellow-striped hose held halberds—tall poles topped with wickedly curved blades. Despite the silly clothes and anachronistic weaponry, the Swiss Guards had trained for over five hundred years to defend the Vatican. Selene had little doubt they carried more advanced weapons out of sight, just like her.

She wore the most nondescript outfit she owned—loose pants with plenty of pockets, a dark T-shirt, and, of course, a backpack with her dismantled bow safely stowed inside. She tried to look like a tourist, pulling out her phone to take photos of the colonnade and the saints overhead.

After a few moments, she moved her phone so the camera recorded over her shoulder, where Flint hobbled toward the guardhouse. The soldiers stood at attention, their eyes straight ahead. Flint moved far more slowly than usual, leaning heavily on his crutches. He, too, had dressed for the evening, eschewing his usual somber clothing and long pants for a tourist's Italian flag shirt and shorts that displayed his withered legs.

When he'd emerged from his bedroom that evening, Selene had to bite back a gasp of dismay. She hadn't seen his bare legs since the days when gods and men wore togas. She'd forgotten just how misshapen and pitiable they were. His thighs were barely thicker than his skeletal shins. His knobby right knee buckled inward and his left crooked outward in a mockery of a classical statue's elegant contrapposto. Thick hair grew from the hem of his shorts to his ankles, making him look more like a wretched beast than a man—much less like a god. Flint had caught her staring.

"Thank you," she'd said quickly, feeling her own face warm in response to his obvious embarrassment, "for helping with this. I know you bear no love for my father."

His eyes held hers as he said, "That's true." He didn't say more. He didn't need to. She knew what he was thinking. *I bear love for you. So much that I would reveal all my weaknesses upon your request.* That was the sort of love few men and fewer immortals could offer.

Am I an utter fool not to grab it while I can? Selene wondered as she watched him limp closer to the guardhouse. *What am I waiting for? I don't feel for him the way I did for you, Theo, but maybe that's okay. Maybe love isn't supposed to be as joyful as ours was. Maybe it's supposed to be serious and profound and just a little bit tortured.*

Flint groaned loudly and started muttering prayers in Latin. Her keen hearing recognized the Lord's Prayer; she wondered when he'd picked up that bit of knowledge. Taking her cue, she meandered toward the granite meridian embedded in the ground.

A few feet away from the Swiss Guards, Flint collapsed to the ground with a grunt. He raised one hand heavenward as if imploring Jesus and rubbed his skinny legs with the other. When the guards didn't move, Flint moaned more loudly and pulled a conspicuous silver crucifix from beneath his collar. He attempted to get to his feet but fell clumsily back to the ground, now clutching at his chest.

"Please," he gasped. "I need a doctor."

Selene couldn't help a small, amazed smile. She and Flint had both counted themselves exceptions to their generally histrionic family; she hadn't expected him to do so well with the theatrics.

Sure enough, the guards put aside their halberds and rushed forward to help the fallen man, crouching beside him on the pavement. The few other nighttime tourists turned toward the commotion, leaving Selene temporarily unobserved.

From her backpack, she withdrew a crowbar. This particular

entrance to the mithraeum, she knew, must be ceremonial. *No way the syndexioi can pop in and out of Saint Peter's Square on a regular basis without anyone noticing,* she thought. *Which means this plaque isn't meant to be easily moved by human hands.*

She held the crowbar close to her leg to hide it from casual observation and slipped the end into a slight gap around the slab's circumference. *Good thing I'm not human.*

Repressing a groan of effort, she threw her weight against the tool. At first, it seemed the bar would bend before the stone gave way. Then, with the sucking pop of an opened jar, the marble lifted an inch, then another. She risked a glance toward the Swiss Guards. They were busy struggling to get Flint to his feet—not an easy task with a 250-pound man actively resisting their assistance.

She pressed the crowbar to the paving stones, secured it with her boot, then spun the massive disc to the side. A narrow, dark shaft yawned before her. With a speed no mortal could manage, she slipped inside, braced her feet against the sides of the shaft, and reached overhead to replace the marble.

Blackness.

She froze, suspended within the open shaft, hands and feet holding her steady as she listened to the sounds above. No running footsteps, no cries of alarm.

Relieved that her excavations had gone unnoticed, she turned her attention to her surroundings. Beneath her hands, cold cement.

Scooting gingerly along the circumference, she searched for a ladder with her hands and feet. *Guess they don't want visitors,* she decided when her search failed. *So either I'm right that this is a purely symbolic entrance, or I've just crawled into a sewage pipe.*

She peered futilely into the black void beneath her boots, wondering how deep it went. She dared support herself with just her legs so she could reach into her pocket for a headlamp.

In the light's beam, she saw a dry, concrete floor below her—no wider than a dinner plate from her perch so far above. She let go of the wall, shooting down the shaft with only her boot soles to slow her descent.

She slammed to the ground in a crouch, the smell of burnt rubber wrinkling her nose. Before her, a tunnel led southward. She started down it, adjusting the light more securely on her forehead and readying her bow and arrows. Her quiver held mostly wooden shafts, but she'd packed three god-forged golden arrows as well, the only kind that could actually kill her divine grandfather. Rescuing Zeus was her first priority, but if she happened to run into the Titan on the way out, she wouldn't waste the opportunity.

After a few hundred feet, the tunnel made a sharp right turn, blocking her view of the path ahead. She stepped forward more cautiously and rounded the corner, only to see the tunnel turn again ahead of her. Even as it grew more labyrinthine, the corridor widened. A section of masonry wall interrupted the smooth cement. Old bricks in shades of red and yellow, uneven and chipped, as if made by hand centuries—or millennia—before.

Farther on, she passed another patch of bricks below the fragment of a marble cornice. The floor beneath her feet changed, too, from poured cement to flat paving stones. *I'm walking on the remains of an ancient Roman street,* she realized.

By the time she'd turned three more times, the Huntress— who could navigate through the thickest forest by the feel of the wind alone—had completely lost her bearings in this underground maze.

She had no idea how much time had passed, but she felt sure she'd been wandering the tunnels for at least an hour. She began to long for a man with a gun to show up around the next corner—at least she'd have something to shoot at.

She got a bull instead.

Chapter 17

BULL RIDER

The bull tore through the narrow tunnel beneath the Vatican like a shotgun slug down a barrel. Two thousand pounds of rippling white flesh, a ring through his nose, an incongruous wreath of pine boughs bouncing around his neck, and a pair of wickedly curved horns aimed straight at Selene's rib cage.

She loosed an arrow with more instinct than accuracy. The shaft lodged in the creature's shoulder, only enraging him further.

There was nowhere to hide, no place to dodge. But Selene had honed her fighting skills in the cramped alleys of New York City. At the last second, she dove forward, sliding beneath the beast's belly. His hooves churned inches from her head.

She jackknifed to her feet as the animal clattered to a skidding halt behind her.

He twisted like a mutant dog chasing its tail until he faced her again, nostrils pumping air.

Before she could grab another arrow, he charged. Like the bull-leapers of ancient Knossos, where Theseus once faced the Minotaur in the heart of the twisting Labyrinth, Selene sprang up. She planted one hand on the animal's spine and flipped her legs toward the ceiling, hovering for just a moment in a precarious handstand. The bull bucked beneath her. She pushed off and landed behind him, her bow still gripped in her other hand.

She nocked another shaft. The heaving bull lowered his head just after she loosed her arrow. It sailed harmlessly above the beast's horns.

Without missing a beat, Selene sent another shaft through the animal's back, hoping to slow him down. The beast bellowed, the sound resonating in the narrow tunnel like a war horn blown from the battlements of Troy. Selene cursed under her breath. *So "Lady of Clamors" it is.*

She thought about sprinting back toward the exit and shimmying up the cement shaft, but it was too soon. Flint would still be resting in some clinic, unable to distract the guards while she emerged into the plaza. She'd be thrown in jail and lose any hope of rescuing Zeus before the solstice.

Father, if you're down here, she prayed, *now would be a great time to stage a distraction.* Unsurprisingly, no thunder rocked the underground passage, no lightning flashed before her.

Instead, she heard two men farther down the tunnel jabbering worriedly in German. She knew little of their tongue, only enough to catch something about a bull. *Their prize animal has escaped,* she realized, *but they don't know about me yet.*

The bull himself, unfortunately, knew exactly where she was. Despite his wounds, he closed the distance between them. She sent an arrow into the meat of his chest. He kept coming.

She dodged aside, but he turned his head and pinned her to the wall between his long, curved horns. The bull panted hot against her face like an overeager suitor cornering a blushing virgin. She managed to reach for another arrow. *I never could stand the attentions of smelly men.* She raised the shaft overhead, ready to drive it through the top of the beast's skull.

"Halt!" Two men stood before her in Swiss Guard uniforms, guns raised.

These were no mere Papal soldiers patrolling the Vatican's secret spaces; she knew that the moment one turned to the other and said, *"Sie ist Diana."* Only initiated members of the Host would know her true identity.

"We need that bull more than we need you," the younger man said in English. "So either drop the arrow or we put a bullet through your brain."

Still trapped between the bull's horns, she had little choice but to comply. She put down the arrow but kept her bow, holding it out of sight beneath the animal's body.

The older guard stepped forward to place the barrel of his gun against her head. The other clipped a rope to the ring in the bull's nose and led him away.

Free of the horns, Selene ducked away from the guard's gun and smashed her bow into his knees. He buckled but pulled the trigger—his bullet cracked into the wall behind her, dispelling any last hope that these men had orders to take her alive.

She whipped her bow around to kick the gun away, then back to crack it against the guard's jaw. As his head snapped to the side, Selene sprinted in the other direction. She caught just a glimpse of the second guard reaching for a black device on his belt.

A walkie-talkie, she thought, until two probes shot out faster than even her eyes could follow. They ripped into her neck. Convulsions racked her body.

Darkness slammed her to the ground.

Chapter 18

MAGNA MATER

Warm liquid splatted against Selene's cheek.

Her eyes flew open. She sat up in a circular stone chamber awash with torchlight. Beside her, the marble pine tree from Ostia stood upon an ancient pedestal of cracked limestone.

Selene took a quick survey of her body. Her head and neck still throbbed from the Taser's charge, and steel pinned her wrists behind her back. She wanted to scream her frustration. She'd found the Host only to fall prey to them once more. They'd taken away her low-frequency transmitter—she couldn't signal Flint. And this time, there'd be no Theo Schultz to rescue her. He was four thousand miles away and convinced she was already dead.

Why did I think I could do this alone? she let herself wonder for a moment before angrily thrusting aside her self-pity.

She rose dizzily to her feet and stared at the grate overhead, its openings too small for her to see through. Another drop fell toward her, landing on her upturned face.

Is that...piss? She heard a bellow, a stamping hoof. Her bovine nemesis must be standing overhead.

A Latin chant echoed against the chamber's walls: *"Taurobolium facimus velut Mithras fecit, ut proximum saeculum efficiamus..."*

We perform this Bull Sacrifice as Mithras did, to bring the next Age.

What was it June said about supplicants in the Phrygianum waiting in a pit? she wondered too late.

Another mad bellow from the bull. A knife ripped through flesh.

An instant later, a torrent of blood rushed through the grate, slamming hot and thick against her face. It ran down her scalp, her shoulders, her breasts. It seeped between her closed lips. She retched at the taste of salt and copper and something darker. Some ancient part of her remembered the flavor—and relished it. She retched harder.

"Really?" she hollered when she could speak again. Blood and bile flew from her lips. She sought rage, that old friend, hoping its heat would burn away her fears. "It wasn't enough to steal Jesus? You had to steal the Magna Mater's taurobolium, too?"

At Rockefeller Center, Saturn had dressed Mars up as Aries the Ram before killing him to symbolize the turning of the ages. The Host was obsessed with reenacting the heavens' progress through sacrifice. Such rituals, they believed, helped bring about the final shift into the Last Age—hence the bull blood currently dripping into Selene's eyes. But why bring in the Magna Mater? She might have once been Rhea, Saturn's wife, but how did that help the stars move? She and Flint had never really figured it out.

While Selene's mind whirled, the syndexioi continued their chanting, mixing Mithraic liturgy, Catholic tropes, and references to the Great Mother in their usual synergistic stew.

Mother of Gods, surrounded by bull-destroying lions,
Come mighty power, Phrygian savior, come,
Saturn's great queen, help us move the spheres of heaven.

For like the pine tree, we hold the seeds of our own rebirth.
Water us with your blood.

Blessed are you among women,
and blessed is the fruit of your womb.
Magna Mater, Mother of Gods.

With her hands bound behind her, Selene ducked her chin against her collarbone, searching for Flint's necklace so she could fight her way free of this horror. It was gone. Saturn had seen her use it as a whip and a javelin in Ostia—he'd known to remove it.

They're making me their sacrifice, she knew. *This whole ritual is just preparation for the moment when Saturn cuts out my heart.*

Trying to quash her rising panic, she blinked the blood from her eyes and searched her surroundings for some means of escape. The Phrygianum had been constructed as a place for Rome's powerful and wealthy to offer prayers to the Great Mother. The age of the pine tree's limestone pedestal pointed to the cult's ancient roots. Selene suspected the stolen Ostia sculpture was an ad-hoc replacement for an original cult statue, likely made of wood or ivory, that had disintegrated long ago.

She stood in a cylindrical chamber surrounded by a viewing area where dignitaries could witness the blood pour through the overhead grate and onto the head of the Magna Mater's supplicant. But tonight, the men watching the taurobolium served a very different god.

Here in the privacy of their secret sanctuary, the syndexioi could flaunt their devotion to Mithras. The outfits they wore identified their rank within the Host's strict hierarchy. The lower-ranked Miles, or "Soldier," dressed as a Roman legionary. The mid-level Leo wore a lion mask. The second-in-command, the red-robed Heliodromus, or "Sun-Runner," carried a long cat-o'-nine-tails with which to whip the Sun across the sky.

"If you're going to pretend to pay homage to my grandmother, why not chop off your own balls like you're supposed to?" Selene shouted at them. *Might as well piss them off,* she decided. *They're going to kill me anyway.*

None of the men responded. They turned their masked faces upward instead. A voice floated through the wooden planks. Old and rough but filled with power.

Saturn.

"Hark, syndexioi, to the beginning of the world," he said in Latin. "To Sky and Earth and the children they bore."

She knew this story; she'd heard her own father tell it often enough. But she feared Saturn's version; she remembered how, in Ostia, the God of Time's voice had dragged her backward into another age, making her a silent witness to events she'd only ever imagined. She couldn't afford to tumble into the past, not with her enemies surrounding her in the present. She needed to think, to fight—but Saturn's power could not be denied.

At the dawn of the world there was no Time, the voice began. *Only darkness. Cold. Nothingness.* Khaos.

Selene fought to keep the masked syndexioi before her eyes, but in an instant, she felt herself floating in blackness; the Phrygianum's torches shed no light in this primeval memory. Then, slowly, the ground steadied once more beneath her feet.

From this chasm emerged Ouranos the Sky and Gaia the Earth, the voice continued. *And from their union came Unbounded Time in all his glory. Aion.*

Many-winged, lion-headed, fire-breathing. Protogonos. A primordial son too uncontrolled to govern creation.

Selene caught the merest glimpse of beating wings, of a fanged lion's mouth belching flames to feed a fiery ball that exploded across her vision. When the fire passed, the light remained so brilliant it seemed almost tangible, a great, bright fog slowly melting through a rainbow of colors, from searing red to deepest indigo, before devolving into utter blackness once more.

Next Gaia birthed Kronos, called Saturn. God of Bounded Time, a Titan who bent the curve of the universe into a straight line. Who bound His lion-brother in place. The one true Father who gave life beginning and end.

Slowly, the air around her pricked with stars. Finally, a man appeared before her. Taller than a giant, with hair *khaos*-dark and eyes the layered blue of twilight. In his hand he bore a sickle, the blade serrated with stars.

He knew the world would flourish only under His benevolent rule. So He took His mighty sickle and sliced the manhood from His father, Ouranos the Sky, throwing his stones into the ocean to foam upon the crest of the waves.

Thus did Saturn become King of All, ruling a Golden Age bereft of sin, of suffering, of strife.

But Saturn's wife, Rhea, grew jealous of her husband's dominion.

Selene watched her own grandmother appear. Black hair intricately braided, starry jewels at her wrists and throat, her belly swollen beneath a sheer chiton spun of moonlight and morning dew.

One after another, Rhea brought children into the world, each imbued with a part of Saturn's power.

"Here is Hestia," she said, raising the girl child to her husband. "She will keep the hearth fires burning and bind families to the home." But the wise Father took the babe and swallowed her down, placing her in His own gullet, where she could do no harm to the world. For He alone ruled hearth and home.

Saturn unhinged his jaw like a snake and gulped. Grief blind-sided Selene with its force—a despair too keen for the loss of a distant aunt. She wanted to rip the clothes from her breast, to smear her face with ash. *I'm witnessing the demise of my own child,* she knew, though the thought made no sense.

"Here is Hades," said Rhea, showing Saturn His eldest son. "He will claim dominion over the Underworld."

But Saturn swallowed him down. For He alone ruled the afterlife.

Again, the sharp slash of anguish. Selene screamed in horror as she watched the baby's tiny foot slurped between Saturn's wet lips, but no sound issued from her mouth. She was a silent observer only, though she understood now why Hades' demise caused her such agony. *I don't know how, but I watch through Rhea's eyes*, she realized. *Her broken heart beats in my breast.*

Again and again, five times in all, Rhea presented her children to her Titan king. And each time He protected the world from them. Hestia and Hades. Hera and Demeter and Poseidon. Family and harvest and ocean swells. All swallowed down to remain within the one true God where they belonged.

And then Gaia Earth conspired with Rhea, for they wanted the Father's power for themselves. Saturn's wife gave birth to one final son. A raging child who would cover the world in storm clouds of his own making. Who would bring war and suffering and lightning blasts.

Rhea wrapped a stone in swaddling clothes and raised it up to her husband.

"Here is Zeus," she said. "He will rule the world."

And Saturn swallowed down the stone.

Gaia hid her grandson Zeus in a cave in the depths of a mountain, among goats who succored him with their milk and nymphs who played loud cymbals to hide his infant cries.

Heart bursting with a mother's pride, Selene watched as Zeus grew from babe to man among the familiar stalactites of his cave until his body rippled with power and his beard jutted sharp as a lightning strike.

Zeus sought his father. He ripped open Saturn's gullet and withdrew his siblings. Each emerged full-grown. Ready to steal the world from its rightful God.

A great battle began.

Selene was a silent witness to the story no longer. Saturn had summoned the other Titans to his side, and giants, too, each with a hundred hands and fifty heads. The war with the giants—the Gigantomachy—had raged for so long that Artemis had grown to adulthood before the end. The battle came to her in flashes of double vision as she watched through Rhea's eyes and her own at the same time. The gleaming storm of her arrows striking down her enemies. A queen's long scepter ripping a giant's head from its body. Golden ichor splattering across the carnage. The earth shaking with the force of the clash. The world itself near torn apart.

When the battle was done, Saturn's own children cast Him down into the pit of Tartarus. A prison full of raging monsters, as black and cold as Khaos itself.

Six Olympians remained to divide the world, with their children to divide it still further.

But Saturn never forgot and never forgave. The world suffered with His loss.

And when His children freed Him from Tartarus many eons later, He vowed to take back what they had stolen.

The voice's power finally dimmed, the words just words.

"The Olympians faded, victims of their own blind hubris. They grew weak and mortal—mere bodies of flesh."

Selene slowly came back to the stone floor of the Phrygianum, back to the blood dribbling down her neck. She was in her own body again—but she felt a strange prickle across her skin that had nothing to do with the bull's drying gore. *Someone is watching me,* she thought at first. Then, *No . . . someone is watching through me.*

"I will move the heavens themselves to bring the world into the Last Age," her grandfather intoned. "An Age free of false gods. For I am God and God is One. One in Three and Three in One."

Footsteps on the grate overhead. The syndexioi around her rustled as if to prepare for the next step in the ritual.

"The one responsible for destroying my rule must now suffer the consequences. The Great Mother must be brought low." Saturn's formal incantation became something more personal, more bitter, as he went on. "Rhea no longer walks this earth—my queen is out of reach. And so we imbue her granddaughter with the seed of her spirit instead. We water her with the blood of the bull that she may burst into bloom as the Great Mother herself."

148 Jordanna Max Brodsky

Selene's chest tightened with panic. *My grandmother looks through my eyes. I am not alone in my own body.* She summoned a defiant bark of laughter anyway.

"Well, if you expected me to magically turn into Rhea, it didn't work!" she shouted up to the grate, unwilling to admit to Saturn that his ritual might have succeeded. "I'm just cold and wet and sticky, and the only thing I have in common with Grandma is the desire to rip your fucking stomach out."

The armor-clad Miles brandished his long spear at her and said something in Italian.

"Sorry," she said. "I don't speak the vernacular."

A figure appeared on the stone staircase that led from the overhead grate to the chamber's floor.

"You would prefer English, is that it?" her grandfather asked. "A common language for a common girl."

With his burnt face and white beard, Saturn bore little resemblance to the Titan king in the story. But his eyes still shone like a blue-black sky just before the stars appeared, and he wore his ceremonial garb proudly: a white robe edged in red. His divine sickle hung from his waist, the same curved blade he'd used to slice the balls from his own father. The same blade that had cut Apollo's heart from his chest.

He walked slowly down the stairs and across the bloody floor. Up close, she could tell just how strong he'd become. He might not have swallowed his offspring this time, but their deaths had renewed his power nonetheless. He would be nearly impossible to kill.

That wouldn't stop her from trying.

With her own hatred fueled by her grandmother's ancient rage, she hopped quickly over her cuffed wrists and lunged forward, ready to kill Saturn with her bare hands.

The Miles's outstretched spear swung into her path.

She stopped with its point a centimeter from her chest. The long golden shaft had once belonged to Mars, the God of War.

The Miles might not have any divinely granted abilities—he would wield the spear no better than any well-trained mortal—but the weapon itself, like her golden arrows, had been forged by Hephaestus. No running stream could heal her from such a wound.

"If I'm such a *common* girl, as you put it," she snarled at her grandfather, "why do you keep putting me in your sacrificial rituals?" Chin raised, she stared coldly into his eyes, resisting the urge to wipe away the blood she could still feel trickling down her cheek.

"Because authenticity matters," Saturn replied calmly. "To reclaim my own power, I need to destroy those who took it from me in the first place. Starting with the wife who betrayed me."

"Except she's already dead," Selene said, trying to ignore the niggling presence inside her.

"Indeed. The Great Mother was not so great after all. Nonetheless, I need her for the ritual. I'd planned to kidnap a mortal woman as a stand-in—I hoped the marble pine tree would make up for my sacrifice's inadequacies. But you are *much* better suited to my needs. I can already see your grandmother's soul in your eyes." He smiled tightly, an expression more of anger than amusement. "I didn't think we'd actually catch you a second time, much less be able to hold you. Thank you for proving me wrong. Better to have a goddess for the ritual than any obsolete artifact—and you are both, no?"

"So what now?" she asked, ignoring the insult. "You've used Mithras's rituals, now the Magna Mater's. Are you going to send in the little dancing girls dressed as bear cubs?"

Saturn croaked a laugh. "Like your acolytes in Brauron? No, I think not. I don't need Artemis—I need the Magna Mater." He clapped his hands twice, prefacing a skittering of hooves and pitiable bleating overhead. "The taurobolium is complete. The Age of Taurus is past."

This time, Selene ducked her head just in time, but the ram's blood still slammed against her. Her T-shirt stuck to her skin; the hot liquid dripped beneath her collar and snaked between her breasts, rolling under the waistband of her pants in a parody of intimacy. The syndexioi around her chanted praise for the sacrifice that symbolized the passing of the Age of Aries the Ram.

"And what happens when you end the Age of Pisces?" she asked, wiping bloody strands of hair from her eyes with her cuffed hands. "It's going to take a damn big fish to get a good blood shower."

Saturn didn't smile. His eyes traveled hungrily to the gore still drizzling from the overhead grate. "Every time we reenact the heavens' progress, we move one step closer to the Last Age."

"You can't actually change the sun and the stars, you know," Selene snapped. "*None* of us have that kind of power anymore—if we ever did."

Saturn gave her a look of mild surprise. "The stars? No, we cannot move the stars."

"Then why the *fuck* are you bothering to pretend you can? Why the obsession with the Age of Aquarius?"

"The Age of Aquarius…the Last Age. They're one and the same. The stars will move with or without us, you are right—we merely channel the power of that movement for our own purposes. Great shifts in the heavens lead to great shifts on earth. We have waited two thousand years for the next moment of turning. Only now can the Last Age arise. But first we must rid the world of the last few tired remnants of the Olympians. We must restore the One God to his rightful place." His chin lifted; he stared down his nose at Selene. "And to do that we must destroy the old King and make way for another."

She shivered despite the hot blood coating her skin. "You mean killing my father."

"Precisely. Zeus has, after all, had it coming for millennia."

"He should never have released you from the pit of Tartarus," she growled.

"No, he shouldn't have," he agreed with a nod. "And you should never have come here to rescue him. But too late for regrets now, is it not?"

She balled her fists; Saturn noted the gesture with a flare of his nostrils. "You dream of bursting free of your chains and striking me down. But you know now I'm far stronger than you."

"You think I care?"

"Not at all. That's why I'm going to leave this corporeal body behind once and for all. That's what none of you have understood. You mourn your fading flesh, your graying hair. You want to return to youth and power and glory. I want to move beyond all that. The Hebrew god had the right idea, you see. If you never take human form, you can never be hurt, never die. This body is a tomb, granddaughter. One I'll escape soon enough."

He motioned to the Miles, who jabbed his spear toward Selene, herding her out of the stone chamber. Saturn led the way into a long hallway studded with doors.

"This temple of ours is far more ancient than the one we constructed in Manhattan," he explained, as if he gave such tours every day. He stopped at one of the doors and pulled a key from his pocket. "More powerful, too, of course. But we never planned to hold the Olympians captive here—we knew you'd all left Rome after the Diaspora—so no fancy fortified cell this time, I'm afraid." He opened the door. "This was once a schoolroom, where we taught new syndexioi the beauties of our faith. Perhaps now, in your last moments, it might teach you something as well."

"So you *are* going to kill me?" A small part of her had hoped he meant to keep her alive to witness the turning of the Age.

"Of course," he said, looking genuinely surprised. "The taurobolium implanted you with the seed of your grandmother, remember? In a few hours, you will burst into bloom as the Great Mother, and I will prune you from your stem. I just haven't figured out the best cutting method yet."

Selene swallowed hard. Would her body transform, her

stomach swell, her hair coil? Would her mind, her heart, her very soul fall sway to the spirit of a grandmother she couldn't even remember?

Saturn didn't give her the chance to ask. He gestured to his Miles, who pushed her inside the schoolroom. The door locked behind her.

The first thing that caught Selene's attention in the small, dim chamber was the fresco on the ceiling. A beatific young man wearing the seven-rayed crown of the rising sun and a star-studded cloak: Mithras-as-Jesus, the Sun and the Son. Beside him, some syndexios had painted a bearded, older man carrying a sickle in one hand: the Father bearing the symbol of Saturn. The third figure Selene had never seen before, but she recognized him from Saturn's story: Aion, the primordial God of Unbounded Time, a creature with a lion's head, four wings, and a snake coiled around his naked human body. The two Roman keys the figure held against his chest reminded her of the Vatican's coat of arms.

"God is One in Three and Three in One," said a gravelly voice from nearby. "The Father, the Son, and the Holy Spirit."

She spun toward the sound. Crouched in the corner of the room sat a very old man, his nakedness covered only by a thin, ragged blanket. His patchy white beard drooped to his bent knees, and his scalp showed pink beneath his wispy hair. An age-spotted hand patted across the floor until it found a pair of broken glasses. He fumbled them onto his face and peered up at her with rheumy gray eyes, one obscured by a shattered lens, the other enormous behind the thick glass.

After a long moment, she recognized him.

"Father…"

In answer, the barest hint of a smile curved his thin lips. "Deer Heart."

A moan escaped her as she staggered forward and fell to her knees before the King of the Gods.

Chapter 19

PSYCHOPOMPOS

Theo's mouth felt sticky, his back ached, and he had no idea what time it was, but none of that mattered. Soon, he'd either be dead or with Selene. *Or maybe both.*

Twenty hours after he'd left New York, Theo watched Scooter Joveson bound toward the visitor's entrance to Saint Peter's Basilica. Beneath the watchful eyes of the countless Christian saints carved on the massive cathedral's facade, the pagan Messenger of the Gods disdained Theo's proffered hand and embraced him instead.

For his new career as a cybersecurity expert, Scooter had traded in his rakish movie-producer suit for dark slacks and a crisp checked shirt. He'd slicked his unruly black curls into a short ponytail, revealing a high widow's peak that made the famously youthful god look just a little past his prime. Thick-framed blue glasses contributed to the overall "serious nerd" facade, an illusion quickly shattered the moment he pulled a brightly patterned Hermès handkerchief from his pocket and fanned his face with it.

"If we're going to do this thing," he carped, glancing around the sunbaked piazza, "let's at least do it somewhere with air-conditioning."

"Where's Flint?" Despite the burly Athanatos's unfortunate tendency to moon over Selene, Theo was looking forward to having an ally with a hammer. "I thought you said he'd want to help."

"Well, slight hiccup there, I'm afraid. I keep calling, but his phone's going straight to voice mail."

"*What?* He picked *now* to turn hermit again? I thought you'd been in touch with him."

"I have! He hasn't ignored me in months, I swear."

"You think something happened to him?"

"No, no. He can take care of himself." Scooter's perennial smile looked forced. "Except, you know, if the Host attacked him with one of our divine weapons. I mean, it's possible we've been hunting them and they've been hunting us at the same time, so..." He gave a strangled, humorless laugh.

"Okay, no worries," Theo said, more to reassure himself than Scooter. "We don't need the Smith's unbelievably help-ful, pseudo-magical inventions, right? They always come with a massive chip on Flint's shoulder and a side order of surly, anyway."

"Exactly."

Theo patted the bulging satchel under his arm. "I've got what we need. We'll be fine." *Or not. But I'm too close to stop now—I'm not going to wait around for Scooter to summon some other relative for backup. Selene's waited long enough already.*

"Glad to hear it. Now tell me you have a plan besides walk-ing up to Pope Francis and demanding he let you into the secret pagan cult temple in the attic."

"Not the attic," Theo said with a smile. "The basement."

"Oh. Much better."

"The mithraeum has to be underground, since the cult always placed its sanctuaries in hidden spaces or caves. And it has to have a relationship with death and the afterlife, so I'm thinking we start our little treasure hunt in the necropolis."

Scooter cocked a quizzical eyebrow, and Theo had to remind himself that the gods hadn't kept up with contemporary archeological discoveries. They'd left during the Diaspora and, for the most part, never looked back.

"In the 1930s, while the rest of Europe was worried about a little thing called the future of the world," he explained, "the Vatican was navel-gazing into its own past. They started excavating underneath the basilica, looking for the grave of Saint Peter, the disciple who spread Christianity to Rome—the guy they consider the first pope. Smacks of fascism, honestly, like Mussolini reviving old Roman Empire symbols for his parades, but since it resulted in some pretty remarkable archeological finds, I guess I can't complain."

Theo kept talking as he led Scooter into the massive, vaulted sanctuary of Saint Peter's and headed toward the center of the nave. "The excavators found the remains of a necropolis—an ancient street of mausoleums. Seems Emperor Constantine, everyone's favorite Christian convert, buried the whole thing in the fourth century AD and then used it as a foundation for his first basilica. Twelve hundred years later, a pope knocked that down and stuck *this* basilica on the same spot. Which means the original necropolis is about thirty feet below us right now."

"What do we want with a Christian graveyard?"

"It's older than Constantine, remember? It's a *pagan* necropolis. A perfect meeting place of religions old and new, all centered on the portals between life and death. How can Saturn resist putting an entrance to his mithraeum right there?"

"Uh-huh." Scooter looked doubtful. "And how are we supposed to get inside?"

"Easy." Theo gestured to a line of people waiting beside a small sign labeled VATICAN EXCAVATIONS. "We just take the tour." He opened the satchel wide enough for Scooter to glimpse the dark helm inside. "And since no one will see us in the first place, they'll never notice when we slip away."

A few minutes later, they were scuttling arm in arm behind a tour group.

"Stop stepping on my feet," Theo whispered in Scooter's ear.

"You don't need to hold me so tight!" the god hissed back.

"I don't think it'll work for both of us if I'm just holding your pinky!"

He couldn't see Scooter's expression—wearing Hades' Helm of Invisibility, Theo couldn't even see himself—but from the exasperated sigh, he could imagine it.

They squeezed down the stairs to the ancient necropolis. The alleyway ahead looked much as it had seventeen centuries earlier—except for the low ceiling and LED spotlights. On either side of them stood walls of layered brick with travertine lintels marking the entrances to the various mausoleums.

"Any idea what we're looking for?" hissed Scooter as they peered into the first doorway. The tour group had already moved on, leaving the two invisible prowlers to scope the scene in peace.

"I'm hoping we'll know it when we see it."

They stepped inside the small chamber. Layers of earth had protected its walls for so long that the frescoes' colors remained bright. Red-breasted birds with wings of brilliant blue flew above pomegranates and lilies. Dozens of rectangular and semicircular niches, each bordered in ochre paint, lined the room. The smaller cubbies once held funerary urns, the larger ones corpses. The entire mausoleum looked like a very crowded apartment house for the dead. Now all the niches stood empty. Theo was grateful—he didn't need any further reminders of his own impending doom.

They moved on to the next mausoleum. A black-and-white floral mosaic covered the floor, sagging in the middle like an old mattress. With no other visitors around, Theo released Scooter's arm.

"Finally," the god grumbled as he popped into sight, rubbing at his elbow. "You've been gripping me like a movie ingenue at her first premiere. Tense much, Theo?"

"You think?"

Scooter's eyes skimmed right past him. "Hearing your voice without seeing you is giving me the creeps."

"Get used to it. I'm not about to go to my death with a Swiss Guard's halberd up my ass—I've got other plans for my demise."

Scooter made a sound of choked protest, clearly still not on board with Theo's plans for suicide.

Theo ignored him, crouching down to examine the floor. In each corner of the room lay small marble panels with a round hole cut in their center. "Any idea what these are for?"

"These what? I can't see you, remember?"

"Sorry, the holes in the floor."

"To pour libations to the ancestors. Or to the chthonic gods of the Underworld. At least . . . I think. It's been a while."

Theo lowered himself to all fours and pressed his eye to the hole. Nothing but darkness. He took a sniff but smelled only dust. Shining his flashlight through the opening, he saw a layer of packed dirt a mere foot away.

After knocking on the inside walls of all the tomb niches, looking for hidden panels inside the frescoes, and even tapping out random codes on the mosaic tiles, they finally gave up.

Scooter reluctantly grabbed hold of Theo's waist again, and they walked back into the alleyway. The tour group emerged from one of the mausoleums far ahead, talking excitedly to each other before heading up the spiral stairway at the far end of the necropolis.

"That one must be good," Scooter whispered. "Let's say we skip the boring part and head for the main attraction."

Still wary of being seen, they scurried forward arm in arm and entered a chamber much smaller than the last. Theo took an astonished breath and turned in a slow circle, gazing at the brilliant yellow mosaic that covered the walls.

"I thought you said this was a *pagan* necropolis," Scooter said with a huff.

"It is."

"Then why, pray, is Jonah here?" Scooter broke free of Theo's grip to jab an accusatory finger at a depiction of a man swallowed headfirst by a sea monster. "And if the fisherman behind him isn't a Christ symbol, I don't know what is."

"It's pagan because of *that*," Theo said, pointing upward. Then, at Scooter's exasperated expression, he added, "On the ceiling."

The vault curved into a shallow dome above them. In the center gleamed a mosaic depicting a man in a chariot drawn by four white horses. On his head sat a seven-rayed crown.

Scooter whistled. "All hail Sol Invictus, the Invincible Sun."

"Who just happens to be a common manifestation of Mithras. *And* occasionally mistaken for Christ. This mausoleum isn't exactly Mithraic, but it sure as hell isn't fully Christian. Which makes it the perfect place for our cult."

Together, they scoured every corner of the small room. Mosaics of dark green grapevines twined across the ceiling and walls, framing the images of Jonah on one side and two fishermen on the other. *Is the ivy a Dionysus reference?* Theo wondered. *Perhaps even Orphic?* Yet despite the intriguing meld of religions, they found no sign of secret entrances.

Theo glanced at his watch before he realized he couldn't see it. "Shit. What time is it?"

Scooter looked at his own watch—something heavy and expensive, Theo couldn't help noticing—and let out a yelp. "Almost six. We've got to hurry up or we're going to be locked down here all night."

"Is that a problem for the God of Thieves? I thought you were a master of the lock pick."

"Sure, except when it's the *Vatican*. Their security goes a little beyond the usual five-pin tumbler. I'm just saying, I've got a reservation at a very exclusive nineteenth-century villa for us tonight, and I've already booked a massage, so if we could hurry this up—"

"Scooter," Theo interrupted. "I know life to you is just a series of adventures punctuated by stays in luxury hotels, but I'm not leaving here without Selene. Either we find the mithraeum and I do it there"—He couldn't quite bring himself to say what "it" was—"or we don't, and I just pick my favorite mausoleum and take the chance that it's good enough." He looked once more at the Christ-as-Sol-as-Mithras mosaic and the curling grapevines. "Honestly, this one may be our best bet."

"Hold on, we've got a few hours before the solstice—June twenty-first doesn't start until midnight," Scooter said quickly. "Let's go back and check the other mausoleums that we skipped before you go all 'Romeo at the apothecary' on me." Despite his quips, his smile looked plastered on.

He has no intention of letting me kill myself, Theo knew. *He's only playing along until we find the mithraeum.* Theo had no brilliant plan to avoid Scooter's protectiveness. He just knew that when the time came, he would find Selene. And nothing, not even Hermes, the legendary Trickster, would stop him.

They examined each room in turn. One held plaster statues of the Olympians—Scooter looked peeved the whole time that there was no effigy of Hermes among them. Another was decorated with delicate frescoes of gazelles and birds.

Finally, they stepped into a larger mausoleum with a mosaic floor bordered on two sides by libation holes. Theo stood at its base and examined the design. A slow smile spread across his face, even while his heart began to trip with fear. This was it. He could feel it. The image on the floor was Hades, Lord of the Dead, in a chariot drawn by black horses. A naked Hermes stood before him, the Psychopompos guiding the way to the Underworld with his snake-twined caduceus. A perfect symbol of the journey into death—and back to life.

Scooter stepped into the center of the floor, tilting his head at his own nude image. "That's more like it. I'm liking the six-pack, although the cock is *way* too small."

Theo ignored him. "The entrance must be here." *Or it's not in the necropolis at all,* he admitted silently. He couldn't bear the thought that he'd been wrong, although it certainly wouldn't have been the first time.

"All right, Makarites, I hear you," Scooter said, already beginning to examine the tomb niches. Theo peered into a few of the libation holes, but once again found nothing but dirt a few inches below the surface. He moved on to the frescoes, checking each one for signs of recent disturbance.

After nearly an hour, Scooter sat gracefully on the ground, pulled his silk handkerchief from his pocket, and wiped his brow. The gesture seemed more a learned affectation than anything else, since Theo didn't see any sweat on the god's forehead, but it got the idea across. They hadn't seen or heard any more tour groups, and the basilica had officially closed a half hour earlier, so Theo finally removed the bronze helm. It had stopped emitting its usual frosty chill and had instead become just as hot and sweaty as any other incredibly heavy, totally non-breathable metal bucket. He rubbed at the broad indentation carved into his forehead.

"Oh, Theo, you've looked better."

"Thanks. Not exactly worried about my nonexistent online dating profile at the moment." He reached into his satchel, pulled out a bottle of water, and took a much-needed swig.

"Always prepared, I see. Any for me?"

Theo tossed Scooter the bottle, but whether due to his unusual exhaustion or his typical lack of athleticism, it fell two feet shy of the mark. The cap snapped off, and water glugged out across the floor. Theo leaped to his feet.

"The mosaic!" Two-thousand-year-old art about to be destroyed by his clumsiness.

"No, wait." Scooter held up a hand to stop him. His eyes were fixed on the water now streaming through a libation hole—one Theo hadn't bothered to check. "Listen."

The unmistakable sound of liquid splattering onto a surface from a great height. A very great height.

At the same time, the two men scrambled forward and nearly knocked heads trying to peer down the hole. Theo angled his flashlight once more. "I can see the reflection off the water," he said, his voice hushed with awe. "It's got to be at least a hundred feet down."

"So it's a tunnel?" Scooter asked excitedly.

"No, it's too narrow. Just a pipe—maybe a foot across."

"So it's not an entrance." Scooter sounded disappointed. "Maybe it's just a drainage hole for rainwater."

"The mausoleum always had a roof. So why have a drainage hole?" Theo got down on all fours, craning his head to see the interior of the pipe, and then sat up with a smile. "Also, the Romans didn't build with PVC pipe, as far as I know."

"You think the Vatican put it in?"

"Nope. They wouldn't disturb the floor that way. The Host, on the other hand, has no problem destroying ancient artifacts for their own purposes."

"Sure. But *what* purpose? Why bother?"

Theo didn't have an answer for that one. He sat cross-legged in front of the hole and stared at it intently, willing it to divulge its secrets. Scooter tapped an impatient rhythm on his own knee, his eyes roaming the room like a fidgety schoolkid's. Theo tried to ignore him—Olympians could be the best of allies and the most useless of ones.

Finally, Theo picked up the nearly empty water bottle and poured the last of its contents in a careful stream through the hole.

"What are you doing?" Scooter asked, coming to stand beside him.

"Offering a libation. That's what the hole was for, right? Well, the Host believes it's practicing an authentic ancient cult. Libations were an essential component of nearly all Greco-Roman religions, so why not—"

"Shh!" Scooter grabbed Theo's arm. Deep below the ground, a soft *clonk*, like a piece of machinery moving into place. "It's working."

They both peered around the room, fully expecting a secret entrance to swing open. Nothing happened.

"Pour some more."

"I'm out of water."

"Pour something else!"

Theo reached into his satchel for his toiletry bag and took out a travel-size mouthwash. Feeling increasingly guilty for defacing priceless antiquities, he poured the liquid through the hole. It splashed far below, but no machinery clanked in response.

"Ouranos's balls," Scooter cursed. "Guess a Listerine libation's not good enough."

"You think it matters what sort of liquid we pour?"

"Of course! When I was a god, if you tried to offer me that shit I'd make your cattle's teats go dry. *If* you were lucky. I demanded wine or water—no substitutions."

"Well we're out of water, and unless you're holding back on me about your god-powers and can magically turn shampoo into wine, we're out of luck there, too. So if Mithras's taste in libations is as picky as yours—" He stopped, openmouthed.

"What?"

"He's the god of the tauroctony. The bull sacrifice. He's the god of blood."

"Theo, *wait*—"

But he'd already pulled the divine sword from his satchel. The blade of Orion, who now lived only in a pattern of stars but once had hunted wild boar at Artemis's side. A blade of untarnished bronze forged by the Sea God Poseidon, still razor-sharp, its seashell pommel glinting gold. Before Scooter could stop him, Theo drew the blade across his wrist.

A thin stream of blood spurted into the libation hole like air escaping a punctured balloon. He heard the splatter as it struck the pooled water below.

Scooter lunged toward Theo's wrist, his face pale.

"Calm down," Theo said. "I'm not going die here. I just want to see if—"

The scraping of metal interrupted him. The splatter ceased, as if a panel had opened to allow the blood to pass through. A moment later, a terrible grinding of stone heralded their success.

The back of a grave niche slid open.

A narrow tunnel stretched into blackness.

Chapter 20

FATHER OF THE GODS

The King of the Gods' hand trembled as he held it out to his daughter.

Selene crossed the Mithraic schoolroom and knelt beside him. "What have they done to you?" she begged. Filth marred Zeus's once proud visage, staining his deep wrinkles brown. A long white ridge trailed from cheekbone to chin, and heavy purple bags shadowed his eyes. He rocked back and forth like a child trapped in a closet, afraid of the dark. His ragged blanket smelled like stale piss.

"Did they beat you?" Selene asked, afraid of what she might hear. "You're covered in scars."

"Scars?" he asked, sounding confused. He touched the ridge on his face. "Time," he said after a moment, as if the import of her words had finally made it through a brain grown slow and stiff. "Time carved these." His voice, which once had rumbled like thunder, now wheezed weak and thin.

"Time," she said bitterly. "You mean Kronos. Saturn."

He chortled wetly. "Time is"—he searched for the word—"unstoppable." He moved a hand, his ring finger as crooked as a wind-sculpted branch, and traced the lock of white hair at his daughter's temple. "You understand that."

She could only nod.

"Still," he went on, "you came. For me." In his voice, she heard the gentle warmth that fearsome Zeus showed only to his children. Now, when the titles of King, Lightning Bringer, Raging One had all been lost, *Father* remained.

"Yes, I came for the love we have borne each other." She nearly choked on the words. What did love matter when it couldn't save his life?

His magnified gray eye squinted at her blood-caked cheek. "What did they do to you?"

"A taurobolium."

It took him a moment, but eventually he nodded, the gesture made sloppy by the tremors that waggled his chin. "Rhea's rite. Greedy."

"Greed has served the Wily One well so far," she said bitterly. "He stole you, didn't he? And now—somehow—he's turning me into Rhea so he can destroy the two gods who stole his crown so long ago. I don't know what hope we have."

For months, she'd pictured every moment of her father's rescue: She would strike down Saturn with a single golden arrow, destroy every remnant of his perverted cult, and lead Zeus to safety while he showered her with his thanks. She'd never imagined failing. The reality felt like a bull's horn goring her stomach.

"What about your friend?" he asked, patting her hand in a weak attempt at comfort.

"The Smith?" she asked, raising her head. *If Flint was captured by the wrong Swiss Guards,* she realized suddenly, *he might be down here somewhere, too.* Her heart sank still further.

"No, no." Zeus shook his head, irritated. He'd never liked his wife's bastard son. "Your mortal Makarites. Did they catch him, too?"

"Theo?" she asked, baffled. "He has no idea I'm here. How do you know about him?"

"*Zeus Moiragetes. Zeus Semaleos.*" He spoke the old epithets slowly, as if savoring their taste. *The Leader of the Fates. The Giver of Signs.*

"You can still prophesy?"

Again, that phlegmy chuckle. "No. I have no oracle at Delphi as your brother Apollo once did. But the dreams...they come whether I will them or not. I saw you in a mortal man's arms."

Selene's cheeks burned, but her father went on, his speech growing more sure even as his gaze grew vague. "I saw brazen-armed Mars struck down like an animal. Dark Hades slaughtered on a bull's back. Tortured Prometheus burnt in a lightning bolt's fire. Bright Apollo sliced from this world. And when I woke"—he slapped his chest weakly—"a piece of my own soul had ripped away. With each god's death, I grow weaker." As if to prove his point, he doubled over in a sudden fit of coughing.

Selene helped him sit up straight and pulled the blanket more firmly around his body. Futile gestures, she knew, when she saw the red speckling his lips. Her father was dying, even before Saturn's sickle did its work.

"I don't understand," she begged. "Why would our deaths make you weaker, when they make Saturn *stronger*?"

"The Titan always feared sharing his power. I did not."

Saturn claimed his children's births had threatened to split his domain asunder. Zeus, on the other hand, had happily granted each of his children and siblings a separate domain.

"You gave me the wilderness and the mountainsides," she said softly. "The shaded forests and the secret meadows."

"Yet in my dreams... you hunt through city streets." Zeus didn't look surprised, just saddened. "You gave up your birthright?"

"Because I couldn't bear it," she admitted. "To see all I once ruled and know it's mine no longer. Better to turn aside than be reminded of how far I've fallen."

Her father didn't scold her. "I did the same. Years in my cave, turning my back." His lips tightened, as if to hold back his emotion, but the trembling of his chin only increased. She remembered the pile of goat bones, the dripping stalactites. With so much solitude, it was a miracle her father retained any sanity at all.

"Saturn still sees strength in you," she insisted, "or he wouldn't seek your death. You're the only one left who stands in his way. When you're gone, he can truly become God the Father."

"Me?" He blinked through his glasses. "I stand in no one's way." He slumped against the wall, looking half the size of the god she'd known. "Let him have what title he wants."

"How can you say that?" she nearly shouted.

Zeus flinched, drawing his crooked hands close to his chest as if to shield himself from her wrath.

She went on more calmly. "He would raise himself above us all. He would become one with the Christian god. Incorporeal, omnipotent, eternal. What would that do to the world?"

Zeus's mouth chewed for a moment on his answer before the words emerged. "What have we to fear from the Christian god that he has not done already?"

"*We* may not fear him, but what of the millions of Christians who will find themselves worshiping a cruel, all-powerful god they never dreamed existed?"

"He may be powerful, he may not. Mankind sees their 'God' everywhere and nowhere—I have never seen him at all. Have you?"

"No. But—"

"The Jews, do you remember how we laughed at them for their invisible god? No statues, no paintings?" He gave a rattling snort. "If they'd never seen him, why did they think he existed?"

"And yet that invisible god now rules the world."

Zeus shrugged. The filthy blanket slipped, revealing skeletal shoulders. "Or perhaps he exists only in some other plane. Do you remember how we existed in more than one world?"

"Yes," she said hesitantly. "I have memories of walking the earth, memories of riding the sky, but much is fuzzy in between." As Artemis, she'd contained multitudes. A thousand versions of herself, worshiped by a thousand different peoples. Now Rhea's memories tugged at the edges of her mind, too, turning her already hazy grasp of the past into a swirling mist of impressions that she couldn't begin to fathom.

"You're confused," Zeus said, "because our half-mortal minds"—he tapped swollen knuckles against his skull—"can't understand true godhood...not any longer." He knocked his head again, harder, as if punishing himself for his failings. Tears pooled in his eyes, the sight made more conspicuous by the magnifying effect of his glasses. "If Saturn wants to be...infinite... maybe he'll simply disappear. He won't bother us any longer."

"Except that he's going to kill us both before then," she retorted. Her father's theories were all well and good—they might even be right. But she couldn't take that chance. Her goals hadn't changed: rescue Zeus, stop Saturn. "I doubt Grandfather will be patient enough to grind us down into willing sacrifices as he did to Mars and Apollo and the others. Now that he's so close, he'll want to kill us both on the summer solstice—that's *tomorrow*. We have to escape before then."

"I've tried. How I've tried. There's no way out of here, child."

No offense, Father, she thought, *but you're not the man you once were. I will succeed where you failed.* "I destroyed the cult in Manhattan by convincing one of its initiates that their precious Pater Patrum was not who he always claimed to be. The lunkheads here know he's a god, but they think he's the one and only. If I can convince them he's just another petty Athanatos intent on reviving his own power—"

Zeus shook his head sadly. "That won't work. I've heard them talking: Their ancestors have been soldiers in the Host stretching back for generations. They can't question their leader now.

You know how thanatoi are—they need a purpose to live. They won't let you take that away from them. At least a dozen of the Swiss Guards are more loyal to my father than to the pope himself."

"Does the pope know there's a conspiracy right under his basilica?" she demanded.

"No. The Wily One is too clever for that. His syndexioi speak of keeping their movements secret, so even if earlier popes were members of the Host, the current one isn't. And most of the Swiss Guards are just what they appear: young Christian men serving the Catholic Church."

"Deeply oblivious young men whom we can't count on to rescue us," Selene said with a grimace.

She rose to her feet and began to pace the small chamber. She could never compete with Saturn in a battle of wits, that much was clear. She'd have to use force. Which was just as well—she was much better at breaking things anyway. "This whole place is over a hundred feet below street level," she said. "Which means they must've built ventilation shafts somewhere. Otherwise, we'd suffocate."

Zeus didn't even watch her prowling. He kept his eyes on the stone floor, scratching at it with an overlong pinky nail. "There are no vents."

"True, they're probably in the hallway. But the ducts have to run nearby. If I just knock a hole through the wall, then through the ductwork—"

"You are still goddess-strong?" He looked up eagerly.

"I'm stronger than most mortals," she replied. "But as strong as I once was? No." Saturn's taurobolium might have somehow implanted her with Rhea's spirit, but it hadn't increased her physical strength. Zeus was right: Even if she could locate the ducts, she'd never be able to break through the plaster and brickwork, much less the metal. Still, she was no common girl, as Saturn named her. And she had not come this far just to let her father die.

She searched the room for tools or weapons but found only dust. The syndexioi had removed every item in her copious pockets. Her gold bow and arrows no doubt lay locked away in some Mithraic armory, ready to be used against her. Saturn had already recovered Mars's spear—how many other divine weapons might he have access to? She bit back a groan of helplessness.

Her keen hearing picked up footsteps approaching the door of the schoolroom, and sudden fury chased all her doubts away. She had only the clothes on her back—but that would have to be enough.

She grabbed the hem of her T-shirt and ripped off a length of fabric with her teeth. As the door opened, she leaped toward the armored Miles guarding her grandfather. She wrapped the fabric around Mars's spear and yanked it from the syndexios's grasp before he even realized what had happened.

Without missing a beat, she spun the shaft and rammed its point through the man's throat. She wrenched it back out, blood flying. Then wheeled toward Saturn.

But the Wily One had slipped past her. He stood in the center of the room, his sickle already held to Zeus's throat.

"Do you remember?" he said quietly, his mouth bent to his son's ear. "How you held your blade to my stomach in the dawn of time? How you cut out the children I had swallowed so they might rule at your side?" The story sounded ludicrous now. Hunched Zeus stood a full foot shorter than his Titan father, his body birdlike and shrunken in the stronger god's grasp.

Saturn raised his eyes to Selene. "Now it's my turn to slice open a god. Shall I do it right now, granddaughter?" He narrowed his gaze. "Or should I say...*wife*?"

Selene's vision doubled, her stomach clenched. She saw Zeus

before her both as the frail father she'd sought for so long—and as the glorious son she'd saved in the dawn of time. She loved with two hearts. Daughter and mother. Neither would allow her to risk Zeus's life.

No matter how many of his men I kill, she realized, lowering the spear, *as long as Saturn threatens Zeus, he can always make me surrender.*

She didn't bother resisting as three other syndexioi pounded up behind her, ripping away Mars's spear and fastening chains tight around her ankles. Only then did Saturn lower his sickle. Zeus bowed his trembling head, but not before Selene saw the shame on his face.

Another man entered the room, the red-robed Heliodromus with the cat-o'-nine-tails. Without his mask, Selene recognized him by the constellation of moles on his cheek as the syndexios from Ostia. She'd taken his Swiss accent for a German one. In New York, a similarly garbed man had been Saturn's second-in-command, capable of wielding several divine weapons. This man was younger than his American counterpart but no less fierce.

He knelt beside the slaughtered Miles and stared up at Selene, lips bared in a snarl. His hand moved toward the thick whip at his waist, but Saturn stopped him with a gesture.

"I've decided what to do with you, Diana," the old man pronounced. "I would've waited for the solstice—sent you and your father off together—but I see the Great Mother's spirit has already bloomed within you. The first time my traitorous wife died, it was a waste. Ignorant mortals scrabbling and gnawing at her like a pack of sharp-toothed rats until they finally brought her down. Her death was pointless. Squandered. This time, she will perish in a fitting sacrifice, and her power—*your* power—will become mine. Just as it always should have."

The last thing Selene saw before the Heliodromus threw a

hood over her face was Zeus's crooked hand reaching toward her. A father's futile attempt to protect her. A son's desperate plea for help.

She struggled as all four men dragged her from the schoolroom. She fought until her wrists were bloody from straining against the handcuffs. Until her lungs burned with effort and the hood stuck to her face with her sweat and the bull's gore. She fought until they drove the prongs of their Taser three times into her temples and sent her plummeting into darkness once more.

Chapter 21

PRETENDER

After several hundred yards of crawling through the tunnel behind the grave niche, Theo emerged into a small brick antechamber, spitting cobwebs from his mouth. His sliced wrist ached, dust coated his pants, and his hands shook with a toxic mix of anticipation and dread.

He stood with Scooter before a locked wooden door.

The God of Thieves whipped out his ever-present lock picks and went to work while Theo held him by the waist to maintain their invisibility. Scooter uttered a variety of creative curses at having to work without seeing his own hands, but before long the door swung soundlessly open.

Theo could hear the smirk in Scooter's voice. "So much for high-tech security at the Vatican."

"I guess the blood libation was security enough."

Scooter humphed. He clearly still hadn't forgiven Theo for slitting his wrist.

A low-ceilinged passageway sloped downward before them, its walls hewn from the archeological past—a conglomeration of brick layers, paving stones, marble slabs, and raw earth. Potsherds and bits of broken statuary peeked out from amid the layers like lettuce between slices of ham. *Steve Atwood would be salivating,* Theo thought. But he couldn't muster any enthusiasm for archeology with his own death staring him in the face.

After another hundred yards, the rough passage dumped them into a better-preserved corridor of well-matched brick punctuated by several other hallways branching in every direction. He had no idea how to find the mithraeum's main sanctuary, but at least no guards patrolled the corridor. He had time to search.

"Where is everybody?" whispered Scooter.

"Maybe off at some pre-solstice ritual," Theo answered under his breath. *Let's just hope they're not all gathered inside the sanctuary. Otherwise, I'm going to have to die very, very quietly.*

Theo walked cautiously toward the end of the corridor, where a door half again as wide as the others indicated a room of some importance. He pressed his ear against it. Nothing. He took a deep breath and pushed.

The foul stench of iron and rot slammed against his senses. He took a step; the sole of his shoe lifted with a sucking pop. He switched on his flashlight and took off the Helm of Invisibility so the beam could illuminate the ground. Dried blood.

Trying not to gag, he raised the beam to illuminate the walls. Any hope that he'd found the mithraeum's sanctuary vanished when he saw the shape of the chamber: round instead of rectangular, its floor a wooden grate rather than the usual mosaic aisle.

"What is this place?" he whispered.

"I don't know," Scooter said, his voice hushed and nervous. "It looks like a charnel house."

Theo moved the flashlight lower, staring across the chamber's floor. A single wide brown eye stared back.

A bull.

It lay on its side like a felled mountain, its beige tongue protruding obscenely between its jaws. A slice in its neck gaped like a second mouth, this one coated in sticky red that ran down its white breast like a matador's cape. A ram lay beside it, the pale curls of its pelt drenched crimson. Theo took an involuntary step back.

Scooter tightened his grip on Theo's elbow. "Careful. We don't want you to be the next sacrifice."

He peered over his shoulder to find his heels an inch from the top of a precipitous stairwell. The grate beneath their feet hung suspended above another chamber. More blood coated the lower floor in a wide, dark puddle, its splattered edges reaching for the walls with inky tentacles. Droplets peppered the flagstones, the walls, the bottom steps. Selene had once explained to him how the police used blood splatter evidence to investigate crime scenes, but Theo didn't need a cop to tell him that the animals' blood had poured through the grate in a waterfall of gore.

A marble pine stood at the chamber's focal point like a Christmas tree hung with bloody tinsel. Theo understood now. "It's a Phrygianum," he whispered. "A sanctuary for the Magna Mater."

Red footprints led from the puddle to a door in the chamber's wall. *Someone,* Theo realized with a shudder, *stood in the path of this carnage.*

The smell of death poured down his throat in a gagging cloud, an undeniable reminder of his fate. This was no game, no adventure. He forced himself to look at the dead bull once more. *That's going to be me. Staring eyes and stony flesh and silent heart.*

The reality he'd resisted ever since he'd left Dennis's bacchanal now brought him to his knees. He felt the cold blood seeping through his pants and didn't care. Scooter's voice in his ear, begging him to stand up, seemed very far away. He closed his eyes, reaching for a vision of Selene. The sweep of her black hair. The smile in her silver eyes. He could almost feel her hand in his, her fingers long and cool and strong as they faced life together. She should never have died. He should never have let her go.

There, a kneeling petitioner in an ancient temple, his hands clasped against his chest, he offered up a silent prayer to whatever god or God might listen: *Let me find her. Let me bring her back where she belongs.*

The last words he spoke aloud. "Let me hold her in my arms once more."

The door slammed open.

As light flooded the room, Scooter jammed the helm back on Theo's head. Four syndexioi burst in dragging a limp woman between them, her hands bound, her head covered with a dark sack. They threw her forward. Her body slammed against the bloody ground, forcing the air from her lungs in a faint moan.

"She'll wake up soon enough," one of the guards grumbled.

"She better," returned another. "The Pater wants her conscious for the next ritual."

"Then we should go get the good chains."

They left again, a bolt clanging into place as they shut the door behind them.

Theo wasn't sure what was going on, but he removed the helm and hurried forward, pulling free of Scooter's grip.

"Wait," the god urged, sounding suddenly panicked, but Theo paid him no heed. He wasn't about to let Saturn's men hurt anyone else, not if he could help it. And no matter who this woman was, she didn't deserve what the Host would do to her.

Scooter's hand shot out, grabbing Theo's arm to stop him in his tracks. "Theo, you have to listen. Let me explain."

The fallen woman groaned and sat up, pulling off the hood with her bound hands.

She raised her head, her black hair falling away from her face to reveal a pair of silver eyes, glowing with fury.

Theo's prayer had been answered.

———— ◇ ————

Selene snarled at the closed door and rose to her feet, stumbling a little as she fought the effects of the Taser's charge. She had every intention of ripping the door from its hinges.

She was stopped by a scent.

A thin thread, barely perceptible beneath the stench of stale blood. A wisp of something so faint only the Huntress could've detected it.

She froze, sniffed the air once more, wondering if she could trust her senses with Rhea's memories still clouding her brain. Perhaps she was hallucinating. Or still unconscious. *It must be a dream. That's the only explanation.*

But the scent was too real, too familiar. Wonder and fear and shock sent cold sweat prickling beneath her arms.

"Theo . . ."

A clatter of metal on stone. Selene wheeled around in time to see Hades' helm rolling down the steps—and Theo hurrying past it.

Her heart leaped. *You came to rescue me. I knew you would.*

"Selene," he gasped, rushing toward her with outstretched arms. Her scholar, always so logical, so practical, looked like a man in a dream, his eyes wide and mouth open in reverent awe. "I prayed, and you—"

He didn't bother finishing the sentence. His lips crushed hers; his hands threaded through her bloody hair. Every fiber of her ached to step into his embrace, to feel the curve of his shoulder blades beneath her palms. Her body hummed in response to his touch. Her mouth softened, opened. *He thinks I was really dead,* she realized, but his lips soothed away her tremor of foreboding. *I can explain it all when we get out of here. We will have time.*

She extricated herself gently, pushing against Theo's chest with her bound hands. Then she noticed Scooter for the first time. "The only way I'm going to forgive you for letting Theo come here," she snapped at him, "is if you get us *all* out alive."

Her half brother gave her a sheepish grin and brandished his lock picks. "Sorry I didn't follow your orders. Handcuffs first. Recriminations later."

Theo looked from Selene to Scooter and back. "Your *orders* . . ."

In an instant, the joy on his face crumbled into confusion. Then horror. Selene's dream crumbled along with it. "You..."

He stood only three feet away now, but she felt as if a mile-wide chasm had cracked open between them. Blood from her lips had stained his. He looked, in every way, like a man who'd just had his teeth knocked out. "You weren't..."

"Theo..." she began, the word desperate, beseeching. *Not now,* her mind screamed. *Don't make me face this now.*

He stumbled backward, repulsed. His shoes slipped on the bloody stones, and he sat down hard. She could hear his teeth clang together with a hollow echo, but his eyes never left her face. "Six months. Six months. I almost died."

"Theo..." she tried again. A broken record, stuck on the same useless groove. After so many months of silent conversation, now she had nothing to say.

Footsteps in the hallway. The guards returning. Too soon. She jerked toward Scooter. "Too late for me. Just get him out of here," she hissed. Her half brother nodded, scooping up Hades' helm just as the door swung open behind her.

Theo tried to rise, but Scooter dashed forward with all his preternatural speed and slammed the helm over his head. They winked out of sight before the guards entered the room.

Selene turned calmly toward her captors, trying in vain to erase the shock written across her features. Six of them now, not four, and one carried an armload of iron chains. They clearly weren't taking any more chances with her—the barrels of five assault rifles rose toward her face as the men fanned out into tactical positions around the room.

The Heliodromus strode forward. "You look distressed, Diana. Finally realizing your fate?"

His eyes flicked around the chamber, and Selene held her breath, waiting for him to notice something amiss, some hint that Theo and Scooter stood close by. Instead, he simply smiled, his nostrils raised as if enjoying the scent of decay. "This morning's blood libation worked. You are both Huntress and Great Mother now. Glorious, no? We will send your spirit to the one true God—you will make a most powerful sacrifice."

He ordered the other men to secure her. One grabbed her arms, another held her legs in place, while a third wrapped a heavy chain around her ankles. Together, they hoisted her into the air like a log. She let them do it all; if they fired their weapons in this room, Theo would surely be hit.

"And you know the only way to send your spirit heavenward, don't you, Pretender?" The Heliodromus took a step closer to her, resting a finger on her chin to tilt her face toward him. "On a pillar of smoke."

Selene heard Theo's intake of breath. *He's going to scream,* she realized, *and they'll find him.*

So she screamed first.

They hauled her chained body out the door. Writhing, shouting, sobbing. It took the undivided attention of all the men to handle her. None of them even heard the stifled shout, the crash of wrestling bodies, the tortured moan issuing from the seemingly empty room behind them.

Chapter 22

PROTOGONOS

With Scooter's hand pressed against his mouth and nose and his arm squeezing the air from his lungs, Theo couldn't breathe. Part of him was happy enough to suffocate so he wouldn't have to face the truth. The other part of him wanted to use all his growing rage to beat Scooter senseless. But mostly, he wanted to race after Selene. To save her. To scream at her. Both.

Theo slammed an elbow into the god's invisible stomach and wrenched from his grip. Scooter burst into view, his face drenched in sweat, looking more panicked than guilty.

"They were armed," he insisted. "They would've killed you."

A thousand thoughts whirled through Theo's head. *He lied to me. She* lied *to me. All my grief, my suffering. All a lie.* But one thought pierced through the cacophony like a siren's wail.

They're going to burn her alive.

And though the voices in his head cried out in furious warning, he felt like a tractor trailer without brakes, unable to stop hurtling toward her even when he knew he should leap to safety. Selene was about to be taken away from him. Again. And he couldn't let that happen.

He scrambled to his feet and ripped open his satchel, grabbing Orion's sword.

"Stop!" Scooter cried, his eyes scanning the empty air before him. "I can hear you pulling out that sword. You can't go after her, Theo! We have to find Zeus and then get the hell out."

"Zeus?"

"Saturn's got him trapped down here."

"Something else you didn't tell me," Theo snarled. "Afraid I'd get too close to the truth, huh? Afraid I'd realize Selene was alive this whole time?"

"She hid herself to protect you."

"Stop it. Stop lying, *Trickster*." He made for the door.

"I told her I'd get you out!" Scooter begged.

Theo spun toward him. "*Now* you're a man of your word?" He hefted his sword, resisting the urge to slam it through Scooter's chest. "Come or don't. But don't get in my way."

———<o>———

The syndexioi carried Selene into a sanctuary far larger than any she'd seen in her hunt through Rome. Feasting platforms decorated with intricate mosaics of stars and planets lined the wide aisle. Overhead, darkness shrouded a ceiling too high to see. A massive sculptural tauroctony sat beside the altar, Mithras in his seven-rayed crown proudly straddling his bull. Beside the altar stood Saturn in his crisp white robes, tapping the handle of his sickle in his palm. And on the altar itself...

A careful pyramid of wooden logs surrounding a tall stake. The reek of lighter fluid burned her throat.

The Heliodromus and his men dragged her forward and onto the pyre. They looped more heavy iron chains around her waist and chest, securing her to the stake. Saturn hadn't gagged her, no doubt wanting to hear her scream again. Selene refused to give him the satisfaction.

A wheezing music began, the strange, atonal melody a counterpoint to her own sucking breaths. A hydraulis, she saw now. An ancient Roman water organ.

A veiled syndexios crouched beside the instrument, pumping water into its base, while another dressed in a crow's mask sat at the keyboard. Copper tubes rose from short to tall, like the reeds in Hermes' shrill pipes. The song that emerged was no shepherd's tune, but a dirge for Rhea, the Mother of Gods. A dirge for her.

Yet even then, even when the Heliodromus struck the match and laid it against the wood, when the smoke curled like blood in water and the rising flames licked at the toes of her boots, Selene didn't really believe she would die. After all, she never had.

"You think you're still an Athanatos." Saturn raised his voice above the gasping music and the crackling flames. "But this is no wound, no bruise, no broken bone. There will be no rushing river to heal your flesh. Not when there's no flesh left."

He gestured for his syndexioi to join the crow-masked musician in song. The hymn to the Magna Mater grew louder, more insistent, rising along with the flames.

The first finger of fire reached the cuff of Selene's pants. The fabric smoldered for a moment before igniting. She kicked her feet against the chains, but the jerky motion only fanned the blaze. The fire reached her skin an instant later, the sensation like a thousand bees stinging her ankles one after the other. She still didn't scream.

Then the door at the end of the aisle opened, and two men dressed as Roman legionaries appeared, dragging Flint between them.

He screamed in her stead.

A ragged, desperate bellow as his bloodshot eyes met hers. He struggled in vain against the thick iron binding his arms to his chest and crisscrossing his pitiful, withered legs. The veins popped on his forehead, his face flushed as red as the flames of his forge. They threw him to the ground like a sack of flour.

He lay prone, craning his neck to see her better, even as the tears coursed down his cheeks and into his beard.

Saturn looked down at his grandson, his mouth twisted in distaste. "The next time I command you to fashion weapons for my army, you won't refuse. You see now what happens to those who try to stand in my way."

Flint kept hollering, his words an unintelligible roar of fury and anguish.

Saturn shook his head and motioned for the Heliodromus to gag the Smith.

Forgive me, Selene wanted to beg as she watched Flint spasm beneath his chains. Her friend, her stepbrother, and now somehow her grandson, too. *Forgive me for dragging you into this.* The gag cut the soft flesh of his mouth, and his strangled cries soon flecked the cloth with red. *For not loving you enough.*

But the smoke poured thickly down her throat, and when she opened her mouth she could only cough.

She lost sensation in her ankles as the flames seared her nerves; the pain migrated to her calves, her thighs instead. She couldn't see the devastation—black smoke billowed before her eyes. She tried to hold her breath, then gasped, sucking in superheated air and smoke and the flying ashes of her own flesh before coughing it all out again.

Now she'd lost all sensation in her legs, but as the heated air rose, it blistered the skin of her arms, her chest, her face—an agony far more painful than the flames' kiss.

I'm going to die. And I'm not ready. Three thousand years and I'm not ready.

There was still so much left to do. She would never free her father. Never see Saturn brought to justice.

Never hold Theo again.

I thought I'd have time.

She couldn't see the smoke anymore. Her eyes were open, but the cone of flame had scorched her corneas. She reached inside herself—*Rhea, Grandmother, Cybele, Great Mother!* she screamed silently to the presence in her heart. *If you're there . . . rise up! Come with your charging lionesses and your queen's scepter. Lend me your strength to rip from these chains! Please . . . please help me . . . help me . . .*

But Rhea was as powerless now as she'd been the first time mortals burned her at the stake in a Prussian village so many centuries before. June had said her mother lived for days after her incineration . . . *I won't have days,* Selene knew. *I have minutes.*

She opened her mouth to shout a final curse at Saturn, but no oxygen remained to fill her lungs. She sank against the chains, her leg muscles no longer thick enough to hold her weight. A mortal would have died long before, but her semi-divine body still clung to life.

She remembered her own mother, Leto, whose death had come so peacefully in the arms of her children. *Let me have the strength to go as gracefully as she did,* Selene begged.

As her mind slipped into unconsciousness, she clung to one final prayer. *Perhaps I will see those I love again.*

I'm coming, Apollo.

———◇———

Theo raced down the hallway in Hades' helm, barely aware of Scooter still clinging to his arm. He couldn't think about the last six months or even the last six minutes—only about finding Selene before it was too late.

He knew the Host would take her to the main sanctuary—the only place sacred enough for such a sacrifice. But where was it? He dashed down one branching corridor, then another, falling deeper and deeper into the underground maze. He tried each door. Some opened onto training rooms and storage closets or crumbled chambers of brick unused for centuries. Many more were sealed; he didn't leave Scooter time to pick the locks. Why bother locking the door of the sanctuary if all the Mithraists were inside?

He ran until his lungs burned and then ran some more. Finally, he stumbled to a halt, panting hard. *Stop. Think,* he commanded himself. Mithraists believed in orbits: celestial spheres whirling in their prescribed paths, the equinoxes shifting with regular precision, the solstices cycling in perfect symmetry. If the sanctuary dedicated to the Great Mother lay on one end of their complex, then the mithraeum, dedicated to the Father, must lie on the other.

"The Phyrgianum was..." he began, turning in a slow circle.

"That way." Scooter pointed to the far wall.

"You sure?"

"God of Travelers, remember? Great sense of direction."

"Then take me to the exact opposite end of the complex—as far from the Phrygianum as we can get."

Scooter didn't question him, just veered right, then left. Theo followed, barely keeping up.

After a mind-boggling series of turns, they stood before a wide door flanked by two statues: torchbearers wearing Phrygian caps. One carried his flame upward; the other stood with his pointed at the ground. Cautes and Cautopates, the Mithraic minor divinities symbolizing Birth and Death.

They could hear the crackle of flames on the other side.

Theo rushed toward the door, his invisible sword outstretched.

It opened before he reached it, and a tidal wave of heavily armed syndexioi poured out, dressed in robes of red and black, some masked like lions or crows, others veiled, still others in legionaries' armor. Saturn walked in their midst, but Theo paid the scarred old man no mind. Only one thing mattered.

With Scooter invisible at his side, Theo slipped into the room just before the heavy door slammed shut.

He froze.

A gentle rain fell from overhead sprinklers onto a tall pyre. The water doused the flames to embers and raised a thick column of smoke that billowed toward an unseen vent. Still Theo found himself choking, gagging, as if he stood within the pyre's heat.

He could just make out the figure tied to the stake. A blackened corpse, her head thrown back, her hair burnt away, her familiar square jaw clenched shut. Her long arms looked like the remnants of a proud tree after a raging forest fire. Her eyes were hollow pits. The chains across her waist and chest glowed yellow hot. As he watched, the heavy iron links dragged a long sheet of charred flesh from her body; it fell into the embers in a torrent of sparks.

Theo couldn't move. Scooter slumped against him, silent. He could feel the furious racing of the god's heart against his own spine. They stood together like supplicants at a shrine, praying that they might unsee the epiphany before them.

A ragged moan floated toward them over the sprinkler's hiss.

Flint lay bound and gagged on one of the mithraeum's wide feasting platforms, staring at the smoldering pyre with bright red eyes, his beard flecked with mucus and foam.

The sight of the Smith broke Theo from his stupor. He pulled away from Scooter, dropped the helm unceremoniously to the ground, and walked to the pyre. Ignoring Flint's confused moans, he clambered onto the still-smoking logs, heedless of the smell of melting rubber rising from the soles of his shoes.

With a single swipe of Orion's divine sword, he cleaved the last of the iron chains in half, then sliced through the handcuffs that bound his former lover to the stake. Her body fell toward him.

He grabbed her shoulders—her flesh sizzled against his. He pulled off his shirt and wrapped it around her waist so he could pick her up. She was light. So light. Embers and ashes and air. He knew as he carried her off the altar that pieces of her were floating away, and he didn't let himself look.

When he reached the mithraeum's aisle, he laid her down gently. Scooter, face drawn and coated in sweat, had removed his stepbrother's gag and unlocked the chains with his picks.

Flint didn't speak; he bellowed. Animalistic and hoarse and full of volcanic wrath. He crawled across the platform, dragging his withered legs behind him, then tumbled into the aisle beside the corpse. He grabbed one blackened hand, his flesh hissing—he only held on tighter, even as a thin coil of smoke rose between his palm and hers. He lifted crimson eyes to Theo.

"I couldn't stop it," he panted. "I'm the God of Fire. And I couldn't stop it."

Theo had no words for Flint. Even Scooter sat silent, frozen, his legs dangling over the platform's lip, his eyes trained on this black mannequin. This ravaged statue. This cracked *thing* that could not possibly be Selene.

When Theo had lain in a hospital bed after the battle on the Statue of Liberty, Scooter had told him that he felt Selene pass from the world. *The tides moved,* the Trickster had lied. *The moon cried.*

And now? When she was truly gone? Where was the ripple effect on the world? *We're too far underground,* Theo realized. *There is no moon here to weep, no animals to mourn. She's simply gone. As if she never existed. Her death no more momentous than that of a mortal woman.* Even thinking the words felt like a betrayal.

"No," he said aloud. "No. She's not gone for good."

He cast a quick glance around the mithraeum. Large frescoed panels of snakes and starry night skies hung on the walls, their crumbling borders showing where they'd been ripped from their original locations. Slabs of mosaics displaying the attributes of different Mithraic ranks covered the aisle. A hydraulis sat in the corner, ready to play hymns worthy of Orpheus himself. In a niche beside the tauroctony stood a statue of Aion, the lion-headed god with his crossed keys, promising entrance to another world.

"Mithras, Orphism, Birth, and Death—it's all here," Theo murmured. "This is the place."

"The place for what?" Flint demanded.

"Theo..." Scooter began warily.

"This is why I'm here." Theo fumbled through his bag. The moment he pulled out the case of syringes, Scooter hopped down into the aisle, ready to stop him. "If you want Selene back," Theo ordered Flint, "stop him."

Flint obeyed. He snatched Scooter's ankles, tumbling the slighter man to the ground, and pinned him in place with a massive forearm and a deeply terrifying scowl.

"What's your plan?" Flint rasped.

"The same one I had when I came down here. Nothing's changed," Theo answered. *Everything's changed,* the voice in his head screamed in protest. But he kept talking, drowning out his own doubts. "I'm going to inject myself with the concentrated venom of a Greek sand viper."

"No," Scooter wheezed from beneath Flint's arm. "Don't."

"Snakes have always held the secrets of the Underworld," Theo went on, willing his voice to stop shaking. "They understand the mysteries of death and healing. Dennis says they hold the boundaries of Time itself." He raised his eyes to Flint. "They'll take me into the Underworld."

Flint nodded silently. All the jealousy that had once flared between them was now extinguished by their determination to bring back the woman they'd both loved.

Scooter groaned. "This is absurd! If you're dead, how is that supposed to help Selene?"

"I'm not going to *stay* dead," Theo shot back. "Give me five minutes and then inject the antidote in the second syringe, okay?"

He retrieved a container of raw beef heart, procured from a local butcher. "I'm using the Orphic ritual." He unwrapped the makeshift bandage from around his sliced wrist and let a few drops of his own blood mix with the bull's. He kept talking, kept explaining, like a lecturer instructing his class, the familiar cadences lulling his rising fear into submission. "I'll recite the Orphic hymn on the way in to guide my steps. And I'll have

Dionysus's instructions once I'm there." He held out the dripping heart to Flint. "But right before you use the antidote, eat this. The Orphics believe consuming the heart can join spirit to flesh once more. It'll help me—and Selene—get back."

"I told you I'm not going to let you kill yourself," Scooter nearly shouted, shoving against Flint's weight.

In response, Theo handed Orion's sword to the Smith, who pressed it against his stepbrother's throat.

"Oh, come on," Scooter scoffed. "You're not going to kill me."

"Try me," Flint growled.

"But it's not going to *work*. And we're wasting time. It's too late for Selene, but not for Father."

Flint shifted the sword, scraping it against Scooter's bobbing Adam's apple. "Not until we get her."

"But—"

"Orpheus almost got his love back," Theo interrupted. "And Dionysus rescued his mother. I can do this."

He produced a long match and a small dish of myrrh. The Orphic texts were very clear on the importance of using the correct incense to accompany different incantations. He lit the balls of aromatic resin, grateful that his hands had almost stopped shaking, then removed the first syringe from its case.

"Do it, Schultz." Flint's voice carried the rumble of a god's command. "Bring her back to us."

But Theo barely heard him; he was too focused on the needle resting on his palm. He pulled the stolen ivy leaf pendant from beneath his shirt. The faint Greek characters on the surface were still indistinguishable. There was nothing he could do about that now.

He clasped the pendant. He knelt before the statue of Aion.

In the background, he could hear Scooter and Flint shouting at each other, but he didn't pay attention to their words. The thick scent of incense made him want to sneeze.

He focused his energy on Aion, on the snake that coiled from his lion head to his bare feet, the guardian of the mysteries of life and death. He looked to the Roman keys that would open the locked precincts of the Underworld—and then allow him to leave again. In careful Greek, he began a hymn to the proto-god. He'd altered the words, but he sang the melody he'd learned from Dennis—the same one Orpheus himself first played upon his lyre as he walked through the Underworld, seeking passage back to life.

Upon lion-headed Protogonos, I call:

You fly through the world on waving pinions,
All-spreading splendor, pure and holy light,
Dispelling darkness from our darkened eyes.

For this I call you Aion, Unbounded Time.
Shine your joyful light upon my holy sacrifice.

With Scooter's desperate protests loud in his ears, Theo slid the needle into his vein and pressed the plunger.

Nothing happened at first, only a sharp ache in his arm. Then nausea, rushing from gut to throat in a convulsive wave. He heaved out the airplane breakfast, the morning coffee, and what looked like his stomach lining, the yellow liquid dripping through lips suddenly thick and swollen. Dimly, he watched Scooter twist away from Flint's blade and crawl forward. But Flint slammed the sword's pommel against the other god's head, stunning him into submission.

"It's too late, Scooter," Theo slurred as the corners of his vision turned black. His heart felt strange in his chest. As if it pumped molasses through his veins, sluggish and dark. He slumped to his side on a feasting platform, pillowing his head on both arms—one swollen and throbbing, the other slick with cold sweat.

His throat tightened. His tongue lay like a fat, dead snake against his teeth. *The sand viper crawled inside my mouth*...he suddenly knew. He willed his heart to panic, to race. It squeezed out a single beat instead.

He waited for it to beat again, suspended in agonized anticipation.

It didn't.

Chapter 23

LETHE

Like a man in a dream, the tall figure with sandy hair had no knowledge of how he came to be in the vast meadow of waving grass. He knew neither his own name nor that he should remember it.

Naked, he walked forward through the waist-high grass with only one goal in mind—to see what lay beyond it.

Figures passed on all sides of him, their features unclear, their bodies blurred. When he looked down, he saw that he, too, was a bleeding watercolor, a brushstroke away from eternal formlessness.

This did not seem strange.

He walked until a tall cypress tree broke through the featureless plain. White and glowing rather than dark green. At its base, blurred figures bent to drink from a spring gurgling into a small pool.

Throat raw with thirst, he knelt at the pool's edge. He reached his hand into the cool water. Only then did he notice the glint of gold reflected in the pool's surface.

Curious, he lifted one blurred hand to his throat. A pendant in the shape of an ivy leaf. The inscription glowed sharp and clear, brighter than the leaf itself, as if penned by a hand of fire. The words scrolled across the small leaf like a Times Square news ticker.

You will find in the halls of Hades a spring on the left,
and standing by it, a glowing white cypress tree;
Do not approach this spring at all.
Find the Lake of Mnemosyne, refreshing water flowing forth.

He looked at the figures around him with new eyes. As soon as they drank, all color drained from their bodies; they became no more than pockets of vaguely man-shaped darkness in the world. Shades.

They moved away from the spring in a great herd, passing farther into the meadow, where one great hole opened in the heavens and another in the earth. Most of the shades walked forward into the earthly portal. Very few ascended through the celestial gate instead. He watched them impassively. Some small part of his brain recognized the portals as exits from this netherworld.

That's the goal, isn't it? he wondered. *To get out of here?*

An indistinct figure, vaguely woman shaped, knelt eagerly beside him and plunged her face into the pool to suck the water. Despite the leaf's instructions, he wanted to join her. *If I drink,* he suddenly understood, *I can leave through one of the portals.*

He cupped his hand in the water and lifted it to his lips. The woman beside him straightened up, now no more than a shadow.

Lethe, he realized. *This spring is Lethe, the River of Forgetting.* The moment he drank of its waters, he would lose whatever it was that made him... *Theodore Schultz.*

Yes, that was his name.

If he walked through the lower portal, he would return to life, but as someone—some*thing*—else. *But what is Theodore Schultz, anyway?* he wondered, searching his own fading memories. *I read* *old books,* he remembered dimly. *I have friends who love me. Students who depend on me. I have a home and a dog. A great lumbering, brindled dog with eyes full of grief.*

The image sparked something in him, and he fought through the cobwebs in his brain to latch onto the memory, but all in vain. He tried to reach further back. To remember his childhood, his parents, but it was all too hazy. *It's as if I'm a different person, trying to remember a different life.*

A woman's voice echoed in his mind, bright and ringing while all other sounds were muted. *My memories of godhood are like images seen through a forest pool.*

Who'd said that?

With that single question, Theo remembered his purpose.

"Selene." He spoke her name aloud; like a spell, the fog lifted from his mind.

His memories rushed back, as sharp and clear as the leaf's gold words: Selene alive in his arms, Selene falling through the night like an arrow piercing the clouds. Selene kneeling on a bloody floor, the answer to his prayers. Her stunned face, as the dream faded to nightmare. Her charred husk smoldering before him. The mithraeum. The syringe.

His anger returned—anger at Saturn. Anger at her.

He stood up abruptly and shook Lethe's water from his fingers as if it burned. While the shades flocked toward the portals, their memories forgotten, Theo headed back the way he'd come at a run, shouting Selene's name, half pleading, half enraged.

He walked against the tide of the faded dead. Back into the waist-high grass. He felt like a sailor in an unending sea, searching the waves for sign of his drowned love.

He had no idea how long he wandered the plain. Hours, days. Years, perhaps. No sun crossed the blank gray sky, no moon either. Time had no meaning.

He thought of Scooter and Flint in the mithraeum. Had the syndexioi found them and confiscated the second syringe? *Or maybe,* Theo thought, *they've already injected me with the antidote— and it didn't work.* He made a conscious decision not to panic. *I'll be stuck here for eternity with Selene. That's not such a bad idea—it will take that long for me to find a way to forgive her.*

Thirst tore at him like a lion. He could barely move his cracked lips. Yet drinking from the River of Forgetting would mean giving up on Selene. And somehow, despite everything she'd done to him, he couldn't do that. Not yet.

Finally, he returned to where he'd first emerged. There, the grass dissolved into a great wall of darkness, infinitely tall and infinitely wide. The surface eddied, black upon black, like a whirlpool of ink.

The River Styx, Theo realized. The border of the Underworld upon whose waters the gods swore their most solemn oaths. Vast and impenetrable, rushing in every direction at once—across the ground, toward the sky, beyond the horizon.

A hand emerged from the swirling black, then a foot. A figure stepped through, quickly resolving itself into the hazy outline of a man. He didn't look confused or lost. He simply strode slowly forward without noticing Theo standing nearby and joined the herd of other ghosts headed in the same direction.

They're all drawn straight to Lethe, he realized. *Just as I was. Selene will go there, too.* Panic quickened his pulse. *She won't know not to drink. She'll return to the world another woman. Forgetting she was ever Artemis. Forgetting that I ever loved her.*

He raced back toward the spring, fear driving him faster, faster. *I can't be too late,* he begged silently. *Not again.* He'd never believed in destiny—but if Artemis was real, perhaps the Fates were, too. *There has to be a reason I went into the necropolis just before Selene was killed. It can't have been for nothing. The universe would not be so cruel.*

He reached the white cypress and ran from one blurred ghost to the next, grabbing them by formless shoulders, looking for the woman he'd loved. *She can't have drunk from the spring,* he decided. *She'd know, somehow, that I was coming for her. She would wait.* But his faith in Selene had already crumbled in the Phrygianum.

He searched a hundred bland faces—but none were the one he sought.

He felt like a man pushed from a cliff, clutching at air he knew to be empty.

Finally, for the first time since he'd come to this place, Theo sank to the ground in despair. The grass closed above his head, transforming his world into a colorless prison, just as it had been for the last six lonely months. Had his sacrifice been the gesture of a man desperate for meaning in a world that had none?

His adrenaline finally drained away. The obsessive need to find Selene settled into weary recognition that his epic quest had been no more than a fool's errand. Because even now, when he'd come so far, she didn't *want* to be saved. She'd drunk from Lethe's waters and moved on, happy to forget.

For a long time, he sat with his head in his hands and simply mourned.

Finally the spring's gurgle penetrated his fog of despair. It seemed to be whispering to him.

You can forget, too.

He stared at the water, obeying the desperate thirst urging him to rise. To kneel before the pool. To reach a hand into the shining deep. To finally forget his sorrow.

Chapter 24

THE FACE OF DEATH

The slender, black-haired woman emerged from darkness into a vast meadow. She stood naked, staring at the blurred outline of her own body, slowly coming to understand that all the nebulous figures streaming by were dead—and so was she.

Around her, the ghosts passed by in an inexorable tide, dragging at her like a lodestone. Some small part of her begged not to go with them. *You've never followed the herd before—don't start now.* But the urge to move was a physical ache. She felt like a droplet in a stream, bereft of will, unable to withstand the unceasing flow around her. She lifted a foot—and a whisper of melody froze her in place.

Like a flower turning its petals to the sun, she pivoted toward the sound. She couldn't hear the words, only the gentle rhythm pulsing in her blood, as if the song existed within her more than without.

She took a single step toward the melody, and the sound grew louder, the wisp of tune humming in her bones. She still didn't know her own name—but she knew the song.

Another step. Another.

She passed through the waving grass, onto parched ground. She could hear the words now.

Hear me, O queen,
Zeus's daughter of many names,
Torch-bearing goddess, bane of monsters fell,
Huntress, Giver of Good Counsel,
Come, dear Goddess. Be my savior.

Over and over the hymn played, urging her onward.

Torch-bearing goddess.
Huntress.
Counselor.
Savior.
Hear me, O queen.

"I do," she answered. "I hear you."

She could see each name, each title, spiraling upward into the featureless sky. She grabbed hold of that rope of linked names and followed it back to herself.

Back to Artemis.

To Diana.

To Selene Neomenia.

Memory returned, slow and fragile at first, like petals falling from a tree. Her father's cracked eyeglasses. Theo's shocked face. Rhea's silent helplessness. Flint's horrified cries. Saturn's grim smile. *The scent of blackened meat.*

As the rest of the memory scorched through her, she nearly buckled under the remembered pain. Her hazy body showed no sign of the pyre's many-tongued kiss, but she felt it nonetheless. She stood rooted to the ground as if iron chains still bound her fast, trapped in the memory of flames flaying the skin from her bones. But worse than the pain was the thought of what she'd left behind. Of Flint, trapped and chained. Of her father, bound for sacrifice. Of Theo, whom she'd tried so hard to protect, now caught amid his enemies. The men she loved most in the world, now in mortal danger. And she could do nothing to help them.

Yet still the song continued. She reached for it, a drowning woman seeking a lifeline. She followed it backward, climbing hand over hand along the rope of names, following it to its source.

To a wide lake, its waters smooth and mirror bright.

To a naked young man who stood silhouetted before it with a gold lyre in his hands.

Like all the figures in this world between worlds, the outline of his body blurred; his flesh seemed without substance. His once bright curls were near colorless. Yet she knew his face. She had known it since it floated beside her in their mother's womb.

Apollo, the God of Light and Music, ran toward her.

When he flung his arms around her, she felt only the barest hint of sensation, haze brushing haze. *I prayed to see him again,* she remembered dimly. *So why do I feel so little joy?* They had always been two sides of the same whole. Sun and Moon. Civilization and wilderness. Male and female. Yet she felt as if Saturn's pyre had burned away both Artemis and Rhea and left her no more than a shell that even her twin couldn't fill.

He stepped back to stare at her, and his face, too, was full of grief. "Has that much time passed, Moonshine, that you have finally lost your immortality? Or have the Fates cut short the thread of your life as they did mine?"

"Not the Fates. Grandfather."

Apollo's expression hardened. "And so he has killed us both." He spoke in the formal language of a deity. Little sign remained of Paul Solson, the moody indie rockstar he'd been before his death. "He has finished his rituals, then? Is he truly God the Father?"

"Not yet," she managed. "But soon."

"What of the others?" he urged. "Surely Hermes and Hephaestus and Theodore will not—"

At the mention of their names, her blurred hands pressed against eyes too unformed to weep.

Apollo gripped her shoulders, though she could barely feel his touch. "Artemis, I beg you. Tell me what happened."

And so she did. From the battle against Saturn on the Statue of Liberty to her time in the flames beneath the Vatican. She told him of abandoning Theo and finding him again. Of Rhea's soul mingling with her own. Of Zeus and Flint captive in the Host's prison. Of her own failure to keep any of them safe.

"I am no *Savior*," she cried. "Those names you sing...they're mine no longer. And I'm not the Great Mother either. Saturn finally got what he wanted—Rhea's soul isn't inside me anymore. She's nowhere. Nothing. Wiped from the earth, from memory, from existence itself. And so am I. So if you must speak of me, don't sing my glory." Her voice turned hard, bitter. "Call me by my other epithets. Call me Stormy, call me Despoiler, call me the Face of Death."

She went on, repeating the long litany of all the titles she'd tried to forget until her words became a chant. Apollo sang with her, but with words of his own. A hymn of praise for his glorious twin. Dirge and paean twined in counterpoint, until, when Selene's throat was raw from sobbing and every limb felt too heavy to lift, Apollo put his arm around her and drew her close.

"You said Theodore has Hades' helm and Orion's sword," he murmured.

She nodded.

"And Hermes is with him."

"Yes."

"Then you must not underestimate them, Moonshine. The Makarites is smart, the Trickster cunning. They will find a way to rescue the others. You must trust in that."

"You know trust has never been easy for me."

The corner of his lip twitched. "Yet you learned to trust me in the end. Trust me now. They will survive."

"Do you have the gift of prophecy again?" she asked, not daring to hope.

"No." His eyes roamed the parched ground and the mirrored lake. "This place is no Delphi. Here, I have only my music. And my faith."

"Faith in *what*?"

"In you, of course." Apollo lifted a narrow brow. "The others whom Saturn killed—Hades, Prometheus, Mars—passed through like any other shades. I alone have remained. And I knew you would do the same. We entered the world together. It seemed only fit that we leave the same way."

"You've been . . . waiting for me?"

"I have not been too lonely. Song makes memories strong enough to withstand the ravages of time. It made the world and it can unmake it, too."

He rested his fingers upon his lyre, coaxing forth his hymn once more—the same tune that had drawn her from across the Underworld. A song, she realized, he'd been playing for the last six months.

But this time, another man's voice sang the words she had chosen.

"Stormy. Despoiler. The Face of Death."

Theo's voice. Ragged, hoarse, as if the words tore at his throat.

Dread choked the breath from Selene's lungs. But her heart cried out one word over and over. No. *No. NO.*

She looked to her twin, whose gentle face had twisted with new misery. "I am so sorry," he said.

"You were wrong," she managed, the words more lamentation than accusation. "He didn't make it."

She turned to face the hazy outline of the man she'd loved. He stood naked before her, his fair hair falling across his forehead in a blurry sweep, his green eyes, always so keen, now mere smudges in a face devoid of its usual angles. Only his voice remained sharp.

"Selene…" When Theo had spoken her name in the mithraeum, it had been an awesome gasp. Now it was a command.

She opened her mouth to respond and no words emerged.

Her twin's arms around her shoulders were no comfort at all. Not when her brilliant, laughing lover was dead.

Selene felt as if her body were still a charred husk, so fragile that the grief burning within would split her apart. A cry of anguish fought against her clenched lips. Apollo couldn't soothe her now—only anger could tame the sorrow that threatened to break her. But what good was wrath when the one who truly deserved punishment was herself?

She tried to speak. Choked. Tried again. "How did—"

"I was about to drink from Lethe when I heard your song." His eyes shifted to Apollo, his tone softening for an instant. "Hey, Paul. Nice to see you again."

"No, I mean—" Selene began.

"There's no time," Theo cut her off. "Somewhere in another existence, Flint's waiting with a syringe full of antidote. We've got to move."

"Antidote," Selene managed. "Saturn didn't kill you?"

"No," he said shortly.

Apollo looked at him, confusion brightening into awe.

That's when Selene understood. *I prayed you'd come to rescue me. But please, not this time. I beg you, Theo, not like this.*

Horror twisted through her stomach like a many-coiled serpent, threatening to tear her apart from the inside. Then, something deep within her switched off. A circuit breaker tripping. A sluice gate slamming shut. In the place of devastation she felt only numbness.

Apollo still watched Theo, a bittersweet smile on his lips. "What a song I could write of your love."

Theo looked like he might vomit. "My love," he spat. "Is that what this feeling is?" But when his gaze flicked back to hers, some of his rage melted away. In her coldness, he seemed to find an icy calm of his own. His chest rose and fell in a single deep breath. "Come on," he said. "We're going. Now."

Something in his tone brought Selene to her feet. But Apollo only shook his head sadly. "It doesn't work that way. You can't just walk out."

"Sure I can," Theo said. "Orpheus did."

"There are no Queen and King of the Underworld anymore to grant you passage. Hades himself is gone."

"I don't need his permission. I have this." Theo held up a gold leaf-shaped pendant.

Apollo fixed his eyes on the thin sheet of metal like a starving man seeing bread for the first time. "Is that—"

"Dionysus's instructions."

Apollo turned to his sister, hope flaring in his familiar gold eyes. But even before Theo had shown her the pendant, Selene had already made up her mind. He had killed himself. For her. She still couldn't allow herself to feel the true import of that gesture—the force of it would crush her, body and soul—but she could make sure he had not sacrificed himself in vain.

She gripped Apollo's hand. "We're getting out."

"He came for *you*," her brother replied hesitantly.

"Well, he's leaving with both of us," she said in a tone that brooked no argument.

She shot a glance at Theo, who nodded in solemn agreement. "Fine. But we don't have time to waste."

He turned away from her, all business. He looked down at the pendant, then back up at the mirrored lake before them. "It says to go to the Lake of Mnemosyne. So far so good."

He stepped to the lake's edge and reached down. The lapping water receded before him faster than any wave. He took another step; the water retreated still further.

"You can't reach the lake here. There is only one entrance," Apollo explained. "I know where it is—at a stream that runs from the lake to the Styx—but the Gods of Birth and Death guard it well. Still...if we could enter, to drink from Mnemosyne is to drink from Memory itself. We would return to life with all our past intact."

"So we just have to get past Birth and Death, huh?" Theo said, a grim smile crooking one side of his mouth. "No problem."

Apollo led the way. Theo followed without looking back at Selene. But the flicker of his old wit rapped against the wall she'd thrown up around her emotions, a jeweler's hammer tapping out a familiar tattoo. As she walked along the edge of the lake, her feet marched to its rhythm, and she felt, for the first time since Saturn's men had dragged her to the pyre, a glimmer of hope.

Chapter 25

GOD OF UNBOUNDED TIME

Selene walked along the water's edge for what felt like hours but might have been seconds. To her right, the parched ground stretched into hazy distance. To her left, the vast Lake of Mnemosyne lay calm and still, reflecting the featureless sky. In either direction, nothing held the eye.

This is what it means to be dead, she thought. *To exist within nothingness.* Apollo had wandered this netherworld for six months—half a year that might have felt like centuries or minutes. Only his music—and her memory—had kept him sane.

Selene fixed her gaze on her twin and Theo, latching on to them as the only anchors in an empty sea.

Finally, they came to a narrow stream that swirled with color like oil in sunlight. Where it joined the lake, two men stood guard. Selene recognized them from the carvings in so many mithraea: Cautes and Cautopates, the Torchbearers. They were twins, their expressionless faces like bronzes cast from the same mold. Only the direction of their torches differed—upward for Cautes, guardian of Birth; downward for Cautopates, guardian of Death.

Between them stood a lion-headed man, the same figure she'd seen on the ceiling of the Mithraic schoolroom, the one Saturn had called Aion, Unbounded Time. He stood ramrod straight, clasping two foot-long keys against his chest. A snake writhed around his nude body and up his torso, its head resting above his lion's mane for a moment before it slithered back down to retrace its twining path. An undulating double helix, twisting into the shape of life itself.

None of the three guards paid any heed to the blurred ghosts standing a few yards away.

"Dennis said we need to be Releasers," Theo murmured. "That must mean getting our furry friend to use the keys to unlock the way forward."

"The Torchbearers will not let you pass," Apollo said in a hushed voice.

Theo tapped the gold pendant around his neck. "We'll see."

Neither Cautes nor Cautopates looked at him as he approached, but when he tried to pass between them, their meter-long torches slammed together like a gate.

Theo looked down at his pendant and read aloud carefully, as if reciting a passphrase:

"I am the child of Earth and starry Heaven, but my race is heavenly. I am parched with thirst and I perish, but give me quickly refreshing water flowing forth from the Lake of Mnemosyne."

To Selene's amazement, the guardians uncrossed their torches in response. Lion-headed Aion took a step back and raised his two keys overhead, as if to unlock the sky itself.

Theo motioned for Selene to follow. "Do what I do," he urged. "We're almost there."

He passed beyond the guardians and quickly bent to sip from the rushing rainbow stream. Selene grasped her twin's ghostly hand in her own and strode quickly between the guards. Cautes and Cautopates let her through—but their torches clashed together behind her with a shower of sparks, blocking Apollo's way.

"He may not pass," they said in unison.

Aion merely growled, his long teeth bared.

"Why not?" Selene demanded. Her hand still clutched her brother's, their outstretched arms reaching between the crossed torches.

"Only souls newly arrived can depart," the Torchbearers intoned. "You may go. He may not."

"Where I go, he goes." She squeezed her twin's hand, trusting her own nebulous flesh to convey her message. As one, they swept their clasped hands upward to knock aside the torches, moving so fast the flames barely licked their skin.

Selene yanked on Apollo's arm to drag him through, but Aion stood before them, barring their path to the stream. He lowered his keys with a roar.

Theo stepped forward to help, then jerked to a halt as if he'd run into an invisible wall. His shell of calm determination cracked open. "Aion locked the way!" He pounded his fist against thin air, desperate, panicked. "I can't get back to—"

Apollo's warning shout drowned out Theo's words. Selene wheeled toward her twin just in time to see him dodge the torches swinging toward him from either side. Cautes and Cautopates moved in perfect symmetry, their flaming brands streaking the dim gray sky with light.

"They move as one," she cried, "but we don't have to!"

Releasing Apollo's hand, she hurtled toward Cautes just as his torch swung toward her. She ducked the fluttering flame and seized the bundled reed handle instead.

"They call me Torch-Bearing Goddess," she snarled, ripping the reeds from his hands. "But I prefer She Who Helps One Climb Out."

She jabbed the torch into the ground, dousing the flames against the rocky earth.

Cautes stared down at the blackened reeds, his hands limp at his sides, a robot with his batteries removed.

Selene risked a glance back to her twin. Apollo had trapped Cautopates's torch in the strings of his golden lyre. He wrenched the instrument to the side, shearing the torch in half. The flame tumbled to the ground. Selene stamped it out with her bare feet, the pain nothing compared to her time upon Saturn's pyre.

The torchbearers both stood slumped and unmoving, their strength doused along with their fire. The shape began to leech from their outlines, the color from their skin and clothes.

But the fight was not yet done.

Aion roared his anger, dragon flames spouting from his fanged jaws. Selene ducked beneath the plume of fire and slammed a roundhouse kick into the creature's stomach. His flesh was solid and unyielding beneath the sole of her foot; her kick seemed to have as little impact as a butterfly's wing. She reached for his keys instead, but he bolted into the air. His four feathered wings flapped noisily, taking him—and his keys—out of reach.

Saturn's story came back to her. Primordial Aion, limitless and infinite, finally pinned in place by Saturn, God of Bounded Time, who bent the universe into a straight line.

If I want to reverse my own death, she realized, *I have to make Time limitless once more. I have to unbind him from his serpent coils.*

The snake hissed down at her, its tongue a mocking flicker. Selene snatched a rock from the ground and hurled it like a shot put. It crunched against the snake's skull.

The serpent unfurled, slipping off Aion's naked body and spinning to the ground. Selene snatched it up, the coils heavy and rough. It blinked slowly, barely alive. She grabbed its neck, ready to finish the job.

"Wait!" cried Theo. "Dennis said *release* Time from the snake. Don't kill it! We don't want to resurrect *all* the dead!"

Selene held the snake up to Aion like an offering. He swooped down to retrieve the prize.

She yanked it back at the last moment. "Drop the keys, and I'll give you the snake."

Aion growled, smoke billowing from his jaws.

She held the beast across her body like a shield. "Burn me, burn your pet."

The lion blew sparks from his nostrils and bared his fangs— but he held out the keys.

The voice of the Torchbearers surprised her. She'd thought them too stunned to speak.

"If you take them," Cautopates began.

"No one will ever pass through Mnemosyne again," finished Cautes.

"So be it." She grabbed both keys from Aion. Then she hurled the snake away from the stream with all her strength. The lion-headed man flapped after it, bellowing his distress. She tossed one key to Apollo.

Theo stood at the lake's edge. He still hadn't entered the water. Perhaps he couldn't.

"Here, Theo, you take it," she said, preparing to toss him the other key.

"I didn't come all this way to leave you behind," he said tightly. "Besides, I have another way out. Flint's going to—" His hands shot to his throat. His eyes bulged as he drew a wheezing, terrified breath.

"Theo!"

For an instant, his amorphous form turned solid, color flooded his cheeks—and then he disappeared.

Chapter 26

MNEMOSYNE

Theo felt as if his lungs were on fire. That was nothing compared to the ache in his heart.

Scooter loomed over him in the aisle of the mithraeum, his face contorted in desperate concentration, his hands still resting on Theo's torso from the chest compressions. The empty syringe of antidote lay beside him on the platform.

"You must've been doing something important over there," the god gasped with a relieved grin, "because I didn't think you wanted to come back." His bloody teeth, stained from eating the raw heart, only added to Theo's sense of turmoil. What world had he returned to?

He sat up slowly, urging numb limbs to obey a numb mind's commands. His ribs felt bruised from Scooter's ministrations, vomit coated his bare chest, and he couldn't bend his fingers or toes.

A large hand grabbed him hard by the shoulder, nearly knocking him backward again. "Where's Selene?" came Flint's growled demand. He rounded on Scooter next. "I told you not to bring him back yet!"

"He said *five minutes*," Scooter snapped. "We gave him seven."

Theo blinked, willing his eyes to focus. A black husk lay beside him on the ground. Selene.

Still dead.

"No," he choked.

"Where *is* she?" Flint levered himself upright on the lip of the feasting platform so that he stood as straight as his bent legs would allow.

"She was . . . She was right behind me."

———◇———

"Do not fear," Apollo told Selene as she stared dumbfounded at the spot where Theo had stood a moment before. "He has returned to the world of the living."

Selene took a breath she hadn't realized she'd been holding. "Then let's go join him."

With the keys outstretched, they passed easily to the stream's edge. But just as they bent to drink, the rainbow water at their fingertips shuddered with the force of Aion's roar. A searing wind swept against Selene's bare shoulder blades.

The lion-man, his snake slung about his shoulders but not yet binding his body, rocketed toward her. His fiery breath had relit the broken ends of the Torchbearers' reeds. With their attributes restored, they stormed toward the stream, screaming curses.

"The lake!" Apollo leapt into the stream. "Get to the lake!"

Selene ran upstream beside him, the hip-height water dragging at her legs. When she reached the edge of the lake, she tried to spring forward, but the ground disappeared from beneath her feet and she plummeted downward instead. A single gasped breath and the water closed over her head.

She tried to swim for the surface, but the weight of the foot-long iron key dragged her down. She dropped it—it quickly disappeared into the murky depths. But despite her frenzied struggles, she hovered in the water, her body refusing to rise.

She peered in vain through the darkness for any sign of her brother, wondering if he, too, had been trapped. The oxygen fled her lungs and her thrashing slowed. Finally, she opened her mouth, gasping, and swallowed the water. It was warm and sweet on her tongue.

It's not a lake, she decided. *It's a womb.*

She no longer needed to breathe. The first time she'd been born, Apollo had floated beside her. Now she was utterly alone.

Not Artemis. Not Diana. All trace of Rhea gone, too.

As the warm water sluiced down her throat, Mnemosyne—Memory herself—unrolled an intricate tapestry before her eyes. Images of her long past slid by in a single heartbeat, restoring her to herself.

Her mother's arms, her brother's smile, her father's laugh, her nymphs' song. The leap of a stag, an arrow's flight. The keening of maidens and the cries of men. The baying of hounds. The fall of Troy, the heights of Olympus. Thousands of women defended, thousands of men destroyed, from medieval villages to the streets of Manhattan. A hundred dogs to love, a hundred names to call her own.

Then her mother torn away, her twin torn away, Theo still holding her in his arms above a moonlit harbor. Flint's shoulder beneath her palm as they swayed together on a dance floor. The anger in Theo's eyes as he stared at her across the Phrygianum.

All in an instant.

A sunbeam struck her closed eyes, and when she opened them, light streamed through the water, showing her the way back to the world of the living. This time, when she began paddling for the surface, her body moved effortlessly.

I'm coming, Theo. I'll make it up to you.

Yet she halted once more to look for Apollo. He floated a hundred feet below her, eyes closed. He held neither lyre nor key.

She dove, lungs bursting, and grabbed his empty hand. But

when she pivoted to paddle upward again, the sunlight had disappeared. Everything returned to blackness.

Forgive me, Theo . . . forgive me, she begged, knowing she'd lost her only chance of escape. She could feel Apollo's hand in her own, but she couldn't see his face. Then a faint glow appeared—more a softer shade of black than true illumination.

It's coming from the bottom *of the lake,* she realized, *not from the surface.*

Then again, she no longer knew which way was up. She struck out toward the dim light, dragging Apollo behind her.

After only a few strokes, she broke the surface of the water and emerged not in the lake but in a pool no more than chest-deep. She hauled her twin up beside her.

The jagged walls of a cave rose around them. A spring fed the shallow pool, then burbled toward the faint daylight at the cave's mouth.

Selene lay half out of the water. Next to her, Apollo still breathed, although his eyes remained shut. He looked strangely peaceful.

She gripped him under the arms, then almost dropped him in surprise. His flesh burned like black basalt in the noontime sun. Worried, she clenched her teeth against the pain and gently settled him on the driest patch of ground she could find before walking to the cave's entrance.

She stood in a cleft of rust-streaked limestone, the rock dropping twenty feet below to a narrow gorge shadowed by rustling poplar trees. Beside her, the stream arched from the cave in a narrow waterfall, disappearing beneath the canopy of trees.

Beyond the gorge, the mountainside sloped precipitously into a wide valley carpeted in low pines. Scattered cypresses towered over the other trees like sentinels guarding the forest with their spears.

She felt as though she stood on the edge of the world. Across the valley, more mountains marched into the distance. Rosy-fingered Dawn cast her blush upon the nearest peaks, while those farther away disappeared into a soft blue haze. *Wherever this is, it certainly isn't Rome. But it isn't the Underworld either.*

She allowed herself to hope. *We did it. We're free.*

She felt surprisingly strong considering she'd just been burned at the stake, passed through Death, and emerged on the other side. In fact, she felt better than she had in a very long time. She flexed one bare foot against the rock and then another, noticing the ripple of strength in her legs.

From the gorge below, the murmur of voices arose, but she couldn't pick out any words, nor could she see the speakers through the leafy canopy. She looked down in dismay at her nude body; she didn't intend to let a bunch of hikers see her naked. Still, she needed to find a bus, steal a car, hitch a ride—*something* to get herself and her twin back to Rome, where they belonged. Surely if Theo had been revived in the mithraeum under the Vatican, then he was still there—and still in danger. Flint and Scooter were still trapped, her father too. They would need her help to escape.

She ducked back into the cave to check on her sleeping brother. Then she cut a few stems from a chasteberry bush near the mouth of the cave and fastened the long, flexible lengths around her waist and chest. *I look like a Christianized statue,* she thought ruefully, *sanitized with fig leaves.*

Digging her toes into the craggy limestone, she descended the rock face with practiced ease. The stone was cool beneath her fingers and toes, but already the rising sun warmed her back.

She reached the ground moments later and darted from tree trunk to tree trunk, as fast and lithe as a dryad. She could hear the babbling of water now, the stream from the cave reappearing somewhere nearby. But the susurrus of voices nearly drowned it out, a mass of people all whispering at once. *There must be a school group camping in the woods,* she decided, creeping closer.

Styx, she cursed as the crowd came into view. *Forget the school group—make that an all-male skinny-dipping society.*

Twenty naked men stood around a fountain cut into the side of the limestone gorge and ornamented with marble railings and finials. Some splashed their faces and arms with the spring water from the basin. Others submerged themselves completely, emerging like newborns, glistening and pink in the dawn light. No one spoke above a whisper. More men stood waiting for their turn at the fountain; the line trailed off into the trees, making the exact number difficult to count.

A pile of discarded sheets, white and yellow, lay between the roots of a nearby pine. Selene snatched two pieces while the men were busy at their bath and slipped back into the woods to clothe herself. Using the chasteberry stems as a belt, she wrapped the white fabric around her waist and shoulder like a chiton. The tightly woven wool felt like silk. She scrambled back up the cliff with the other piece of fabric.

"Sunbeam." She spoke the old nickname gently, laying a hand on her twin's shoulder to wake him. His skin still burned, but his eyes snapped open, glowing faintly golden in the dim light. "We did it," she told him. "We're alive. But we have to leave."

"Where are we?" he asked, sitting up and squinting in the dim cave.

"No idea. Somewhere in the countryside. Maybe south of Rome." She helped him wrap the yellow fabric around his waist, her hands rough from urgency. "All I know is it's going to be a long walk back to Vatican City."

"How did we get here?"

"Don't ask me. I followed you deeper into the Lake of Memory, and this is where we wound up. I thought maybe you chose this place."

As they emerged into the sunlight, Selene looked at her twin, impressed. For just having been dead, he looked amazing. In fact, he looked better than he had in years. The streak of white in his hair had vanished. His body gleamed as if oiled, and any hint of age had vanished from his face. He looked eighteen years old, a perfect specimen of masculine beauty.

Selene lifted a hand to her head, wondering if her own journey through death had erased the matching white streak from her hair—and found her usual chin-length bob transformed into a black curtain brushing her waist.

"When did my hair grow?" she demanded.

"What do you mean?" Her brother looked confused. "It's always been that length."

"No, it hasn't," she snapped. She hadn't had long hair since the 1920s. "You did drink from the lake, didn't you?"

"The lake?"

"The one we just swam through," she pressed, increasingly worried.

"I drank. I drank so much..."

Selene had the sudden suspicion that it was possible to remember so much you remembered nothing at all. "We need to get you back to civilization."

She messily bound her long tresses into a loose chignon with another stem of chasteberry, then led the way back down the cliff to the fountain.

"Autobus a Roma?" she called to the crowd in her best attempt at Italian. *"Veloximente!"*

The men turned to stare, their faces at first uncomprehending, then ashen. One by one, they fell to their knees and bowed their heads.

One man raised his arms high in the air and called out in perfect Ancient Greek:

"Khairete o pythie Apollon kai iokheaira Artemi."

Hail to Pythian Apollo and his immortal sister Artemis.

"Ummmm. Sunbeam?" Selene whispered, her heart sinking as she looked ahead through an opening in the trees to the countryside beyond. From her new vantage point, she could see the line of men stretching all the way back to a wide road that hugged the mountain. Those closest to the spring had already disrobed, but the rest wore Greek chitons. Many held laurel branches or libation bowls. Others clutched small terra-cotta figurines of bulls, goats, or rams.

On the sunbright limestone cliffs to the west, below a mountain with a distinctive double peak, perched a sanctuary cluttered with columned buildings of marble and bronze. A long temple, the statues on its pediments painted in bright shades of turquoise and carnelian, dominated the center. Next to it loomed a sixty-foot-tall statue. Completely covered in gold, it burned so brightly in the newly risen sun that Selene had to shield her eyes to see it better. A young god, his perfect beauty revealed by his nakedness. In one bent arm, he clutched his most famous attribute: a golden lyre.

Selene knew in that moment that they could only be in one place:

Delphi. The sanctuary of Apollo on the slopes of Mount Parnassos north of Athens, where the most famous oracle in the history of the world granted prophecies to the masses.

And since I know that statue was melted down long ago, we can only be in one time, she realized with a start.

The fifth century BC.

"Remember when I said it'd be a long trip back to the Vatican?" she asked her brother from the corner of her mouth, uncomfortably aware of the staring crowd. "I think that's putting it mildly."

Chapter 27

PYTHIAN GOD

Apollo, god of the Delphic oracle, strode forward toward the waiting crowd of worshipers without a backward glance. Only when he drew close to them did Selene realize that her brother now stood at least ten feet tall.

And so did she.

She followed Apollo's lead, ignoring the gathered supplicants entirely and walking toward the road. Bent on one knee, the already tiny mortals seemed even more insignificant. Few dared raise their eyes to the passing gods. The legends were clear, although exaggerated: Anyone who looked upon the undisguised glory of an Athanatos would be reduced to ashes. A faint yellow glow surrounded her twin. At first, she'd taken it for the morning sun streaming through the dew-filled air. Now she knew better. Apollo had regained his divine aura.

She looked at her own arms, noticing for the first time the pale silver light emanating from her flesh.

Mortals lined the road, but the surrounding woods held worshipers of another sort. The leaves rustled as Selene passed; her very presence had summoned her acolytes. Deer and hare, jackal and lynx, all gathered at the forest's edge to bow before the Mistress of Beasts. She could imagine her chariot waiting for her among the trees, her wide-antlered stags yoked to the reins. *If I asked, would they carry me to the Moon and back?* she wondered.

As if in answer, a black hawk keened overhead. She watched it float in lazy circles, its presence a reminder that if she joined it on high, she could see the whole world. All the helpless confusion of her half-mortal life, the futile wandering into dead ends, the struggle for understanding, the constant battle to survive, would mean nothing to an omnipotent goddess.

But she turned back to the dirt path ahead. If she went to the Moon, she would never return to Theo and the others.

"I hope you know where we're going," she said to her twin, confident that the worshipers would be unable to understand English. They'd probably think it a secret language of the gods.

"Home," Apollo replied, the English sounding suddenly strange coming from lips so divine.

"New York? That's an even longer trip, Sunbeam."

He cast her a mildly curious glance, as if he had no idea what she was talking about and didn't much care. He pointed one long finger at the brightly painted temple on the hill. "Home," he said again.

The line of men curved back on itself as those who'd already purified themselves at the spring awaited their turn to enter the sacred precinct and consult the oracle. Delphi only permitted such consultations on the seventh day of every month, so the crowds had likely accumulated for weeks.

As the gods passed by, men lowered their heads in reverence, but beside the sanctuary's gate, they lowered them more slowly. These were the richer folk, those privileged enough to be granted places at the head of the line. Many were accompanied by slaves holding goats and honey cakes for sacrifice. Others carried more permanent votive offerings: not terra-cotta figures like the poorer men, but finely wrought sculptures in gold or silver, tripods of bronze, reliefs of carven ivory, helmets and shields, the spoils of war.

Apollo nodded beatifically as he passed some men, frowned as he walked by others. Occasionally he would offer a simple yes or no: *"Nai"* or *"Ou."* At first, Selene didn't understand, then she realized that he answered their questions before they even asked them. The God of Prophecy plying his trade.

At the front of the line, the gate to the sacred precinct remained closed. The oracle had not yet started business for the day. A single boy—he seemed a mere toddler from Selene's lofty height—scurried ahead and pounded frantically on the gate.

"Apollo and Artemis are here! Open! Open!" he called in Ancient Greek.

Apollo didn't slow his step; the portal just opened before him as if by the magic of his presence. The bearded priest on the other side, garbed in a long purple himation, stepped backward and raised his arms high.

"Phoibon, Khrysokomes," he chanted. Soon the whole crowd took up the hymn:

> *Bright One, Golden Haired,*
> *Who on the split-cragged seat of Parnassos*
> *Arrives at Delphi, the prophetic hill,*
> *And shines forth prophecies to all the mortals.*

As Apollo walked into the precinct along the Sacred Way, a faint smile curved his lips, not unlike the smiles on the two marble kouroi that flanked the path. These were old statues, faintly Egyptian in their stiff poses and almond-shaped eyes. Hundreds of other, more classical figures lined the street beyond. Marble and bronze effigies of kings, gods, and heroes competed for space atop long plinths. On one pedestal stood a massive wooden Trojan Horse. On another, a bull plated in silver with gilded horns. The inscriptions identified them as offerings to great Apollo from different city-states, the wealth of an entire civilization on display.

It's like Times Square and Fifth Avenue and Epcot Center all rolled into one, Selene thought, her head swimming at the sight of so much decadence.

Cities as far away as Syracuse had built entire treasuries within Delphi's walls, their columned porticoes heaped with gold and silver booty—all gifts to the god. Selene wondered, awestruck, if her own sanctuaries had been so laden with wealth. She thought she'd long ago forgotten such details of her past, but to her surprise, an image of Brauron came to mind, the town south of Athens that had housed the priestesses and young girls dedicated to Artemis.

Yes, I had my offerings inside within a small temple, she recalled, *but they were gifts from families asking for the protection of their daughters. Simple statues of me, my family, the girls themselves. Nothing,* she had to admit, *half so grand as this.*

She tried not to feel jealous as they continued up the hillside, but jealousy came easily to the gods. Although the Selene part of herself felt nothing but revulsion at the idea of massive crowds of men standing at her gate, Artemis's pride came surging back. *I deserve such treasure,* she decided, even as she fought against the thought. *I REQUIRE worship.*

They passed more buildings, more pedestals—a limestone boulder dedicated to their mother Leto, a marble sphinx perched three stories high atop an Ionian column, a massive bronze tripod balanced on a serpentine pillar—until finally they stood beneath the colossal golden statue Selene had seen from the road. Its straight nose, generous mouth, and soft jaw mirrored the features of the man beside her.

This is not the first time my twin has visited his holy city, she knew, struck by the statue's verisimilitude. *They have seen his face before.* The next thought came unbidden: *I will have to remind my own worshipers to build me a statue even taller.*

Between the statue and the painted temple stood a tall gray altar piled with wood. From higher up the slope, a priest came running down the path leading a kid goat. The animal bleated mournfully. The other priests tutted and clucked like nervous hens, clearly afraid the kid would balk at such a pace: An unwilling sacrifice would be a great affront to the god. Bad enough on a normal day of consultation—the entire oracle would be canceled and the hundreds of supplicants forced to bide their time for another month—worse yet to show such disrespect to the epiphany of the god himself. But the priests need not have worried. Apollo raised a hand and the animal instantly quieted; its sharp hooves rang merrily on the stones as it trotted obediently toward the altar.

With a single slice of the knife, the kid met its end. Rather than burn only the fat and bones as usual, Apollo's priests tossed the entire animal onto the altar, added a small fortune's worth of myrrh, and lit the pyre.

Selene stood beside her brother as he inhaled the sweet smoke. She tried to do the same, expecting it to fill her with power. Instead, she had to stifle a cough, reminded suddenly of the 1980s, before New York City's cigarette ban, when smoke clouded every restaurant. This burnt offering was not meant for her—it could give her nothing. Yet Apollo only breathed more deeply, his aura brightening.

He walked up the wide ramp into the temple's vestibule. Selene followed, taking it all in. Chasing the young syndexios through Ostia, she'd been able to recall snatches, images, of what life in that city had been like two thousand years before. But actually walking through the past was a completely different experience. The colors were brighter than she'd remembered. No crumbled marble could possibly compare with the brilliantly painted pediments of Apollo's temple or the man-high piles of glittering offerings heaped beside its soaring Doric columns. The odor of burnt flesh and myrrh titillated her senses, but she tried to think of the temple as no more than a museum. A place to tour—and then leave.

I cannot let myself enjoy this. I cannot want to stay, she thought desperately.

Overhead, scores of votive shields and cuirasses—even a few entire chariots—hung from the temple's rafters. On the walls of the vestibule, over a hundred sayings were etched in gold. Wise words from wise men. The largest simply proclaimed, KNOW THYSELF.

Easier said than done, Selene thought, staring at a nearby fresco that reached from marble floor to coffered bronze ceiling. The painting depicted a battle that felt all too familiar after Saturn's retelling: the Gigantomachy. The Olympians battling Saturn's giants at the beginning of the world.

Zeus stood at the center of the fresco in all his glory, his thunderbolt raised to throw like a javelin. Beside him stood his brother Poseidon with his trident, Dionysus wielding his pinecone-tipped thyrsus like a spear, Athena cloaked in her tasseled aegis with Medusa's Gorgon face emblazoned across her chest. The painting's Artemis, her bow drawn and her arrow aimed at a hundred-armed giant, bore a familiar stony gaze and square jaw.

No, Selene reminded herself. *That's not me anymore. But if I stay here any longer . . . it will be me again.*

She eyed the portrait uneasily. "Please tell me this temple is the way back to Rome."

"Why would you want to go to Rome?" Apollo sounded bewildered. "It's a place of clay temples and warring tribes. They won't build their marble monuments to us for many years."

"Theo's there," she reminded him. "And Flint and Scooter and Father. They *need* us. That's where we belong. This isn't our time anymore."

"We are timeless," he responded, ignoring the rest of her pleas.

In the center of the chamber, a sacred fire crackled in a round hearth between two altars. Nearby, a short staircase led into an open pit. Selene followed her brother down the steps, unsure what else to do. She'd arrived in this world because Apollo's soul had taken her there.

He would need to lead the way back out.

Dirt covered the pit's floor, not marble, for the oracle had once belonged to their great-grandmother Gaia, Mother Earth, and from her all prophecies arose. Gaia, so the story went, had placed the dragon Python to guard the oracle. When Apollo slew the monster, he claimed the site—and the prophecies—for himself. Now, when the priests of Delphi chose a woman to serve as the oracle's prophetess, they titled her "Pythia" in honor of the slain beast.

The prophetess sat hidden in the pit behind a woolen curtain. No supplicant to the shrine could be allowed to see her face. Yet Apollo pushed aside the curtain as carelessly as he might open the drapes in his New York apartment. This was, after all, his house.

The male priest who served the prophetess inside the oracular cell started with alarm, then instantly knelt when he saw the nature of the intruder. He held a tin tablet and stylus in his hand, ready to record the Pythia's words so they might be taken back to whatever city had sent a delegation to consult her. But seeing the Athanatoi before him, he put the stylus down.

Apollo walked over to a tall bronze tripod—a three-legged stool topped by a round bowl. Usually, such tripods held oil or flame, but this one held the Pythia herself atop its basin, her legs dangling a foot above the ground. The elderly woman wore a simple knee-length white dress and a wreath of Apollo's sacred laurel around her brows.

The only other objects in the room were two golden eagle statues and a limestone rock the size and shape of a distended womb—or the top of an egg. A net of lambswool beaded with gold couldn't hide the stone's cracked surface, striated gray and orange like the cliffs around Delphi. Selene recognized it: *the Omphalos—the Navel.*

In the beginning of time, so it was said, Zeus had released two of his sacred eagles. They flew around the sphere of the world in opposite directions until they met again on this very rock, marking Delphi as the navel of the world, the place from which mankind would be reborn.

In the next age, men descended into barbarism, murdering their own kin, lying and stealing with impunity, and ignoring the gods. Finally, the Olympians released a great flood to wash away the human race and start anew. Later, the Hebrews would tell of Noah, but the Greeks knew that only Deucalion and Pyrrha survived the deluge. The pious couple landed their boat safely right here in Delphi, atop the summit of Mount Parnassos.

Now I, too, have washed up on these shores, Selene realized. *A vestige of another world.*

A new scent mingled with the heavy myrrh, rising through three small holes in the ground around the Omphalos. Sweet and pungent like overripe fruit. The Pythia breathed deeply, inhaling the vapors, and her eyeballs darted back and forth beneath closed lids as if she walked through a dream.

When Apollo spoke, the Pythia chanted in chorus, her lips mirroring his. Her voice was resonant, rough, the voice of a chthonic spirit, not an old woman.

She speaks for Apollo, Selene remembered. To consult the oracle at Delphi was to consult the god himself. The Pythia's trance was more than just visions brought about by the underground vapors. She was *en-theos,* "with the god," a state far more profound than mere enthusiasm.

"*Here I inhale the breath of Earth herself,*" god and prophet chanted together. Then a pause, as if they waited for the supplicant to ask a question.

If mortal men consulted the oracle for a thousand years, Selene figured, *I guess I can, too.* "Tell me how to get back where I belong," she said in the ancient tongue. "Tell me how to get to the other world."

The Pythia took another deep breath. In one hand she held a woolen thread tied to the Omphalos's netted covering, in the other, a branch of laurel. Her entire body began to vibrate, and the leaves of her branch clattered like the flapping of crows' wings. Her voice emerged even hoarser than before as she and Apollo said as one:

"The bridge between worlds hangs on lyre's strings."

Selene waited for more. The Pythia continued to tremble. Apollo merely stood above the holes in the floor, breathing the vapors with a look of sublime tranquility.

"I don't know what that means," Selene said finally. She dared not interpret the Pythia's words carelessly: That always led to disaster.

She still remembered the story of King Croesus, legendarily wealthy ruler of the Lydians, who'd once asked the oracle whether he should march against his neighbors. The reply: *"If you do, a great empire will fall."* Croesus heard only what he wanted to hear and promptly invaded, assured of success. But the empire that fell was, of course, his own.

Better to look at the answer more critically, as the great Athenian general Themistocles had done when told how to defend his city from the Persians. *"A wooden wall only shall not fail,"* the prophetess had said. Themistocles wisely interpreted the "wooden wall" as the Athenian navy, and he successfully defeated the attackers at sea.

I am not as arrogant as Croesus nor as wise as Themistocles, Selene thought. *The inscription on the temple wall said, "Know thyself"—as if that's the key to understanding the oracle. Good luck with that. I'm not even sure who I am anymore—goddess or mortal or something in between.*

The vapors from the ground were beginning to make her head spin. She felt a stab of despair, quickly overcome by irritation.

"I have no time for riddles," she snapped at the old woman. "I just need to save an Athanatos from death, or the past, or whatever this place is. I want to go home—is that too much to ask?"

The oracle raised her arms toward the ceiling and threw her head back. At the same moment, Apollo mirrored her gestures in reverse, reaching toward the ground and bowing his head.

The voice of Gaia herself, deep and rough and filled with power, spoke through their mouths:

"Seek the Wise Virgin. Not in Athens is her seat, but where the Virgin is tall. There the cure is the spear that can conquer the greatest foe."

"Great. Thanks. But wisdom's never been my strong suit," Selene insisted in English. "And I'm ridiculously tall right here. Look at me!" The male priest, she noticed, was surreptitiously inscribing the oracle's words on his tin tablet, clearly wishing to preserve them for posterity.

"Stop that!" She kicked his stylus aside with her oversized foot. "You don't need to write it down, because it doesn't make any sense."

The man cowered, his hands over his head. He couldn't understand her words, but everyone in the ancient world understood her wrath.

Selene just rolled her eyes and took her brother by the elbow. "Let's go."

Apollo wouldn't move. "This is my womb," he intoned. The Pythia echoed his words.

"No, it's not. This may be the navel of the world, but you were born of *Leto's* womb. Our mother, who lived out her life in New York, loving us until the end. We were there when she died, remember?" Anger hid the desperation in her voice. "She was in a hospital bed. In Manhattan. Your name was Paul Solson, and you sang to her as she left the world."

A flash of confusion marred the serenity of his expression, and he didn't resist as Selene dragged him out of the Pythia's chamber, through the temple, and back into the daylight.

A thousand people crushed close to the temple's foundations; word had spread that an epiphany was at hand. No doubt as soon as the deities disappeared, the priests would carve the footprints of the gods onto the temple steps to remember the moment. Selene ignored them. She wished desperately that she had a magic gold pendant like Theo's that would tell her how to return to the present. She'd rather fight any number of winged, fire-breathing guardians than wander helplessly in this past where she didn't belong.

I entered this world through the pool in the cave, she decided finally. *Perhaps I can leave through it as well.*

Apollo's hand in hers, she'd started back down the temple ramp when she noticed a lyre amid the other offerings in the vestibule.

The bridge between worlds hangs on lyre's strings.

"Styx," she cursed. She wasn't sure she'd have made the connection if Theo hadn't mentioned Orpheus in the Underworld.

Dragging Apollo behind her, she snatched up the lyre. *I will make sure Theo succeeds where Orpheus failed.*

She thrust the instrument at her brother, who took it eagerly. Like the one he'd held beside the Lake of Memory, the lyre was covered in gold, but this man-made object was far more ornate. Tiny embossed figures of silver and electrum danced across its arms; ivory crows' heads served as tuning pegs; the gut strings burned carnelian red.

"Play something," Selene ordered. "Something that will bring us home."

"I told you, this is my home."

"This place isn't real. And even if it's real in this past, it isn't real in our present."

"Please," her twin said, his voice plaintive, insistent, no longer the confident prophet but rather the petulant boy she'd known in their childhood. The boy who wanted everything for himself—a bow and arrows, the love of any nymph he desired, his great-grandmother's sacred oracle. "I like it here," he whined, his golden eyes welling.

"Too bad."

"I wouldn't know what to play. If I did, don't you think I would've played it to get out of the Underworld?"

"There, you were little more than a shade," she reminded him. "Here, you're a god. Now act like one."

"But—"

"Orpheus was a mere mortal. Yet he escaped the Underworld by softening the hearts of Hades and Persephone with his song of grief. I can't sing, Apollo, so you must do it for me. Sing of *my* sadness if you can't find any of your own. Sing of my grief at losing you. I watched Saturn slice your heart out with his sickle, and I felt my own soul cleaved in two. I mourned as only a twin can."

Apollo's fingers brushed against the lyre strings as she spoke. No melody yet, but a plaintive chord of longing.

"Life goes on without you," she continued. "But it's a life lived only in prose."

He cast a glance at the silent crowd, the statue-clogged sanctuary, and she knew he still longed to stay in this Delphic past.

She let desperation leak into her voice. "Once you led the Muses. Do you remember?"

He picked out the simplest of tunes as he recited all nine of their names from Calliope through Urania. "Of course I remember."

"Since I lost you, I've walked often with Melpomene, learning all she has to teach of tragedy. I have danced for Terpsichore; I have studied the stars for Urania; and today we walk through history with Clio. But what is a life without Euterpe's poetry, Thalia's comedy, Erato's love songs, or Polyhymnia's hymns? Without them, without *you*, I live in black and white and splashes of red. Bring back the rainbow, Apollo."

"Do you really need me anymore?" He squinted, as if trying to remember something in the distant past. "I told you to find love in the arms of a mortal man, did I not?"

She laughed. "I did as you counseled. Then I threw that away, too. And I'll never get it back again if I'm stuck here. So help me return! Help me save Theo. Help me rescue our father before Saturn kills him. Do it for me, even if you won't do it for yourself."

His golden eyes bored into hers, their old connection fused anew. His fingers danced upon the strings. His lips didn't move, but she heard the song in her mind as only a goddess could. A song woven not by Greek words, nor English, but by the language of emotion. Not grief, as she had asked for, but love.

He dropped his hands from the lyre, yet the song went on. Selene wrapped her arms around her twin, and the song enveloped her like the lake, enfolding her in warmth and safety and light. Apollo's skin grew hotter and hotter beneath her touch until it felt like holding the sun itself. But her own divine flesh could not burn.

She gripped him harder as the song grew louder and deeper, thrumming through every bone, turning her skeleton to a sounding board, her limbs to lyre strings, her heart to a tuning peg.

Above her, the sun grew brighter and larger. The Greeks shielded their eyes and bowed their heads in fearful awe, but Artemis and Apollo turned their faces to the light.

The world flashed into blinding, white brilliance.

Yet Apollo remained before her, his golden face the only color in a blank world. He looked at her with infinite regret and pressed her to his breast. They had never needed words, these two. She saw the truth in his gaze.

"No..." she whispered. "You're not coming..."

"Even your love cannot pull me back after so long away."

"But—"

"At least this time we get to say good-bye. This time, when you're ready, I'll be waiting right here, in Delphi. For you."

She could do nothing but nod. She felt the relentless pull of another universe. At any moment, she'd be ripped away.

Apollo backed away slowly, his hand still trapped in hers.

"But don't come too quickly. Take what time you need. And Moonshine—when death comes for those you love, *remember my prophecy.*"

Her hand slipped from his grip. Already, he was fading from view. He whispered one last request:

"Live your life in song. Promise me."

Selene placed her hands over her own breast in a silent vow. Her heart pounded in time to the rhythm of Apollo's hymn.

She was reborn in the aisle of a mithraeum, staring upward into Flint's tear-streaked face.

Chapter 28

ARROW-
SHOWERING

Selene felt her limp body yanked into Flint's strong arms.

She remained hollow, unreal, unsure of who or what she had become.

The world spun. Her limbs felt heavy and numb, while her heart knocked against her rib cage like a desperate fist. She lay naked, although a few scraps of charred fabric fell away from her as she moved. For once in her life, she didn't care who saw her bare flesh.

"What happened?" she managed.

"A minute after Theo came back, your body just...changed, like a snake shedding its skin. And then you were here." Flint clutched her to his broad chest, his arms like iron bands.

Another voice added, "There are more worlds than we know of."

She turned to see Scooter sitting cross-legged, his face more grave and his voice more solemn than she'd ever heard it. "And the portals between those worlds are not yet closed."

Theo sat nearby, shirtless, his chest streaked with vomit. He stared at her gravely. Only he understood what had just happened. "Apollo?" he asked.

She shook her head, blinking back tears. "It'd been too long. He . . . couldn't come back."

"I'm sorry," Theo said with a tenderness Selene knew she didn't deserve.

There was so much more she needed to say to him, but now that he stood waiting, listening, she couldn't find the words.

"Here." Flint shrugged out of his T-shirt and handed it to Selene. She tried to put it on, but her hands wouldn't obey her commands. He gently lowered it over her head; it reached to mid-thigh. Even as Flint maneuvered her into the shirt, his hands didn't leave her body for more than a breath at a time. He seemed unable to stop touching her, staring at her.

"We have to find Father and get out of here," she said, extracting herself gently from his grip. "Before they kill him."

The mithraeum's door suddenly swung open, freezing her in place.

Saturn strode through, accompanied by two syndexioi dressed as Swiss Guards. Despite Flint's voluminous shirt, Selene felt naked without her bow. From the corner of her eye, she saw Theo lift a familiar dark helm, grab Scooter's arm, and then pop out of existence before the guards noticed them standing at the back of the room.

Saturn regarded Selene, slack-jawed. For once, the Wily One looked completely astonished by someone else's ruse. "How?"

She didn't bother responding. Thinking they'd come for Flint, the guards carried only tall halberds. More important, Saturn had left his sickle behind. A jolt of adrenaline cleared some of the fog from Selene's mind and the heaviness from her arms. She scrambled to her feet, ready to claw out the guards' eyes with her bare hands if they came at her.

Luckily, she didn't have to.

Saturn's head flew back, an invisible hand grabbing him by the hair. His eyes widened as a thin line of blood crawled across his throat. The guards started toward their Pater just as Scooter materialized before them, pressing the barrels of two semiautomatic pistols against their foreheads.

"Drop your weapons!" he shouted at the guards, "or my invisible friend slices off your Pater's head with his divine sword. And trust me, no one will bother to get *Grandpa* back from the Underworld."

The guards dropped their halberds. Selene stumbled forward and snatched up one, Flint the other.

A pair of open handcuffs lay nearby on the ground. Fighting off a wave of dizziness, she bent to retrieve them. Then, feigning a calmness she didn't feel, she fastened them around her grandfather's wrists. From the pocket of his white robe, she pulled out the key to the schoolroom. Not deigning to meet his eye, she looked over his shoulder instead, where she knew Theo stood with his invisible sword at Saturn's throat.

"I'll get my father. Then we can leave." To Scooter, she said. "Get rid of this old man before I come back. I never want to see him alive again."

Despite her wobbliness, she willed her body to move in the semblance of an assured stride. As she entered the hallway, she held the halberd like a queen's scepter, finding confidence in the feel of the shaft in her hand. No doubt other syndexioi lurked in the mithraeum's depths, but she had a weapon now. Saturn would die. Her father would be free.

Theo's furious, but we're both alive, she reasoned. *I'll have a chance to make amends.*

She counted the doors until she reached the schoolroom. The key—an old L-shaped iron rod like those Aion held—opened the heavy door. Zeus stood just inside, as if waiting for her. Something like pride beamed from his overlarge eyes.

She took his arm, fragile as a chicken bone beneath her fingers, and led him back to the sanctuary. He moved with a shuffling step, and she matched her pace to his. "I'm going to get you out of here. Get you some clothes, something to eat. You'll never have to go back to that cave."

Zeus said nothing, but a small, eager smile crossed his lips.

She opened the sanctuary door to a scene of chaos. Saturn crouched in a fighter's stance—the broken and twisted handcuffs dangling from his wrists a clear sign that mortal restraints could no longer hold him. Though his grandsons had backed him into the corner of the room, he remained calm—even smug.

Flint now held one of the pistols; Scooter had the other, along with the divine sword. But the stepbrothers aimed their weapons at each other.

Selene could barely make out their words for the shouting. The two Swiss Guards stood sandwiched against the wall, a single halberd pinning them both like mounted butterflies, its length sheering through one man's shoulder and into the other's. Despite their pained groans, no one paid them any heed.

Theo, who'd removed Hades' helm, looked from one squabbling god to the other with an expression that veered between rage and disgust.

Beneath the clamor, Selene's keen ears caught the thread of whispered words unspooling from Saturn's lips.

"Hephaestus tumbled through the air, thrown off Olympus by wrathful Zeus, and no god reached out to help him. Hermes laughed at his distress—"

Before the words could suck her into the past, Selene thrust the blade of her halberd at her grandfather's mouth, ready to silence him forever. Scooter's warning cry stopped her with the tip an inch from Saturn's teeth.

"Not yet!"

"Why not? Don't you see what he's doing?" With her halberd's blade leveled at his mouth, Saturn snapped his jaws shut. For the first time since she'd known him, he looked afraid, his eyes darting from one grandchild to the next. "His power as the

God of Time is back," Selene shouted at her brothers. "He's making you all remember how much you used to hate each other."

"I don't need to be reminded," Flint growled at Scooter.

"I'm trying to tell you," Scooter insisted angrily. "He could be useful!"

"Useful?" Flint spat. "For what? For trying to murder our family? Twice? Have you forgotten how he swallowed his own children in the beginning of time? And then killed Mars and Hades and Apollo? How he *burned Selene alive*? Saturn needs to die. Use the sword, Scooter. Now."

"No," Zeus croaked, finally emerging from the doorway. He took two slow steps closer to Saturn. "Even if you use the divine sword, if we kill him here, in the mithraeum, he might come back."

At the sight of Zeus, Flint looked only angrier, but Scooter's face broke into a broad, relieved grin. "Pop's right," he offered, sketching his father a quick bow. "The mithraeum's all about rebirth."

"I stole the lion-headed god's keys, Father," Selene insisted. "There's no coming back for any of us anymore."

Some of the old tone of command reentered Zeus's voice. "The worlds are more connected than we know. The Wily One might find a path others forgot."

"So you'd keep him alive?" Selene asked, incredulous. "This man who murdered your children? Who grew stronger from their blood?"

"We keep him alive only for now, daughter." The gentle, frail father she'd talked to only hours before now spoke with a new ferocity, as if her own victory over death had given *him* strength as well.

He said our deaths ripped him apart, she remembered, *so perhaps my resurrection has put him back together.*

"Don't worry," Zeus went on. "Saturn will get his just reward soon enough. But for now, we need him alive."

"If we don't kill him," rumbled Flint, "his followers will chase us across the world to get him back."

"No they won't." Scooter pivoted toward the back wall and fired his pistol. The guards stopped their thrashing, a single bullet driven through both their skulls.

"Hey!" Theo shouted. "What'd you do that for?"

"Flint's right," Scooter said mildly. "They'll come after us."

"You just killed two defenseless men," Theo protested. "Why don't we just tell the other Swiss Guards that their brethren are secret pagans and have them come down and arrest these guys?"

"Because they burned Selene alive," Flint said coldly.

Theo blanched. He looked sick, rather than appeased, but he shut up.

"What about Saturn?" Selene began. But before she could form her argument for killing him, Scooter turned his pistol on the old man, squeezing six shots into his heart. She felt no shock—only relief.

Her father, however, hadn't given up on his plan to keep Saturn alive. He cried out in anger as the Titan fell.

"Relax, Pop!" Scooter said with a laugh. "Grandpa's gotten plenty powerful in the last year, and my guns are no divine weapons. What would kill one of us will only knock him unconscious for a while. He'll wake up good as new. But in the meantime, we won't have to deal with his time travel bullshit on the way out of the mithraeum."

Scooter handed Orion's sword back to Theo and heaved his grandfather's limp body over his shoulder. He started into the hall.

Flint yanked the halberd from the wall; the guards' corpses slid to the floor. Using the bloody shaft as a crutch, he hobbled after Scooter, a scowl deepening the lines on his face. Selene followed. She wasn't happy that Saturn would live, but she had more important priorities at the moment. Like getting Theo and her father out of this hellhole before more syndexioi showed up.

Theo offered his arm to Zeus. He regarded the god's frail form with far less curiosity than she would've expected, as if still numb from his ordeal.

Theo and I have just come back from the dead, she worried. *Flint's lame, Scooter's carrying an unconscious body, and my father's still an old man. There's no way we're getting out of here.*

But Scooter seemed impervious to fear, swinging his gun around like an action hero in one of Theo's movies, and her father sounded surprisingly confident when he said, "Stop here" before a wooden door.

Scooter kicked it open, revealing a small armory. Among the rows of modern guns stood a locked glass case—easily opened by the God of Thieves—containing several divine weapons. Two of them Selene had never thought she'd see again: her own golden bow, stolen when the guards captured her the day before, and Flint's necklace.

Beside the bow lay two finely tooled quivers. One held five gold arrows—not the modern kind that Flint had made her, but slender shafts tipped with leaf-shaped blades and fletched with black feathers from Artemis's sacred hawk. Inside the other quiver were three silver arrows of a similar design, the feathers plucked from a rare white crow. Apollo's divine shafts.

Yet it was Zeus who reached into the case first and withdrew a narrow, two-foot-long bundle of twisted bronze, copper, silver, and gold. His thunderbolt. Forged by the monstrous one-eyed Cyclopes in another age. Saturn must have retrieved it from the site of the battle on Liberty's torch.

In the faded Sky God's hands, the bolt remained plain metal: Zeus was far too faded now to wield its magic. But Selene had seen it imbued with its true power—a brilliant streak of light, capable of incinerating man and god alike. She still bore its scar upon her chest.

She gathered the necklace and her weapons, wondering at

the arrows. Flint peered at them curiously. "I made those in my forge at Lemnos before the Diaspora. I never had a chance to give them to you. I'd thought them lost."

"More like stolen by Grandpa," Scooter said, tapping Saturn's skull with the butt of his gun as it dangled over his shoulder. "Guess we know where I inherited my light fingers."

Selene collected her twin's silver arrows next. Flint grabbed Poseidon's whalebone trident to replace his bloody halberd. True to form, Scooter slid several things into his bag before she even noticed what they were. But even the God of Thieves didn't dare touch the final item: a folded goatskin cloak edged with a hundred feathery gold tassels. From the center of the cloak stared a woman's face. Her mouth contorted in a scream, and dead serpents hung from her head like limp hair. The image was no appliqué or embroidery, Selene knew, but rather the flesh of the Gorgon, Medusa, skinned alive and sewn upon the cloak by a goddess equally skilled with both spear and needle.

"Is that..." Theo began, sounding thunderstruck.

Scooter whistled. "Athena's aegis. Grandpa is good."

No god moved to pick it up. Athena, the Goddess of Wisdom, had never allowed anyone else to touch her famous garment, which served as both cloak and shield, without permission.

Finally Zeus reached for it. His arms sagged beneath its weight, but he managed to drape it across one shoulder. He didn't disappear or grow taller or burst into flames. Whatever supernatural properties the aegis might still possess would never work for a god as diminished as he; for the most part, only a Makarites like Theo could elicit such power from a divine item. Yet beneath the golden tassels, the King of the Gods' skinny bare legs no longer looked quite so pitiful.

As Scooter led the way back out of the armory, Selene ran her fingers over the divine arrows' fletching. *This is what I wanted,* she knew. *To be an army again. Reunited with my family to bring justice to our enemies.* Yet something felt incomplete and out of place. Not just Apollo, whose absence still felt like a gaping wound, but Theo, whose angry stare burned against her back.

Footsteps pounded toward them from around the corner, and Selene had no more time to worry. With fingers devoid of their usual deftness, she fumbled for an arrow—one of Apollo's silver crow-fletched shafts—and nocked it to her bowstring. Three syndexioi stormed forward, guns drawn.

Before Selene could shoot, Scooter had brought down two of them with his pistol. Selene sent her arrow into the third man's stomach.

Black boils swelled upon the guard's neck. His face grew white, his lips blue, and he cried out hoarsely as he clutched at his throat. Red veins burst in his eyeballs, pus leaked from the boils. Only then did he collapse.

Selene whispered her twin's most fearsome epithet. *"Plague-Bringer."* The thunderbolt might not work for her father, but clearly she could still wield Apollo's arrows—even summon traits unseen since before the Diaspora.

She looked down at her own black-fletched shafts, wondering what power they might still hold.

She found out when a door opened behind them; the armored Miles appeared, holding Mars's golden spear. Scooter's first bullet bounced off the solider's breastplate; the second flew just past his ear and shattered the brick wall beyond. Selene raised her bow, willed her hands to steady, and sent a black-fletched arrow slicing down the hallway.

The Miles spun to the side, bringing his spear in front of his face like a shield. The arrow sailed harmlessly past him; she reached for a second one, but before she could aim, her first shaft turned in midair like a heat-seeking missile, reversed course, rose higher—and struck the Miles in the soft flesh of his neck.

No one spoke as the Miles skidded down the wall, blood gurgling from his lips. Selene's gut clenched as she stared at the remaining arrows in her quiver. *No one should have this much power anymore.*

Scooter ripped Mars's spear from the dead man's grip, grinning fiercely. He passed the weapon to Flint. "Your brother would've wanted you to have it." Next he pulled the black-fletched arrow from the other man's neck and tossed it to his sister. Selene caught it more out of instinct than desire.

The lights in the hallway began to flash. A belated alarm wailed. A door slammed open, followed by several others along the length of the corridor. A dozen men streamed forth, some in their Swiss Guard uniforms, others in the costumes of their Mithraic rank. The Heliodromus bore his cat-o'-nine-tails aloft. The others carried guns.

"Protect Father!" Selene shouted.

Instantly obeying, Flint ripped Zeus from Theo's grip and slammed his broad shoulder into a nearby door, bursting through the wood and dragging the old man to safety.

Theo donned his helmet and winked out of sight. Scooter let Saturn's body slip to the ground so he could shoot more freely. His movements were a dance: The Many-Turning One spun in the air, leaping and dodging as the bullets flew thick around him.

Selene shot without bothering to aim. She had never felt weaker, yet the arrows continued to soar with supernatural accuracy. One after the other, the syndexioi fell before the Huntress's grievous shafts.

With her focus on the men with guns, she didn't notice the Heliodromus until he was hard upon her, his thick whip whistling through the air toward her face. Still shaky from her time in the netherworld, she dodged out of the way no faster than a mortal; she couldn't prevent the barbed tips from striking her cheek and drawing blood.

She took a step backward and loosed an arrow—but the Heliodromus flew to the side like a marionette yanked offstage.

She heard Theo's grunt of effort just before his helm rolled off and he materialized on the ground with the Heliodromus captive beneath him. Selene's black-fletched arrow jerked, pivoted ninety degrees, and hurtled toward the Heliodromus's heart. Nothing could stop its flight.

Not even Theo.

Chapter 29

THE UNSEEN

Holy FUCK, Theo cursed in silent agony as he tried to yank himself free of the arrow pinning his arm to the dead Heliodromus. The pain of his movement nearly blinded him; he gave up on stoicism and shouted aloud. His cry reverberated in the sudden silence. The gunshots had stopped, the syndexioi all fallen. Even the blaring alarm had ceased. There was no one left to summon.

Selene dropped to her knees beside him and reached for the arrow's feathers. Black feathers, he saw now. One of her nightmarish, magical, leaf-bladed arrows.

"No, don't—" he began, envisioning her dragging the arrowhead back through his arm. But she merely steadied the shaft with one hand and pulled the dead Heliodromus away with the other. The arrow stayed in Theo's arm, but at least he was free of the corpse.

"I didn't mean to..." she started, her cheeks flushed.

"You've done worse," he said through gritted teeth. In fact, accidentally shooting him was about the least horrible thing she'd done to him all day.

She flinched but didn't bother defending herself. She reached for the bloodstained arrowhead protruding from the bottom of his arm and tried to snap it off, but even she couldn't break solid metal.

Scooter huffed in dismay. "Those arrows are a little *too* good."

"Flint!" Selene called, her voice rising in desperation. "Can you break this?"

The Smith emerged, somehow managing to support Zeus with his shoulder while using Mars's spear and Poseidon's trident as crutches. "I don't have my hammer. I left it back in our apartment."

It was Scooter who strode forward, holding one of Apollo's gruesome silver plague arrows.

"Hey!" Theo backed away.

"Hold still," Scooter demanded. He held the gold shaft in one hand and sliced the head away with the silver blade.

Selene drew the shaft up and out by the fletching so fast that Theo barely had time to shout with pain. She ripped the hem from her already dangerously short T-shirt and bound his arm with expert speed. Theo could only shake his head at her obvious concern. "*Now* you're worried about me."

Scooter had the nerve to laugh. "Let's just be glad that wasn't one of Apollo's plague arrows. You'd be bleeding from more than your arm."

Selene rounded on him, but her father put out a hand to stop her.

"Please," he begged weakly. Between the half-shattered glasses and his spindly bare legs, Zeus looked like an escapee from an especially barbaric nursing home. Nothing like what Theo had expected from the King of the Gods. Then again, he was getting used to disillusionment.

"There's no time to fight each other," Zeus warned. "With all the noise, the other Swiss Guards might finally find this place. We have to hurry."

"The Makarites will use the helmet to take us up," Flint said. "We'll go with him one or two at a time, so we remain invisible."

"Good idea." Scooter holstered his pistols. Neither he nor his stepbrother, Theo noticed, bothered to ask if the Makarites *wanted* to help. As usual.

Scooter hefted Saturn's limp form back onto his shoulder. "We should use the necropolis exit. It'll still be empty this time of night."

I should just leave, Theo thought. *Let them figure out their own escape.* But for all the other Athanatoi's treachery, Zeus had done nothing wrong. After everything the old man had been through, he deserved help.

And so, despite his bleeding arm, throbbing wrist, and vomit-covered bare chest, Theo made two trips back through the tunnel, into the necropolis, then out into Saint Peter's Square with a pair of gods in tow. First Scooter, carrying Saturn's limp body, then Flint and Zeus. Finally, only Selene remained.

She slipped her hand into the crook of Theo's good elbow. She wore a dead syndexios's pants and boots and held out a stolen shirt. "I don't know what happened to your other one."

He started to answer, then thought better of it. How could he explain that he'd wrapped it around his hands so he could pull her still-smoldering body from the pyre? He hadn't had the stomach to put the ash-smeared shirt back on. He accepted the new shirt from her without a word.

As soon as he donned the helm, he couldn't see her anymore. For that, he was grateful. If he had to look at her for another minute, he might break apart. When her charred body had shed its black crust and Selene had emerged, whole and alive, on the mithraeum floor, Theo had never felt so relieved. Or so angry. The two emotions warred within him so fiercely that he felt as if he'd injected himself again: The venom's cold chill pumped through his veins, surging ever closer to his heart, threatening to stop its beating. This time for good.

As they walked awkwardly through the necropolis, the cypress smell of her surrounded him. Her unseen hand tightened on his flesh; it was all too familiar, this sensation of being dragged down by her invisible presence. He'd felt that way for half a year.

They emerged into Saint Peter's Square, where the other Athanatoi stood waiting for them in the shadows of the colonnade, and he felt Selene stop. Her disembodied voice whispered so close to his ear it sounded like his conscience.

"Theo..."

He'd never heard her plead like that. He stopped walking and waited for her to go on. Yet she said nothing more. As usual, she wanted him to do the talking. He had no intention of fulfilling that request.

"Let's go," he said gruffly, pulling her toward the others.

Only once they were hidden by the columns did he remove the helmet. He caught Selene staring at the gold and silver arrows in her quiver, many of them bright with the syndexioi's blood—one broken shaft stained with his own. Narrow red lines striped her cheek from the Heliodromus's cat-o'-nine-tails. She looked haggard, dismayed, exhausted.

Zeus looked even worse, holding his hands out as if to steady himself on a rolling ship. A second later, his face turned the color of clay. His eyes rolled back in his skull. Scooter grabbed him before he could slam into the ground.

Selene rushed to her father's side. "He's still breathing."

A scowl carved a deep trough between her brows. Theo understood—he still remembered every nuance of his lover's expressions. She wasn't angry at her father, just at herself for not protecting him better.

"We need to get him somewhere to recover," she insisted. He could hear the unspoken entreaty in her voice: *And you will come, too, won't you?*

"I'm glad you're both safe," he managed. That much was true. He looked down at the dark helm in his hands. Its cold surface pulled the water from the humid air. The black metal wept.

He wanted to give the helm back to the gods, but to what

end? Faded as they were, they couldn't use it. Selene might be able to command her twin's terrible arrows, but she couldn't wield the helm of Hades, the Unseen One, any more than she could her father's thunderbolt.

Regretfully, he placed the dark helmet back in his bag beside Orion's sword. He would keep both for now, but he didn't intend to ever wield them again. Too many men had already died, victims to the gods' manipulations. He wanted no part of further killing.

"Theo—" Scooter called after him as he walked away.

"Whatever you're going to ask of me," he interrupted, not bothering to turn around, "the answer is no."

Let the gods fight their own battles. I'm done with heroism.

Chapter 30

PANTHEON

I have a new diagnosis for you . . .

Theo imagined some shrink with an Austrian accent, peering excitedly over the rim of his glasses.

First you exhibited all the symptoms of obsessive-compulsive disorder. Then manic depression with suicidal ideations. And now . . . The shrink would nod wisely and stroke the little gray goatee on his chin. *Classic masochism.*

Ah, come on, Doc. It's not that bad . . .

The shrink would gesture to their surroundings with a pensive frown.

Then tell me, Mr. Schultz, why are you sitting in a temple to the Olympians if you just want to forget them all?

Theo stared up at the sky through the round oculus in the domed ceiling, searching for an answer he already knew: In all his many visits to Rome, he'd always made a pilgrimage here.

The Pantheon.

The great Roman temple to all the gods, still intact nearly two thousand years after its construction. Within its enormous, vaulted sanctuary, he'd felt most in touch with the ancient world.

For much of his life, that meant he'd felt most fully himself. It had been a place of peace and meditation to him—the closest thing he knew to a sacred space.

The massive twenty-foot-tall bronze doors remained firmly locked this late at night, but his time with Selene had taught him a thing or two about sneaking in through side entrances.

Only a few small lights illuminated the interior of the temple. In the dimness, he could easily ignore the crucifixes and oil paintings of saints—reminders of the building's current function as a Catholic church—and fall under the spell of the original Roman design. The geometric pattern of green, gold, and red porphyry across the floor. The soaring coffered dome of concrete, a masterpiece of Roman engineering. At the very apex, a large circular opening to the sky: the oculus—the eye. In the daytime, as clouds drifted by against the backdrop of pure blue and the occasional bird swooped through like a messenger from the heavens, he'd always thought it a window onto the gods themselves. Now he knew better.

Theo lay down on the floor directly beneath the opening. The marble cupped him gently, worn concave from centuries of libations poured by the Sky. He stared straight up into the infinite black of space. The stars, he knew, told the stories of Artemis and Zeus—the heroes they blessed, the monsters they created. Yet from inside the temple-turned-church, Theo could see only a smattering of pinpricks, the constellations as broken and hidden as the lives the gods now led.

Is this what I want? he wondered. *To no longer know the gods' stories? To imagine them as lost figments and fractured tales rather than breathing, feeling flesh?*

When he heard the side door creak open, he knew it was no night watchman. He could smell the sudden breath of pine on the summer air. Her appearance didn't surprise him. She was the Huntress; she'd always track him down, no matter how far he ran. Perhaps he'd even come to the Pantheon because he wanted to be found. Because he needed to hear the words from her own lips: *I had a choice to love you—or to break you. I chose the latter.*

He wondered whether he should sit up. Stand, perhaps, so he could look her in the eye. But what was the point?

To his surprise, Selene lay down beside him on the floor, her body a careful foot from his.

She didn't speak at first, and he didn't turn to look at her.

"Saturn is still unconscious, but we've got him under lock and key," she said at last. "And my father's resting back in our apartment."

She said "our" apartment, Theo noted. *Hers and Flint's.*

"I have my father back in my life. Alive and safe. That's because of you."

"Don't thank me," he retorted. "I didn't go there for him." He left the rest unsaid.

They fell back into a tense silence that he steadfastly refused to break. He could hear her breathing, its slight hitch the only sign of her distress.

"I'm not going to apologize," she said finally.

Of course not.

"I was trying to protect you," she continued. "If I'd held on to you that night above the harbor, we would've both died. I let go to save you. I was ready to die for that."

The thought of her in his arms, making that fateful decision, instantly grabbed at his heart. He knew something about dying to save the one you love. He took a deep breath before saying quietly, "I know."

"Then why are you so angry?" she asked. Her voice had sunk to a defensive murmur. He didn't believe for a second that she didn't know the answer to that question, but he couldn't help himself from laying it all out for her anyway.

"Because when the Fates smiled on us both and spared your life, when you washed up on the shores of New Jersey or Staten

Island or wherever it was, you could've come to me and saved me again."

"You *were* saved." From the corner of his eye, he watched Selene prop herself on an elbow to stare at him. "I made sure of that. Scooter kept tabs on you for me. I wouldn't have let anything happen to you."

At that, Theo sat up. She did the same, looking at him with an expression more indignant than apologetic.

"Except I died, Selene! And I don't even mean today, for God's sake, although *that too*. I mean when I woke up in a hospital bed after crash-landing in Lower Manhattan and I remembered I'd never see you again and I couldn't save you—I died. I couldn't feel anything except pain. For months. I didn't care about my friends, my students, nothing."

"That's not true, the arrow—" She broke off, looking suddenly ill.

"*What* arrow?"

"Nothing."

He stared at her until she relented. He'd learned that technique from her.

"I asked Philippe to make sure you didn't suffer too much, that's all," she muttered.

"You told the God of Love to shoot me with one of his damn darts?"

"It worked!" she insisted. "I watched you look at Ruth and you seemed better. I thought you'd learn to love her and forget about me."

"You watched." He wanted to scream, but the words came out as cold and hard as anything Selene had ever said. "You had to have your way with my emotions even then."

"I was trying—"

"You thought I'd love Ruth." He couldn't let her speak. He needed to release his own words first. "I *wish*. She's everything

I thought I ever wanted in a partner. Kind. Brilliant. Generous. Thoughtful. *Loyal*." He spoke the words like accusations, and he knew that to Selene, they would be. "But if you thought a god's powers would make me forget about you, then you were wrong. I didn't find any pleasure in life until I decided I could bring you back. That's what's kept me going these last months. Not Ruth. *You*."

"Theo," she began, her face suddenly full of pleading. He knew she understood what she'd done, but he wanted to press home the point. To wound her with an arrow as unerring and terrible as her own.

"I learned my lesson from Orpheus and Eurydice: True love requires trust. By coming back to life, I think you finally accomplished what you never could've by dying. If you could sit there and watch me grieve, knowing it was in your power to save me, and decide to walk away, then you no longer deserve my love." He got to his feet, feeling incredibly weary. "I don't need a love dart this time to help me get over you, Selene. You're doing a damn fine job all on your own."

Before he turned away, he caught a glimpse of her stricken face. For all his brave words, he still felt the pull of her grief. But this time, he obeyed the pull of his own instead.

Chapter 31

LEADER OF THE FATES

An old man stood in the shadows of one of the Pantheon's wall niches, a pitiful simulacrum of the statues that once paid him homage.

Theo wanted to just keep walking. Leave the temple and all its gods behind. Yet something about Zeus's faded majesty compelled him to pause. He felt, somehow, that he owed at least that much to his former self, the one who'd dreamed of coming face-to-face with the deities he'd read about his entire life. The eager classicist who gave a shit what the King of the Gods might do or say.

Zeus walked slowly forward. In a Flint-sized trench coat, he looked even smaller than he had wrapped in his blanket from the mithraeum. He still smelled faintly of urine, and his half-shattered glasses made him seem cyclopean, blinking at the world through one enormous, visible eye.

He held out a hand. His fingers, despite the swollen knuckles, remained half again as long as a normal man's—the sort of hand that once needed a lightning bolt to look complete. Theo took it warily.

Selene got to her feet. "Father, what are you doing out of bed? You should be resting."

"I asked the Messenger to bring me here," he replied. "I needed to speak to Theodore." Still holding Theo's hand, he walked slowly to the center of the room and cricked his skinny neck awkwardly to look up through the oculus. He stood that way for a long time before he finally spoke. "You see stars up there. I see my half-mortal children—the heroes who once walked the earth." He squinted nearsightedly at Theo. "You are not my child. Yet you are as much a Makarites as Hercules or Perseus."

"Not anymore."

Zeus made a sound between a chuckle and a cough. "It's not something you can turn off."

"Well, I can damn well ignore it."

"For my sake, I'm glad you haven't." Zeus smiled like a doting grandfather reveling in his grandson's report card. "It takes a Makarites to wield my brother Hades' helmet. I hear you earned the title of 'Blessed One' through study. Now you earn it over and over through heroism."

Pin a gold star on my chest and let me get the hell out of here. "I've already booked a flight back to New York. It leaves tomorrow morning, and I plan to be on it. Blessed One or not, I'm going home."

"I have one more favor to ask of you."

He needs me to find a Golden Fleece or battle a Minotaur or cut off my own balls, Theo thought. He wanted to protest that he'd done the gods enough favors for his one mortal lifetime, but he waited, curious.

"Saturn must be punished for what he did to my family."

Theo felt mildly queasy. "Look, I know my opinion here doesn't matter, and I certainly want to make sure he can't hurt anyone again, but I'm not exactly pro–death penalty. Selene said you've got him locked up, and he's still passed out. If you're asking me to use Orion's sword to execute him while he's unconscious—"

"No, no." Zeus looked flustered. "He's spent centuries with his resurrection cult. Who's to say there aren't more syndexioi somewhere else who would find a way to bring back their Pater? No, there's only one way to control my father. One prison that only *we* have the keys to." He clasped his gnarled hands together like a man in prayer and stared at Theo intently. "Tartarus."

Theo couldn't stop himself from gaping. He wondered if Zeus's mind had grown as feeble as his body. "You mean the mythological pit where you cast your father the last time you deposed him? That Tartarus? The one full of the terrifying monsters you conquered in the Gigantomachy?"

Zeus nodded, the slight tremor in his chin making a mockery of his grave expression.

"But, Father," Selene interjected. "Surely Tartarus doesn't exist anymore. If it ever did."

"Of course it existed."

"But so much of our past is just tales the poets told," she pressed. "If Tartarus is one of those—"

"Has your mind grown so narrow?" he said sharply, spit flecking his lips.

"Has yours grown so confused?" she shot back.

Zeus thrust out his skinny chest in a pathetic attempt at pride. He pushed back the lapels of his trench coat to display the golden tassels of Athena's aegis. "Do Gorgons walk the streets of Rome today? No! And yet Medusa's face screams from this cloak. You deny that?"

"No," Selene admitted stiffly.

"The arrows from the armory—they defy this world's laws."

"Yes."

"Then don't talk back to me." He sounded like a senile old man, snarling at his well-meaning nurse. Yet the force of his own convictions gave his wheezing voice a new resonance. "We can open a portal to Tartarus. We can cast Saturn through."

"Uh…" Theo had to ask. "Who's 'we'?"

"Men still worship wine and thievery and the ways of the flesh—many of my children will stay strong for decades, centuries even. But the Sky?" Zeus looked up through the oculus once more, a grim smile on his face. "Mankind does not worship it, doesn't even notice it. All those stars, planets, the immensity of the universe. It might as well be"—he paused, as if searching for a vile enough description—*"wallpaper."* He sniffed, a sound more of illness than scorn.

"As for my other domains—fate, kingship—no one believes in them anymore." He looked down at his own shaking hands, the constant reminder of how old he'd grown through man's disdain. "For such a mighty task, we'll need all the gods, strong and weak alike. Only a united pantheon can finally defeat the Titan who has always been a cancer, eating away at what little worship remains." He linked his fingers together as if to stop their trembling. "With him out of the world, we may regain what we have lost."

"You're saying Saturn's death will bring us strength." Selene took a step back. Theo couldn't tell whether she felt disgust at her father's ideas or at his wretchedness. "No. We can't sacrifice him for that. That's what *he* tried to do to us. To use our deaths to become invincible. I won't become that, Father. None of us should."

"Have you listened?" he demanded, his voice cracking. "We do not *sacrifice* Saturn—we just open the door to Tartarus and cast him in." He flung an arm forward weakly, a parody of a hurled thunderbolt. "And we do it together, our strength combined as one. Tartarus is a place of old powers and older magic. A place full of monsters and gods. When we open it once more, some of that magic will seep out—a divine wind, a whisper of *pneuma*. We will be there to breathe it in, and it will bring strength to us all." He raised a gnarled hand to stop Selene's protests before they could begin. "We won't be invincible or omnipotent—such power is impossible in this world—but we will not be so old, nor so weak. Look at me! I have dreamed my own death, child." His voice slipped from demanding to pleading. "Even without Saturn's sickle to cut me asunder, I am not long for this world. Six months, perhaps. A year. Two at most. And every day I grow weaker."

Selene's face crumpled. Her mouth worked in wordless protest as her father went on. "If I do nothing, I will slip away into eternal sleep, just as your mother did. But if we go to Olympus..." A racking cough cut short his words. Selene stepped forward, her eyes bright with unshed tears.

Zeus held his hands out to his daughter. "Do not deny me this chance, however slim it may seem."

"But it makes no sense," she said gently. "How would you even open Tartarus in the first place?"

"With a Great Gathering on Mount Olympus, where we were always strongest." He turned to Theo. "You must be there, Makarites, to bear witness to this conclave. Well you know that our stories don't survive unless there are poets to tell them. You may not be able to share the tale with the world, but it will live on in your mind—your very presence will give the Gathering power. That is the favor I would ask."

"That sounds..." Theo wasn't sure what to say. Moments before, he'd decided he wanted nothing to do with any of them. But perhaps Zeus still retained some power as the Leader of the Fates, because Theo suddenly realized that he'd decided to go as soon as the words "Great Gathering" crossed the old man's lips. "It sounds like something I should see."

"Theo, it's insane to—" Selene began.

"Any more insane than thinking I could kill myself, stroll into the afterlife, take you by the hand, and stroll back out?" he retorted. "Honestly, my bar for crazy has gotten pretty damn high."

Selene's expression of dismay was barely perceptible; Theo noticed it anyway.

Zeus clapped his hands, as if it was all settled. "Good. There's a flight at noon tomorrow to Athens." He no longer sounded senile. "Theodore will take it. I will stay here one more day, gathering the other Athanatoi."

"Wait," Selene began. "We should think about this first."

"No. We must act quickly—the Wily One cannot be held for long." He threw back his stooped shoulders. "In two days' time, we will stand together: Artemis and Hephaestus, Dionysus and Hermes, Aphrodite, Poseidon, Hera, Demeter, and Hestia."

"Um. Didn't you miss one?" Theo asked.

"Mars is dead," Zeus said solemnly.

"But what about Athena?" When he was a child, the gray-eyed Goddess of Wisdom had always been his favorite deity. She was not only the patron of scholars but also a goddess of crafts, creativity, and justified war. To Theo, she embodied the best of human civilization.

Zeus's posture deflated. "That daughter is lost to me."

"I've heard that before," Theo interjected. "But it seems like someone always knows where the Athanatoi are hiding."

"Not Athena," Zeus insisted. "She was always the smartest of my children. Even Hermes, Messenger of the Gods, cannot find her. If she wants to stay hidden, she will."

"But you said the whole pantheon had to be there to open Tartarus," Selene said, her brow furrowed. "Will it work without her?"

"We will have to hope so." Zeus cleared his throat wetly. "Now, we have much to do. Much to plan."

"What can I do?" Selene asked. "I still don't see how it will work, but I'll do whatever I can. Let me help."

"No, no." Zeus patted her on the shoulder like a master reassuring his dog. "You saw what happened in the mithraeum. You came all that way and got yourself killed, my reckless child. We must both rest. Recover from our ordeal. We need to be strong for Olympus."

He turned away and shuffled slowly out of the temple. Selene stood like a statue. Zeus had not offered his daughter a single word of thanks or praise for coming to rescue him. Theo had never seen her so casually dismissed by anyone. He thought that she would shout something biting at her father's back. Or that her face would turn to stone as she closed her heart to him. Instead, she blinked back tears. Her shoulders slumped. The fierce Huntress seemed little more than a chastened child.

Theo felt an overwhelming desire to go to her, an electric pulse that spurred his feet to move and his arms to open wide, to assure her that her father didn't know what he was talking about.

He swallowed back the words. Selene would be just fine without his comfort—and it was about time he was fine without hers.

I will see her on Olympus, he resolved, bending down to gather his satchel and purposely avoiding her gaze.

Then I will never see her again.

Chapter 32

LADY OF THE TIBER

Selene ran.

She ran from the Pantheon. From her father's decline and Theo's disgust.

And eventually, as the sun cast its first piercing beams across the city streets, she found herself drawn once more to the River Tiber to heal the wounds to both body and soul.

The Host in Rome would never threaten her again, and with Saturn gone, any other secret branches of the cult would collapse. But death still stalked her father, and she couldn't quite believe his Tartarus plan would work. As for Theo... *It's not the lack of his love that hurts,* she told herself. *I wanted him to find happiness with another woman—I truly did, for his sake. It's the loss of his respect that feels like a javelin's point drilled through my heart.* With no passersby in sight, she sprinted onto the arcing bridge and stopped in the center, panting. *I've stopped talking to him, even in my own mind,* she realized. *Why bother, when now I know he doesn't want to listen?*

She climbed over the stone railing. And jumped off.

She floated there for a moment beneath the river's surface, her head suspended in sun-warmed water, her feet dangling in the murky cold. Her heart pounded with the memory of her near-drowning in the Lake of Mnemosyne, but she forced herself to stay submerged for another few seconds, letting the power of the fresh running water dispel her weariness and heal her battered body. With the familiar invocation to the Tiber's rushing flow, she felt the whip slashes on her cheek knit closed. A warm surge of power flooded her limbs, returning the strength that Death had stripped from her.

She kicked her way to the surface and, bracing her hands on the ledge, hauled herself from the river. She sat on the lip, her feet dangling, water dripping from her hair and clothes to puddle around her.

The flowing water had fixed her body. Her heart still felt broken.

She'd run from the Pantheon, but she didn't want to go back to her apartment either. How could she bear to face Flint's pleasure when he realized she'd failed so utterly with Theo? Or Scooter's grief when she told him their father was still in danger?

I want to go somewhere dark. Quiet. Deep in a forest, where there are no people to protect—or disappoint. Perhaps it's time to change my name again. I wouldn't even tell Scooter or Flint. I could just disappear.

But her father needed her to join the rest of the pantheon in his crazy quest, and she hadn't freed him from the Host only to abandon him now. She hung her head and stared down at her hands. Such long fingers, their strength renewed by the Tiber's waters. *It will be many years yet before I fade away completely. And as long as I'm here on this earth, I have work to do.*

There's only one problem—I'm not sure what that work is anymore.

She closed her eyes and tuned her ears to the sounds of the just-waking city. Somewhere, she was sure, a woman begged for help. A child needed protection. A dog howled in pain. The Protector of the Innocent would hear their cries.

She sat there for a very long time. If the people of Rome called out for her aid, she couldn't hear them.

Eventually, the sun set fire to Saint Peter's gilded dome and dried the river water from her clothes. Traffic hummed along the streets; pedestrians crowded the bridge above her. Still, Selene didn't move.

A steady flow of tears tracked silently down her cheeks. She leaned her elbows on her knees, her head bent above the river. The drops ran off her nose, disappearing from view before they joined the Tiber's languid flow.

I miss New York, she finally admitted to herself. *I miss my dog. I miss my river. I miss my island.*

I miss Theo.

It took her another several minutes before she found the strength to return to the apartment where her family waited. Despite her newly strong legs, the five flights up had never felt so long.

To her relief, Scooter wasn't there. She wasn't sure she could bear to see him without losing her composure; he loved their father as much as she did. And he'd been the one to urge her to seek Theo out in the Pantheon in the first place.

"I'll take care of Pop," he'd said when they'd finished settling Zeus after returning from Saint Peter's. "Go find your thanatos."

"Why in the world would I drag him back into something he clearly wants to be done with?" she'd demanded.

Scooter laughed. "You really think he wants to be done with you?"

"That's exactly what I think."

"Then you're a fool, sister mine. He loves you. He gave his life for you more than once. He might be pissed, but trust me, he's willing to be convinced. Just shake your pretty hips and—"

Selene shot out a hand to grab Scooter by the jaw, gripping tight. "You forget who you're talking to."

Her brother wrenched away. "Ouranos's balls, Selene, you're a pain in the ass. I just mean that he may be a Makarites, but he's only human. He can be persuaded."

"Even if that was true—which it's probably not—why would I try?"

Scooter rolled his eyes. "Because you *love* him."

"I..."

Her brother had looked over his shoulder toward the living room and lowered his voice. "You've lived with Flint for how long now? Six months. And in all that time, did you ever feel for him what you felt for Theo?"

"It's not—"

"Yeah, that's what I thought. Flint may be damaged goods, but he's got the shoulders of a god, he can't keep his eyes off you, and I've heard he's got a certain hairy appeal. Yet you haven't fallen for him. In fact, if I remember rightly, you've fallen for two, and *only* two, men in your entire overlong life. Orion the Hunter and Theo the Nerd. One of them's dead, and one of them's waiting for you to come get him right now."

She laughed now at the memory; she'd been a fool to believe Scooter. Her bitter humor quickly stuttered into a choked sob as she pinwheeled from self-loathing to grief. *This emotional fragility is probably just another effect of my journey through the Underworld,* she decided. *That's what's wrong with me.* She felt new and raw, her emotions bubbling too close to the surface for comfort.

Despite the early hour, Flint was awake, sitting at the dining table in the center of their small living room. For once, he didn't have a pile of gears and wires in front of him. Nor did she see Mars's spear. Flint had never condoned his brother's bloody ways; no doubt he'd stowed the divine weapon somewhere where it couldn't be used to hurt anyone. He looked tense, as if the whole time she'd been sitting beside the river, he'd been here waiting. His eyes went first to her bare neck—she hadn't put back on his necklace. Hurt flashed across his face, but she didn't have the will to explain. What would she say? *It feels wrong to wear your gift with Theo back in my world?* Why should that matter when Theo wanted absolutely nothing to do with her?

"Schultz isn't coming back," she said instead, "in case you're wondering."

Flint's shoulders lowered; his face relaxed. She could've sworn he hid a smile beneath his beard. His obvious pleasure made her angry. But angry was better than despondent.

"Did Scooter get back from the Pantheon with Father yet?" she asked.

"Yeah. Then he went out again. Your dad's taking a shower, and Saturn's still locked up and unconscious."

"Fine." She considered telling Flint about Zeus's Tartarus plan, but she knew the Smith would want nothing to do with it. Saving her father from brutal murder to prevent Saturn's rise was one thing—saving Zeus from the inevitable decline they all faced was another. Eventually, she'd have to convince Flint to come so they could complete the pantheon, but she couldn't quite summon the strength for that argument yet.

"Oh, and Father just brushed me off like a useless puppy," she said instead. "So in case you're keeping score, two more men I care about are leaving my life. More room for you. So congratulations."

Flint's lips tightened. He didn't shout back at her or tell her she was being unfair. He didn't need to. But a hint of red colored his cheeks, and his massive hands tightened on the edge of the table before he pushed himself upright. He wasn't wearing his leg braces, and he had to hold on to the furniture to support his body. His withered legs buckled and twisted as he hobbled toward his bedroom.

I'm punishing him, and myself, for the pain I've caused, she knew. *Theo doesn't think I deserve to be happy—I'm making sure he's right by pushing Flint away.* She could reach out to him instead, seek solace in his strong arms and unquestioning devotion. But that felt like one more betrayal to add to her list of sins. Instead, she simply crossed her arms on the tabletop and buried her face in her elbows.

Exhaustion overtook her. *Maybe Father was right. I need to regain my strength before Olympus.* She couldn't fathom the idea of climbing a mountain anytime soon. Zeus had said he had months, maybe years, before the fading overtook him. *I should try to convince him to wait a bit and think this through,* she mused wearily. His plan to rush off to Olympus and break open a mythical pit that might not even exist seemed half-baked at best. *If I think he's being reckless, then he's really in trouble.*

She didn't realize she'd fallen asleep until a loud crash ripped her from her nightmares. She rushed toward the bathroom as Flint charged out of the other room in his leg braces.

Zeus lay naked beside the bathtub in a steadily growing pool of blood, the red brilliant against the white tile. One leg lay awkwardly over the tub's lip, the papery skin of his calf torn open on the sharp rail of the glass door. He wasn't unconscious, not yet. His eyelids fluttered, and his mouth worked wordlessly. His entire body seized and jerked, sending splatters of blood across Selene's face as she bent over him.

"Help me," she gasped to Flint, grabbing a nearby pillowcase and making a quick tourniquet on Zeus's leg. Flint pressed another piece of linen against the wound. She held her father's head in both hands so he would stop knocking his skull against the floor.

"It's okay," she said uselessly. "You just overdid it by going to the Pantheon. You're going to be fine. Calm down, calm down, Father," she begged. But she knew the spasms weren't under his control. His chest heaved; water droplets ran down the stark tracks of his ribs to pool in his hollow stomach. She couldn't avoid the sight of his penis—a limp, curled worm, nearly hidden by a nest of gray hair. Proud Zeus, lover of a seemingly infinite array of gods and mortals, now unable even to care for himself. She grabbed the bloodied bath mat and laid it gently over his lap.

Flint fetched a first aid kit from the medicine cabinet. In a matter of seconds, he'd bandaged the wound; Zeus wouldn't die from blood loss. Yet the seizures didn't stop.

"Please, Father," Selene whispered, over and over, until finally, after what felt like an hour, his body stilled and his eyes stayed closed. She could hear his heartbeat from where she sat, but she pressed her ear against his chest anyway, wanting the closeness. "It's erratic," she said. "And very faint."

Flint helped her hoist him into the bed. She dried him as best she could, then tucked an extra coverlet around his frail form. Another image flared to mind: her mother in a hospital bed, an old woman swaddled in a thin blanket like an infant. For all the pain of her mother's passing, at least Selene hadn't faced it alone: She had her twin beside her.

What would Apollo do now for our father? she wondered desperately. But then she remembered how he'd comforted her when she found him beside the Lake of Mnemosyne—with melody. Selene had never been much of a singer, even in her days as an immortal. The careful constraints of melody and pitch had been her civilized brother's domain; she preferred the wild abandon of the dance. But now she reached back for a nearly forgotten hymn and sang.

"*I will sing of Zeus, chiefest among the gods and greatest. All-seeing, the lord of all, the fulfiller who whispers words of wisdom*— Help!" she begged Flint. "Sing with me."

The Smith tried, adding his own tuneless, rough voice to hers. Finally, Zeus's eyes crept open. He stared blankly at the ceiling above him.

She kissed his scarred cheek. "I thought you were gone," she murmured hoarsely.

He clutched tight at her hand. "I will be," he said, his voice barely audible.

"Stop it. Don't say that."

"I tried…" His face twisted with effort. "I tried to tell you. What little strength I have comes in fits and starts, but I'm dying, daughter. I thought I'd have at least six months, but I was wrong. I dreamed again of my fate—my death comes swiftly. Two days.

Mount Olympus…Tartarus…It's the only way. The only cure that can defeat death." He slipped once more into unconsciousness.

"Seek the Wise Virgin," Selene whispered. She chafed her father's hands, willing him to wake up, to come back to her. "Not in Athens is her seat, but where the Virgin is tall. There the cure is the spear that can conquer the greatest foe."

"What are you talking about?" Flint asked.

"It's the prophecy." She explained quickly how she and her twin had emerged into classical Delphi in their journey from the Underworld. Flint listened, wide-eyed. "I'd asked how to save an Athanatos from death," she added. "I thought the oracle was just telling me how to get home, but maybe it actually explained how to save Father. The Wise Virgin holds a cure to conquer the greatest foe—death itself."

"So then what was your father saying about Tartarus?"

She related Zeus's plan to open the ancient prison, throw Saturn in, and let the divine *pneuma* escape to strengthen them all.

Flint grunted. "I thought we knew only sacrifice could return a god's lost strength."

"I know, but my father is the King of the Gods. He may know something we don't. I thought we had more time, but obviously I was wrong. We have to try to save him."

"But if he's right about the *pneuma* from Tartarus, why do you need some wise virgin's cure?"

"I don't know! But Apollo told me that when death comes for those I love, I should remember his prophecy. He spoke as the Pythian God, and it was one of the last things he said to me—I can't ignore the warning. But I didn't understand Apollo's prophecy then, and I understand it even less now. Who holds the cure? The Wise Virgin—I assumed the Pythia was talking about me." She shook her head. "But no," she answered herself. "I'm not a virgin anymore."

She saw Flint tense, but she didn't care anymore who knew her secret.

"The *wise* virgin." He growled. "That doesn't sound like you either." He shifted away, as if he couldn't stand to be close to her. "The oracle must've meant Athena."

Selene flinched, surprised that his words could hurt. He was right; wisdom had never been one of her attributes. And yet she couldn't help feeling he'd just called her stupid. Anger—more at herself than at him—flattened her lips. *Since when do I let a man's opinion of me matter?*

Before she could form a retort to Flint's insult, Zeus moaned in his sleep and began to shake. All Selene's ministrations could not soothe him. His heart continued to beat unevenly and too slow. No singing or prayers seemed to help. Flint stayed in the room, but he had no words of comfort or advice.

"Maybe you should just leave," she snapped at him finally, frustrated by his looming presence.

"I don't want to leave."

"Then *do* something."

His jaw twitched. "Tell me how to help and I will." He sounded like a man compelled by forces outside his control. But he didn't leave. Even now, when he knew she'd shared her body with Theo, he stayed beside her, bearing the blows of her anger like a caged bear with a broken spirit. *And I'm the cruel mistress with a whip,* Selene thought with a stab of guilt. She felt tears prick at the back of her eyes and took a deep breath to center herself. Flint must have seen the shame on her face because he didn't ask her to apologize. He simply reached for a glass of water on Zeus's bedside table and passed it to her.

"Drink," he ordered. "Your body is still recovering."

She obeyed, then found the strength to say calmly, "If Athena is the only one who can help, then we need to find her."

She watched his nostrils flare above his pinched lips. *Just like Theo, he wants this to be over with. But unlike Theo, he isn't walking away.*

"The problem is," she continued, "that she's been in hiding

for thousands of years and doesn't want to be found. I warned my father that we might need her to make the ceremony on Mount Olympus effective—that must be what the oracle meant. She's the only one who can cure Father. We have the clues to find her. Her seat is where she's *tall*. What does that mean?"

"For Athena, I would've thought that meant the place with her colossal statue—atop the Acropolis in Athens."

"Except the Pythia said specifically, '*Not* in Athens is her seat.'"

Flint grunted, clearly frustrated. "Then I have no idea."

"What about all your fancy technology?"

"She's the Goddess of Wisdom. If she wants to stay hidden, there's no way she's got a damn Twitter presence."

Selene dropped her head in her hands. "You're right. If it was that easy, Scooter would've found her a long time ago."

"And even if you could find her," Flint said defensively. "You wouldn't convince her to come. You remember Athena never liked you, or me, or any of the other Athanatoi—especially your father. She won't listen to us."

Flint was right. As a virgin like Artemis, Athena had nothing but disdain for the male gods of the pantheon. Her relationship with their father, Zeus, had been strained to say the least. And she was equally competitive with most of the goddesses. It was the battle of egos between Hera, Aphrodite, and Athena that had started the Trojan War. But there was one group to whom Athena had always shown favor: men like Odysseus and Perseus. The great Greek heroes who relied on the Gray-Eyed Goddess to help them in their epic quests, to lend them her cunning, her strength of arms, her indomitable will. All those men had shared the same title: Makarites. Blessed One.

Selene groaned aloud. *Theo doesn't want to help,* she knew. *And I certainly don't want to ask him.*

But it looks like neither of us has a choice.

Chapter 33

PARTHENONA SOPHEN

It wasn't hard to find Theo in the Rome airport. Selene went straight to the bookshop closest to the gate for his Athens flight. He wasn't in the history section—she suspected he was tired of dwelling on the past. Instead, she found him tucked in the corner beside the single shelf dedicated to English-language science fiction novels.

She stood silently for a moment, watching him read. His glasses slipped down his nose; he pushed them back up. She'd seen that gesture a hundred times. Never before had it made her want to cry.

This is a terrible idea, she thought, taking a wary step back. *I should never have come.* But she thought of her father, so close to death, and cleared her throat. "Looking for a little escapism?"

Theo jumped.

"Christ, Selene! You scared the crap out of me." He slammed his book closed, wincing at the movement. *The arrow wound in his arm,* she remembered guiltily. *That's not going to help my case.*

"What the hell are you doing here?" he demanded. Then his anger swiftly dissolved into desperate misery. "Please don't tell me you're on my flight."

"No," she said, pretending his expression hadn't felt like a stab from Mars's spear. "I'm not meeting Scooter at the base of Olympus for another two days. No point in getting there earlier—it'll take him that long to help Father assemble the other gods. So I'm not going to Athens yet. It's the only place I know I don't need to search."

He glared at her suspiciously. "Search for what?"

"More like for whom." She didn't elaborate. This was a bear better lured with bait than trapped with force.

She watched the conflict play out over Theo's face. Finally, he shoved his book back onto the shelf and crossed his arms. "All right. For *whom*?"

"The Gray-Eyed Goddess."

"I thought Athena couldn't be found."

"Has that ever stopped us before?" she asked calmly.

"*Us?* You're kidding, right? Why would I possibly help you?"

"Because my father's life hangs in the balance." She described Zeus's worsening health. When she'd left the apartment that morning, his heart had slowed even further, and his skin was icy cold.

"I'm sorry about your dad," he said, and from the softening of his gaze, she knew he spoke the truth. "I'm trying to help—I'm going to Olympus so a mortal can witness the Gathering, remember? But I don't see how Athena can do more than the rest of us."

"I *know* she can. Because the Delphic Oracle told me so."

"What? When?"

"After we defeated Aion and the Torchbearers, Apollo and I passed through classical Delphi."

Theo's eyes grew huge. "You *time traveled* to classical Delphi and you didn't tell me?" He threw up his hands. "Didn't anyone ever tell you not to bury the lede, Selene?"

"I thought you didn't want to talk to me," she said a bit sullenly.

"I didn't. But..." He groaned loudly, his customary loquacity finally surrendering to wordless frustration.

"Come on, Theo," Selene urged. "Help me find Athena. Don't you want to meet her? I thought she was your favorite goddess."

"I've learned that even favorite goddesses can disappoint you," he snapped.

I deserved that, Selene knew, biting back a retort. "At least help me figure out where to look. The Pythia said, 'Seek the Wise Virgin. Not in Athens is her seat, but where the Virgin is tall. There the cure is the spear that can conquer the greatest foe.' But if she's not in Athens, then where? Where else would Athena be tall?"

Theo's lips pressed together, and she could sense his resistance. He still didn't want to get dragged back into her problems. But some combination of his sympathy for Zeus and his usual insatiable curiosity got the better of him. "You received the prophecy in Delphi, so it was in Ancient Greek, right, not English? Tell me the Greek version."

"Um..." She took a second to retranslate. *"Zetete ten Parthenona Sophen. Ou de en Athenais to hedos, alla Hagne pou eukteanos, ekei to akos to akontion hoi ho megistos enantios nikethesetai."*

"To akos to akontion," Theo mused. "The cure is the spear."

"Yes. When we find the Virgin, her cure will be the spear we use to conquer death—the greatest foe."

"So you're taking 'spear' and 'foe' metaphorically."

"Of course. The Delphic oracle should never be taken literally—you know that."

Theo raised a skeptical brow. "More like you should never trust your first interpretation. Apollo spoke the prophecy in ancient Delphi, after all his immortality had been restored—why would *death* be his greatest foe? The Olympians' traditional enemy wasn't dying; it was the giants."

"The ones we locked away in Tartarus after the Gigantomachy." Selene sucked in a breath as she imagined what could happen on the summit of Olympus when the gods gathered to reopen the ancient prison.

Theo echoed her thought. "I've been standing here for the last hour, waiting for my plane, trying to distract myself from what we're about to do in Greece. Because the more I think about opening Tartarus, the more I think Zeus might not have thought carefully enough about what comes out."

"Father thinks a whisper of *pneuma* will escape from the chasm, but along with it—"

"Comes a whole army of hundred-armed giants." He looked grim. "I think your prophecy is telling us *all* how to survive. Athena was called the Giant Killer. That's why we need her. And her spear, too. Because there's not much point if the *pneuma* comes whooshing out and Zeus is miraculously healed, but then we all die at the hands of your ancient enemies anyway."

"True. But whether the spear is metaphorical or literal— whether she defends us with her weapon or heals Father with a cure—we still need to find her hiding place. Think."

Theo raised a brow at her impatience. "I'm working on it." He rubbed the dimple on his chin. "The *Parthenona* in the prophecy definitely refers to the virgin Athena—that much we agree on. She's the one with the Parthenon and the spear, after all. But I'm not so sure about *'alla Hagne pou eukteanos.'* You translated that as 'where the *Virgin* is tall.'"

"Because that's what it means," Selene said quickly, annoyed that he might accuse her of messing up her mother tongue.

"Sort of. But *Hagne* is more like 'Chaste One.' Pure, holy, inviolable. Any woman who hasn't had sex—even just a *young* woman—can be a *parthenona*. Only one actively resisting sex is a *hagne*. That's why *Hagne* is more commonly used as an epithet for—"

"Me," Selene finished for him. She could almost see the scene playing across his memory—all those nights he spent in her bed, abiding by her strict rules, until she finally tossed them away one frozen, moonlit night by the banks of the Hudson. Before the thought could derail him—or her—she pushed on. "So Athena can be found where the Chaste One—*Artemis*—is tall? Where the hell would that be?"

"*Eukteanos* . . . Tall like a tree," Theo began, his eyes roaming the shelves of the bookstore. "Something tells me I'm not going to find an Ancient Greek lexicon hiding amid the Italian paperback thrillers, but I want to look up the definition. I feel like Aeschylus uses the same word to mean—"

"Wealthy," Selene interrupted with a groan. "*Styx*. Not 'where Artemis is tall,' but 'where Artemis is *wealthy*.' When we were in Delphi, I wasn't thinking about dual translations," she admitted. "It felt perfectly natural to me to just assume I understood the prophecy in English, too. But Ancient Greek is full of words with multiple meanings."

The corner of Theo's mouth quirked. "Like I said, never assume you understand the Delphic oracle."

"True," she agreed. "Like when King Croesus asked whether to invade—" She stopped in mid-thought. "King Croesus," she repeated slowly.

Theo's eyes lit up. "You mean 'rich as Croesus'? That King Croesus?"

She nodded, finally slotting the pieces together. "The legendarily *wealthy* king who built one of the biggest temples in the history of the world to honor the Chaste One."

"The Temple of Artemis at Ephesus in Turkey." Theo's broad grin brought out the dimples on both cheeks and sent Selene's heart skittering. She never thought he'd smile at her again. "You weren't wrong, Selene. The prophecy just holds multiple meanings at once. The Wise Virgin's seat is the place where the Chaste One is *wealthy*—"

"And *also* where Athena is *tall*—"

"Because *that's* where your sister is living today."

They stared at each other for a long moment, the thrill of discovery coursing between them like an electric current.

"Aegean Air flight fifty-four to Athens, now boarding through gate fifteen."

Theo started visibly. He glanced down at his watch, then at Selene, then back at his watch.

Selene looked at the departure board. For once, she felt as if the Fates were on her side. "There's a flight in forty-five minutes to Izmir, Turkey. That's the closest city to ancient Ephesus. We have a day to find her and a day to get back. I'm going. Now."

"Athens passengers, please have your boarding passes and passports out."

Theo pulled out his boarding pass and stared at it for a moment before he blew out a loud breath. "I'm going to come with you, aren't I? I'm going to help you find Athena and convince her to come to Olympus."

Selene just smiled.

Theo crumpled the boarding pass in his fist. "But that doesn't mean we're partners in any other sense, okay? If we need a hotel, you get your own room, and we don't talk about *us*. I'm coming as a scholar—is that clear?"

Her smile drained away, but she nodded. She'd never begged a lover, a worshiper, or any other man to want her.

She wasn't about to start now.

Chapter 34

INTERMISSIO: THE TETRACTYS

A cacophony. A discordant clamor to shatter the ears.

At least that's how it must have sounded to the others in the mithraeum below the Vatican.

But shortly before the hidden temple descended into bloody carnage, the long months of tailing Theo Schultz had finally paid off: The Tetractys had reunited with the Father he'd lost months before. And despite everything that had happened since, despite the killings and the terror and his own frenzied escape, he finally heard the melody line above the chaos. Sharp and clear, ringing through his mind like a trumpet call the moment he'd looked upon the Father's face.

A face more ravaged than he remembered, battle-scarred and aged, but imbued with great power nonetheless. *Nothing will stop us,* the Tetractys had thought, his heart leaping at the sight.

"No matter what happens to me," the Father had assured him long before. "No matter how weak I appear, have faith in our plan."

But the Tetractys no longer felt quite so confident. After overhearing the professor's conversation in the Pantheon, he'd decided he could finally stop his chase—Schultz was on the right path. The end was in sight. But now it almost seemed that the professor was following *him*. At the airport, he'd spotted Schultz boarding a plane to Turkey with Selene Neomenia.

The Tetractys had ducked behind a kiosk selling miniature plastic Coliseums just before they noticed him. He'd crouched there, frozen with indecision.

I could easily get them stopped by the Italian authorities, he reasoned. *A gun planted in their carry-on luggage would do the trick.* Then again, he couldn't risk the professor getting stuck for too long in Italy. In two days, Schultz needed to be in his appointed place. The entire plan depended on it.

So the Tetractys had let him go. He'd boarded his own flight, trusting Schultz's word that he'd be present at the gathering on Mount Olympus. Surely his curiosity would draw him there, even if the Huntress had temporarily lured him off on some mysterious errand.

The thought of the conclave gave him a shivering thrill. *All of them in one place, just as the Father always wanted. He truly has foreseen everything.* He took a swig from his tiny bottle of whiskey and reclined his first-class seat a little further. *They're playing right into our hands, no matter how dire things seem right now.*

Still, he couldn't repress a thread of anxiety. He pushed the call button to summon more whiskey from the flight attendant. *Two days,* he thought. *Two days to accomplish so much.*

He wanted more time. And, at the same time, he wished it was already done. The new Age would be so much better than this one—he could barely stand the wait. It would be glorious to behold. *Too bad Schultz won't live to see it.* He forced down a pang of regret. There was nothing he could do about the professor's fate.

He stared out the window of the plane. His own reflection stared back. "I *will* be forgiven, in the end," he murmured, trying to convince himself. The reflection grimaced—even his own face didn't believe his words.

He looked past himself, to the landscape below—to the task at hand. The mountains here didn't look that different from those in Greece. Their slopes were covered with green, their peaks sharp and barren. *But these mountains are silent,* he reminded himself. *Mount Olympus will sing.*

"We just need the musicians to play their parts," he said aloud. Then he focused once more on his reflection and smirked. "And one damn fine conductor to keep them in tune."

Chapter 35

THE BLESSED VIRGIN

Selene watched while Theo slept through the flight to Turkey. He slept through the wait at baggage claim. He slept through the long cab ride from Izmir. *Either he got no sleep last night,* she surmised, *or he just doesn't want to talk to me. Probably both.*

She would've appreciated a nap herself. Yet the thought of her father lying close to death left her too agitated to rest.

An hour after they left the airport, the taxi's hum finally lulled her into a light doze. She popped back into wakefulness as they made an especially sharp turn on a hillside. The red roofs of modern Selçuk spread across the valley below her. The blue Aegean gleamed in the distance. Farther inland, she could see a large archaeological site. Broad marble streets, a wealth of crumbled buildings, a massive Roman amphitheater.

"Is that Ephesus?" she asked the cabdriver.

"Yes," he replied. "You must see. Very beautiful." He slowed the car and pulled into an overlook.

She considered waking Theo, but decided he needed sleep more than sightseeing. She stepped into the glaring heat and stared down at the ruined city below. A memory pricked at her consciousness, but the town had changed too much over the millennia to evoke anything specific. Yet there was something about the theater especially that looked familiar. She stared at it a moment longer.

"Artemis."

She spun at the whisper of her old name. But Theo was still asleep, and the cabdriver had eyes only for his cell phone.

"Artemis! Artemis! Artemis!" Not just one voice. Thousands. Their gathered cries both a furious roar and a barely heard murmur. The chant came from within her own mind, yet as she turned back to the view, Selene felt sure it rose from the theater far below, the sound climbing up the mountainside like fog lifted with the sun.

The voices dissipated. She returned to the taxi. When she closed the door, Theo finally awoke.

"Where are we?" he asked groggily.

"Almost there."

He straightened his glasses and peered at her. "You okay?"

"Yeah. I'm fine." She was surprised he noticed her distress—even more surprised he seemed to care. Unsure how to deal with it, she leaned forward to speak to the cabbie instead. "Drop us off at the Artemision." She turned back to Theo. "The Temple of Artemis was the heart of the ancient city. That's where we should start looking for Athena."

"I was there a few years back. The temple hasn't exactly fared well," Theo said cautiously.

"Are you worried my feelings will be hurt?" Her words came out more disdainfully than she'd intended. "I'm used to looking at ruins."

Theo only shrugged and turned to stare out the window.

The cabbie let them out on the side of the road. A single, bedraggled souvenir vendor stood at the site's entrance. They walked down a narrow, weed-covered path into what seemed at first glance to be a swamp.

The great Temple of Ephesian Artemis had been one of the Seven Wonders of the Ancient World. One hundred and twenty-seven columns, each the height of ten men, had supported a building longer than a football field.

Theo was right to warn me, Selene realized, swallowing hard as she stood before the ruin.

Only a single column remained erect. The broken bases of a dozen others poked above the marsh grass in a rough rectangle.

Selene stared. "I don't even know what I'm looking at."

"The standing column is from the enormous temple built in the fourth century BC," Theo said gently. "The earlier building— the one commissioned by our favorite King Croesus—was still huge, but not quite as big. It was burned down by an arsonist the night Alexander the Great was born three hundred miles away across the Aegean. Do you remember that?"

She shook her head. The story didn't sound familiar.

Theo went on. "There's a legend that Artemis, Goddess of Childbirth, was off in Macedonia helping Alexander's mom in her labor that night. Otherwise, she would've been here protecting her temple better."

A groan escaped her lips.

"Selene?" There was more concern in his voice than she deserved.

"I couldn't protect it. I couldn't protect anything or anyone." She gestured helplessly at the ruins. "They abandoned me. I knew that already, but to *see* it..."

"But look." He pointed to a large nest perched atop the lone standing column. The head of a baby bird peeked over the edge, cheeping plaintively. From the west, a wide-winged stork soared toward the nest with a strip of fish in its long bill. It landed on the column and bent to feed its chick. Only then did Selene notice all the other birds in the swamp. Large orange-footed geese waddled at the column's base; black swallows looped through the air; tiny sparrows trilled merrily in the undergrowth.

She closed her eyes for a moment, listening. She heard a snake slithering through mud. A large turtle trundled down the footpath. Cicadas buzzed in counterpoint to the birdsong. The wind whistled among the reeds as merrily as any tune played on Hermes' pipes.

"Potnia Theron," Theo said quietly. "Mistress of Beasts. Your oldest epithet. If mankind no longer worships you, at least the animals still do."

An ungainly bee hummed its way toward her and landed on her bare forearm. It crawled there for a moment, searching for nectar, before lumbering back into the air.

"The bee..." she murmured, grasping at a memory fluttering just out of reach.

"The people here embossed their coins with bees," Theo offered. "A symbol more apt for Artemis of the Ephesians than Artemis of the Greeks."

Artemis! Artemis of the Ephesians! The distant chant echoed once more in her mind. And somehow, this time, the thought of the bee brought the memory flooding back.

She placed a hand beneath her ribs and ran it down her stomach. "I had bees here, on my gown," she said. "And a necklace of pinecones. Here." She tapped her collarbone. "Deer. Griffins. Bulls. All standing in neat rows down the front of my skirt. Lions standing proud on my bent arms, like those that guarded the Magna Mater's throne. Three strings of bulls' testicles hanging pendulous like breasts around my neck."

Her voice grew wistful as the memory returned. "They were warm, soft, heavy against my chest. My worshipers would cut them from the bulls and throw them on the lap of my statue— just like the Magna Mater's priests did when they castrated themselves." She touched the top of her head. Dimly, she knew the sun had turned her black hair hot, yet she felt cool ivory beneath her fingers instead. "I wore a crown carved with more animals," she continued. "Bordered by flowers and bees, topped by a columned temple stretching heavenward." She remembered the crown's weight on her skull not as a physical sensation—she wasn't even sure she'd ever actually worn such a thing—but like a heavy dream. "The night Alexander the Great was born I couldn't have left the temple, because I carried it always on my head. That sounds silly, but I know somehow it's true."

"You're describing the statues of Artemis made here in Ephesus," Theo said, his voice hushed with awe. Whatever anger he still harbored toward her seemed to have dissipated with the return of his customary fascination with the ancient world. "The people of Asia Minor had an original Potnia Theron of their own—a prehistoric Earth Goddess not unlike Cybele, the Magna Mater. Then the Greeks brought Artemis the Huntress, and the two goddesses merged into one. Did you only just remember that?"

She nodded, as confused as he was. In Greece, so Hera had explained, it was Selene's grandmother, Rhea, who had taken the Great Mother's worship for herself. Selene had completely forgotten that across the Aegean, Artemis had earned that honor instead. "When Saturn placed me beneath the bull's blood, I felt the Magna Mater take root within me. But after the Underworld, her spirit left me. I didn't remember we'd ever been joined before—I usually only remember my Greek incarnation. Occasionally the Roman one. Homer, Ovid, Aeschylus—theirs are the versions of myself I know."

"You were created by the poets," he said softly. "I forget that sometimes. If the Ephesians ever wrote hymns to their goddess, they didn't survive. Even the image of you with your animal-studded gown isn't well-known anymore outside of Turkey—the Ephesians may have molded you of marble and silver, but their goddess was too mysterious, too bizarre, too *eastern*, to catch on in the rest of the world. The bulls' balls especially were a bit much. The Greeks preferred their lithe huntress; the Romans liked their moon goddess."

"You said the Ephesians molded me of silver," she said. "I remember rows and rows of silver statues, no more than three inches tall, at the silversmiths' booths in the marketplace."

"You saw those?"

She nodded. "When I came to hear a man named Paul preach."

"You mean Paul the Apostle?" Theo asked, his eyes bright with curiosity. She knew he could barely refrain from whipping out a pen and paper to write down her words.

"Yes." She understood now why the bearded Jew whom Saturn had spoken of in Ostia had seemed so familiar. She'd seen him in Ephesus, years after that fateful day on the road to Damascus. The man had taken his god's commandments to heart. He'd spread the good news as far as Artemis's holy city.

"Saint Paul talks about preaching to the Ephesians in the Bible," Theo prodded. "You were actually there?"

"I was everywhere," she said slowly. She started walking away from the swamp and back toward the road, letting the memory of a different walk unfurl as she went. "I traveled up the marble street from the harbor, disguised as a mortal man. A merchant, with grain to sell. It was night, and oil lamps lined the colonnade along the street, gilding the marble. A great crowd streamed ahead of me, and I followed them into the theater. Thousands, tens of thousands, filled the benches. A bearded man stood in the center of the orchestra, his face lit by torches. He looked like a madman, ranting about how I was an instrument of the devil, and Christ alone could save them."

"You must've been pissed."

"No...I thought it was funny. I had no idea how dangerous it was. I thought of punishing the man, of course—he shouldn't be allowed to show such disrespect—but I didn't have to. My people did it for me. A silversmith stood up in the middle of the theater, holding aloft his icon of me with my towering crown, and yelled, 'Great is Artemis of the Ephesians! Great is Artemis of the Ephesians!' The whole crowd took up the chant. All twenty thousand of them. And then they streamed down the aisles like an avalanche and descended on the preacher. They beat him half to death."

Theo chuckled uncomfortably. "One of the great moments of Christian persecution and you're smirking."

"They didn't actually kill him," she retorted defensively. "The Roman soldiers stopped the riot. But they eventually sent the apostle into exile. Meanwhile, my city stayed my city." She stood by the souvenir stand now, and the grizzled vendor stared at her blankly. To him, she was just another American tourist. "At least for a little longer."

"The Ephesians never really forgot about you," Theo said. "When Christianity finally took over, they buried your cult statues; they didn't destroy them. The one in the museum here in Selçuk is in perfect condition—temple crown, bull balls, and all—except the arms have been broken off at the elbow." He reached for a figurine on the table, a six-inch copy in white soapstone. "Like this, see?"

The vendor perked up. "Twenty lira, but for you, fifteen."

"Oh." Theo reached into his pocket. "I only have dollars."

"Fifteen dollars, then, no problem." The man grinned broadly.

Selene thought about telling Theo that three Turkish lira were one dollar—she'd seen the exchange rate posted at the airport—but decided the vendor needed the money. Besides, a statue of Artemis should be worth at least fifteen dollars.

While Theo paid for the figurine, Selene examined the other items on the table. "What's that?" She pointed to a small clay model of a veiled woman standing in the exact same pose as the Ephesian Artemis statue. Even her arms had been broken at the same place.

The vendor's eyes brightened as he smelled another sale. "That's a copy of the statue of the Blessed Virgin."

"No, it's not," Selene retorted. "Artemis never wears a veil."

"No, no, the *Blessed* Virgin. Mary, Mother of Jesus."

Selene stiffened. Could they have been interpreting the prophecy wrong? Theo turned toward her, looking alarmed, and she could hear his silent question. *Was Mary the "wise virgin" who could save Zeus?*

No, I refuse to believe that, she decided. *Mary isn't even a goddess, just a long-dead mortal woman. Bringing her into my sacred shrine is nothing but an insult.*

"Why are you selling Mary's statue here?" she asked.

"Because this is her home."

Selene rested her hands on the table and leaned toward the man threateningly. "Is the word *Artemision* so hard for you to translate?"

The man reached hurriedly for a pamphlet on his table. "Here, see? The House of the Virgin Mary. It's only twenty minutes away."

Selene snatched the pamphlet before Theo could. The cover photo showed a small brick chapel surrounded by olive trees. Walking quickly toward the road with Theo beside her, she read aloud: "Ephesus is considered to be the last home of the Blessed Virgin, the Mother of Jesus Christ."

Theo leaned closer, reading over her shoulder. The pamphlet explained how Mary had supposedly left Jerusalem after Christ's crucifixion and lived out her days in Asia Minor even before Saint Paul made the journey.

Theo, annoyingly reading faster than she did, pointed to the end of the first page. "The Council of Ephesus, in 431 AD." He sounded awestruck. "It took place right inside your city."

"So?"

"That's when the leaders of the Church officially declared that Mary was the Mother of God, and therefore not just a woman or even a saint—but actually divine herself." He laughed shortly.

"Catholicism has been bending the knee to the Holy Virgin ever since, all because the people of Ephesus so loved their goddess that they decided Christianity wasn't complete without her."

"I see," sneered Selene. "They're monotheists, but god is three in one and one in three and has a mother who's basically a goddess. Sounds like a whole damn pantheon to me. They even made their statue of Mary look like their statue of Artemis."

"You know, if you'd stuck around Turkey after the Diaspora, you might have retained some power."

Selene rolled her eyes.

"Listen to this part," Theo went on. " 'The Orthodox villagers, the descendants of the ancient Christians of Ephesus, passed from generation to generation the belief that the Assumption of Mary occurred in this place.' "

"What's the Assumption?"

"It's when Mary dies and gets sucked up into heaven in a beam of light to take her place next to God and Jesus."

The rest of the pamphlet included a long list of scriptural and historical justifications for why the little brick house in the middle of nowhere might actually be the final home of Mary. Selene snorted. "Their obsession with presenting the evidence only proves the Christians know it sounds far-fetched."

The last paragraph seemed the most absurd of all, describing how a nineteenth-century nun who'd never left Germany received detailed visions of the hills of Ephesus and the house of the Blessed Virgin. When a scientific expedition journeyed to Turkey, they found the brick house, miraculously identical to the one in the German nun's visions.

"I'd bet my whole damn quiver that this is why Athena's here in the first place," Selene grumbled. "She couldn't stay in her own city of Athens—our father specifically prohibited it when he sent us out of Olympus. So she stole *my* city instead. She could never be a Mistress of Beasts, so she took Ephesus by setting herself up as the Virgin Mary: a protector of mortals, a holy virgin, an intercessor on behalf of the cities of men—all the things the Gray-Eyed Goddess embodied in the old days."

"That's awfully conniving." Theo looked more impressed than dismayed.

"*Styx*. She might even have *been* Mary in the first place. Maybe not the one in Jerusalem who gave birth to Jesus, but the one who showed up on this mountainside in Asia Minor claiming to be Jesus's mom."

"You think she's been here that long?"

"Why not? For all I know, even before the Diaspora, she was sneaking off to set up a nice little retirement plan, just like Saturn. She convinces the local Christians of her 'assumption' and enjoys their reverence for a while. Holy Roman Emperor Theodosius prohibits worship of the Olympians in the 390s—that's when we all left Greece and Rome to wander the world as mortals.

"But it only takes my sister another forty years to get herself deified—again—at this Council of Ephesus. She's sitting pretty for another thousand years, at least, hanging out as the local saint. Then finally, when the rest of us are really starting to lose our powers, she sends a vision to that nun in Germany, or poses as the nun herself, or maybe just shows up in a bedsheet in the middle of the night at the foot of her cot and pretends to be an angel. Then *wham*, just like that, her little house in Turkey becomes a site of international pilgrimage."

She stepped into the road and hailed a passing taxi. When the driver pulled over, she slapped the pamphlet against his window.

"Take us here. Now."

Chapter 36

GRAY-EYED

Let's just hope Selene doesn't burn the whole place down before we find Athena, Theo prayed as they followed the shuffling crowd toward the House of the Virgin Mary, waiting their turn to enter. Selene's face bore one of those sneers that could morph from implicit disdain to explicit violence with startling alacrity.

He rested a hand on her elbow, just for an instant, resenting the little jolt of electricity he felt every time he touched her skin. "Hey, try to stay cool, okay?" he muttered as they entered the chapel. "We don't want to get dragged out by security guards."

"Don't worry," she hissed back. "The only way I'm leaving is with Athena over my shoulder."

That is not *comforting,* Theo thought with a sigh. Still, he'd known what he signed up for when he agreed to come to Turkey: *stubbornness, fury, and an uncanny ability to piss off everyone around her.* But he had to admit that he'd also gotten a good dose of mystery solving, adventure, and first-person accounts of ancient history. He'd even managed to shunt aside the worst of his bitterness, ignore the continuous throbbing of the arrow wound in his arm, and focus on the task at hand. So far, at least.

The tiny sanctuary had room for only a few wooden stools

and a small altar table. In a niche at the front of the chapel stood a small bronze statue of Mary facing forward with her feet together. While it was clear she'd once held her palms outward in a gesture of peace and welcome, now they ended in hollow stumps just below the elbow, just like the little statue of Ephesian Artemis he'd bought from the souvenir vendor.

The pilgrims stood in reverent silence before the shrine, some crossing themselves, others moving their lips in prayer. Theo scanned the room for signs of Athena, but saw only Greek Orthodox icons and photos of visiting Catholic popes.

After a few moments, they filed out again to stand on the terrace, grateful for the shade beneath a row of trees. *Olive trees,* he noted, looking at them more closely. *Might be a sign that Athena is here somewhere—or just that Turks like olives as much as Greeks do.*

They walked farther down the terrace, past trays of flickering votive candles and a prayer wall thickly carpeted with fluttering paper petitions. He sat heavily on a stone railing. The prophecy pointed to this as the right place, and yet they'd found no evidence that Athena actually lived here.

Two sunburnt women with bright-pink lips to match stood before the prayer wall. One scribbled something on a scrap of toilet paper.

"You really think Mary's going to answer your prayer if you write it on TP?" asked her friend in a broad Cockney accent.

"Shut up, Dottie. I'm not writing it for Mary, I'm writing it for the woman on the hill. They say she cures people just by touching them."

"Oh come on. You believe that rubbish? There's really a woman up here who's some sort of miracle worker? You're not even Catholic!"

"Never hurts to cover your bases." The two women continued bickering, but Theo had stopped listening. Selene met his eyes, clearly thinking the same thing.

Silently, she pointed to a small gate marked NO ENTRY. Beyond it, a narrow path continued into the woods. She raised her eyebrows at him meaningfully, and he nodded in agreement. While none of the security guards were looking, Selene hopped the three-foot-tall fence in one quick jump then helped Theo clamber more awkwardly over it.

They avoided the path and pushed up through the undergrowth toward a small complex of buildings. *Houses for the priests and caretakers,* he decided. *And—let's hope—one former Greek goddess.*

Selene leaned close to whisper in his ear. "When we find this *miracle worker,* you need to talk to her."

"Me?"

"She's the Protectress of Cities, remember? Friend to Makaritai. She'll listen to you more than she would to me. And I trust that you can talk your way in to see her."

Theo nodded, feigning confidence. In truth, his heart was racing. Not with fear—Athena wasn't known for irrational anger, unlike Artemis—but with anticipation.

Selene dropped to a crouch and scuttled silently around the side of a building, peering in each window. Theo followed, keenly aware of the loud crunch of dried pine needles beneath his sneakers.

He tried to imagine what Athena would look like when they found her. After so many centuries—millennia even—of stealing worship meant for the Virgin Mary, she must have remained impossibly strong. Would she still be able to speak to the owls? To wield her spear as deftly as any warrior? He knew by now that the gods were never what one expected, but he'd dreamed of this moment since he was a little kid hiding under his blanket with a flashlight, rereading myths about his favorite goddess's legendary wisdom and bravery. Athena was, in many ways, his first love.

His most recent—and possibly current—love stood on her tiptoes to peer into a small window set high in a wall. She dropped back down, eyes wide, mouthing, *I found her.*

He put his hands on the sill and leaned over to look, knowing it was crazy and yet still expecting Athena to be standing inside with a golden helm and bronze shield.

He hadn't expected her to be a nun.

Theo spent the next twelve hours at the feet of a saint. Or at least that's what the priests would've said. He felt like he'd spent twelve hours sitting with a madwoman. Sister Maryam, they called her, and so far, that was the only name she'd answer to.

"Your father needs you on Mount Olympus," he'd said to her when the priests ushered him into the small, cell-like workroom. It had taken all his powers of persuasion—not to mention his credentials as a Columbia professor—to convince the Church officials to let him see Sister Maryam in the first place. He'd made up a very impressive-sounding treatise on the correlation between modern miracles and biblical references to the Virgin Mary written in the original Greek.

"The university dean thinks I'm a gullible fool," he'd claimed. "You know these bastions of liberalism—no respect for the sacred. But I heard about the Sister's miracles, and I want to prove they're authentic." He knew Catholics could never resist a scholarly exegesis that just happened to "scientifically" validate their dogma. They'd granted him a single day's audience.

Sitting in a thin sunbeam streaming through the window, Sister Maryam had smiled faintly, barely glancing up from her worktable when Theo entered. Piles of ruddy clay and wooden sculpting tools covered the surface before her.

Over the black arms of her nun's habit, she wore white sleeve garters streaked with dried smears of red clay like bloodstains on a priestess's robes. She plucked a fistful of clay and began to mold it between hands stained equally crimson. "The Lord sends many to me in their time of need." Her voice was low and warm, but so soft he had to lean forward to hear. She spoke in unaccented American English, and he suspected it was only one of a dozen languages she'd mastered.

"Yes, the Lord…" Theo looked out the open door, making sure no priests were standing outside in the hallway. "The Lord of the Sky."

The nun nodded, her eyes flicking to the small painting sitting in a frame on her windowsill: a pastel-hued Mary with baby Jesus on her lap. "He is the Lord of all."

She began to shape the clay with a thin wooden tool. She flipped it in her fingers, using first the spatula end and then the point, smoothing then sculpting, trimming then incising, back and forth, back and forth, nearly too fast for his eyes to follow. It reminded him of how Selene wielded a javelin.

"I'm not sure we're talking about the same Lord," Theo pressed.

"There is only one Lord." She sliced the bottom of the figure flat and placed it on a tray, barely looking at it before grabbing another ball of clay and beginning the process over again.

"Right," Theo said slowly, looking at the tiny sculpture. The Virgin Mary. Her bent arms broken just after the elbow, her feet together. A modest veil covered her hair rather than an ornate crown. A simple face, merely the suggestion of a mouth and eyes, a slash of nose, but carved with such skill that it expressed both tranquility and mercy. He sat in silence, watching her make another identical figurine. He'd seen a whole row of them in the gift shop down by the brick chapel. For only sixty lira you, too, could own a sacred relic handmade by the former Goddess of Crafts.

Sister Maryam didn't ask him why he'd come. The priests had made it clear that supplicants often came to receive a blessing from the holy sister and to ask for her prayers on their behalf. Many miracles had occurred, they said in hushed tones. When the sister passed on, she would no doubt become a saint.

But from what Theo could tell, Sister Maryam wouldn't pass on anytime soon. Her face was that of a young woman. Her bold jaw resembled Selene's, but her blade of a nose was larger, her brow firmer, giving her a slightly masculine appearance. Yet her lips were full and soft, the ends curving into a maddening Mona

Lisa smile that Selene would've found unbearably simpering. Whatever hair she had was tucked tight beneath a black wimple. Her hands alone looked old, but only because of the clay that stained every crease. She wore a simple gold band on her left ring finger, a symbol of her marriage to Christ.

Yet Theo never doubted for a second that this was Athena before him, even if she wouldn't admit it. "Gray-eyed" didn't do her justice: She looked at the world through lightning-lit thunderclouds, brilliant silver and dark iron, more like layered agate than simple granite.

He tried one more time. "Zeus needs you," he said. "Your father's dying, and you may be the only one who can save him."

Any other nun would surely have reacted with shock—or at least confusion—at the mention of the god's name. Sister Maryam didn't even look up. That's how Theo knew she understood.

He tried a different tack. "How about a blessing? Maybe a little laying on of hands?" He didn't mean to sound sarcastic, but his patience for her false piety was running thin.

"Do you mean to heal your arm?" she asked calmly.

"How did you…" The sleeve of his shirt hid the wound from Selene's black-fletched arrow completely.

"Come, my child." She put aside her clay.

Awkwardly, Theo knelt at her feet, unsure if he should pray or chant or just look penitent. Maryam laid a hand on his arm. He felt a tingle of warmth—or perhaps he just imagined it. When she moved away, he noticed the wound had stopped throbbing. Amazed, he pulled up his sleeve. The gash was still there beneath its bandage—it just didn't hurt. "So you *can* do miracles. Sort of."

The words of the oracle came back to him: *To akos to akontion. The cure is the spear.* Maybe he and Selene were both right: Athena's healing powers could cure Zeus while her spear could defend them from the giants when they opened Tartarus to imprison Saturn. The message was metaphorical and literal at the same time, just like any good prophecy.

Maryam went right back to her sculpting. "God works through me. I do nothing."

"Oh, come on. Stop pretending! If you can help me, you can save your father!"

She didn't take the bait. She just bent closer to her little Mary and added a tiny beatific smile to its clay face.

By the early evening, he resorted to playing the Makarites card. "If I'm a Blessed One, aren't you duty-bound to help me on my quest?"

Sister Maryam merely fingered her crucifix and said, "Only God can help you." He was ready to rip the clay from her hands and throw it out the window. Selene, he knew, still crouched beneath the sill, no doubt listening to every word. She'd probably catch the clay and throw it right back at him, furious at his failure.

He glanced over at the row of Mary statues. *Time for a miracle,* he thought, *and I don't care what faith it comes from. What do you say, Mother Mary? Want to help a guy out?*

Whether through divine inspiration or not, an idea blossomed. He reached for the pile of clay. Sister Maryam's eyes followed the gesture. As she sculpted the arms on yet another statue, Theo rolled his clay into a flat pancake, then added a nose, eyes, and mouth. *It looks like a third-grader sculpted this,* he thought ruefully, nudging the nose into something slightly less Wicked Witch of the West. But he'd seen clay votive offerings the ancients had left at their gods' shrines; they'd been crude, too, and the gods never seemed to mind.

He plucked off some more clay and rolled out seven long snakes, poking holes for the eyes. He attached the snakes to his clay face, coiling them like hair. Then he sat back and admired his handiwork. A Medusa.

He moved his sculpture into Maryam's line of sight.

"Ovid tells us that Medusa was a priestess of Athena," he began, as if speaking more to himself than to the woman across the table. "A beautiful maiden serving at a temple on a cliff above the wine-dark sea. A sacred virgin with beautiful black hair that fell past her waist in oiled curls. Beauty wasted on a maiden pledged to chastity—or so blue-haired Poseidon thought as he gazed up through the watery depths. The one they call Earth Shaker, Horse Breaker, Lord of the Sea, burst inside Athena's temple on a wave of foam and took Medusa there beneath the Virgin's statue of gold and ivory."

From the corner of his eye, Theo noticed Sister Maryam had finally stopped sculpting. A statue lay half finished in her hands, the clay on her fingers drying to a burnt orange crust. He kept talking quietly.

"To punish the maiden for desecrating the temple, Athena turned Medusa's long black hair to long black snakes. She became a Gorgon. Her face retained its beauty, but those who looked upon it were turned to stone. Such was the justice of Athena, who punished the victim, not the perpetrator."

He pushed the clay face a little closer to Maryam and waited until her eyes fixed upon its snaky tresses. "I've always wondered if that's why Athena placed the Gorgon head upon her aegis. Not, as some would say, to protect herself with its stony gaze— but to remind herself of her own cruelty."

Maryam placed her clay-covered hands over her eyes. Theo made no move to comfort her. It took a very long time, a very long silence, but finally the tears ran through her fingertips. The dried clay dissolved to liquid blood.

Only then did he lean forward. "I've seen the Gorgon head. It still adorns your aegis—an aegis stolen by Saturn, but returned now to your father's hands. Zeus wants to give it back to you."

Maryam lifted her head, her eyes flashing with fierce greed. Theo couldn't help the grin that pulled at his mouth. "There you are," he said. "I was beginning to think you'd never come out."

"Medusa..." Athena began. "I remember every tear she shed as Poseidon tore her apart. She cried even harder when I made her a monster...I don't *want* to remember." Her voice suddenly grew fierce. "I don't want to remember *any* of it. Do not make me." She wiped angrily at her face, smearing the red clay across her cheeks. "I do only good now. I try to..." Her voice faded away, and the slightly sleepy smile returned. "I try to do the Lord's work."

Sister Maryam reached once more for the clay.

Chapter 37

WISE VIRGIN

"Athena's not what I expected." Theo reached under his glasses to rub his eyes like a man wishing to unsee the last few hours.

"That's an understatement." Selene had been crouched beneath Maryam's windowsill the whole time, listening to him fail to convince her half sister to join them. She'd nearly stood up a dozen times and started hollering in frustration. When he finally gave up, she'd circled around the building to meet him at their appointed rendezvous point further into the woods.

"I thought at first she was just pretending to be a nun up there." Theo gestured to the church residences behind the trees. "But I'm not so sure. It's like the good Sister Maryam really believes she's married to Christ now."

"Don't believe her shtick," Selene said dismissively. "Remember, this whole place is her scheme."

"Maybe," he admitted. "I saw a glimpse of the real Athena, but she didn't seem to have complete control. She was like some woman on a made-for-TV movie in the seventies, a schizophrenic bouncing from pious nun to wrathful goddess and back for the sake of the Emmy voters. I don't understand. If Sister Maryam is keeping herself powerful through a connection to Mary, just like Saturn fed off the Host's devotion to their warped Christian trinity—then why did she look so...daffy? You'd think with all the billions of Christians in the world, she'd be living like a queen, not a nun."

"I told you once that if I'd tried something similar—embraced the Christians' love for their Virgin as just another aspect of worship for me—I would've had to take on Mary's characteristics, too."

Theo snorted. "I believe you said you'd be 'weak and mild and impregnated by a shaft of heavenly light.' You think that's what happened to your sister?"

"Yes. Saturn gets to be God the Father: vengeful, powerful, scheming. The Virgin Mary has to be humble and helpless. That's why her powers could barely heal you—and I doubt they're what can save our father."

"She's been bit by her own snakes, so to speak."

"Exactly. But that doesn't mean we can't find the antidote. Even if she can't cure him through her 'miracles,' our other interpretation of the prophecy still stands: Her spear can defeat our greatest enemy. This pallid version of Athena's useless, but if we can get her back to the sister I remember—the Goddess of Justified War, the One Who Musters the People—we might have a chance."

"What do you have in mind? She didn't care that I was a Makarites. And I showed her the Gorgon, tried to appeal to her conscience, and that didn't do anything."

"Reminding her of her self-loathing won't be enough. We need to speak to her strengths."

"Since when do you advocate persuasion through such benevolent means?" he asked with a raised eyebrow. "Aren't you the one who usually beats people up instead? Or have you already forgotten the story you just told me about the mob attacking Paul the Apostle?"

"I'm more flexible than you think. And I can learn from my mistakes."

Theo lifted a skeptical brow, his eyes the color of marsh grass, bright green in the light of the setting sun. He didn't trust her. He didn't actually think she could change. "Then you talk to her next," he challenged.

Selene scowled. She and Athena had never gotten along, despite the virginity they shared. Selene had chosen chastity because of her complete disinterest in motherhood, a desire to run wild, to hunt. Maidenhood had given her the freedom to pursue those desires unencumbered. But for Athena, virginity had a moral dimension. She believed herself the embodiment of everything pure and just in the world, a strangely priggish argument among Greeks who generally saw sex as a pleasure, not a sin. But Athena had thought herself better than all men, mortal and immortal alike. Better, in fact, than just about everyone.

"You know I'm no good at talking," Selene protested. "How about we just kidnap her and let Scooter figure out how to convince her to help. He's the one with the silver tongue... although yours isn't bad either." She immediately realized how that sounded; a sudden memory of Theo in her bed in New York, his cheek resting on her thigh, sent a flood of heat to her face—and elsewhere.

Theo gave her a lopsided grin. "Why, thank you."

I guess the humiliation's worth it for the smile, she decided. She'd missed his dimple. Despite the danger facing them, she found it surprisingly easy to slip back into their old banter. *Maybe there's hope for us after all,* she couldn't help thinking.

"Come on, Selene, let my silver tongue convince you to talk to your sister."

She nodded grimly and walked back through the twilit woods. She gestured for Theo to stay put and peeked through the window of Maryam's room. The nun lay fast asleep on a small, hard pallet on the floor.

Selene hoisted herself through the small window, nearly knocking over a framed painting of the Virgin Mary sitting on the sill. Clay figurines stood like ranks of soldiers on their tray. She reached for a wooden chair, then thought better of it and settled herself cross-legged on the ground beside the pallet instead.

"Sister," she said softly.

Maryam's eyes flew open. She squinted at Selene, a look of alarm passing across her face. Then her eyes widened in recognition. Just as quickly, her expression dissolved into gentle curiosity.

You can't fool me, Selene thought. *You know exactly who I am. Otherwise you'd be screaming for help right now.*

Maryam sat up. She'd taken off her black outer habit and wore only a simple, sack-like sleeping shift. The pure white of it glowed in the dim light, making her look more saintly than ever. A large wooden crucifix hung around her neck.

"What can I do for you, daughter?" Maryam asked gently.

Selene nearly choked at the condescension but forced herself to smile back. "Oh no, call me sister, Sister."

"You have also taken holy orders?" Maryam asked, her voice just a hair too innocent.

"Something like that." Selene nodded toward the figurines. "Nice statues. They remind me of someone I knew once."

"Oh?"

"Metis. Her name means 'Wisdom,' in case you've forgotten," Selene added lightly.

Maryam's jaw tensed.

"She was lovely like this." Selene picked up a statue. This was not a recollection of her own, for she hadn't witnessed it herself, but rather a story retold by gods and man alike—paired with just a little educated guesswork. "A Titan goddess with bright gray eyes and features as strong as a man's but as beautiful as a sea nymph's." She turned the statue so the last rays of light played over the sharp nose and jutting jaw. "So beautiful, in fact, that Zeus loved her in the dawn of the world. But he received a prophecy that if Metis bore him a son, the child would steal his throne—just as he himself had deposed Kronos, and Kronos had overthrown Ouranos.

"Zeus could take no such chances, so after he lay with her, he swallowed Metis whole. Nine months later, a headache drove him to such distraction that he asked the Smith to open his skull with a hammer to relieve the pain. And when his skull cracked open, a goddess emerged, full-grown and dressed in gleaming armor. If she'd been a man, Zeus would have killed her to prevent his own overthrow. But she was a woman—imperious and fierce, but a woman nonetheless—so he had nothing to fear. He embraced his daughter and gave her a seat upon Olympus, where she could defend both gods and men with her shining spear."

Selene passed the statue to Maryam and looked her sister hard in the eye. "At least, that's the story I know. But I always wondered, what happened to Metis? When Hephaestus split open Zeus's skull, why didn't Wisdom come out, too? Surely, Athena, the Goddess of Justified War, would have thought her own mother worth fighting for."

Maryam's hands clenched, turning the statue in her fist into undifferentiated clay. "Mother made me the armor," she said finally. She looked down at the lump in her hands and slowly released it back onto the ground, as if afraid of what she might do if she held it any longer. "She made the armor inside my father." She frowned and repeated, "Father... *Father.*" She shook her head, as if to dislodge the word, then clapped her hands over her ears and squeezed her eyes shut. "No, no, this isn't me. Stop hammering! *Stop it!*"

Selene leaned forward and clasped Maryam's clay-stained hands. "Shhh. We don't want the priests barging in here. It's okay, Sister. Tell me about the hammering." Maryam began to shake more violently.

Am I pushing her too far? Selene wondered. *If I force her to remember what she's tried so long to forget, will she crack apart further than she already has? Will Athena disappear forever into the chasm that emerges?* But she couldn't stop now.

"Go on," she urged again. "What hammering?"

"My mother's hammer on the anvil, beating bronze into armor." Maryam's words rushed out, as if they needed speed to break through the barrier of her mind. "Mother hid the sound beneath Father's own heartbeat. *Bah boom. Bah boom.* Our whole world vibrated. Between every heartbeat, every stroke, she whispered to me, her unborn child, 'Be a Savior. Be a Savior.'"

Tears streaked her face, softening her features rather than swelling them. She looked more like the Virgin Mary than she had before, yet her memories as Athena continued to come. "After nine months of ceaseless work, Mother said it was time for me to leave her behind. She would be trapped forever in the mind of the Sky God, destined to provide him wise counsel whether she willed it or not. And there was nothing, *nothing* I could do to change that."

Selene pressed her half sister's hands harder. "You could do what she asked of you. You still can."

"I've tried—" Maryam whispered, her voice shaking.

"She made you a warrior," Selene interrupted impatiently. "She clad you in battle armor so you could save people. So you could save your father."

"The father who swallowed my mother?"

Selene winced. "He's done many unforgivable things. But he loves you. He loves me. He loves all his children. And now he's grown so old, so sick. You . . . you wouldn't recognize him. He's dying."

"I can't heal him," Maryam protested. "I can barely heal a mortal, only provide some comfort in their time of need. That's all the power Mary has."

"I don't need Mary! I need *Athena*. Father says that opening the pit of Tartarus is the only thing that can save him, but he can't do that without *your* spear to defend him from the giants that will pour out. Please, Maryam. I know you usually only care about mortals, but aren't we all little more than mortals now? Father will die just like any old man. He needs you."

"I like helping people," Maryam said hesitantly. "I've *always* liked helping them. Odysseus, Heracles, Pers.... Pers..."

"Perseus," Selene supplied impatiently.

"Yes! That was his name," she exclaimed. "He was the one who slew Medusa. I gave him my shield, and he used it as a mirror so he wouldn't be turned to stone." Her face fell as she looked at the Gorgon sculpture Theo had made. "But when he gave me the Gorgon's head, I remembered Medusa as the young woman she'd been before I... before I..." Her tears sprang anew.

"Oh, for heaven's sake," Selene sighed. "That was at least three thousand years ago. If it even really happened. Trust me, I know how easy it is to succumb to guilt for the things we did in a different age, but you have to move past it. Father is in danger *now*, and you're no use to him if you just sit here sniveling. I need you to be strong on the summit of Olympus."

Maryam shrank under her scrutiny. "I don't remember how."

"Well think harder! They called you Giant Killer! Have you forgotten? Where is your helmet with its shining crest?" Selene rose to her feet and loomed over her sister. "Where is your armor? Where is your *spear*, Athena?"

Maryam shook her head, looking desperate. She clasped the wooden crucifix around her neck. "I don't know. I don't... I don't remember. I think I lost it."

"You what? Are you an *idiot*?"

And that, finally, brought Athena, Goddess of War, of Wisdom, of Crafts, Protectress of Cities and Savior of Men, to her feet.

"The Goddess of Wisdom is no idiot!" she roared.

Her hands clenched into fists as if she fought against raising them—whether to cover her own mouth or to slap her sister,

Selene couldn't be sure. The wood of the crucifix gave an audible crack as it splintered beneath Athena's white-knuckled grip. The muscles of her arms stood out beneath the loose fabric of her nightdress.

"Good. Now prove it."

"But I have no spear," Athena seethed.

Selene refused to give up, not when they'd come so far. "Problem solved, sister. I know just the god to make you a new one."

Chapter 38

LADY OF CLAMORS

This was not supposed to be so hard, Selene thought as she stalked across the roof of the National Archaeological Museum in Athens with a black-feathered arrow in her hand.

She, Theo, and Maryam had flown in that morning from Turkey, and they were due to bring Flint and Zeus to the base of Mount Olympus that afternoon. Scooter had promised to meet them there for the journey up. "I'll bring Grandpa—don't worry," he'd assured her in a rambling voice mail. "His bullet wounds are all healed, but I've been keeping him unconscious with a little mix of morphine and gin. He won't know what's going on until he wakes up on the summit, about to be thrown into Tartarus. And with a little cajoling, I'll get the rest of the family there, too, ready to help. You guys just make sure you're on time!"

Selene hadn't thought the timeline would be an issue; she'd blithely assumed that Flint could just remake Maryam's spear, forgetting that he hadn't made it in the first place. It was Metis who'd forged the armor for her daughter, and the Smith no longer possessed the supernatural ability to craft divine items from scratch unless they were copies of his original works.

Selene had briefly considered giving up on finding a divine

weapon for her sister, thinking perhaps any old spear would do. But when she'd seen her father at the Athens airport, she knew she had to do everything in her power to arm Athena with a true Giant Killer's spear. Flint had wheeled Zeus off the flight from Rome in a wheelchair. He was barely conscious, still mumbling about Tartarus, and he hadn't recognized Selene when she tried to speak to him.

Maryam had placed her hands on their father's chest; he rested more calmly for a few minutes, but then returned to his delirium. If anything, he seemed worse after her ministrations. *Of course,* Selene had thought, *a Christian saint can't help a Greek god, not when her kind helped destroy him in the first place. I need the real Athena, armed and armored, to save him.*

"Since I can't remake her weapons, we'll just have to get the real ones," Flint had said when she pulled him aside to explain the situation.

"Except she lost them. Don't tell me they were sitting in Saturn's armory under the Vatican and we didn't see them."

"Just the aegis, which Scooter took with him for safekeeping. But the helmet and spear were buried on the slopes of the Acropolis."

"How do you know that?"

"I didn't keep track of most of the divine weapons, but Athena's were...special. Where do you think I learned to smith? My own mother certainly didn't teach me."

The thought of June trying to wield a hammer in her wobbly diadem and matronly wedding dress almost made Selene laugh.

"When I cracked open your father's skull," Flint went on, "and saw Athena emerge, I was more impressed by the armor than the woman. I'd never seen craftsmanship so beautiful. I studied it for centuries."

"So why'd you let it get buried?" Selene asked, annoyed.

"The Gray-Eyed Goddess didn't give me permission to use it, and you know how she gets." He glanced down the corridor to where Maryam sat beside Theo and Zeus in the baggage claim area. She certainly didn't look threatening at the moment: She still wore her black nun's habit and wimple, although she'd left her shattered wooden crucifix behind and removed her wedding ring. On the flight over from Turkey, she'd stared fixedly out the window as if she'd never flown in an airplane before.

Selene's first time had been only a few months earlier, when she traveled from New York to Rome. Like Maryam, she'd been captivated by the view. *Is this what it looked like when I rode the moon across the sky?* she'd wondered, gazing out at a landscape carved of clouds. But whatever Maryam was thinking, she didn't say. Her stony expression bore no resemblance to the gentle nun's, nor did she evince any of Athena's anger or pride. It seemed her entire personality had fallen away—and she looked to the sky to find it again.

As for Theo, the awkwardness between them had returned as soon as their quest to find Athena was complete. He, too, had barely spoken on the flight to Athens; this time, he'd succeeded in buying a science fiction novel at the airport, and he'd kept his nose in the book the whole time. Occasionally, she'd catch him glancing warily in her direction, but he always turned back to the book without speaking. Such uncharacteristic reticence worried Selene more than any vitriol he could hurl at her. He didn't even engage with Maryam. He seemed to have given up on the Olympians entirely. She would've thought him content to escape into his world of aliens and spaceships and the rest of his beloved nonsense if it weren't for the fact that despite his usually phenomenal reading speed, he'd barely gotten through the first twenty pages by the time they landed. Nonetheless, he had the book open again in the baggage area, reading aloud to Zeus in an effort to calm his feverish murmuring. So far, it seemed to be working better than Maryam's "miracles": Either her father was a closet sci-fi fan, or Theo's book was incredibly soporific, because the King of the Gods sat quietly dozing.

Selene turned back to Flint. "So Maryam's spear and helmet are buried. Please tell me you know exactly where, or am I going to have to dig up the entire Acropolis to find them?"

"The archeologists already beat you to it. Her weapons are on display in the National Museum."

"You're going to say *I* have to steal them, aren't you?" Selene asked with a sigh.

Flint raised a grizzled eyebrow. "The whole crippled thing means I'm no good at cat-burgling. And something tells me your professor wouldn't approve of stealing priceless artifacts from a scholarly institution."

Yet when she told Theo the plan, he didn't object. Nor did he volunteer to help. He said only, "Sure. Have fun," as if he'd stopped caring one way or the other. "I'll be right here with my book." He gave her a tight smile and continued reading aloud to Zeus.

Now, on the roof of the museum, Selene dropped to all fours and peeked over the edge to see the night watchman— watchwoman, actually—exit the building. The rest of the staff had gone home an hour earlier, finally leaving Selene an opportunity to sneak in.

The search for Athena's armor had meant missing their promised rendezvous with Scooter at the base of Olympus that afternoon. But the actual Gathering of the Gods wouldn't occur until midmorning the next day. They still had time.

The guard took out a pack of cigarettes and checked her watch. Her contract probably allowed ten minutes for a smoke break. *Thank goodness for Europe's strong union rules,* Selene thought, affixing one end of a rope to an exhaust pipe on the roof. She rappelled down the side of the building to reach a second-story window. Thankfully, due to austerity measures imposed during the recent financial crisis, the Greeks didn't have the money for the sort of security systems richer nations could afford.

She unlatched the window with a narrow blade and crawled

through. Silently, she padded through darkened offices filled with dusty books and dustier potsherds.

When she reached the main gallery, she paused for a moment to reconnoiter. No guards, that was good, and the woman on her smoke break wouldn't be back for at least another six minutes.

Darkness shrouded the vast hall, rendering any security cameras nearly useless. Unlike a professional art thief, Selene hadn't brought infrared goggles, but nor did she need them; the green light from the exit signs provided more than enough illumination for She Who Roams the Night.

She sprinted full-out into the hall. The weaponry display, according to the map Flint had shown her, was at the far end, and she didn't intend to stop until she reached it.

Yet she skidded to a halt when the King of the Gods emerged from the darkness.

Her father stood in the center of the hall, feet spread wide, one arm cocked to throw a weapon and the other extended before him to point to his target. He didn't move.

It's just a statue, she thought, catching her breath. Yet it perfectly captured Zeus at the height of his power. His sharp beard jutted forward, his lips unsmiling. The muscles of his lean, naked body were molded in high relief, taut and chiseled. The sculptor had cast the figure in bronze, and the eerie light of the exit signs only intensified the green of the metal's swirling patina. Where the statue's inlaid eyes of ivory and precious stones should've been, only empty holes remained, and his right hand grasped empty air rather than a braided lightning bolt.

Your stormy gaze is gone, Father. You can no longer wield your own weapon. The statue made a mockery of all her father had become—trembling and age-spotted, his mind creeping forward where once it had soared on eagle's wings. *But all hope is not lost,* she vowed to Zeus's image. *Your daughters will be your eyes. We will be your strong right arm. Together we will cast Saturn into Tartarus and save you from death.*

At the end of the gallery, a large case held a trove of weaponry. Selene's heart sank as she scanned the artifacts inside. The arrow points and spearheads were mottled green, their edges pitted and blunt, brittle enough to shatter in a strong wind. The bronze helmet in the center of the case was dented and black with corrosion. No divine items would decay like that. Yet Flint had been clear: *Take the helm and the largest spearhead.*

She removed the glass cutter the Smith had whipped up at the airport using a compass, a suction cup, a carbide blade, and a small reservoir of lubricating oil. Scooter, as the God of Thieves, would've probably had the right equipment on hand, but he was already at Olympus, waiting with the other Athanatoi he'd gathered from around the globe. She placed the cutter on the case and sliced out a perfect circle of glass.

She reached in and pulled out the spearhead. Sixteen inches long, tapering like an elm leaf. Flakes of bronze fell like green snow. Even if Flint could somehow remove the corrosion, it wouldn't be much use without a shaft, but she took it anyway. She wrapped it in an old shirt and placed it into her pack with a small smile of satisfaction. *Hah. Who needs Scooter? Piece of cake.*

She reached for the helm next. It was far more ornate than Hades' simple dark headgear. Its long, curved cheek guards had been flipped upward like wings, and several narrow, broken stumps protruded from the crown—the remains of three griffin statues that had served as its crest. Selene lifted the helm an inch off its stand—pulling at a steel filament that immediately triggered a screaming siren.

A panel of overhead lights at the other end of the hall snapped on, then the next panel, and the next, a wall of light cascading toward her. In less than a second, she'd appear on the security camera overhead.

She tried to rip the helm from its tether, but the steel held fast. Cursing, she let it drop back onto its stand and dove for cover beneath a large Roman table of purple porphyry marble, crouching behind a wide, lion-clawed leg as the lights burst on above her.

Pounding feet echoed on the marble floor. She could see the guard now, a stout woman with a walkie-talkie in one hand and the remains of a cigarette in the other. The watchwoman skidded to a halt in the middle of the hall, spinning in both directions, looking for the intruder. She finally dropped the cigarette, called for help on the walkie-talkie, and drew a gun from her belt.

Selene sighed. Another Athanatos would've just shot an arrow through the woman. That would've made things easy. But after accidentally wounding Theo in the mithraeum, Selene couldn't bear the idea of maiming an innocent woman just for doing her job. She'd have to come up with some more creative way of escaping—without getting shot herself.

The guard stutter-stepped down the length of the hall, gun held firmly in both hands. Selene scooted a little further beneath the large table and reached carefully for her pack, thinking to knock the gun from the woman's hand with an arrow. But the sound of the zipper would have the guard running forward before Selene could remove and assemble her bow. She cursed silently, then pulled Flint's gold necklace from her pocket and unclasped it. She grabbed one end while the other telescoped silently outward into a long golden whip.

The guard's footsteps came closer. Selene dared not lean forward to see, so she depended on her ears alone to judge when the woman stood only a few paces away. She slung the whip forward. The tip lashed out, wrapping around the guard's ankle and yanking her leg out from under her.

The woman slammed face-first into the ground with a cry, twisting backward to squeeze off three shots as Selene ducked once more behind the table leg. Chips of purple marble flew from the table like hail. Selene kept one hand on the whip and held her pack like a shield over her face until the guard ran out of bullets.

Selene reeled in her whip, dragging the guard beneath the table like a fish on a line. The woman released the gun to grab onto the slick floor, but Selene didn't give her the chance. As soon as the tabletop hid the guard from the camera's view, she lunged forward and pinned the woman's cheek to the ground, her rolling eyes averted from Selene's face. A very strong grip on the woman's carotid artery knocked her unconscious in seconds.

Selene grabbed the walkie-talkie from the guard's belt and said with exaggerated casualness, *"Pseudopura. Pseudopura,"* hoping the Greeks hadn't changed their word for "false alarm" some time in the last two thousand years. From the bewildered, panicked voices on the other end, she was out of luck. Beneath the continuing din of the museum's security system, she could hear the police sirens, still far away but getting closer by the second.

With a curse, she peered out from beneath the table at the brightly lit hall. She couldn't afford to have the Greek police seeing her face; she'd prefer if they didn't even know their thief was a woman. She unwrapped the whip, twisted the handle so it shrank back to necklace size, then assembled her bow and grabbed a fistful of wooden arrows. Shooting from beneath the table, she knocked out three of the security cameras in quick succession. Only the one closest to her hiding place remained, and she couldn't aim for it without crawling out and exposing herself to the camera's eye.

At least, not with a normal arrow.

She looked at the hawk-feather shafts lying inside her pack. She'd left Apollo's silver plague arrows behind—her twin had long ago rejected his role as the Plague Bringer. He'd tried to live as the Healer, instead, and using his arrows felt like a betrayal of his memory. But she'd kept her own leaf-bladed, black-fletched arrows. *If I shoot one,* she wondered, *will it somehow curve back on itself to kill the guard?* The squeal of car tires outside the front entrance decided for her. She pressed her face against the floor so she could just see the camera from the corner of her eye.

Okay, listen up, arrow, she prayed. *I'm aiming for that camera way up there, even though it may not look like it.* She loosed the shaft.

It shot straight across the ground, then swooped upward in a hyperbolic arc. The second she heard the camera lens crack, Selene dashed from beneath the table, arriving just in time to pluck the tumbling arrow from the air.

A minute later, she was back on the roof, reeling in her rope. She took off along the ridgeline at a trot, then slipped down a gutter pipe and into a thick evergreen hedge. She crouched there until a small troop of cops jogged past, then crawled out and ducked onto a side street. She patted her pack, making sure she still had the spearhead, and called Flint. To her surprise, Theo answered instead.

"What?" he demanded without preamble.

She tried not to feel the sting of his disregard. "Mission accomplished. Mostly. Why are you picking up—"

"Flint's busy."

"Well, tell him to come get me and we'll head to Mount Olympus. If we leave now, we'll still make it to the summit before the Great Gathering tomorrow morning."

"We can't really do that right now." He sounded distracted.

"Why not?" They'd had a very specific plan, and it wasn't like either Flint or Theo to ignore it.

"Because we're chasing after Sister Maryam."

"Chasing? I left her sitting meekly next to you in the airport! Where'd she go?"

"All of a sudden she sort of woke up and looked at a map on the wall and then just took off. To the Acropolis. We couldn't stop her. We're on our way up there now."

"What about Father?"

"Don't worry—he's asleep in the rental car. We parked below and slipped up the path while the guards were all distracted by news of a break-in at the museum on the other end of town."

"Ah, see, setting off the alarms was all part of my master plan."

Theo snorted, unamused. "So the Lady of Clamors shook the hornet's nest. They're below us now, swarming all over the base of the Acropolis. You'll never get past them."

Selene was already hailing a taxi. "I'll bet you one very unimpressive ancient spearhead that you're wrong."

Chapter 39

ATHENA

The Acropolis, the "High City," loomed five hundred feet above the modern buildings of Athens. Floodlights warmed the pale limestone slopes of the massive butte, illuminating every detail of the ancient temples still perched atop it.

The gate to the main path up the Acropolis was locked for the night—and thick with panicked guards besides. Selene directed her cabdriver instead to the Odeon of Herodes Atticus, the mostly preserved Roman theater that hosted performances all summer long on the Acropolis's southern slope. At eleven, the show was just letting out—*Aida*, from the posters. Actors in Egyptian costumes mingled beneath the Odeon's towering Roman facade, snapping selfies with the audience members in a disconcerting juxtaposition of modern and ancient. For a moment, she allowed herself to imagine coming back someday after things with Saturn and her father were finally settled. Apollo would want her to let art into her life. *I wonder if Theo even likes opera?* she found herself wondering before quashing the thought. *It doesn't matter. Because as soon as this is all over, he's gone. He made that perfectly clear.*

Selene took cover in the crowd, threading through the thick

of it before ducking off the terrace and into the undergrowth. Scaling the tall chain-link fence took her seconds. From there, she hurried to the steepest part of the cliff, far from the path used by both tourists and guards.

She stared up at the sheer rock face. *This is why the ancient kings of Athens built their citadel on top,* she thought ruefully. But it would take more than a little rock climbing to stop She Who Dwells on the Heights. The only challenge lay in avoiding the floodlights.

Selene shimmied her way up a shadowed cleft, bracing hands and feet against the dusty limestone, then levered herself onto a shelf of rock no wider than her boots. The cliff continued above her with no visible handholds or accessible shadows. This time, there were no security cameras to worry about—just the millions of Athenians gazing lovingly up at their Acropolis from roof decks across the city.

If I'm going into the light, she decided, *I better be falcon swift.*

She eased her pack open, assembled her bow for the second time that night, and chose a steel-tipped wooden arrow. Fifty feet overhead, a single olive tree grew crookedly from the bare rock. From the width of its trunk, she figured it had grown there for at least three hundred years. *Let's hope it stays put just a little longer,* she prayed as she tied her rope to the arrow shaft and aimed at a branch. She sent the arrow straight up with a gentle pluck of her bowstring. It reached its peak just above the top of the tree, then fell back toward her, fletching first, missing the branch entirely and nearly striking her in the face.

Her phone rang as she reeled back in the rope.

"What about 'I'm sneaking up the Acropolis surrounded by guards' do you not understand?" she hissed.

"That's what vibrate mode is for," Theo whispered back. "You need to hurry. Maryam's losing it. She wants her spear."

"Yeah, yeah, give me a minute." She hung up and traded her wooden arrow for a hawk-fletched one. *Does it make me less of a*

Far Shooter when I have arrows that do all the work for me? she wondered as she aimed for the tree again. The gold shaft rocketed into the sky, then curved in midair and flew around the trunk in a perfect circle. It looped two more times for good measure before burying itself six inches deep in the bark.

"Holy Roman Empire," Selene muttered under her breath, borrowing Theo's favorite curse.

Hand over hand, she scurried up the rope like a spider on its web, so fast an observer might've mistaken her for the shadow of a cloud passing before the moon. From the olive tree, it was a short, steep scramble to the top.

Several guards roamed the plateau with flashlights. After all, this was the biggest tourist destination in the entire country. During Athens's Golden Age, the Acropolis had housed the city's most important temples and shrines. Now it was the symbol of the modern nation.

The Huntress had come here often in antiquity. She had a shrine right beside Athena's—a long stoa dedicated to the Goddess of Girls, an offshoot of her sanctuary at Brauron. Here, too, young girls dressed as bear cubs had danced in homage to Artemis. But as she stalked from temple to temple, ducking out of the guards' line of sight, she noted that no trace of the Brauronia remained, only an expanse of bare rock and a few low, crumbled stones.

Not far away, Selene remembered, had stood the bronze statue of *Athena Promakhos*—Athena the Frontline Soldier. It had towered three stories in the air, its spearpoint and helmet crest so bright that sailors forty miles away off Cape Sounion could see it winking in the sun and know they were almost home. Looters had no doubt carried it off long ago—the courtyard stood barren. Selene thought of the corroded spearhead in her pack. *Will it be enough to make Athena the tallest goddess once again?*

She passed beyond the courtyard, where the mighty Parthenon dominated the plateau. Even with much of its facade covered in scaffolding, the floodlights still illuminated the yellowed marble so brilliantly that the entire building glowed with the power of a goddess's aura. Statues of Athena and Poseidon no longer adorned the pediments, but the thick Doric columns remained, their careful proportions—swelling in the middle, tapering at the top—lending an illusion of lightness to the massive facade.

Three walls of the temple's inner sanctuary, the cella, remained intact. A Venetian cannonball had collapsed the fourth wall in the seventeenth century, when the occupying Ottomans had used the Parthenon as a gunpowder depot. The Athenians, it seemed, had been trying to reconstruct the temple ever since. More scaffolding filled much of the interior, and a line of tarps obscured the far end of the cella.

Selene stole up broad stairs worn smooth by countless Athenian pilgrims and ducked under the scaffolding. The murmur of urgent voices floated from behind the tarps.

She pushed aside the plastic sheeting to find Flint and Theo standing on either side of Sister Maryam, who knelt with her hands clasped before her, every inch the prayerful nun, right down to the black habit and wimple.

"What the hell is she doing?" Selene asked in an angry whisper.

Flint just grunted in answer.

Theo, of course, was more specific. "We tracked her up here, but now she refuses to leave." His eyes kept roaming to the tall walls of the cella. Despite the precariousness of the situation, he looked positively enraptured. All signs of his earlier apathy had vanished. With the temple's interminable restoration, even a classicist of his stature had likely never stood in the Parthenon's interior. "This is where her statue was, you know," he said, his voice hushed with more wonderment than caution. "*Athena Parthenos*, Athena the Virgin. A spear in one hand and winged Victory in the other. Forty feet tall with flesh of elephant ivory and a helmet and gown of beaten gold."

"Yeah, I remember," Selene said, unimpressed. "But it's long gone, just like the bronze statue of her as the Frontline Solider that used to stand in the courtyard—the *Athena Promakhos*. The Athenians ripped the gold sheets off their Virgin to pay their army in the third century BC. They probably abandoned my Brauronia even earlier." She strode over to her half sister. "So whether you're praying to your Christ or your missing statue or someone else entirely, snap out of it, Maryam. Because none of it's real anymore."

To her surprise, Maryam looked at her with an expression more wrathful Olympian than pious Christian. "I'm not praying to my missing statue. I'm listening to the *Athenians'* prayers to it."

Selene looked around the empty cella. "You can do that?"

Maryam closed her eyes. "As Athena, I heard their prayers. As Mary, I did the same. You might've stopped listening long ago, but I never did."

She said it more as a fact than an accusation, but Selene felt its sting nonetheless. Until recently, she'd shown little care for the mortals around her.

Maryam's head tilted as if to listen more closely to voices only she could hear. Flint opened his mouth to protest, but Selene gestured him to silence.

After a moment, Maryam's stern mouth softened into a smile. "They never stopped praying to Athena," she murmured. "They come by the hundreds of thousands to my Parthenon, even now. They visit by day; they light it up by night." She took a quick breath, her eyes twitching beneath closed lids as if watching history play out before her. "The Nazis occupied it—they knew what it symbolized. But rather than lower the Greek banner that flew over the Acropolis and raise the swastika, an Athenian soldier wrapped himself in his country's flag and jumped from the cliff. Freedom or death." She shuddered visibly. "That's what this place means to those who still bear my name." Her eyes flew open, and she thrust her arms straight out before her. "Give them to me now," she said urgently. "My spear and helmet."

"I don't have the helmet," Selene whispered to Flint while digging through her pack. She unwrapped the pitted spearhead. "But the prophecy only mentioned the spear, so let's hope this does the trick."

Flint pulled his hammer from the sling across his back and an awl from a pouch at his waist. Wielding the massive hammer with a jeweler's care, he began to knock away the green corrosion from the blade. Selene and Theo both moved closer to watch.

Theo whispered, "I thought divine weapons never rusted."

Flint grunted. "They don't." He didn't explain further.

"Wow." Theo cast an awed glance at Maryam. "At some point, she must've covered it in normal bronze to hide its true nature. That's pretty brilliant."

Selene rolled her eyes, trying not to feel jealous of his obvious admiration.

"Stop talking, Schultz," Flint said. "And find me a shaft."

He chipped away another large flake of green. The centimeter of gold beneath gleamed brilliantly even in the dim light. Selene caught her breath as the full spearhead came into view: Now she knew their delay in Athens had been worth it. The blade was smaller than it had looked when encased in bronze, but sharper. It bore no intricate engravings or inlaid designs. Instead, Metis's hammer marks had rippled the gold like the surface of a sunbright lake, glinting and glimmering while hinting at a vast depth and darkness underneath.

Theo unfastened a long wooden support pole from one of the scaffolds and handed it to Flint, who widened the blade's base just enough to slip the pole inside. He handed the spear to Selene, who placed it in her sister's hands.

Maryam's fists closed over the shaft. The light from the spearhead played over her face, illuminating its sharp planes. "Where's my helm?"

"I...couldn't get it," Selene admitted.

Maryam's lips tightened. She reached for her nun's wimple and pulled it off. She ran a hand still stained with clay over hair as black as Selene's but chopped short against her scalp. "My mother gave me this, too. It will be my only helm."

She rose to her feet in one graceful movement and turned to stand before her kin. With her spear clutched in one hand and the other outstretched toward them, she mirrored her ancient statue's pose. But surely no creation of ivory and gold, even one forty feet tall, had eyes that flashed like storm-shrouded lightning.

"Take me to Olympus. You have found your *Promakhos*."

Chapter 40

SHE WHO DWELLS
ON THE HEIGHTS

Hiking boots. Hiking boots. Hiking boots, Theo thought every time the blisters on his heels slammed against the back of his canvas sneakers. Which happened every time he took a step. And he'd taken hundreds of thousands of steps so far. He took another step anyway.

Next time, don't travel without hiking boots, because you never know when you'll be scaling the highest mountain in Greece while carrying one end of a stretcher holding a hundred and fifty pounds of god-flesh. Without Scooter to help, he and Selene had decided to simply carry Zeus up the mountain on their own. They'd lugged the litter straight uphill for six hours, and they still weren't above the tree line.

I should be taking careful notes, he knew. Zeus had summoned him to bear witness to their conclave—to record it as the ancient poets had done. But all he could think about was the pain in his feet. *Carrying the damn stretcher is giving me blisters on my hands, too,* he decided, clenching his teeth against a gasped, "Are we there yet?" *I'm only thirty-three,* he reminded himself. *I am a fit person. I really am. I'm not going to pass out.* But hiking with a goddess was enough to make any man question his abilities.

Neither Selene's knee-high leather boots nor the fact that she'd been carrying the heavier downhill end of Zeus's litter seemed to have any effect on her. In fact, he'd rarely seen her looking so at home.

Of course, he realized. *This* is *her home. Not just Mount Olympus, where she theoretically had a palace above the clouds, but all mountains were home to She Who Dwells on the Heights.* Selene no longer seemed a jaded New Yorker, closed off to everything around her. The higher they climbed, the more at ease she appeared. Only when she glanced down at her unconscious father on the stretcher did the usual scowl crease her forehead. Otherwise, she barely looked like the woman he'd fallen in love with. It made it easier to remember he wasn't in love with her anymore.

The last two nights, he'd lain in his hotel bed—first in Turkey and then for a few hours in a small town at the base of Mount Olympus—knowing that Selene lay on the other side of the wall. The tiny soapstone Artemis statue he'd bought in Ephesus stood on the bedside table, staring at him sternly from beneath her tall crown. He imagined the real Selene wasn't asleep either—she'd always been nearly nocturnal—but he could picture her trying to rest, her long limbs sprawled across her bed, her breasts falling to the side as she rolled... *Stop it,* he told himself sternly, taking another step up the mountain.

He'd found it disturbingly easy to slip back into their old partnership during their hunt for Athena. Piecing together clues with her reminded him of their first week together, when he'd learned to love her. He'd spent the flight from Turkey to Athens repeating the same phrase to himself: *Don't do it, Theo. Don't forget that she lied to you and never apologized. She doesn't even really understand that what she did was wrong—which means she'll just do it again. Let her go.*

A dozen times the night before, he'd almost gotten up and knocked on her door anyway. He wasn't even sure what he'd say to her. *In case you're lying there wondering—yeah, I'm still pissed.* That was one possibility. *Screw you for hurting me like that.* That was another. Or, he could just take her in his arms and run his hands down her back and bury his face in her neck and tell her how much he—*STOP IT.*

He took another step. Then another. *Hiking boots. Hiking boots.*

————⟨◦⟩————

Optimism was a new emotion for Selene. Fierce confidence in her own abilities—yes, that she could usually summon. But blind faith that everything would work out all right, even things beyond her control? *That* was something she'd lost around the time Emperor Constantine converted to Christianity. Yet the minute she'd stepped foot on the mountain, she couldn't suppress a surge of elation. Everywhere in Greece had changed over the millennia—except here. Mount Olympus had always been a wild place, and it still was. No temples or shrines had graced its slopes; the mountain itself was a temple, its towering pines and jagged spurs of rock the only columns it required.

She knew Theo was still angry. He'd barely spoken to her all day, just trudged before her, dutifully carrying the other end of the stretcher. But neither his reticence nor their delayed arrival on Olympus could dampen her spirits. *Theo will forgive me,* she knew somehow. *And Father will be strong again. The mountain will make it happen.*

They'd started their hike before dawn. They needed to arrive at the summit before the almost daily storms moved in to make the ascent impossible—there was a reason Olympus was known as the home of He Who Marshals Thunderheads. But despite slowing her pace to match Theo's, Selene felt absolutely sure they'd make it to the top in time. There, they would reunite with Scooter and the other Athanatoi. *With Maryam and her spear,* Selene decided, *we will cast Saturn into Tartarus and cure Father of his weakness at the same time.*

As the sun rose, the mountain burst into color around her. Wildflowers carpeted the slopes: bright clusters of sunny yarrow, waving stalks of magenta fireweed, delicate chandeliers of purple and white columbine. She passed a patch of sky blue flowers no bigger than raindrops. She could almost hear them whispering their name to her: *Forget-me-not, forget-me-not, forget-me-not. We've been here all along,* they seemed to say. *You abandoned us. Don't do it again.*

I won't, Selene thought, breathing the scent of the pine trees, the hot earth, the blooming flowers. Of Theo's sweat, floating toward her on the warm air. Musky and sweet and familiar.

She looked down at her sleeping father on his stretcher. The wind tossed his beard, its strands only a shade darker than his chalky face.

"We're almost there," she murmured to him. "You're going to be just fine."

"I know you're talking to your dad," Theo panted without turning around, "but I'm taking that as encouragement for me, too."

"Go right ahead." Selene looked at Theo's sweat-drenched neck, knowing he was struggling under the weight of the stretcher. *Maybe it's a good thing he refused to lug Orion's sword and Hades' helm up here, too,* she decided, despite trying to convince him otherwise that morning. *"I'm done with divine weapons,"* he'd insisted. *"I'm here as a witness, not a warrior."*

So far, despite his obvious exhaustion, Theo hadn't complained. *He wants to help bear my burdens—what better sign that he still cares? Either that or he's persevering out of sheer stubbornness.*

Stubbornness was certainly all that kept Flint going. Despite his titanium leg braces, he was obviously in extreme pain. He'd fallen farther and farther behind over the last hour. She glanced through the thinning trees to watch him plodding up the switchbacking path at least half a mile back.

Maryam fared better. She walked just behind Selene, using her spear as a trekking pole. Unsurprisingly, she'd somehow managed to procure sturdy boots, lightweight hiking pants, and a large pack—she'd always known how to plan ahead. After the dramatic investiture in the Parthenon, Selene had expected Maryam to act like the Athena she remembered: smug, self-righteous, and maddeningly bossy. But instead, despite her newly sensible outfit and the spear at her side, the former nun walked silently, head bowed like a penitent. Selene found her obliviousness to the landscape's beauty personally offensive. Athena had always been a city goddess, but how could anyone be unmoved by the mountain's glory?

"Hey," Selene said, drawing Maryam's attention. "The shelter isn't far away now. How about you go down and help Flint while we carry Father the rest of the way?"

Maryam looked thoughtful, then said, "Yes." She turned around abruptly and marched back down the path.

Selene wondered if Theo found the Gray-Eyed Goddess as odd as she did, but from his labored breathing she got the feeling he cared only about his next step. She shifted her hands on the stretcher handles to take a little more of the weight. *We'll have time to compare notes about my family when this is all over,* she decided.

After another twenty minutes, they finally reached the mountain shelter at the edge of the tree line, where hikers could spend the night before their final ascent. A wooden building roofed with solar panels stood in the center of a wide terrace. The slope dropped off before it, allowing a view back down the gorge, and rose precipitously behind, promising a steep climb to the summit.

Scooter lay on his back on a picnic table, basking in the sun. He bounced up when Selene called his name and yelped, "Where have you *been*?"

Before she could answer, he looked at their father, eyes widening. "You said he'd gotten worse. You didn't say he looked like Bela Lugosi on a bad day." Despite his levity, she caught a flash of real concern on his face as he stared at Zeus's unconscious form. "Why'd you carry him all that way when you could've just taken one of the mules?"

Theo gave a sound halfway between a shout and a sob. "Are you kidding me?" He collapsed on a nearby bench and eased off his backpack. "*What* mules?"

Scooter jerked a thumb toward a small paddock holding a dozen pack animals.

Selene glared at her brother. "You're such an asshole."

Scooter threw up his hands. "Don't blame me! I *told* you to meet me at the base of the mountain *yesterday*. Mules for all and a nice overnight in the shelter! Not to mention a helicopter for the final ascent to the summit."

"Helicopter, huh?" Theo asked eagerly.

"Yup. We already took a trip hours ago. That's how I got the old folks up to the top—*including* Saturn. He's all ready for his little joyride to Tartarus. Just waking up from his gin and morphine cocktail. But don't worry; he's tied up tighter than a Botoxed forehead, and I left our blue-haired uncle to guard him. I gave him back his trident, and he's having way too much fun poking the tines into Grandpa's spine whenever he gets feisty."

"Please tell me the helicopter's coming back for us," Theo pleaded.

"Sorry, my friend. Way too late in the day—not enough visibility for a flight. And the mules can't do the final ascent, so we'll have to hoof it on our own." Scooter narrowed his eyes at Selene. "Why *are* you all so late anyway?"

"We made a little detour to fill out the pantheon." Selene was looking forward to seeing his face when Athena arrived.

"Finding our missing kin is *my* job, darling." He looked mildly offended. And worried. "Who did you—"

"Bonjour, mes amis!" a cheerful voice interrupted. Philippe Amata—previously known as Eros, God of Love—stood in the doorway of the mountain shelter, waving his lit cigarette merrily. Blond hair as spiky as usual, slender frame garbed in formfitting jeans and an even tighter shirt. He hurried forward and kissed Selene soundly on both cheeks before she could stop him, then repeated the process with Theo, who stiffened in his embrace—no doubt remembering the love dart Philippe had shot into his arm after Selene's "death."

Philippe held Theo at arm's length with a bashful smile. "I'll have you know I *told* her not to lie to you."

Selene wanted to tell him he wasn't helping, but Philippe had already turned to Zeus with a gasp of dismay. "He looks terrible!"

"I know," Selene growled. "Which is why we don't have time to waste. We're only stopping here long enough to gather everyone together. Then we keep going. Helicopter or no."

Philippe nodded. "But where's Papa?"

"Your stepfather's about half a mile behind us," Selene told him.

"Ah, *merde,*" he cursed. "I will go help." Philippe trotted off to the paddock and led the sturdiest mule back down the path.

"There goes my angel. Always so full of *l'amour* even for those who don't deserve it," said a woman emerging from the shelter in a high-waisted 1940s safari suit. Her crystalline blue eyes flicked to Selene. "It's been too long, Huntress."

Or not long enough, Selene thought, smothering a groan. *Aphrodite.* As the Chaste One, Selene had a pathological aversion to the Goddess of Erotic Love. She could almost feel her optimism leaking away. Nothing about this trip was going to be as easy as it seemed.

The goddess sashayed onto the terrace, tucked a stray blond curl back beneath her brightly patterned Hermès silk kerchief—no doubt a gift from Scooter—and walked to Zeus. She knelt gracefully beside the stretcher to brush a kiss on the lined forehead of the man who had been her king and, like all the male Olympians, her sometime lover. "I wouldn't have recognized him with all his beauty gone," she said worriedly, as if his looks mattered more than his ragged breathing.

She rose to her feet in a single sensuous movement and, ignoring Scooter and Selene entirely, made straight for Theo. She gave him her hand palm down, clearly expecting him to kiss it.

"Esme Amata," she introduced herself, her voice a throaty, seductive murmur. Unlike her son, Esme had no French accent, although Selene suspected she could speak in whatever accent she chose, depending on the whim of the man she was trying to seduce. It seemed one Athanatos, at least, hadn't changed a bit. "You're the handsome Makarites my son was raving about."

Theo took her hand, clearly flustered, and shook it firmly. Selene tried and failed not to notice his eyes widening as he took in the voluptuous perfection of Esme's figure, the coral-shell hue of her generous mouth, the dove-soft luster of her skin. She no longer looked like the young, nubile woman she'd been in her prime—she looked *better*. Maturity agreed with her.

Esme took a bold step closer to Theo. "I've heard all about you. The Huntress doesn't know what she threw away, does she?"

One more step toward him, Selene seethed silently, *and I'll throw away her next. Right over the side of this mountain.*

Theo started to stutter an answer, but Esme talked right over him. "I like a man who likes strong women. And, unlike some relatives of mine, I'm not scared of a little"—she blinked languorously—"intimacy."

Selene's fingernails had carved deep crescents in her palms. *I told Flint he didn't get to own me. I don't get to own Theo,* she reminded herself. She felt a sudden moment of empathy for Flint nonetheless. Possessiveness came naturally to the gods.

A puff of smoke wafted from the door of the shelter. A pungent mixture of marijuana, mint, and pennyroyal. Which could only mean one thing.

"Dennis is here?" Theo sniffed the air.

Selene's mood blackened further. She still hadn't forgiven the God of Wine for encouraging Theo to kill himself.

Scooter shrugged. "Pop said he wanted his whole family, right? I'm just following orders."

"Any more surprises?" Selene demanded. "Are all the aunts and uncles already on the summit?"

"Of course!" His self-satisfied smile shrank a centimeter. "Well...those that are left, anyway." He lowered his voice as he spoke their true names. "Demeter, Hestia, and Hera. Uncle Poseidon, like I said, is guarding Grandpa. And Cora's there, too."

Cora, once called Persephone, was their sister-cousin, the off-spring of Zeus and his sister Demeter. As the Goddess of Spring, Persephone had once looked younger even than the perennially youthful Apollo and Artemis. But her status as a minor goddess, bereft of the name recognition the Olympians enjoyed, had consigned her to more rapid fading than the others. When Selene had last seen her, Cora had looked like a woman in her sixties. The Mithraists' brutal murder of her beloved husband, Hades, the God of the Underworld, could only have aged her further.

"How'd you manage to convince Aunt June to come? She had no interest in helping Father. You tore her away from her honeymoon with young Mauricio?"

"Kicking and screaming." Scooter grinned. "But hey, no one can resist a Great Gathering of the Gods."

"Speak for yourself."

Another cloud of reeking smoke drifted from the shelter. Esme thrummed a chuckle and batted her lashes at Theo. Selene grunted.

She returned to Zeus's side, laying a hand on his clammy forehead. "You're going to owe me one, Father," she murmured to him. "There's nothing like a family reunion to make me want to disown ninety percent of my relations."

Chapter 41

GODDESSES OF OLYMPUS

Scarlett Johansson's sex appeal... Marilyn Monroe's glamour... Cate Blanchett's elegance...

Theo was running out of beautiful blond celebrities, and he still hadn't described Aphrodite to his own satisfaction. Normally, he would've enjoyed meeting another Athanatos. It was, after all, why he'd accepted Zeus's invitation in the first place. But despite her blandishments, Esme Amata made him feel like he'd time traveled back to 1999, when a gawky, pimpled, teenage Theo Schultz hadn't yet learned to wield his humor like other boys wielded their football prowess. *At any moment, I'm going to ask her to prom, and she's going to laugh in my face. Or she's going to shove me into a broom closet and have her way with me.*

I'm not even sure which is worse.

He made a half-hearted excuse to leave the terrace and retreated into the mountain shelter, looking for blister treatments.

Sprawled across a bench in the dining area with one hairy-knuckled bare foot propped up beside him and his knee spread wide to display the crotch of his too-tight denim shorts, Dennis Boivin's unsightliness only threw Esme's beauty into sharper relief.

The Releaser's eyes widened when he saw Theo. He puffed two thick lines of odiferous smoke through his nostrils like a seething dragon, then scrambled to his feet and threw Theo against the wall.

"Hey!" Theo shoved back, hard, but for all his apparent lassitude, Dennis had an Athanatos's strength.

"Think you can steal my golden leaf, little fucker?" Dennis growled in his ear. "Bet you felt smart, huh? Clever Professor Theo, always the quick study." The god slipped his hand under Theo's shirt, ripped the pendant free, and dangled it in front of his face. "Guess I got the last laugh, though. Whole thing's just some useless Orphic bullshit."

"Orphic bullshit that got me into the Underworld and back out, with Selene in tow."

Dennis immediately released him. "No shit!"

Theo rubbed his bruised chest. "Yeah shit."

Dennis stepped to the window and looked out to where Selene crouched worriedly beside her father. "I thought no way you were going to go through with it. You committed suicide and everything?"

"Piece of cake. You should really try it sometime."

Dennis just guffawed at the insult, all his ire immediately dissolving into his usual insouciant derision. "And look at you now, up on Olympus with the big boys. Bet you're wetting yourself with excitement."

"Remind me, is it the *big boys* who needed a mule to get up here?" Theo asked casually. "Because it seems—"

"Don't remind me of those horrible beasts," Esme interrupted, appearing in the doorway. "The whole trip smelled like dung. Not at all what I'm used to."

What is she used to? Theo wondered. *Rose petals underfoot and naked young men fanning her with dove feathers?*

"What do you do, Esme?" he couldn't help asking. "For a job, I mean."

Clearly bemused, she replied, "Why would you think I have a job?"

"Selene's a private investigator. Philippe runs a dating website, right? So I just assumed—"

Esme waved a dismissive hand. "Selene needs the money. Philippe likes the distraction. I don't need either of those things. Love is the best distraction you can ask for. And as for money"—she chuckled throatily—"I get plenty of that."

For the first time, Theo noticed the ring she wore. A diamond the size of a marble. "You're engaged?" he asked her.

"Oh, perpetually," she said, the corners of her coral lips turning up. "To one man or another."

"But not...married?"

Dennis and Esme laughed. Theo couldn't help feeling they were laughing at him.

"You're adorable," Esme said. "The Goddess of Erotic Love couldn't possibly get married." She batted thick black lashes at him. "That would defeat the purpose, wouldn't it?"

Her limpid blue eyes turned hard, just for an instant, and Theo suddenly understood why Aphrodite had betrayed her husband, Hephaestus, and chosen Mars for her lover. To her, Love was War. A series of conquests and pillages. Storm in and take their hearts, take their diamonds, and then move on to the next battle. She hadn't, he noticed, even acknowledged that she *was* in fact still married to Flint. The Smith believed in building things slowly, carefully. That was as true for his relationships as it was for his complicated mechanical inventions. He'd taken centuries to craft his bond with his stepson, Philippe. Even longer to finally reveal how he felt about Selene. Theo felt a surge of sympathy, remembering how Flint, despite all his surly reserve, had fallen prey, over and over, to his wife's wiles. Theo squared his shoulders, determined not to suffer the same fate.

Esme stepped closer. He'd expected her to smell like flowers; instead, the tang of a woman's sex and the faint musk of sweat wafted toward him, as if she'd enjoyed a marathon session of lovemaking just before he arrived. He cast a suspicious glance at Dennis's bulging crotch and wondered if that could actually be true.

In the myths, he remembered, Aphrodite and Dionysus had a son named Priapus, the God of Fertility. He'd seen a fresco in Pompeii of Priapus placing his two-foot-long penis on a scale, where it easily outweighed several bushels of grain. As Dennis's grad school roommate, Theo could testify from firsthand observation that Priapus's father wasn't as well-endowed—not quite, anyway. He shuddered at the memory of Dennis's disturbingly frequent naked rambles through their apartment.

That got Theo thinking of Dennis's orgies, which made him think of his own crotch, which made him look again at She Who Turns to Love, who'd unbuttoned the top of her shirt so that two perfect hemispheres of creamy flesh swelled into view, which made him turn to the shelter's reception desk and pound the bell in a desperate SOS.

The manager appeared, a harried woman with unwashed hair.

"*Kalimera,*" Theo greeted her. "Could I get a blister pad and a pitcher of cold water, please?"

The woman dashed sweat from her forehead. "There is no water. No toilets, no drinking water, no showers." She sounded angry. "The spring that feeds the shelter has run dry."

"Climate change?"

"That's what started it. Not enough snow this winter. But then the government came in and tried to help. Brought in a whole bunch of machines to dig deeper channels, but that just made it worse. Now there's nothing." She reached behind the desk and retrieved a pack of blister plasters and a bottle of water from a cooler. "Ten euros."

At this point, Theo would've paid twice that. He took his bottle of water, downed half of it in one gulp, then found himself standing uncertainly in the middle of the room.

Esme had moved to sit with Dennis, and the look that passed between them signaled it wouldn't be long before they returned to their erotic pursuits. Theo didn't intend to play voyeur, but he didn't particularly feel like going out to talk to his former girlfriend either. Looking at Esme just made him more aware of his desire for Selene, not less.

"Do you think we're making him uncomfortable?" Esme asked Dennis, not bothering to lower her voice.

"Theo-bore's always uncomfortable," the God of Revelry replied, looking straight at him. "You should've seen him in grad school, gasping like a shocked schoolmarm when I'd bring home some heroin and some women for a little nighttime snack. I swear he used to go into his room and secretly call the cops on me."

"No wonder the Chaste One likes him so much. They're a perfect match."

Theo downed the rest of his water, now thoroughly confused. Hadn't Esme been coming on to him a moment before?

"Oh, he's embarrassed!" Esme said with a peal of laughter. "He thought I wanted him!" She finally addressed Theo directly. "I just wanted to remind the Huntress how she feels about you. I'm awfully good at matchmaking, as you can imagine."

"Do you expect me to thank you?" he asked stiffly. "Because I don't even—"

"I didn't do it for you."

"You did it for Selene?"

Esme snorted delicately. "I just don't want *Hephaestus* to have her. He is still my husband, after all."

Theo felt exactly like the prudish schoolmarm Dennis had so derided. All these "gods," these hypocrites, these greedy *assholes*. They manipulated each other; they manipulated him. Selene had done it, too, asking Philippe to shoot that love dart into his arm after she'd faked her death. *I can't trust any of them,* he decided, growing angrier by the second.

He stormed out of the shelter, then froze on the terrace, unsure where to turn. Maryam was just arriving, followed by Flint, who rode on a mule led by his stepson. The two men went to speak with Scooter and Selene, who'd already started making preparations to continue their trek. Selene glanced up from securing her pack and caught Theo's eye. Heat flashed between them before he looked away. Perhaps Esme's little ploy had achieved its desired effect. He couldn't help hoping it had—and then hating that he cared one way or the other.

Maryam sat by herself at a picnic table, massaging her feet. *Perhaps I finally found the one goddess I can relate to,* he decided, heading toward her. He'd felt little kinship with Sister Maryam back in Turkey, and the *Athena Promakhos* atop the Acropolis had seemed far too intimidating for small talk, but now, seeing her so isolated from the other Athanatoi, he felt a tug of empathy.

As he made his way toward her, he noticed the construction site on the border of the shelter. A sign in Greek and English explained that an American company had sponsored the "spring relocation" project that would ensure a continuous water supply for the shelter in the face of climate change. Beside it sat a backhoe and a bulldozer. He pitied the poor mule that had to lug the machinery up the mountain.

He walked to Maryam's table. "I see you're not twirling around the mountainside Maria von Trapp style, huh?" he ventured. "Not that kind of nun?"

She looked mystified by the reference. It seemed American musicals had never made it to the convent. He tried a more direct approach. "I've got some blister bandages if you need them."

"That would be useful," she said.

Useful, Theo mused. *Not "nice." Not "good for my evil plan to manipulate all my relatives." This is a woman devoted to practicality above all. What a nice change of pace.*

He handed over half his supply, then reached to pull off his own sneakers and cotton socks. "Honestly, I wasn't sure how hard the hike was for you," he said, watching her apply the adhesives to the backs of her heels.

"Hard enough."

"But you...you're still worshiped. After a fashion. I thought maybe your strength..."

"Strength to stay young, yes. Strength to perform the odd miracle or two for the penitent, yes. Or at least, to make them believe I'm performing a miracle," she admitted. "But physical strength? The Virgin Mary doesn't climb a lot of mountains. Nor is she used to lugging such weight anymore."

Theo looked down at her enormous hiking pack. He'd assumed that, since she didn't complain, Maryam had shouldered her burden easily enough. "Now that we've got more people to carry the stretcher, I could help with your pack the rest of the way," he offered.

"You think you'd be helping me," she said matter-of-factly. "But once the oxygen thins, the extra weight would slow you down by at least thirty percent." She glanced at the sloping path to the summit. "Perhaps thirty-two if I judge that gradient right. We'd need to leave you behind to get to the top before the storms move in, but Selene wouldn't do that without protest, and I predict it would take at least fifteen minutes to convince her otherwise." She glanced at her watch. "My uncle and aunts are already waiting up there with Saturn. We can't afford any more delays." Then, for just an instant, this new, scarily smart Athena disappeared once more behind Sister Maryam's gentle smile, and she added, "But thank you for your kindness."

"Um. Anytime." He wasn't sure what made him more uneasy: the mathematical precision, the jarring personality shift, or the fact that she thought Selene could be convinced to abandon him in fifteen minutes.

Either way, when Selene announced that they'd be continuing

their ascent, and Maryam hoisted her huge pack onto her shoulders, Theo made no move to help.

Neither did Scooter, who'd been staring at his half sister with an unusually chilly expression ever since she'd arrived. He sauntered over to the picnic table. "This is quite a surprise. *Maryam*, is it?"

Theo wondered if Scooter's aloofness resulted from bruised pride. As the god tasked with keeping track of the Olympians, he wouldn't appreciate Maryam sidestepping him.

"I came here to help Father," she said calmly. "Selene said I was needed."

"Yes, so I heard." He gave her a strained smile. "The more the merrier."

Turning to the assembled crowd on the terrace, he said, "Okay, ladies and gentlemen and Dennis. This is the last push. We need to get up there before eleven in the a.m. After that, we're hiking through a torrential downpour, and the whole plan's kaput. So let's be quick like little mountain goats, yes?" He glanced up at the summit, already shrouded in clouds. "Unfortunately, no helicopter in this weather and no mules. So Philippe, you and Selene should take Pop's stretcher. That way, our brave Makarites can be rested when he gets to the top."

"I don't need—" Theo began, but Scooter talked right over him.

"I'll lead the way, okay, and no stragglers." He winked at Flint, who glared back as if he might break the slender man in half.

Theo hitched his own pack higher on his shoulders and tried to ignore the tension swirling around him. *Selene's staring daggers at Esme,* he couldn't help noticing. *Philippe's scowling at Scooter; I want to throttle Dennis; Scooter's giving Maryam the stink eye; Esme keeps batting her lashes at me; and Flint is clearly furious at every single one of us. Forget the storm up ahead. We'll be lucky if we don't incinerate each other right here on the trail.*

Chapter 42

CLOUD-COMPELLING ONE

The line of gods stretched down the slope like a sacred procession, passing through the rolling clouds as if emerging from a dream.

Scooter walked at the front, a hierophant leading his initiates. To Selene's surprise, he'd chosen to wear his winged cap. After it'd been struck by lightning during the battle atop the Statue of Liberty, it didn't fly anymore, not even for a Makarites like Theo. Yet the soft light of the mist-shrouded mountaintop obscured the dents and broken feathers, and Scooter made a surprisingly convincing Hermes, Messenger of the Gods.

Selene urged Philippe to walk faster so they could get upwind of his mother, whose unmistakable musk filled her with a discomfiting mélange of nausea and titillation. Dennis, who somehow managed to move with languorous slowness and still keep pace with the swifter gods, walked just behind Esme. He carried two large plastic water bottles—undoubtedly filled with something other than water—attached to a fanny pack he'd probably owned since the eighties. He used his thyrsus—a pinecone-tipped staff twined with vines—as a walking stick.

Maryam plodded along beneath her heavy pack, her eyes on her feet. Theo came next, wincing with every step. Flint hobbled behind them. Selene could hear his heavy breathing as he struggled to keep up, but wondered if part of his pacing was purposeful. He hadn't spoken to his estranged wife, and he seemed careful not to get anywhere near her.

It took nearly an hour for the whole lumbering party to make it up the steep, boulder-covered slope to the start of the Skala plateau that marked the penultimate portion of the trail. Beyond it, only the final ascent remained.

The word "plateau" was misleading. "Skala," after all, meant "stairs." The expanse sloped continually upward, and at nearly three thousand meters above sea level, the thin oxygen sapped even Selene's strength. Philippe, too, struggled with the other end of the stretcher, sweat making his spiky hair spikier. Only Scooter seemed unfazed. His swift pace soon took him over a slight rise and out of sight.

The summit, where Selene's aunts and uncle waited with Saturn, never seemed to get any closer.

There were no trees this high on the mountain, just an unrelenting field of gray gravel. *This is no longer my mountain realm,* Selene realized. She felt as if they walked through the Sky instead, the ground the same color as the clouds that blew across the plateau and blocked the sun. She'd thought she'd feel like a goddess up here; instead, she felt like an intruder. *This isn't where I belong,* she decided. *This is my father's turf.*

She looked down at the stretcher, expecting to see Zeus open his eyes. Surely just being here would give him strength. But he remained unconscious, his breath rapid and uneven. She quickened her steps to make it over the rise ahead of them, then slowed once more when a figure appeared in the distance, obscured by the thick clouds. She could make out a protruding limb, a towering head, something that looked like a trident. *Poseidon?* She tensed at the thought. *Does my blue-haired uncle know I killed his son Orion last year?* she wondered belatedly. *Is he about to attack me with his trident, seeking vengeance?*

She looked around for Scooter, hoping he'd already dealt with the situation. But the Messenger of the Gods was nowhere to be found.

"Scooter?" she called. Her voice sounded strange and muffled in the wet air. "He was just ahead of us—did anyone see where he went?"

Esme patted her sweating upper lip delicately with the edge of her silk kerchief. "I wasn't looking."

Philippe shrugged. "You know how he is. Probably just ran ahead to show off his speed."

The clouds scudded past, revealing the open ground ahead of them. The strange figure, she saw now, was no god—just a construction mechanism. Some sort of telescoping drill.

"That's mine," Flint said, coming up panting beside her.

"What do you mean?"

"I invented it. It can drill up to three hundred meters deep, but runs on solar power and is ultralight for easy transport though difficult terrain. It's supposed to drill wells in villages in Africa."

"Then why's it on top of Olympus?"

Flint narrowed his eyes. "Because the man I sold it to must've brought it up here."

"And who's that?" she pressed.

"Scooter Joveson."

Selene shrugged. "Maybe he's going to use it to help open Tartarus."

Theo joined them, already shaking his head. "No, it's for the spring relocation project. I saw the signs down at the shelter. Listen, you can hear the water."

Flint scowled at him. "There is no spring this high up. It starts at the shelter and runs downhill from there."

"But Theo's right," Selene said, listening. She and Philippe laid down the stretcher. She followed the sound. Not far from the drilling machine, she found a narrow hole. She couldn't see the water inside, but she could hear it burbling.

Flint crouched down as far as his leg braces would allow. "Scooter somehow redirected the spring water up to the plateau. That's an engineering feat that even I'd have a hard time with. It must've taken all year—and it certainly wouldn't help the shelter's water supply." He gave her a grim look. "Scooter must've been working on this since well before we freed your father from the mithraeum and heard about his plan to open Tartarus. What does he know that we don't? This doesn't feel safe."

Esme frowned. "You're being paranoid. We may all enjoy our little plots and ploys"—she ignored Theo's indignant snort—"but Scooter would never put me in danger. He loves me." She smiled a little smugly.

Flint gave his wife a black look. "Then what the hell's he doing with the water?"

"If you're so distrustful," Selene snapped, too tired to bother tempering her tone, "then why come?" One look at his face and she knew the answer. He'd come for her, of course.

Philippe put a hand on his stepfather's arm. "I'm sure Scooter just wants the same thing we all do, Papa," he said gently. "To help Zeus. Trust me when I say he loves his father." He gave Flint's arm an affectionate squeeze. "I know real love when I see it."

Maryam's brow furrowed. "And yet there is much here we do not understand. We should consider turning around, synthesizing this new information about Scooter and the water flow, and then examining our options from several angles. We will miss our chance for the summit today, but we can spend the night at the shelter and try again tomorrow if we decide it's prudent."

On his stretcher, Zeus moaned and turned his head, then settled once more. His skin was the same flat gray as the stony ground.

"He won't make it," Selene insisted. "Two nights ago he told me this is all the time he had left. If we don't get Tartarus opened today, then it's too late." She looked at each of the Athanatoi in turn, coming to a decision. "I've spent too long questioning my own siblings. Esme and Philippe are right: Scooter wouldn't hurt Father. Or us. If he's building some contraption up here, then it's part of his plan to help. He's the Giver of Good Things, remember?"

Maryam and Flint still didn't look convinced, but neither did they protest.

"We have greater enemies to battle than each other," Selene went on. "Death. Saturn. The giants. *That's* who we should be worried about. So let's be prepared."

She took off her backpack and drew out the parts of her bow. Flint scowled, but moved the massive hammer on his back into easy reach. The others followed suit: Philippe removed his own child-sized myrtle bow from his satchel, along with a quiver of tiny darts; Maryam opened her enormous backpack and, to Selene's amazement, pulled out a complete set of bulletproof tactical armor. The Goddess of Love had no weapons Selene could see—Esme had never needed anything besides her own beauty. But Selene noticed she took a step closer to her son.

Dennis leaned on his thyrsus, watching with a lopsided leer. "This is finally getting good. Much more interesting than screwing my ten thousandth undergrad."

Selene barely managed to restrain herself from sending an arrow through her half brother, but she somehow managed to keep her shafts—both wood and hawk-feather fletched—securely in the quiver at her hip. *Greater enemies to battle . . .* she reminded herself as she slung her bow across her back and hoisted her end of the stretcher again. She and Philippe started back up the path.

This time, Theo walked beside her. Despite her confident words, she shivered with apprehension as they continued up the slope. He seemed to sense her unease.

"You're going to save your dad," he said, for her ears alone. "I know it." He put a hand on her arm. It was the first time he'd touched her with any warmth since that first passionate kiss in the Phrygianum.

"But if Flint's right, and I just brought Father into danger, instead... *Styx*, if I brought *you* into danger..."

A spark flashed between them when he met her eyes—yet he didn't pull away. "You didn't bring me. I came."

Another thick cloud moved across the plateau, sucking the warmth from the air and the light from the sun. Selene could see no more than ten feet ahead.

She paused to pull a fleece blanket from her pack and tuck it around her father. Flint had already donned a thick sweater. Maryam's body armor protected her well enough. Theo simply clutched his bare arms across his chest; he hadn't brought any other layers. Philippe put on a light windbreaker but looked like he barely minded the cold. *This is a sure sign of who's seriously fading and who's not,* Selene thought.

Dennis kept walking, clearly impervious to the temperature, while Esme simply tightened her silk kerchief around her face, probably just to protect her coiffure from the wind. Selene hoped Scooter had provided plenty of warm clothing for the Olympians he'd already helicoptered to the summit. Zeus's siblings—Demeter, Poseidon, and Hestia—were likely as frail as their brother, and Aunt June hadn't looked like a woman used to frigid temperatures either. Selene found the damp chill in the air more annoying than debilitating, but the hair on her arms stood up nonetheless. *I'm cold more from worry than the weather,* she knew, forcing herself to stay calm.

She glanced at Theo's shivering form, reminded of just how frail his mortal body really was. He'd already died *twice* since she'd known him.

She wanted to tell him to turn around. His little adventure

to meet the other gods might become something far more complicated, and Theo shouldn't be there. *Why did Father even invite him?* she wondered belatedly. *It can't just be to help record the Gathering.* But one look at Theo's determined face and she knew any protest would be useless. Besides, hadn't he just reminded her that coming to Olympus was his decision? The last time she'd tried to shield him from pain he'd wound up dying anyway. He knew as much as she did about what they were facing. If he wanted to turn back, he would.

He caught her staring at him and crooked her a faint ghost of his old familiar smile as if to say, *Don't let the shivering fool you—I'm perfectly content right where I am.* She found herself smiling back. Still, she wished he'd agreed to bring his divine weapons along.

Maryam followed Selene's gaze to Theo. Without a word, she pulled a foil emergency blanket from her pack and handed it to him. He wrapped it around his torso, a billowing silver cloak for a shaking Makarites.

They walked on, scree crunching beneath their feet. Even Selene's usually sure steps sent shards of rock skipping down the hill behind her, raising a cloud of dust and eliciting several yelped protests from Esme.

The stretcher's weight only made Selene's footing worse. Her boot slipped on a large stone; she looked down to see that the moving gravel had uncovered a large capped pipe sticking up two inches from the ground. She stopped to look at it more closely just as the last ragged edges of a cloud passed by, clearing the landscape again and revealing at least a dozen more pipes marching across the plateau.

Flint caught up to them. "Scooter's not just bringing the water to the plateau," he warned. "He's diverting it all the way to the summit."

"But we still don't know why," Selene said, looking to Maryam for an answer.

The Goddess of Wisdom and Crafts just looked down pensively at the pipe without speaking.

"Okay, then," Selene said brusquely. "We keep moving."

They followed the trail, the pipes growing more frequent on either side. She couldn't hear the water anymore, but she imagined it running uphill beneath her feet, an inexorable, impossible river carrying her toward the unknown.

Chapter 43

INTERMISSIO: THE TETRACTYS

The Tetractys sat cross-legged on the summit of Olympus, counting aloud.

"One and two. Two and three. Three and four."

One and two. Two and three. Three and four.

Over and over he counted, trying to lose himself in the sacred numbers so he could forget what was about to happen to his friend Theo.

He watched his siblings wind their way up the slope beneath him, each one an ant carrying its own heavy burden.

Guilt, shame, grief, loneliness, weakness, despair.

He had tried to doff those loads time and again, to forget the past and make his way in the ever-changing mortal world. But his family had suffered. Even those who still retained their youth today would eventually fade away entirely. His family was dying.

The Tetractys couldn't let that happen.

He'd always been a Trickster, but he was a Helper, a Shepherd, and a Giver of Good Things, too. The Father had given him a chance to help his family when they could not help themselves.

For years, the Tetractys had worked with the Father on this plan, although he didn't want to admit that. His siblings would know how long he'd lied to them, and they'd find it harder to forgive him when they learned of the sacrifices that had been made along the way—not to mention the one still to come.

In a few minutes, everything he'd worked for and dreamed of for so long would finally become reality. He'd rushed to the summit, unable to wait any longer, and anxious to make sure the other Athanatoi were still in place. His instincts had served him well—Hera was about to back out when he arrived. Despite her complete lack of mountaineering skills, the woman who called herself June had started climbing down the summit on her own, claiming something didn't feel right, and she should never have agreed to come in the first place. It had taken all his famed skills of persuasion to convince her to stay.

Now his hands shook with excitement—and trepidation. *This is my moment of triumph,* he knew. *We will all enter the new Age together.*

Yet he couldn't help wondering if his family would see it that way. Selene certainly wouldn't—not when the man she loved had to die to make it happen.

He reached into the pocket of his jacket and pulled out a set of reed pipes. *I am the Tetractys. I am the perfect number,* he reminded himself. *I am the harmonies that will remake the world.*

"One and two. Two and three. Three and four," he counted as he played the sacred notes. Over and over until his own guilt floated away on the wings of melody.

Chapter 44

SHE WHO TURNS TO LOVE

"Mytikas," the Greeks called Olympus's peak—the Nose. But from the crest of the plateau, it looked more like a crown.

An oval slope rose before Selene, surrounded by great jagged spires of rock like a diadem's points. The center looked carved by an ice-cream scoop, smooth and steep and impossible to climb.

From where she stood at the plateau's edge, the Mytikas peak seemed to float in space two hundred yards away. But when she moved closer to the lip, a knife's edge of rock appeared, connecting the plateau to the peak. One wrong step across that bridge would spell certain death, even for an Athanatos. Carrying Zeus's stretcher across would prove extremely difficult—getting it up the slope to the summit itself would be nearly impossible.

Standing beside her, Theo gave a nervous smile. "Please tell me you smuggled a divine jet pack up here, because I don't see a path."

Selene pointed to the rock face. "There are red dots painted on the stone to show you where to put your hands and feet."

Theo squinted, but clearly his mortal eyes weren't up to the task. "Hands? You mean we've got to climb?"

"Yes, although you won't need ropes. You might *want* them, but you don't need them. And it's your choice—you don't have to come," she couldn't help saying.

"Please—and miss all the fun? I'm like Dennis; undergrads are getting boring." He laughed shortly. "Teaching them, that is, not...you know."

"I figured."

He gazed at her, suddenly sober. "I'm coming. Not just to bear witness or for the thrill of meeting Poseidon and Demeter and the others—although, I have to admit, that's pretty cool. But because you—you guys—might need me."

She didn't miss his stumble. He was coming for her, even if he wanted to pretend otherwise.

"So, great Hawk-Eyed One," he went on. "Do you see the rest of the pantheon up there?"

Selene smiled at the made-up epithet. *His teasing is a good sign.* "Not from this angle. But I can see the storm clouds. The weather's bad up there, and it's only going to get worse. We've got to hurry."

Philippe rubbed at the blisters on his hands. "We can't hurry if we're carrying this stretcher."

Selene knew he was right. "Maybe we go up first without Father," she ventured. "Rig a pulley system—"

Maryam interrupted. "It will take us at least forty-five minutes to get to the top, then another twenty to jury-rig a pulley for the stretcher and haul Father up. We have to take him with us the first time. Otherwise, the probability of success becomes vanishingly slim."

"But how do we get—?" Philippe began.

"I'll carry him." Selene bent down and lifted her father carefully off the litter.

"Even She Who Dwells on the Heights needs to use her hands to climb that slope," Theo protested.

Maryam had already reached into her pack for a long length

of nylon rope. With a speed and ingenuity that put Flint's to shame, she fashioned a quick harness and slung it over Selene's shoulders. With Theo's help, Maryam maneuvered Zeus's limp form into the ropes, his legs dangling around Selene's hips and his arms over her shoulders. His head rested against her neck.

Theo stepped back to admire Maryam's handiwork. "Not exactly Luke and Yoda, but not bad."

Despite the weight of her father's limp form on her back, Selene found herself chuckling.

Theo gave her a puzzled smile as he helped secure the gold bow to Selene's hip so it'd be within easy reach. "What are you laughing at? You don't even know what it means."

"Sure I do. I watched *The Empire Strikes Back* while I was in Rome."

"Without me?" He seemed more disappointed than angry.

She hesitated. "I can watch it again."

He stared at her as if contemplating the offer.

I'm proposing a future together, she realized, *and he hasn't rejected it.* She waited for him to say something more. When he didn't, a wave of regret rushed through her. *I should've said more to him in the Pantheon. I should've apologized for lying to him. I should've admitted how much I'd missed him. How much I love him.* Instead, she said aloud, "It's taking all my willpower not to throw you over my shoulder and carry you off this mountain to somewhere where you can't tumble to your death or be eaten by giants from Tartarus. You know that, don't you?"

He nodded, a smile hovering on his lips. "But you haven't."

She took a deep breath, finally understanding why it seemed to matter so much to him that she allow him to throw himself into danger. Despite her near immortality and his humanity, it made them, somehow, equals.

"I would keep you safe if I could," she said. "Not just today. But every day."

He didn't reply, but she heard the sharpness of his breathing, as if her words had tightened his chest.

"But that's not my job, is it?" she asked.

"Not if it means locking me away in a box, like Eos did to Tithonus."

Selene remembered how Eos, Goddess of the Dawn, had fallen in love with the mortal Tithonus and begged Zeus to grant him immortality. Zeus had complied, but Eos forgot to ask that her lover be given eternal youth as well. Tithonus grew so aged, so weak, that eventually he shrank into a grasshopper. Eos had placed her tiny lover in a box to carry with her everywhere.

I can't decide what's best for Theo. I can't make him immortal. One day, he will grow old. He will die, while I'll barely look middle-aged. I'll have to be okay with that.

She nodded at him, a silent assent to his demand.

Theo's gaze warmed, but he didn't reply.

Esme's throaty giggle broke the sudden silence between them. "Enough flirting, you two."

"Not everyone's thinking about sex all the time," Selene shot back, feeling the blood rush to her cheeks.

Philippe jumped in. "*Oui*, Mama, leave them alone." He put a restraining hand on Esme's elbow to protect Selene from his mother—or vice versa. He cast a worried glance at his stepfather farther down the slope.

Flint shouted up to him, "Do you feel the electricity in the air?"

"Um..." Philippe's eyes darted between Theo and Selene.

"He means from the storm," Selene said quickly. Flint was right; the air seemed to hum as the clouds overhead darkened like a new bruise. "We need to move."

She hitched Zeus a little higher onto her shoulders and started toward the slender ridge that led to Mytikas. The others followed. Flint, she noticed, had donned a rock-climbing harness—not around his waist, but his chest. He carried a long coil of rope over his shoulder, along with a variety of carabiners, ratchets, and a handlebar. He handed another coil of rope to Philippe, who stayed close beside him as they stepped onto the ridge.

"He'll be slow," Maryam stated. "We must keep going."

Selene felt guilty, but she knew her sister was right. Zeus had to get to the summit.

The ridge stretched before her like a catwalk. A low cloud disguised the drop on either side—she wasn't sure if that was better or worse than seeing the valley three thousand meters below. She took a deep breath and focused on the painted red circles marking the path.

Theo's voice sounded strained. "I feel like Pac-Man. Just follow the dots, right?"

"Not sure what you mean this time, but yes." She stepped forward. Normally, the journey would've been simple for someone with her agility and strength, but her concern for her father stiffened her movements, and the combination of his awkward weight and the bow hanging off her body made her balance tenuous.

"Let me take the bow," Theo said.

Selene shook her head. She needed her weapon within reach.

"Or I could carry your dad," he offered, sounding far less confident.

Selene snorted. "You'd topple off the ridge like a drunk bacchant. Besides, this is my responsibility." *I'm the one who knew he was rotting away in that cave for decades and never bothered to go to him until it was too late.* "I'll be fine." She walked quickly forward to prove her point—and almost twisted her ankle on a loose rock. It skittered over the side and plummeted soundlessly into the cloud.

Theo swore softly then turned to Maryam. "You got another line in that pack of yours?" She handed him a length of red climbing rope.

He started to tie one end around his own waist and the

other around Selene, but Maryam stopped him. "You tie terrible knots, has anyone ever told you that?"

Theo quirked a smile at Selene. "Yes, actually."

Maryam refastened the rope to both their waists. "You realize that if one of you falls, there's a very good chance you're just going to take the other down with you."

Selene held her breath, waiting for Theo to untie the rope. Yet when he looked up, he held her eyes and said solemnly, "Yeah, that's the idea."

Selene swallowed hard and nodded. She wanted desperately to rip the rope from his body, but that's exactly what she'd just promised not to do. *If we're truly equals, then he can share my risk,* she knew. *And he* wants *to share it. I never thought he'd feel that way again.*

The red rope stretched between them now, a physical reminder of the link they'd forged, through life and death and back again. Suddenly, she didn't want to free him from its pull; she wanted to reel him in instead. To yank him, hard and fast, into her arms. To say with her embrace what she still couldn't find the words to say aloud. *There will be time for that,* she thought, unable to repress a shudder of anticipation. *When we get off the mountain, we can finally pick up where we left off on that night above New York Harbor.*

Red dot to red dot, she moved carefully across the ridge, Theo's footsteps echoing her own. She could hear his heart tripping in double time.

The ridge wasn't flat; that was part of the problem. It sloped steeply to the right, forcing her to shimmy along, one foot sliding before the other, while trying to prevent Zeus's skinny limbs from scraping against the sharp slabs of rock.

Every time the wind blew, the clouds shifted. She caught a glimpse of clear sky, a brilliant, hot blue heating the valley below, where the temperature would soar into the nineties by noon. Beyond the wooded mountain gorge and rocky slopes, the land flattened until it reached a narrow beach along the Aegean. The sea itself lay beyond, a flat, gleaming expanse that seemed to fill half the world.

"I've never seen the ocean look so vast," Theo marveled.

"I remember this view. We're so high up that we're looking down on the sea instead of out at it."

"But let me guess—the death-defying rock scramble isn't how you guys used to get up to Olympus."

"No. I suspect we flew there in our chariots, although I don't remember exactly."

"Oh, man. I'd give my Harvard doctorate for a flying chariot right about now."

They kept climbing, and Theo kept talking, his voice another rope, stronger than any braided nylon, tying them together. "When we get up top, do I get my own marble palace with a soaking tub and a bowl of ambrosia? Or is that too much to ask?"

Selene laughed. "More like a spiny summit with a Greek flag, from what I can see. Our palaces were never exactly *on* the summit. It's too small for that. They were"—she struggled for the words—"above it. Or...not *of* it at all."

"You mean they were on a different plane?"

"Sort of. It's hard to explain."

"Huh."

Selene knew that if he'd had any more breath to spare, he would've continued to ply her with questions. Once, she would've been grateful for the respite from his curiosity, but now she didn't want the conversation to end. It stopped her from panicking about her father's ragged breaths against her neck. Besides, she'd missed this.

"You know I don't remember everything from my godhood," she said. "Olympus is a little foggy."

"Hah. That's an understatement," Theo said as another bank of vapor rolled past, blocking the view.

Selene surprised herself by laughing.

"Keep talking," he urged. "It's helping keep my mind off the whole tumbling-to-my-death thing."

"Well, I didn't really have my own home on Olympus—I preferred the forests. But my mother lived here in a marble palace my father built for her, as far away from his wife's as possible. I remember her sitting in the sun in the courtyard, weaving, spinning. But whenever Apollo or I would visit, she'd put down her work and listen to our woes. It was...peaceful there."

"I wish I'd had a chance to meet Leto," Theo said gently. "She sounds like a good mom."

"She was the Goddess of Motherhood. I was lucky."

"Do you ever...think about having kids?"

Selene had to stop herself from rounding on him. It wasn't a question she'd ever allowed a man to ask. But the rope that tied them together reminded her she wasn't allowed to push him away again. If she did, she'd only tumble after him.

"After you and I..." she managed. The image of his naked body beneath hers on the riverbank came rushing back to her. *Had sex? Slept together? What do I call it?*

"After we made love?" he prompted, pronouncing the words with careful emphasis.

She cleared her throat and kept her eyes fixed on the rocks as she went on. "After we made love, I didn't get pregnant, in case you're wondering. And since then, I learned that I can't. No goddess can anymore." When Theo said nothing, she wondered if she'd just put a quick end to their nascent reconciliation. *Does* he *want kids?* It was, she realized, a question—like so many others—she'd never bothered to ask.

Theo stayed quiet for a long while. The end of the ridge was in sight now, and Selene was suddenly sure that if he didn't respond before they got there, he never would.

"I'm not sorry," she said, unable to stand the silence. "Motherhood isn't for me. I've been given all the world's children to protect, just not my own. To me, that's a fair trade." She paused and finally looked back at Theo. She'd been honest. Now it was his turn.

He opened his mouth to speak, but Esme, who'd already made it across the ridge, interrupted with a shout. "Stop dawdling! And tell my lumbering husband to get a move on, too!"

The wind picked up around them, tossing the shreds of cloud like ribbons in a maiden's hair. Selene's conversation with Theo would have to wait.

The storm would not.

Chapter 45

ATHANATOI

The mountain climbed steeply upward into a great, twisting, nearly vertical bowl, the spires rising around its circumference like organ pipes.

Selene yelled down to Flint, still fifty yards behind with Philippe, "I'm not sure you can get up this!"

He waved her onward angrily, and Philippe called back, "I've got him. Don't worry!"

She turned back to the rock wall, put one hand on a red marker, and started to haul herself upward. After a moment, Philippe clambered lightly past her with a rope over his shoulder. He hammered a piton into the rock face and looped the rope through it. He threw the end of the line back down to Flint, who attached his handlebar ascender and harness. Then, using only the strength of his massive arms, he began to jerk the handlebar upward, climbing the mountain six inches at a time. He'd removed his thick sweater again, and the wide muscles of his chest and biceps bulged against the fabric of his shirt. His withered legs in their braces hung uselessly below him, swinging as he lurched up the cliff. *His strength may no longer be supernatural,* Selene marveled, *but his tenacity sure is.*

For the next half hour, the procession of gods worked its way up the mountain. The spaces between them widened. Maryam took the lead this time, moving stiffly but surely in her armor, carrying her long spear slung across her back. Dennis climbed at his own lethargic pace, occasionally stopping to take a swig from his water bottle or to banter with Esme. Philippe dashed ahead sporadically, affixing the ropes, then waited for Flint to pull himself up.

All the while, the clouds grew thicker, the air colder, and the hum of electricity more pronounced.

Selene, slowed by her father's awkward weight, dropped back. For the most part, Theo stayed close behind her, helping to stabilize her on the steepest parts of the slope, sometimes scrabbling ahead to help.

While they climbed, he said nothing. But his firm grip on her hand as he helped haul her and her father upward spoke volumes. He was not abandoning her, not yet. For once, it was Selene who couldn't stay silent. "I'd understand, you know. If you wanted children."

His eyes flicked to hers and away again. "There are many ways to have children in your life." He paused for a long breath before he continued. "There's only one way to have you." He didn't elaborate. It wasn't a promise, just a statement of fact. But it finally gave her the strength to say what she should've said long before.

"I'm sorry. For lying. When I fell from your arms that night above the harbor, I didn't expect to survive. I was willing to die to see you live." The words came out in a rush. "When I washed ashore, I wanted to go to you. But I'd almost gotten you killed, and I knew Saturn still lived. If you were with me, you weren't safe. I kept reminding myself of that. I had to, every time I wanted to call or write or just hop on a damn plane and fly across the ocean and back into your arms." She took a final deep breath. "I'm sorry. I should've trusted you."

Theo said nothing, his gaze inward.

She kept talking, finally speaking aloud the words she'd never even admitted to herself. "I thought we'd be all right eventually. That you'd move on, and I would, too. I was wrong. I never stopped wanting you beside me." She hesitated for an instant, hoping he'd say that he felt the same way. But he remained silent, his mouth clenched tight as if he didn't trust himself to speak.

"No matter what happens today," she finished. "I want you to know that."

For once, she couldn't read the expression in his eyes. She didn't think he was angry—maybe just too full of emotion to find the right words. It wasn't the response she'd wanted, but as she clambered up to join Esme, Maryam, and Dennis just below the summit, then lowered Zeus to the ground, she felt like another weight had lifted from her back. *At least I've been honest.*

Zeus's head lolled to the side; she checked his pulse. Slow, faint, and getting worse.

She peered up at the mist-shrouded peak a few yards above them. "Scooter? Are you up here? We need to get the pit opened!"

Beside her, Maryam put down her own pack but held tight to her spear. Philippe and Flint appeared. Sweat had glued Flint's shirt to his body, and he shivered violently. Philippe helped him back into his sweater like an anxious parent.

Scooter popped out from behind one of the rocky spires, still wearing his broken winged cap.

"Hello, darlings!" he called cheerily to his siblings, as if meeting them for brunch at the local bistro. "You made it! And look who's all set for his retirement plan in Tartarus." He yanked on a chain, dragging Saturn forward like a feral dog on a leash.

The Titan wore a thick collar fashioned from his own sickle; even now, the divine weapon's razor-sharp blade dug into Saturn's neck, forcing him to hold his head thrown back at an unnatural angle. Chains bound the god's ankles and wrists. Selene recognized their shimmering links—Scooter had made the restraints from the golden net forged by Hephaestus in the distant past. At the height of his power, the Smith had imbued the net with one very specific property: Only those who loved him could rip through it.

Scooter may not have always loved his stepbrother, but he does now, she realized with some surprise, *or he couldn't have torn apart the net to make the chains.* She gave Flint a pointed glance: *He may be the Trickster, but he's our Trickster.*

Scooter had chosen the fetters wisely: Saturn could never break them. Then again, his greatest power had never been his strength of arms. He was the Wily One, the God of Time, and Selene had not forgotten how his words had the power to suck her into the past. Neither, it seemed, had Scooter. He'd shoved the sickle's thick wooden handle between Saturn's teeth, binding it there with more of the Smith's golden threads. The effect was grotesque. Medieval.

"You broke my net." Flint growled the words, but he sounded impressed. And touched.

Scooter's grin broadened. "Yup."

"And we noticed your other handiwork on the way up." Flint still looked skeptical, but Selene could tell he wanted to trust his brother. "Interesting plumbing job."

"Not bad, right? All part of the plan."

Flint grunted. "A plan you've been working on for a very long time."

Scooter laughed and put a hand to his heart. "I swear I did it all in the last few days after Father told me his proposal. I've turned the whole mountain into an instrument to help us open Tartarus. In just a few minutes, we'll be tossing Grandpa in like a Skee-Ball at the state fair." He kicked the bound Titan with surprising force, eliciting a strangled grunt. "I know, it doesn't seem possible," he went on with a wave of his hand. "But *some* of us are still quite supernatural."

The first drops of rain spat from the sky. Thunder rolled overhead as the clouds darkened to slate, obscuring everything but the shelf of rock on which they rested and the narrow summit above.

A feeble voice spoke, barely audible beneath the storm's growl. "Hermes has always been loyal." Zeus's eyes had finally opened; he stared at Maryam through his newly repaired glasses, seeing his daughter for the first time. His wrinkled mouth puckered with distress. "*He* did not abandon us all."

Maryam stared back at him, silent but unbowed.

"I brought her," Selene jumped in. "According to the prophecy, her spear's the only thing that can defeat the giants in case more than just *pneuma* comes out of Tartarus."

Zeus coughed hoarsely, curling on his side like a slug sprinkled with salt. But he found the strength to say, "We don't need this . . . *Christian*. We have plenty of other gods here."

As if heeding his summons, the rest of the Athanatoi emerged, one by one, from behind the jagged stone pillars on the summit. First Persephone—called Cora—with her dyed-blond hair and sagging skin, looking like she hadn't slept in days. Selene recognized the woman at her side: her mother, Demeter. The Goddess of Grain looked about the same age as her own daughter, elderly but still tall and imposing. She wore her gray hair wrapped around her head in intricate braids. Millennia spent in the fields had turned her skin copper-brown. She wore a thick woolen poncho woven in geometric designs of green and gold and seemed completely unfazed by the weather. *She's been living in Peru,* Selene remembered. *Olympus must seem a mere hill compared to the Andes.* With eyes the color of new wheat, Demeter looked down at her nieces and nephews with more curiosity than affection. She had only ever loved her daughter.

Hestia, Zeus's eldest sibling, wore snow pants and a large hooded parka. A bit extreme for Greece in June—even this high on the mountain—but the Goddess of the Hearth had lived in Tunisia for years; she'd be woefully unprepared for the cold. Selene had heard her aunt was close to death. Indeed, the old woman was hunched so far over her cane that she seemed half her sister's size. The fur-trimmed hood hid her face, but a long wisp of hair had come loose, whipping around her head like a tendril of fog, impossibly long, so fine and white that it was nearly invisible.

Hestia's brother Poseidon supported her by the elbow. The blue-haired god had a white mane now. A beard as long as Zeus's, twined with seashells, covered much of a face as craggy as a barnacled hull. All the Athanatoi tried to retain some of their attributes, but most had abandoned their old costumes for the sake of blending in. Poseidon must've lived far from the eyes of men, because he wore a fishnet cloak, a horsehair scarf, and a sharkskin tunic that made him look like an aging Inuit hunter. He held his whalebone trident before him, the prongs tilting to the side as if he couldn't quite support its weight.

June stood a few steps away from her immortal siblings, bundled in a sensible fleece vest and pom-pommed hat. The sight of Flint on the slope below did nothing to erase the vexation stiffening her features. When she shifted her regard to her frail ex-husband, her puckered frown hardened to a slit-eyed scowl.

"Your mother looks pissed," Selene murmured to Flint.

"She's never trusted her husband, remember?" He didn't remind her that he'd never trusted Zeus either.

On her other side, Theo cast them a surprised look. "That's Hera, Zeus's wife?"

"Yeah. But don't remind her," Selene replied. "Aunt June thinks she's married to a hot Italian boy. Long story."

She bent and hoisted her father into her arms like a babe before scrambling the last few yards to the top of the summit.

Theo helped her lower him back to the ground, propping the old man's back against an outcropping that sheltered him from the worst of the wind and rain.

Zeus could barely sit upright, yet his rheumy eyes were bright with excitement as Scooter dragged over a large duffel and opened it before him. He patted his son on the shoulder. "Thank you, my Giver of Good Things." He pulled Athena's aegis over his shoulders with shaking hands, then dragged out the heavy metal lightning bolt.

He could barely lift his own weapon, much less wield it.

June rested her fists on her hips and barked at her ex-husband, "If you can barely stand, how the heck are you going to open Tartarus?"

"*I'm* not going to." A smile cracked Zeus's chapped lips despite his ex-wife's nagging. "Only one man on this mountain can do that." He stared out—not at his children, but past them. Selene twisted around.

Theo pointed dumbly at his own chest.

Zeus held out his lightning bolt to the professor as another crash of thunder split the sky. "The storm is here, Makarites. Now bend it to your will."

Chapter 46

HE WHO MARSHALS THUNDERHEADS

The pantheon is complete, and I stand at its center.

How the hell did that happen?

Theo stood at the very top of Mount Olympus, Zeus's thunderbolt in his hands, as heavy as a gold ingot and humming in tune to the electricity crackling across the sky. He had come to witness the Athanatoi. Now they witnessed him instead.

Flint and Philippe watched him dubiously. Maryam remained expressionless, although Theo noticed she hadn't removed her armor, and her eyes kept drifting greedily to the tasseled aegis around Zeus's shoulders. Esme, her arm looped through her son's, seemed more worried about the spitting rain dotting her silk kerchief than about what might happen when Theo hurled the lightning bolt. Dennis gave him a thumbs-up, along with a sarcastic smirk.

Theo twisted around to look at Demeter, Poseidon, Persephone, Hera, and Hestia. None of these Athanatoi were what he'd imagined; only Demeter seemed to have retained much of her divine majesty. Despite his maritime costuming, Poseidon looked more like a vagrant beachcomber than a God of the Sea. Hera—June—looked like a middle-aged substitute teacher on an ill-considered summer vacation. Still, Theo found himself trying to memorize each face, each detail of their clothing, their posture, their expressions, as if still fulfilling his promise to Zeus to record the event like Homer or Hesiod.

Yet none of that mattered anymore. Selene mattered.

She stood right in front of him, her brow furrowed with worry, but her feet planted firmly, as if to say, *This could all go very wrong . . . but I'm with you.*

He'd seen the horror on her face when she realized she might be dragging her father—and him—into some unknown danger. It had made him understand just how much she'd been willing to do to keep him safe—even deny herself happiness. All this time, he'd thought she'd easily made the choice to leave him. Now he knew it had nearly broken her. She'd finally told him the truth. And as much as it clearly worried her to watch him take the lightning bolt, she hadn't said a word to stop him. She let him make the decision. Finally, they were equals.

Inch by inch over the past two days, she'd cracked open the doors to his heart, which he'd so carefully sealed against her. Now, finally, they swung wide.

Or, perhaps, he admitted, *I flung them open myself the moment she appeared in the airport, ready to be my partner again.*

He looked down at the twisted metal in his hands. *I can do this. I can do this.* He would've loved to give the honor to Dennis or Scooter or anyone else, but he knew that Zeus's thunderbolt would work only for a Makarites. No faded god could wield it.

He would've preferred some prior notice, of course. Time to prepare for such a weighty task. But he understood why Zeus had kept this part of his role a secret. After their escape from the Vatican's mithraeum, Theo had made it perfectly clear he never intended to use divine weapons again on behalf of the Olympians.

So I've already been manipulated into breaking that vow, he thought wearily, *but I told Selene I'd help save her father.* He tightened his grip on the twisted bolt. *How can I refuse now?*

Saturn, still bound in his golden chains, sat at Theo's feet. Stripped of his Mithraic finery, he huddled shirtless on the bare rock. The lightning that had burned away half his hair on Liberty's torch had also left a swath of tight skin stretching from his face to the center of his chest. There, two tall ridges of older scar tissue formed a perfect "X" that sliced from rib cage to hip.

Scooter had removed the sickle's handle from Saturn's mouth, but the razor-sharp collar still pressed against his throat, a silent reminder that if he dared try to manipulate his children with his words, they'd take off his head.

The God of Time looked up at Theo with eyes full of hate, but he made no move to attack. He merely seethed silently, occasionally casting furious looks at Zeus, the man who'd left the scars upon his stomach when he carved him open and freed the other Olympians so long ago.

"Don't worry about Grandpa," Scooter assured Theo with a wink of encouragement. "He'll be out of the way soon enough."

Zeus struggled to his feet, waving away Scooter's help. He swayed a little but remained upright, then lifted his hands as if to test the raindrops, his face suffused with rapture.

The storm suddenly intensified, and in an instant, the rain turned to tiny ice balls, pelting Theo's head and shoulders. The older gods grumbled and pulled up hoods and cloaks to shield themselves. Selene only scowled. Hail the size of chickpeas stung Theo's face.

Sudden thunder crashed like cymbals beside his ear, followed instantly by a flash of lightning so bright he had to close his eyes. *Not again, not again,* he prayed, remembering the bolt that had nearly killed him and Selene above the Statue of Liberty.

Another lightning bolt, visible even through his closed eyelids, streaked overhead like brilliant ichor in a god's branching vein. Someone shouted at him, but he could barely hear the words above the now constant roll of thunder.

"Open your eyes, Makarites!" Zeus stood before him now. He'd lifted his rain-streaked glasses onto the top of his head, revealing hard gray eyes. The hands he laid on top of Theo's had ceased to tremble. No one could think this man feebleminded. His voice resounded as he hollered, "Use the bolt!"

"To do *what*?" Theo squinted through the pounding hail at the currents that forked and skipped across the sky. "Don't you have enough lightning already?"

"The bolt controls more than that," Zeus insisted. "It controls the wind, the storm, the *sky*. Send the wind into the mountain. Into the plateau."

"I don't know how to do that!"

It was Scooter's turn to press him now. He stepped close enough to shout in Theo's ear, "Did you know how to fly before you wore my hat?"

Theo reached back for the memory of the first time he'd donned the winged cap, the first time he'd picked up Orion's sword or put on Hades' helm. Scooter was right; he was capable of all sorts of magic.

He turned his attention to the metal bolt. He hefted it in one hand, holding it around the middle like he'd seen Zeus do in statues all over Greece. *The bolt wants to be closer to the storm.* Theo wasn't sure how he knew that.

He lifted it higher, forcing himself not to cringe at the thought of holding a metal conductor above his head while lightning streaked from the clouds.

"Hold still!" Zeus shouted at him. "It's coming!"

WHAT'S coming? Theo thought, although he already knew the answer.

This is the end. This is the trap.

Distantly, he heard Selene scream.

A finger of lightning streaked down and slammed against the metal bolt's tip.

Theo didn't die. Instead, he felt the bolt's energy course through him, lifting every hair on his body and surrounding his flesh in an eerie blue glow. In that moment of power, he became the storm itself.

He could no longer hear Selene's shouts nor see her terrified face as she rushed forward, only to be stopped by the force of the sudden vortex that surrounded him.

He stood in the center of a funnel of wind and ice, each particle bursting into fluorescent light like green tracer fire and eddying around him in patterns that suddenly made perfect sense. He reached out a hand to grab the wind itself. He threw it over his shoulder, down to the Skala plateau beyond the ridge. The wind arced in response, gathering force and speed as it whistled past his ears.

He turned to watch it go, a beautiful, bright, cascading stream. With vision as keen as a god's, Theo saw the glowing wind rip the caps from the small pipes dotting the plateau, then pour through them into the heart of the mountain.

A low moan built beneath him, vibrating through the rock and into his feet.

"Keep going!" Zeus's voice rang above the storm.

Theo obeyed, pushing more wind through the sky and into the ground, the currents so luminous he could see them through the rock, could watch them meet the underground lake that had been funneled upward from the spring. The wind collected in the chamber, pressurized by the rising water until it ripped upward to shoot through shafts drilled in the spires of rock that surrounded Mytikas.

It's a hydraulis. A water organ, the last sane part of him marveled, even as he heard Selene dimly screaming, "Stop, Theo! Stop!"

"Now, Saturn!" came Zeus's voice. "Be the God of Time once more!"

From the corner of his eye, Theo saw Saturn glare defiantly at his son. Scooter still held the leash attached to the sickle-collar. A sharp yank and the collar squeezed tighter. A line of blood appeared on Saturn's throat, and the old man lurched to his feet.

"Time of heroes. Time of glory," he began, his voice a resonant thrum. Soon, the roar of the storm drowned out the Titan's words, but Theo still felt their power. With his heightened perceptions, he watched the color of the wind around him darken from fluorescent green to the red of old blood. Its roar shifted, tuned, steadied.

The mountain sang.

The tones rumbled the earth, too low for even divine ears to hear, then rose in laddered chords into a piercing melody too beautiful to comprehend before descending once more. Over and over, the chords resounded. Indescribable. Unbearable.

Electricity pulsed through Theo's body. It didn't sear his flesh like a lightning strike—it burned him from the inside out. A sphere of blue-white heat spun in his gut like a supernova. Ever faster, ever larger, incinerating everything in its path.

And still Theo played his instrument.

———◄◦►———

Selene wept. *This will kill him,* she knew, trying once more to reach for Theo through the swirling funnel of ice and rock that surrounded him. It wasn't the hail that stopped her—she didn't care if it ripped the skin from her body—it was the wind. It flew tornado-strong, impassable as iron.

All around her, the mountain roared. There was no music, no melody, just a continuous rush of sound like a jet passing overhead, growing louder by the second.

The glow around Theo turned from blue to white to a color beyond color, too bright to bear. A mortal surrounded by electricity more brilliant than any god's aura. Theo was the wick at the heart of a flame. Soon he would be nothing but ash.

"What have you done?" she screamed at her father. *He lured me in,* she knew now, *pretending to love me, all so he could get his lightning bolt back—and use Theo to wield it.*

Zeus had eyes only for the storm. His body remained aged, but the gentle old man she'd rescued had vanished. His eyes were eagle-sharp as he watched his plan unfold, and though his body trembled in the force of the wind, he wore the tasseled aegis with all the pride of a mighty god. He raised his arms, the wind whipping his long white beard—and smiled.

Beside him, Scooter stood solemnly, singing along to his grand hydraulis—the colossal successor to the simple reed pipes he'd invented long ago—as if music, not just noise, poured through his instrument. Tears stood in his eyes as he watched Theo's end.

He looked mesmerized by the scene before him, but when Selene lunged toward Zeus, desperate to somehow stop the storm, Scooter moved quickly to block her way. She tackled her brother to the ground, knocking off his winged cap and smashing his skull against the jagged rocks.

"Don't you see?" he gasped. "Theo's sacrifice will be worth it!"

"You *knew* he would die!"

"But it's going to work!"

"*What's* going to work?" she cried, picking him up and slamming him once more into the ground before Maryam and Philippe managed to drag her away.

Scooter staggered to his feet and pointed. "Turn around."

She did. Where Theo had stood, a field of golden barley rippled in a gentle breeze beneath a glorious blue sky.

From somewhere behind her, she heard Philippe's awestruck French cursing.

The storm had stopped, the air hung cold and still, and the sky above the barley blended seamlessly into the sky above Olympus. Yet the field itself seemed to float in midair a few inches above the rocky summit, a vision seen through a frameless window.

A portal.

"Where's Theo?" she begged, even though she already knew the answer.

He was gone. Winked out like a shooting star.

"He was the price—" Zeus began heavily.

Selene didn't wait to hear his explanation. She crossed to her father in a single long stride. This time Scooter didn't stop her.

She grabbed the neck of Zeus's shirt and yanked his face up to hers. "You killed him." She wanted to roar, but the words came out in a ragged whisper, her chest too tight to admit any air. "Theo's gone. And you're *smiling*."

Zeus looked at her with a father's love. "Theodore Schultz was a hero. We will sing his song through this new Age and into all the rest to come."

"His *song* isn't what I—" Selene began.

Maryam interrupted, her voice hushed. "That's not Tartarus," she said, staring out over the barley.

Scooter tittered a half-mad laugh, his spreading smile jarring with his tear-swollen eyes. "Do you recognize it yet?"

Far beyond the field, hazy in the distant glare of the sun, rose a tall rocky butte. A single point of brilliant light shone above it like a beacon.

Selene didn't understand, not at first, but Maryam looked from the distant light to the tip of the weapon in her own hand. "It's the spearpoint on the *Athena Promakhos* statue atop the Acropolis." For once, she sounded awestruck. "You opened a door to ancient Athens."

Selene's grip on her father's shirt loosened. She dropped him to the ground, shock freezing her rage.

Scooter scooped up his winged cap and set it on his head at a jaunty angle. "The new Age is waiting for us. It's just through that portal." He swept his arm toward the sun-warmed barley. "So. Who's going in first?"

Poseidon and Hestia immediately hobbled through. When they turned around in the middle of the field, Selene's breath

374 Jordanna Max Brodsky

caught in her chest. Poseidon's hair had turned a blue so deep it seemed almost purple, as wine-dark as the sea itself. His eyes blazed in a face unmarked by age. The Hearth Goddess dropped her cane and threw back the hood of her parka, revealing a long curtain of chestnut hair. She smiled with a gentleness and warmth Selene hadn't seen on a goddess's face since her own mother had died. Hestia held out her hand to her niece.

"Come," she urged. "Join us."

Chapter 47

KING OF THE GODS

Zeus stood on the rocky summit with a self-satisfied smile, watching as his siblings discarded their frailty as easily as spent rags. Once more, they clothed themselves in the glory of godhood.

Selene wheeled toward him, her fury tempered by a sudden hope. "Step through the portal and you're the omnipotent King of the Gods again, right?" she demanded. "So go in there and use your power to *bring Theo back to life.*"

"No need," a familiar voice croaked.

She spun back to the portal. Theo's arm stuck out from among the barley stalks.

Scooter clapped his hands. "I underestimated you, my friend!"

The lightning bolt, no longer a blaring white column of energy but just a mass of twisted metal, rolled free of Theo's grasp to rest among the grain. He stretched his arm beyond the portal's boundary, out of one world and into another. His fingers floated just above the rocky ground of Olympus, reaching for Selene.

She rushed forward to grab his hand. The portal hovered an inch from her face; she could feel the heated air, smell the rich soil, hear the cicadas hum. She dragged Theo out of ancient Athens and into her embrace. He was solid and real, and although he smelled of electricity and his fair hair waved in a wild halo, he seemed unhurt. She threw an arm beneath his shoulders and helped him stagger away from the field.

"I thought—" she began.

"I know," he finished. "But I'm a Makarites. If Theseus could defeat the Minotaur and Hercules could survive twelve labors, I can get past a little bad weather." He laughed shortly, then caught her gaze in his. "I stood there burning up from the inside, and I made a choice. I'm not leaving this world again without a damn good reason. At least not while you're still in it."

His green eyes were warm. Finally, the answer she'd been waiting for since the moment in the Phrygianum. She tightened her arm around him, desperate to finally restart their life together.

Theo looked over her shoulder at the barley field. "Now will someone explain to me what's going on?"

Cora giggled. "Isn't it obvious? That's *home* in there. And I'm going back to it." She took an eager step toward the open portal.

Selene disentangled herself from Theo, who swayed but remained upright, and grabbed the older woman's elbow before she could pass through. "Wait! We don't know what—"

"I know what I see!" Cora answered, trying in vain to wrench her arm from Selene's iron grip.

Selene turned to Zeus, still refusing to let go of her cousin. "But what about Tartarus? What about Saturn?"

At the sound of his name, the grain shivered, and the God of Time struggled upright. Unlike the others, Saturn hadn't regained his youth. Burns no longer marred his face, but the crossed scars on his stomach remained, and the golden chains still bound his wrists.

Cora waved away Selene's protests. "Look at him. He's not Saturn anymore, beloved god of the Mithraists and Romans. He's just *Kronos*, the Titan that our parents overthrew. He can't hurt us."

As if to prove Cora's point, Poseidon and Hestia grabbed the old man before he could take a step.

This time, when Cora yanked her arm away, Selene let her go.

As she entered the field, Cora's hair tumbled free in soft blond waves; her round cheeks flushed with youth. She was unspeakably beautiful. Tears filled her eyes and rolled down her face to wet her smiling lips.

"Mother!" she cried, stretching out her arms to Demeter. "Do you see? Hurry! Hurry!"

Demeter took a cautious step forward, her face full of longing as she stared at her newly youthful daughter. Yet she paused and looked out over the mountaintops, her gaze resting for a moment on the green valley below.

"I will miss this time, and it will miss me. Yet where my daughter goes, I must follow." Demeter walked into Athens. She moved slowly through the stalks of grain, resting her hands atop the feathery heads of barley.

Cora—Persephone, now—scampered forward to throw her arms around her mother; the two looked longingly westward.

They will head straight for Eleusis, Selene knew. There, the two goddesses had presided over their own powerful cult for thousands of years. *They're going home.*

And if I enter, she couldn't help wondering, *if I walk south to Brauron, will the little girls await me there? Will they don their bear robes and dance at my arrival?* She remembered the rush of power she'd felt striding through the glories of Delphi with Apollo. Would she feel that again?

Zeus put a hand on her shoulder. For now, he was still shorter than she, his fingers crooked with age. She didn't throw him off: All her anger had drained away with Theo's return.

"It's not a trick," he said quietly, answering her unspoken question. "When you enter, you will be Artemis again. Artemis at her best. Not some twisted version born of a cult's imagination, nor a barbaric proto-goddess, but Artemis at the absolute

height of Greek civilization. Worshiped. Adored. Feared. Able
to protect the women and girls of your domain from any threat."

But Apollo won't be there, she thought. *And he is what made Delphi beautiful. Without his love, what do I care for power?*

Her father lifted a hand to her cheek. The pads of his fingertips
were as soft as a baby's. "I've opened a new universe, a new Age.
The Olympians are already there—and have not yet arrived."

Selene shook her head, confused. "Are you saying—"

"I'm saying Apollo may exist there even as he's ceased to exist
here."

She snapped her head toward the portal, searching for her
twin's familiar face. Was it possible? Did his horse-drawn chariot drive the sun above the barley field even now?

Beside her, Theo spoke quietly. "It's everything you wanted."

She had not forgotten his words. He wouldn't leave this world
without her again. "You could come with me," she said quickly.
"We could visit all the places you've only read about."

Dennis cleared his throat loudly. "Hey, sister. You know if
you go through you might not be able to come back, right? It
wouldn't be just a visit. More like a permanent relocating."

"I was in there," Theo said hesitantly. "And Selene pulled me
out again."

Dennis shrugged. "You *made* the portal, dude. And you're a
Blessed One. Different rules for you."

Selene still couldn't move. Every fiber of her ached to seek out
her twin. But she needed more time to think.

Scooter moved to stand before her. "Whatever you decide,"
he said quietly. "Know that I'm sorry. For everything." Selene
looked into her younger brother's eyes. The Trickster. He'd
known Zeus's plan would likely kill Theo. He'd been secretly
plotting with their father about the hydraulis long before they'd
captured Saturn. And he'd lied about the true nature of the
portal—although she wasn't sure why. Yet the regret etched upon

his face made her think his apology referred to an even greater crime.

"I..." she hesitated.

Zeus bent double with a racking cough. Blood spattered his lips. The strength he'd summoned during the storm had vanished as swiftly as the clouds.

"I have to go through," he begged. "Before it's too late."

Scooter held out a solicitous hand to his father, but Zeus waved him away. "Go on, my Tetractys. I'll join you shortly."

With a deferential nod, Scooter sprinted through the portal. The wings of his hat bounced limply behind him.

Theo's hand slipped into hers as she watched her brother go. She clutched it like a lifeline.

Scooter stopped running when he entered the barley field. The wings of his cap straightened and spread. He tilted his head up—and flew.

Dennis grunted, watching Hermes hover high above the field. "Show-off." He twirled his thyrsus. "Wait until I point this thing at the earth and vines start sprouting up to wrench that little twit out of the air."

"You're going?" Selene asked.

"Why not?" He shrugged. "Looks better than this shithole."

"But you..."

"Yeah, yeah, I said you can't come back out. But why would I want to? If *you* want to stay here and get older and weaker in the arms of Theo-bore, feel free, hon."

"I don't know..." she stammered, flustered.

Theo saved her from having to say more. "Dennis, buddy, you've been in grad school for decades. Did you forget already that the Golden Age of Athens lasts for less than a century? Give it another thousand years and the Romans will turn against you, too. You'll just have to go through the Diaspora all over again."

Dennis snorted. "You really think Dad didn't think of that?

Please. He said it's a *new* Age, remember? Not just the same one over again. Don't you see? Mankind's been asking the same question since they looked up at the stars and realized there was more to life than hunting and fucking. The same question *we've* been asking since the Diaspora: How do we transcend these ever-dying meat sacks we call bodies and become something greater? Well, thanks to dear old Dad, we finally know the answer: Don't fight against Time. Just step *through* it. Remake the world. Remake yourself. Sounds good to me." And just like that, he sauntered into the field. He laughed when ivy sprang up around his feet and twined up the barley, the dark, glossy leaves bending the golden stalks beneath their weight.

Theo squeezed Selene's hand a little tighter and leaned close to whisper, "Why did Zeus call Scooter his Tetractys?"

"Maybe it's an epithet I don't know about," she murmured back.

Theo shook his head, but before he could explain further, Zeus interrupted them. "Come, Aphrodite, Eros. Come Hera, my queen. Artemis, Hephaestus. It is time." He did not, Selene noticed, ask Athena to join them. "The portal won't last much longer."

The line between field and mountaintop, she saw now, wavered like the edge of a mirage.

June shook her head, the pom-pom on her hat waggling. "Absolutely not. I have a honeymoon with Mauricio to get back to."

"Hera, my greatest love," Zeus wheedled. "You can rule at my side."

June snorted at the offer, tilting up her chin. Despite the softness of her fleshy neck, she moved like a queen. "I remember your love. It was so *great* it needed a hundred women to satisfy it. Never again."

Esme chuckled. "And I'm not going anywhere near the fourth century BC, but thank you."

Zeus's eyes grew hard. "Why not?"

"Because it's filthy, that's why," she replied. "Animals *every*-where. And did you forget that the men washed themselves in *olive oil*? Slippery is all very pleasurable in the right situations, but I've gotten used to soap." She tilted her left hand so the large diamond caught the light. "Besides, I'm enjoying myself. I cre-ate my own beauty now. I'm not just a reflection of what men *think* is beautiful. And I don't have gods like you telling me who I should and shouldn't sleep with."

Philippe put his arm around his mother's shoulders with a proud smile, but looked at Flint. "What about you, Papa?"

The hunched Smith had eyes only for Selene. His gaze flicked to her hand, held tight in Theo's, and his lips flattened. She watched his chest heave with all the things he wanted to say to her.

She slipped from Theo's grip and moved to Flint. "You have been a true friend."

"But that's all," he grunted. "Just a friend."

"No. More than that. You've been a brother." She searched for the right words. "A partner. The gift of your love..." She swallowed. "It's more than I deserved. More than I could've ever asked for."

Flint stared at her, hard. "And you *didn't* ask for it, did you?"

She could only shake her head.

He balled his massive hands. "I watched you all the way up the mountain. With *him*. He came back into your life and you forgot I was ever in it."

Selene started to protest, but he thrust his palm out toward her angrily, cutting her off. "Give it back."

She wasn't sure what he meant, not at first. Then she pulled the heavy gold necklace from her pocket.

He shoved it roughly into his own. Then, to her shock, he turned and started walking toward the sunlit barley field.

"Papa..." Philippe warned.

"Please..." June begged.

But Zeus spoke over them. "Yes, Hephaestus! Come, my son, I would cure your lameness!"

Flint rounded on Zeus like a trapped bear. "Now you offer that? Now you call me *son*? You, who threw me off the mountain, who watched me fall, who broke me and let me suffer as an ugly, unloved god for my entire existence. *I AM NOT YOUR SON.*"

Selene could breathe again. *He will stay here,* she thought. *He will not leave my life forever.*

Flint unslung the wide hammer from his back. Selene was sure he would raise it against his stepfather. Instead, he held it out to Philippe. "Take it," he said. "To remember me."

Philippe looked stunned, but he clutched the massive tool to his chest. Flint turned back to the portal. He took a single limping step toward it.

To Selene's shock, it was Esme who spoke first. "You think you're unloved," she said matter-of-factly. "You're wrong."

Flint didn't turn to his wife. Instead, he looked down at his withered legs encased in their titanium braces. "Perhaps. But that doesn't change the fact that I hate myself."

Philippe made a sound of strangled protest, but Flint went on. "I can stay here and live another few miserable decades. Or I can try again. Be someone new. Someone whole."

He looked back at his mother, his stepson. "I am weak," whispered the mighty Smith. "Forgive me."

Philippe started forward, but June put a hand on the young man's arm. Her lined face shone with tears, yet she seemed determined to finally allow her selfless son to do something for himself. Selene could not accept his decision with such equanimity. *This is my fault,* she knew. *If I loved him, he would stay. Instead, Philippe loses his stepfather. June loses her son.*

I lose my friend.

She forced herself to stay silent, to respect his decision as Flint hobbled to the portal and stepped inside, though every ounce of her wanted to lunge forward and drag him back where he belonged.

He stood amid the waving barley, facing the distant Acropolis, even as his spine straightened and his grizzled hair darkened to deepest coal. Selene watched his barrel chest heave once, twice, before he reached to rip off a sweater and shirt that could no longer contain his massive torso. Next, he bent and unfastened the braces from his legs. When he finally turned around, she barely recognized him.

Hephaestus was beautiful.

The sculpted muscles of his chest gleamed in the sunlight. No wrinkles scarred his face. His legs were as strong and shapely as his brother Mars's had ever been. But the biggest difference lay not in his restored limbs nor his suddenly youthful features—but his eyes.

"He looks..." Selene began.

"Hopeful," Esme finished.

"You see," Zeus said with a smile. "I tell the truth. The world I've created is brand-new. The mistakes of our past will be wiped away. We can create our own future, our own fate! Wouldn't you like to get your wings back, Eros? The ones you sliced from your own back so long ago? I could make that happen. Aphrodite, you could have any man you wanted!" Zeus swung to Selene next. "Artemis, your twin is waiting for you!"

But it was Maryam who stepped forward, holding her spear now in both hands, as if ready to strike. "Zeus wants this too much."

A slow worm of suspicion crawled through Selene's gut. Her gaze flicked to Flint's glory, then back to her father. "If this is so wonderful," she asked slowly, "why didn't you just tell us the truth?"

"I needed your Makarites," Zeus said easily. "If you knew he could die, you wouldn't have let me have him."

"*I* wouldn't have. But why lie to everyone else? They'd happily trade one mortal life for an eternity of power."

Zeus started to answer, but a cackling laugh cut him off. Saturn, still held captive in the barley field, stared directly at Selene through eyes slitted with deranged hilarity.

"You've almost got it, granddaughter!" he called through the portal. "I see now that I underestimated my son. *He* is truly the Wily One, not I. He needed your professor, yes. But he also needed *me*. And not, old, weak me, mind you, but—"

"Silence, Father," Zeus snarled while gesturing angrily to his siblings. Poseidon jammed the tines of his trident against Saturn's throat. The Titan quieted, but his eyes still bored into Selene, daring her to understand.

"Do it *now*, brother," Zeus called to the Sea God.

Poseidon Earth Shaker struck the ground with his trident. The field outside Athens trembled even as the summit of Olympus remained firm. The barley swayed wildly. A dark gash split the earth. Persephone let out a shocked gasp and clutched her mother's arm.

Smoke issued from the cleft, and heat shimmered against the sky. This was no mere crack—this was the entrance to Tartarus.

Selene reached for her bow before realizing the uselessness of the gesture. If any giants stormed up from the pit, the newly glorious Olympians would defeat them without any help from her. Maryam readied her spear anyway, but Selene no longer believed in the oracle's words. What cure could the Wise Virgin's spear provide that the new Age didn't?

Poseidon and Hestia dragged the Titan to the edge of Tartarus. Saturn dug in his heels, carving great gashes in the earth. "No!" he cried. "You already took my Last Age from me! You promised that if I helped you, I could live in this one!"

"I cast you down once before, Father," Zeus said calmly. "And, against my better judgment, I let you back out. I won't make the same mistake twice."

At Zeus's nod, Poseidon flung their father forward. Saturn

disappeared into the void of Tartarus, leaving nothing behind but a fading cry of rage.

Selene breathed a sigh of relief. *Apollo is finally avenged. My father will be safe in his new world. Flint is happier without me. My job is done.* She should have felt at peace. Instead, Saturn's words echoed in her mind.

Not old, weak me... Suddenly it all made sense. "Dennis had it right, didn't he, Father?" she asked slowly. "He said you'd stopped fighting Time. You *used* Time instead—used his power to help you open a new Age. But for Saturn to truly be the God of Time once more...for him to have that much power in the first place, his cult had to—" She choked, unable to finish the sentence.

June did it for her. "You *let* Saturn kill Mars! You knew his plans and didn't warn us!"

Zeus took a careful step backward toward the portal, both hands extended, placating. "I knew the Host had Prometheus—but he wanted to die anyway. I didn't know Saturn would kill the others!"

Selene's shock quickly melted into rage. "But you knew he *wanted* to. You knew he'd try. All that time in New York while we were hunting down the man who killed our family, *you* knew who it was. And you didn't help. Because you knew that with every death, Saturn only grew stronger. Just like you wanted. Mars. Hades. *Apollo.* Their blood is on your hands."

The other Athanatoi tensed beside her; she could almost hear the discordant symphony of their rising fury. Mars had not only been June's son; he was Philippe's father and Esme's greatest love. Everyone had loved Apollo for his music and poetry. Even Hades, the dark Lord of the Dead, had been brother to Hestia, Poseidon, and Demeter, and husband to Persephone.

The view of the barley field shimmered and began to contract, but she could still see Hermes flying overhead, watching her sorrowfully. Surely he'd known of Zeus's treachery—and helped him anyway.

Zeus looked at the shrinking portal, his eyes panicked behind his glasses. She thought he would run, but he seemed unable to give up on his plan. "Please," he cried, reaching a clawed hand to clutch at the air before him, "I don't want to go in without you!"

Before Selene could react, Maryam aimed her spear at her father's aegis-covered breast, right over the wide-mouthed Gorgon's head that she'd sewn there herself. "We don't have to do anything we don't want to, old man."

Zeus stood well out of the spear's range, inching ever closer to the portal, but he sounded defiant, rather than intimidated. "I don't want *you* to come, *Sister* Maryam. The oracle was wrong. I have no need of you. Or your spear."

"Then I will use it to protect my family from your wiles."

Philippe, still holding Flint's massive hammer, moved to stand beside Maryam. Selene raised her gold bow. Theo stood beside her, fists clenched. Esme flexed her fingers as if she might rip out Zeus's heart with her long, painted nails. June joined them, her maternal rage the sharpest weapon of all. Yet none of them moved to attack the man they'd honored for so long.

"I carried you on my back," Selene said, her voice low and dangerous. "I always thought the father who taught me how to hunt must truly love me. Now I know he would let his own children die. He only loves himself."

Despite her words, Selene still couldn't bring herself to loose her arrow at the frail old man.

Maryam had no such compunction. She charged forward, her spearhead darting out to catch one of the serpents dangling from Medusa's head. She pulled back the weapon, trying to rip her aegis from his shoulders. Zeus yanked it away from her with both hands, falling backward and scuttling crablike the last few inches toward the portal. Maryam lunged after him, but the old man swung one skinny leg over the portal's lip and tumbled into Athens.

Selene held her breath, waiting to see her father's metamorphosis. When he finally arose from the barley, he stood both two meters and two thousand years away from her. He towered in the air, easily three times the height of the old man who'd left Olympus. His hair shone as glossy black as Artemis's, his eyes as stormy gray as Athena's. The snakes of the aegis writhed to life, their beady eyes fixed on their onetime mistress as they hissed an angry curse in Maryam's direction.

The King of the Gods bent to pick up his lightning bolt from where Theo had dropped it in the field. Already, Hephaestus was striding toward the man who'd let Mars die, his youthful face red with fury. Persephone moved from the other side, full of righteous wrath over her husband Hades' murder.

Esme took a step closer to the portal. "He must be punished for what he did to Mars and Apollo."

"Don't worry," Selene assured her, watching as Poseidon, Dionysus, Demeter, and Hestia joined the angry circle surrounding Zeus. For now, they maintained a wary distance, but she knew it wouldn't be long before they attacked the god who'd betrayed his own kin. Even mighty Zeus wouldn't be able to withstand the combined power of so many Athanatoi. "He gave the others back their strength. He's going to regret that."

Maryam rolled her spear in her hands as if itching for a fight. "You sure you don't want to go in there and help?"

Selene watched Theo's jaw clench. He swallowed hard. "You could, you know." His voice was careful, as if he didn't want to sway her decision one way or the other. "Apollo might be in there."

"No," she said, suddenly sure. "Just another of my father's lies. The Delphi I left Apollo in isn't through that portal. It's a Delphi of my twin's imagining, not my father's."

388 Jordanna Max Brodsky

"And Flint?"

She looked at Hephaestus—she couldn't think of him as Flint anymore. Glorious and gleaming, possessed of infinite power, about to finally find justice for his brother's killer. If he was no longer broken, would he still feel compassion for those who were? Had he truly become the best version of himself, as her father promised? And would she even love him if he had?

"You could claim your real name, be Artemis to his Hephaestus," Theo urged, as if reading the conflict on her face.

The sound of her old name filled Selene with certainty. *Regardless of how Flint might change, I know who I would become. I'd be a goddess once more dependent on mankind's worship. One whose identity was constrained by what the mortal world expected of me. One whose absolute divinity would place an insuperable barrier between myself and those who worshiped me.* At the height of her power, she had hurt as many mortals as she'd helped, punished as many as she'd protected—and most had not deserved their fates.

If I pass through that portal, she knew, *I will become like my black-fletched arrows. Deadly and unstoppable, unable to tell friend from foe. A power that no longer belongs in the world I've come to know.*

"My name is Selene," she said finally. "It's the name of the woman you fell in love with. It's the name I chose for myself. That makes it the truest name of all."

Chapter 48

RAGING ONE

Theo's skin tingled. Not with the aftereffects of the lightning, but with the feel of Selene's hand in his as they stood in silence on the summit, watching the angry gods surround Zeus as the portal slowly closed.

"You sure you're staying?" he asked her quietly, still not quite believing it. Seeing Flint regain his magnificence, he'd thought for sure she'd realize the Smith was the better match after all.

"I would rather love those I serve than be loved by those who serve me." Her words were solemn, but her lips quirked in the smallest of smiles. "Hephaestus, on the other hand, deserves some worship after all this time. I'm sure he'll be happier in there. He'll forget me in a week."

"Doubtful. I tried that. It lasted about half a day."

She pulled him into her arms and kissed him without warning. So hard he had to take a step back to find his balance. Her arms came around him, stopping his breath, smashing his glasses against his nose. He felt his whole body sing in response; he clutched at her back, her hips, and drew her closer. He'd imagined this moment for months, and now it was finally here. *She* was here. The Selene he remembered. Fierce and beautiful, warm and loyal.

"I love you, Theodore Schultz," she finally whispered against his lips. "I love you."

Then Maryam hollered a warning.

Selene and Theo pulled apart to stare through the shrinking portal. The three-foot-wide window showed black clouds and storm-tossed grain in the field outside Athens, even as the sky above their heads on the summit of Olympus remained clear.

Zeus, still surrounded by his furious kin, had stripped off his mortal garb and stood clothed only in the tasseled aegis, his naked muscles gleaming and sharp, his lightning bolt raised in one hand. He didn't look penitent. And he didn't look afraid.

He looked like he had a plan.

His voice boomed across the field and onto the mountaintop. *"With the help of his mother, Kronos usurped Ouranos."* A King proclaiming his law to the new world he'd created—and the one he'd left behind.

This was an old story. A familiar story. One he'd made sure his family never forgot. "With the help of *my* mother, I usurped Kronos in turn."

He lifted the bolt higher, and sorrow flashed across his face, as fleeting as lightning. "And with the help of their mothers, I knew that someday my children would try to do the same to me."

Maryam stepped toward the portal, her spear raised. "This is why Father didn't want me to join him."

Theo felt his stomach knot as Maryam's words sank in. "The prophecy Zeus received when Metis became pregnant: Her child would overthrow him. He's never stopped worrying about that."

On the other side of the portal, Zeus turned to glare at his gray-eyed daughter. "The cycle ends here."

Black clouds roiled above his head, shadowing the barley field, turning its gold stalks gray. "Dionysus spoke the truth," he continued. A roll of distant thunder echoed his words. The wind picked up, shaking the field, whipping the Athanatoi's clothes. "I've made this world anew. We won't fade, we won't die. And *I* won't be overthrown. By anyone. Ever. I've made sure of that."

"Mother didn't make me this spear so I could save my father." Maryam continued toward the portal, a *promakhos* ready to defeat her foe. "She made it for me to destroy him."

But it was too late. With a twist of his lightning bolt, Zeus carved the wind into a tornado that roared against the edge of the portal. The gale forced Maryam back, her near-human body no match for a divine storm.

The wind ripped the grain from the ground and sent it swirling into the ever-widening funnel. The tornado circled, faster and faster, its epicenter swirling above the gaping entrance to Tartarus. The Athanatoi in the barley field crouched among the stalks, fighting the force of the wind that threatened to lift them from the ground.

A finger of wind tore between worlds, snatching at Theo's clothes, his limbs, and growing stronger every second. "He's going to pull us in!" he shouted in warning.

"No, he won't." Maryam spun her weapon and thrust it blade-first into the earth, crying, "The cure is the spear!"

The tip struck stone, and all her strength could bury it no further. Selene rushed to her aid. Together, they drove it deep through the solid rock.

The wind picked Theo off the ground, his sneakers floating six inches in the air. He waved his arms like a new-fledged bird, desperate to land—Selene grabbed his shirt with one hand and hauled him back down. Together, they clung to the spear, sandwiched between Maryam, Esme, Philippe, and June like rush-hour commuters sharing a Manhattan subway pole.

Theo peered at the portal through the swirling debris. The Athanatoi on the other side clutched each other, the barley, the earth, but Zeus's tornado, far stronger than the winds buffeting

Olympus's summit, only continued to grow. The funnel snatched them into the air like a deity's fist. Hephaestus, his mighty strength restored, managed to stay rooted to the ground, but Dionysus, Persephone, and the others spun like rag dolls, their clothes tearing apart, their divine weapons ripped from their hands. The Smith watched them go, bellowing with rage.

The wind drowned the Athanatoi's screams as they spun faster, higher, helpless despite the awesome power that had returned to them. Then, in an instant, the tornado sucked them downward like water through a funnel. They were gone. Swallowed whole by Tartarus's gaping maw.

"What are you doing?" Selene screamed at her father, her words barely discernible above the wind. "You're killing them!"

When He Who Marshals Thunderheads replied, his voice carried through the storm as easily as it would through an empty room. "I would never kill them—I love them."

Zeus turned to Selene, and Theo was shocked to see the truth of his words reflected in the sudden gentleness of his gaze. "I love you all. If you die, I would only lose a part of myself. I want you with me forever. I only seek to put you somewhere safe, where you cannot hurt yourself—or me." His face hardened, and he spun his lightning bolt; the storm around him intensified.

Hephaestus's fingers had dug into the earth, but the rest of his massive body swung toward the cleft like a compass needle. He bared his teeth; sweat ran from his brow. Selene cried out. Theo watched her fingers loosen on the spear.

"You can't go in there!" he hollered at her over the wind. "You'll just get sucked in, too!"

She sobbed, but her hand closed back around the shaft.

June, however, could not be stopped. The aging goddess with the pudgy white arms released Maryam's spear with a cry and staggered forward to save her son.

The raging winds tossed her into the air, her round body hurtling helplessly toward the portal. Philippe released his hold on the spear, scrabbling after her with his stepfather's hammer in one hand. But June was already rocketing through the opening between worlds.

Hephaestus lifted one hand from his grip on the earth, but his fingertips only skimmed his mother's as she streaked past, her mouth opened in a cry of horror.

She plummeted into Tartarus.

Hephaestus let go of the ground to reach after her. His huge frame bulldozed the barley as the wind dragged him to the cleft's edge. Theo could hardly bear to watch.

Then Hermes dove out of the sky toward his stepbrother, the metal wings of his cap flapping as powerfully as a raptor's. He looped his own strong arms under the Smith's and lifted him into the air. They swooped heavenward, seeking to outrun the storm.

"Flint will be okay!" Theo shouted to Selene. "Zeus won't hurt Hermes!"

But Zeus proved him wrong. The Raging One raised his lightning bolt higher. The storm grew taller, the funnel elongating into a twisting black serpent, its jaws aimed at the flashing wings above.

Selene finally let go of the spear. Theo seized the back of her jacket before she, too, could fall prey to Zeus's storm, but the wind on Olympus had already begun to subside. The portal gaped no wider than a man's head. When Selene reached to grab the edges and yank it open again, her hands passed through vapor.

"No!" she bellowed, staring through the hole at the black sky.

Through the whirling clouds, Theo could just make out Hermes, still hovering above the ground with Hephaestus in his arms. He kept trying to fly free, but the wind buffeted him back and forth above the sucking heart of the vortex like a shuttlecock volleyed by giants. Selene grabbed her bow and a hawk-feather arrow as Hermes screamed down a single word to his father.

"WHY?"

"I'm sorry, my Tetractys," Zeus called back. "Even you would seek to overthrow me someday. Such is the destiny of the gods." His face crumpled with sadness. "This is the only way."

The gold, silver, bronze, and copper of the braided metal bolt glowed with every color of the spectrum. Small arcs of light jumped from branch to branch, then shot heavenward. Zeus's eyes sparked in concert with the lightning that crackled toward his favorite son. It struck the winged cap with a shower of sparks and a deafening clash.

As Hermes and Hephaestus plummeted through the sky, Selene loosed her arrow. It flew through an opening now little more than an inch wide, but Theo knew the path it would take: straight through the tornado and into Zeus's heart.

The arrow got halfway through before the hole closed around it, slicing the shaft in two. The black fletching tumbled to the rocky ground where the portal used to be, lying as motionless as a bird with a shattered wing.

Chapter 49

THE PERFECT NUMBER

Selene whipped toward Theo. "Open it again! Hurry!"

He took a step back, shaking his head. "I can't. Zeus took the lightning bolt with him."

She spun in a circle, holding out her hands.

"Someone, please! We have to help them!"

But Theo had already seen what Selene did not: Philippe's crumpled body lay sprawled across the ground right where the portal's opening had been. Esme cradled his bloody head in her hands, keening softly.

Maryam ripped her spear out of the ground. "The cure is the spear..." Her voice sounded mechanical, but the weapon trembled in her grasp. "But not for all of us."

"What happened to Philippe?" Selene asked, her face drained of all color.

"He tried to stop June," Maryam said. "He didn't fall in, but that close to the portal, the rocks...the storm." Her clenched jaw twitched. "It was a stoning."

Theo reached out to soften Selene's fall as she sat down heavily on the rock.

"No." She shook her head. "No. Not Philippe too..."

Theo forced himself to look at the bloody wreck that had once been the beautiful God of Love. His legs lay half-buried beneath a cairn of boulders. Esme's fingers stroked the bright yellow hair from cheeks scraped raw by flying debris. His shirt had been ripped to shreds, revealing a grotesque dent the size of a tennis ball where a stone had caved in his chest. Only Hephaestus's hammer, still clutched over Philippe's head, had prevented the rocks from doing the same to his skull.

Maryam moved to crouch beside the young man. She placed her own hands atop his heart and closed her eyes. "He's still alive," she murmured.

Esme turned bloodshot eyes to her cousin. "Help him," she rasped. "Please."

Maryam took a deep breath and moved her lips. Theo wondered if she prayed to Mary or Jesus—or perhaps to Apollo, God of Healing. If she'd renounced her Christian piety, did she still retain any of her miraculous power? But whatever she said seemed to help—at least a little. The blood clotted on Philippe's chest, and the dent grew a little shallower.

When Maryam opened her eyes, she looked paler than she had before; the healing had stolen some of her strength. "He's still hurt badly. But I think his chances of recovery are..." She stopped herself, as if aware that whatever mathematical probability she was about to impart wouldn't help Esme any. "His chances are good."

"You need to get him off the mountain," Selene insisted. "Where he can heal." She reached for the rope harness that had carried her father, clearly intending to secure it to Philippe. But Esme threw her body across her son's and glared at Selene with eyes so red they seemed almost demonic.

"If it weren't for you, Saturn would've killed Zeus back in the mithraeum and none of this would've happened. My husband wouldn't have followed you here like one of your loyal hounds, and my son wouldn't have followed *him*."

"That's not fair—" Theo began.

"And now Flint's gone," Esme spat. "And June, too. My son has done this to himself for nothing. Look at him! Look at what you've done!"

Theo tightened his grip on Selene's shoulders, trying to offer what comfort he could. "This is not your fault," he said to her sternly. Her body was rigid in his arms, as if the force of Esme's rage had pinned her in place. "We *all* agreed to come here. Flint could've walked away at any point. Esme too. She's just lashing out at you because she's mad at herself for not seeing the trap."

"I know," Selene replied stiffly. "But if Flint had known this would happen to his stepson, he never would've come."

He could hear the regret in her voice; he knew she wanted desperately to help Philippe. But Esme wouldn't let her anywhere near her son.

Maryam took the rope harness from her and fastened it onto Esme's slim shoulders. Theo helped them maneuver Philippe's limp body inside. Maryam lent her spear to the Goddess of Love, who used it to balance herself as she headed swiftly down the mountain.

Theo moved to follow them, but Selene stood rooted in place. "I can't leave. This is where the portal opened. If it opens again, I have to be ready to go through."

"It won't open again," Theo said gently. "Even Maryam can't fashion a divine thunderbolt to control the storm, and even if she could..." He pointed to the spires of rock that had served as the organ's pipes. The force of the wind had sliced long fissures along their sides. The hydraulis would never play again.

"Then we get in some other way." She stared at him with just as much determination as she'd shown the first day they'd met. "We've already passed through death and lived to tell the tale.

Will you help me open another rift in the world, Theo? Will you come with me to Tartarus to free Flint?"

Despite everything, despite the loss and the terror and the weeping blisters on his feet, Theo kissed her knuckles and gave her the fiercest smile he could muster. "Just try to stop me."

Twelve hours later, Theo's determination to reopen the portal was fighting a losing battle with his burning need to sleep. They'd made it down the mountain in half the time it took to get up. Esme hadn't said a word the whole way. When they reached the base, she'd simply summoned a taxicab, jumped in beside her wounded son, and taken off.

The others had dragged themselves to a small taverna, seeking somewhere to rest while they planned their next move. The waiter had produced a pot of tea that tasted like earthy chamomile, liberally spiked with honey. "Olympus tea, we call it here, because the leaves grow on the mountain," he'd said. "It's good for everything. Inflammation, fungus, infection. Everything."

But does it cure guilt? Theo wondered, pushing another cup across the table toward Selene and taking a swallow himself. All the fierce joy he'd felt holding her hand on the summit had suffocated beneath the heavy pall of mourning. In that fog of despair, doubts arose. He'd meant what he'd said on the mountainside: It wasn't Selene's fault. It wasn't anyone's. Nonetheless, he couldn't help feeling like he should've seen it coming. Hadn't he already watched both Orion and Saturn try to destroy the gods to regain their own power? He should've known Zeus would do the same.

His own idiocy wasn't the only thing tying a guilty knot in his stomach. When he'd first met Selene, she'd had almost no contact with the other Athanatoi. He'd been the one to urge her to reach out to them, and in the months since they'd met, she'd finally found a family again. Now only Maryam remained.

Right now, the Gray-Eyed Goddess was staring solemnly into

her own teacup. *She's by far the most joyless Athanatos I've ever met,* Theo thought grimly, *and that includes Saturn.* Maryam would never be able to fill the gap the others had left in Selene's life.

And will I? Theo took another swallow of tea, not caring that it burned his throat. He stifled a groan.

"What?" Selene asked. That was the problem with dating someone with preternatural hearing. The slightest shift in breathing gave you away.

"I was just wondering if the Magna Mater was still around somewhere," Theo lied, unwilling to give voice to his other myriad concerns. "If we're going to confront Zeus himself, it might help to have some more allies."

"My grandmother Rhea took over the Magna Mater's worship," Selene said wearily. "June told me she was killed in the Middle Ages, already weakened and forgotten by men."

"But wasn't she the super-powerful Great Mother?"

Selene snorted. "Maybe in the east, but in our pantheon Rhea was the instrument of her own demise." The way she bit off the words made clear that she felt the same way about herself. Whatever guilt Theo struggled with would pale in comparison to her own. "Think about it. Rhea's angry at her husband for dominating the world, so she masterminds the plot to have her son Zeus overthrow him. It works, but that just means that the Titans fall from power and the Olympians arise. Her own daughters become powerful goddesses while she begins to fade into the background. Typical mother—sacrificing her own needs for those of her kids."

"You say that like it's a bad thing."

"Look, no offense to my grandmother—without her help, my siblings and I never would've been born. And when Saturn imbued me with her soul back in the Phrygianum, I felt how much she loved her children. But maybe if Rhea had held on to her *own* power for a little longer, I wouldn't have been born into a world dominated by men." She nearly snarled the last word.

"She let her *son* rule in place of her husband. Why not take it for herself? Or at least help Hera or Hestia or Demeter take the crown? Then we wouldn't be sitting here figuring out how to rescue my family from my own damn father. Notice how *he* didn't sacrifice everything to save his kids—he sacrificed his kids to save himself. All the while claiming he loves us and doesn't have a choice. Typical."

Theo knew better than to rebut Selene's sexist generalizations. In her current mood, it would only make her angrier.

"The Great Mother was more than Rhea," Maryam said, staring numbly into her cup. "More than Phrygian Cybele or Roman Ops. She was a Mistress of Beasts, like Ephesian Artemis. A Queen of the Stars, like Hera. A Mother of Desire, like Aphrodite. A Protectress of Cities, like me. She was all that was best in us."

"Then we haven't been at our best for a very long time," Selene said flatly. "We've *all* been idiots. Me most of all. I should've known my father wasn't the feebleminded fool he pretended to be. He knew too much—said it was his gift for prophecy sending him dreams, and I fell for his bullshit. He was probably getting updates from Scooter for years. I bet he never even lived in that cave in Crete. He just pretended to because he couldn't find Saturn or the thunderbolt any other way, and he needed both of them for his plan. So he lured the Host into kidnapping him, trusting that Scooter and the rest of his children would get him out again. It nearly backfired—the mithraeum was so well hidden that Scooter couldn't find it without help, and Flint and I were almost too late to save him. But in the end, we all did exactly what he wanted us to."

Theo could sympathize with her anger. Scooter and Zeus had used him as carelessly as they would an inanimate tool, first to find the mithraeum and then to open the portal. They'd known he'd likely break to pieces in the process—and they'd done it anyway. "Speaking of your deceitful little brother," he said, "I still want to know why Zeus called him 'Tetractys.'"

"The perfect number..." Maryam said, slowly stirring her tea as if mixing a potion to unlock all the answers.

"Yeah, it's a Pythagorean term."

When Selene looked at him blankly, Theo pulled a pencil from his pocket and began drawing on a paper napkin. Four dots in a line. Three dots above. Then two. One.

"This is the tetractys," he explained, feeling his gut finally relax as his brain took over. "The word means 'fourness.' Ten total dots, forming an equilateral triangle with four dots on each side. Perfectly symmetrical."

"So?" Selene asked, sounding more curious than dismissive.

"The numbers in each row—one, two, three, four—are special: They also form the harmonic ratios." He described how varying the length of a string changed the note it produced when plucked. He wished he had his monochord handy to demonstrate, but Selene seemed to catch on nonetheless.

"If you go down the rows of the tetractys," he went on, "the number of dots mirrors the most pleasant musical relationships." He tapped his pencil on the top two rows. "A ratio of one to two creates the octave; two to three makes a perfect fifth; and three to four gives a perfect fourth."

"All right," Selene said. "Did the followers of Pythagoras ever call a *man* a tetractys?"

"Not that I know of." He looked questioningly at Maryam. Athena had, after all, been the patron goddess of philosophers, although the Pythagoreans, at least, had worshiped numbers more than they did any Olympian.

Maryam frowned at the dots. "Not a man...but the tetractys was more than just a symbol to them. They personified it, prayed to it."

Theo dug through his pack for his research notebook. He flipped to the section on Pythagoras that he'd carefully compiled over the last few months. "I copied down the prayer somewhere." He didn't want to admit he'd memorized it long before, hoping it could help resurrect Selene. "Ah...here we go. 'Bless us, divine number, you who generated gods and men. O holy, holy Tetractys that contains the root and source of the eternally flowing creation. The never-swerving, the never-tiring holy Ten, the key holder of all.'"

"So maybe Father called Hermes the Tetractys because he was the 'key holder,'" Selene offered. "He's the Conductor of Souls to and from the afterlife, and he's the one who opened the portal by inventing a hydraulis."

Theo shifted uneasily on his chair. Something didn't fit right. "But the hydraulis didn't play octaves and perfect fifths, did it? I mean, it's all a bit of a blur, but I remember it was very beautiful. Just not exactly a standard melody."

The women looked at him like he'd lost his mind.

"Melody?" Selene asked. "You heard a melody?"

"It just sounded like a loud roar to us," Maryam explained. "I thought it might've been many chords played at once, like pressing all the keys on the organ at the same time." She leaned forward, gray eyes boring into Theo. "But if you remember a tune, Professor, maybe we can play it again. The portal would reopen."

"Hate to disappoint you, but I have no idea *what* I played. I was a little distracted by the lightning threatening to rip me limb from limb. Honestly, I'm still not even sure what we opened a portal *to*. It wasn't really ancient Athens, right? It was a new Age instead?"

"According to the prayer," Maryam said, "the Tetractys is the key to creation. In other words, Scooter made the pipes, you controlled the breath, and Saturn played the notes. Scooter may call himself the Tetractys, but it took all of you together to make three sides of the triangle. You brought a whole new world into being."

"Like...a parallel universe?" Theo felt himself slipping further out of his depth, wishing, not for the first time, that he'd paid more attention to the science parts of his science fiction novels. "Or...what do the astronomers call it...a 'multiverse'?"

Maryam scowled, looking surprisingly like Selene. "I've been away from science for too long." The usually stoic goddess slammed down her teacup with just enough force to make a loud crash without shattering the porcelain. "I have no answers anymore."

Selene gave her sister a disdainful frown. "That's what happens when you spend centuries leeching off people who think the *Bible* explains everything."

"It's okay," Theo said, quickly fending off another spat between immortals. "Let's just think this through. You know how usually when a god dies they have some effect on the world? At least temporarily?"

"Yes…" Selene said.

"Yet we just watched ten Athanatoi walk through that portal—*nine* of whom wound up falling into Tartarus—and I didn't feel any effect at all. That's because they didn't die—they just left. They exited the universe."

Maryam took a deep breath, as if to refocus her anger, and said, "It's almost like a god's death causes a wreck on the train tracks of time. The next train has to plow through the debris, causing all manner of accidents. But when a god steps through the portal, there's no crash. It's like switching tracks instead. The god takes off in another direction, and there's no sign he was ever on the first track at all."

Selene looked back and forth between Theo and Maryam before saying, "Then we just build another damn track to get them back where they belong. If they exited the universe, they're not dead, they're just elsewhere. I'm going to get them back, even if it means building our own version of the hydraulis and somehow figuring out the right notes to play."

"A normal water organ obviously won't do it." Maryam steepled her hands beneath her chin. "It has to be enormous. Otherwise Scooter wouldn't have spent months digging tunnels through the tallest mountain in Greece."

"And it can't be just any mountain," Theo added. "Scooter always said location matters. He and Zeus chose Olympus because it was the most sacred, most powerful site for the entire pantheon—and for Zeus in particular."

"Fine." Selene pushed herself from the table. "So we find a place that's powerful for *us*."

"Athens," Maryam said immediately.

"No," Selene shook her head. "That's a sacred space for Father, too, or he wouldn't have opened the portal into a field near the Acropolis. No, when we fight him, I want to do it on my turf."

For the first time since the gods had disappeared into Tartarus, Theo found a smile curving his lips. "I like the sound of that."

"Come on." Selene held out a hand to haul him to his feet. "We're going home."

Chapter 50

ONE WHO
MUSTERS THE
PEOPLE

A long flight from Athens and a short cab ride across Manhattan later, Selene stood on the stoop of her brownstone on West Eighty-eighth Street, listening to the unmistakable sound of a woman's footsteps behind the door.

"Is someone staying in my house?"

Theo looked mildly uncomfortable. "Ruth has a key."

How dare she? How dare he? This was not the homecoming she'd imagined. Then again, she hadn't thought Sister Maryam would be tagging along either. Honestly, she'd rarely allowed herself to think of returning at all. When she did, she'd always pictured bursting through her front door and into Theo's arms. Needless to say, she'd never imagined any witnesses.

"Hey," Theo said sternly. "Did you forget that you *died* and left the house to me? That means I can give a key to whomever I want. And who do you think's been looking after Hippo?"

Hippolyta . . .

Crazed barking and the scrabble of claws on the hardwood

added to the tumult of confused voices from inside—not just Ruth speaking, but several women.

Uh-oh, thought Selene as the door swung open.

Hippo barreled through, throwing all hundred pounds of her shaggy weight onto her mistress; Selene had to hold on to the railing to stop from toppling backward.

"Hey, girl," she said as Hippo jumped up to rest her forepaws on her shoulders. "Yeah, I missed you too." She pressed her face against the dog's floppy ear and whispered, "And I'm sorry I left you. You never would've done it to me."

Hippo responded by licking her mistress's entire face as if it were covered in peanut butter. Selene didn't mind—it meant she could avoid the women standing in the doorway for a few more seconds.

She recognized Gabriela Jimenez's incredulous snort. "You're shitting me."

"Theo?" came a smaller, more hesitant voice. Ruth Willever.

"Is that..." another woman began.

Selene dodged away from Hippo's tongue to see an Asian woman with long graying hair standing at Gabriela's side, looking utterly bewildered. Selene recognized her as Minh Loi, the astronomer she'd once helped protect from an abusive boyfriend.

Gabriela crossed her arms over her breasts and stared at Selene. "Oh yeah, that's her. The one who's supposed to be *dead*."

Theo sighed. "Yeah, how about you all let us in, and I'll try to explain. Since, you know, it is Selene's house and all."

That was fast, Selene thought, glad to have regained ownership without a fight. She gently pushed Hippo off her shoulders and strode through her front door.

Ruth stepped aside. She had a rolling suitcase in one hand and a box of plants under the other arm, as if she was just moving in. Or out.

She looked from Selene to Theo. "I was just getting my things," she said quickly. "I'm leaving right now."

"Hey, you don't need to rush off," Theo said, reaching out a hand to her.

Ruth took a step back. "No, I do. Look, I don't know how you did it, Theo, but nothing can surprise me anymore. I'm glad for you. I'm glad you got her back. Please, I have to go." She bent to give Hippo a quick kiss on the forehead, then hurried down the stairs with her luggage banging behind her. She gave a quick, curious glance at Maryam, who stood silently on the stoop, then rushed down the sidewalk.

"That woman has the worst luck," Gabriela said with a sigh. "I mean, she falls for a guy with a dead girlfriend, and then *bam*. It turns out the girlfriend is like actually immortal, not just *sort of* immortal. There's no getting rid of her. Oh, don't give me that look," she snapped at Theo. "Minh knows all about Artemis."

"I told you it was a secret!" Theo protested.

"Yeah, I heard you, but you didn't mean a secret from my fiancée, did you?"

"Yeah, actually I definitely meant—wait, your *what*?"

"I'll take that as a congratulations," Gabriela said. "I proposed while you were off bribing the devil or whatever you were doing to get your girlfriend back from the dead." Her hard stare swiveled back to Selene. "Unless she wasn't dead in the first place."

Selene swallowed.

"Oh, *no*. You lying *puta*..." Despite Minh's restraining hand on her arm, Gabriela's words shot out as violently as any slap. "Do you have any idea what Theo went through these last six months?"

"Gabi, Selene and I have been through all that. I forgave her, okay?"

"Go right ahead, but I plan to hold that grudge on your behalf for a very long time."

"Fine," Selene said, making her way to the kitchen. "But right now your grudge isn't going to stop me from getting something to drink."

"It better be vodka!" Gabriela called after her. "Because you're going to need it when I'm done with you!"

Selene yanked open her fridge. Nothing left but the condiments. Not surprising. Ruth would've cleaned it out so nothing rotted while Theo was away. *She's so damn considerate.* Selene slammed the door shut and poured herself a glass of water from the tap.

She heard Theo piling their bags at the foot of the stairs and then making introductions.

"Maryam is a nun ... or was." He stumbled, settling on, "She's a friend from Turkey. Maryam, this is Minh Loi. She's an astronomer at the Natural History Museum," he went on more confidently. "She helped us work out some of the science behind the Mithras cult's obsession with the zodiac."

"What do you know about multiverses, Miss Loi?" Maryam asked.

"Stop right there," Gabriela interrupted. "Hey, Theo, remember how you almost got me killed, *twice*? Well, don't try dragging Minh into another one of your schemes, okay, because I will kick your ass right back to the little vanilla suburb you grew up in. She's going to be my wife. We're going to have a *kid*—"

"I didn't—"

"And we were going to ask *you* to be the sperm donor." She barreled over Theo's weak protests. "Except now I'm rethinking, because idiocy could be genetic."

"Hey—"

"And who the hell are you, really, *Maryam*? Let me guess ... From the fact that your eyes are so bright they're making my hair stand on end, I'd have to say ... Athena."

Theo groaned.

Maryam just said, "I admire a wise woman."

"Yeah, I'm sure you do."

"Um, Gabi, honey ..." From the tone of Minh's voice, she'd

never really believed her girlfriend's stories about the Greek gods until now.

Selene paced back into the hallway. "Yes, we're real, and yes, I was alive—most of time—and yes, he *still* had to journey into the Underworld to get me." She took a long swallow of water while Gabriela and Minh stared at her, openmouthed. "It's a long story for another day. Right now, I'm going to order some Chinese food, and Minh's going to answer the Goddess of Wisdom's questions. We have a portal to another dimension to open."

Chapter 51

GIVER OF GOOD COUNSEL

Crammed into Minh's small office at the Hayden Planetarium, Theo watched the astronomer scan through book after book on multiverses. Plenty of scientists, it seemed, had proposed their existence. None of them, however, had any idea how to actually get into one.

Gabriela, who sat cross-legged on the desk, looked about to kick them all out and lock her fiancée safely inside, but Minh had insisted on helping. It seemed she couldn't resist an intellectual challenge any more than Theo could. So after eliciting a firm promise that Minh wouldn't be in any danger, Gabi had relented enough to join in the conversation.

"But you guys said you *did* enter another world, right?" she asked, chewing violently on the end of a pen. "In Delphi?"

"Yes," Selene admitted. "I went into the Lake of Memory in the Underworld, then followed my brother deeper into the water rather than swimming for the surface."

"Soooo...it's obvious." Gabi gave her an exaggerated smile. "You just need to kill yourself and jump in the lake again."

Theo blew out an exasperated breath. "Could you try to be nice?"

She shrugged. "Just saying. You did it for her."

From her place standing in the corner of the room, Selene glared at her. "I'd kill myself if it would help, but it wouldn't. When I took the key away from Aion, the gatekeeper, it disappeared. Without the key, you can get *into* the Underworld, but you can't get back out."

Gabriela didn't look mollified, but Selene just continued coolly, "I did manage to get out of Delphi, however, by playing the right notes, just like when Theo opened the portal by playing the hydraulis. Music is the real way to move from world to world. 'The bridge between worlds hangs on lyre strings.' That's what the Delphic oracle told me."

"She's right," Theo said. "That's why the Orphics sang all those hymns, and why the Orpheus myth says he used his lyre to escape the Underworld. He played a dirge for Persephone and Hades, and they were so moved they let him take Eurydice and leave."

Maryam, who'd spent the last few hours buried in Theo's research, put down his notebook and strode purposefully over to Minh's whiteboard. She uncapped a marker and wrote MITHRAISM, ORPHISM, and PYTHAGOREANISM in an engineer's crisp hand.

"Wait," Gabi said. "Why are we still talking about Mithras? Didn't we get rid of those nutjobs already?"

"But Zeus needed Saturn inside the storm with Theodore," Maryam explained. "That's how he made sure the portal opened into the correct time period."

Theo interrupted to interpret for Minh. "Saturn is the Greek Kronos. As in 'chronometer' and 'chronology.' The God of Time." The astronomer nodded, still looking a little overwhelmed.

"But I think Saturn had another role to play," Maryam went on. "From what I've read in the professor's notebook, the Mithraists, despite their scientific inaccuracies, understood the power of the stars. The Host believed Mithras himself brought his followers closer to the Last Age—and to the reincarnation of Jesus—by shifting the heavens." Under the "Mithraism" column she wrote REINCARNATION and CELESTIAL SPHERES.

Theo stood up from his chair and leaned on Minh's desk, unable to contain his growing excitement. "Orphics and Pythagoreans also believed in some form of reincarnation," he said. "When I was in the Underworld, I saw the dead passing through portals—like holes in the celestial spheres—in order to go back to the world of the living."

Maryam nodded and added the words beneath the other two columns. "The two cults had something else in common. Orpheus the musician. Pythagoras the music theorist." She added MUSIC beneath ORPHISM and PYTHAGOREANISM.

"Shit-balls." Theo snatched up a red marker from the whiteboard. He circled MUSIC and SPHERES and then turned to Maryam and grinned. "That's it. That's what we need."

"Wait," Gabi interjected. "What the hell are the Music Spheres?"

Theo laughed. "Music *of the* Spheres."

Gabi just stared at him, both brows raised.

"Imagine you have a ball or a piece of wood attached to a string," he continued. "Like a yo-yo. You swing it around your head in a circle superfast, and it makes a sound, right?" He spun the marker around his head in a futile attempt to demonstrate. "Some Greek cults used it to make a roaring noise in their cult rituals."

Gabi moaned. "You mean there are *more* Greek cults still out there? Spare me, please."

Theo ignored her and pressed on. "The Greeks called it a 'rhombus' from the word for 'spinning'—we still use the word for shapes that look like the piece of wood they whirled around. Well, ancient astronomers figured that, just like a wooden rhombus makes a sound if you spin it on a string, then surely the planets, which are infinitely larger, must also make noise when they're orbiting through the heavens. Remember, in their geocentric model of the universe, each planet had its own celestial sphere. The zodiac and other constellations were on another one. All these spheres are spinning around the earth at different rates. And just like objects on earth, the faster you spin them, the higher-pitched the sound. So, the movement of the heavens creates a Music of the Spheres."

Selene pushed herself off the wall, eyes bright. "And you think *that's* the melody the hydraulis was playing on Olympus?"

"Maybe. Remember the prayer to the Tetractys? It says numbers created the universe."

"But in the Underworld," Selene interjected, "Apollo told me *music* made the world. And can unmake it, too."

"Exactly. They're *both* right. The Pythagoreans knew that numbers and music are essentially the same thing—numerical ratios underlie each chord. The range of pitches is infinite. It's chaos. But when you limit it to specific ratios—octaves, fourths, fifths—you get order, beauty, harmony. Our word for 'cosmos' is just the Greek *'kosmos,'* which means 'order.' So"—he flourished his marker—"it's music that takes limitless *khaos* and restricts it into certain pitches to get limited *kosmos*."

Selene beamed at him. "Music is doing what myth did. Lionheaded Aion wrapped up tight in his snakes. Unbounded Time bound by Kronos himself."

Gabi looked fascinated and bewildered at the same time. "Okay, so the Music of the Spheres sounds pretty cool, but no one can hear it, right? How'd the Greeks explain that?"

"Easy," Theo said, tossing his marker back on the tray. "The sound of the planets spinning on their spheres would be a constant background noise to every moment of our lives, so humans wouldn't even perceive it. It's like how if you live on Broadway, after a while you just don't notice the traffic noise. Pythagoreans thought only one person could hear the music: Pythagoras himself. He was so wise, so learned, that he could perceive the mathematical perfection of the universe in a way no one else could. That sort of knowledge—the ability to see the patterns that form the world around us—is what makes you a true *philosophos*, a lover of knowledge. It connects you to the divine."

Minh waved her hand for him to stop. "Hold up. I was following you until the 'divine' part. I thought this was science, not religion."

Gabi poked her on the shoulder. "I thought you were engaged to an anthropologist. Haven't I been telling you that throughout most of human history those were the same thing?"

"Gabi's right," Theo said eagerly. "The followers of Pythagoras believed only the gods could've created the hidden logic that underlies all of nature. So accessing that logic could bridge the gap between mortal and god. Even the *Christians* believed something similar, although it's gotten corrupted over time. Remember the line from the New Testament, 'In the beginning was the Word, and the Word was God'?"

Gabi and Maryam nodded encouragingly, although he could tell he'd lost Selene the minute he started talking about Christianity. He plowed on anyway. "You hear Christians say it all the time: 'Jesus is the Word.' But the New Testament was originally written in Greek, and the real line goes something like, 'In the beginning was the *Logos*.' Which can just as easily be translated as 'logic.' So it's not that God—or Jesus—created the world. It's that *logic* did. Numbers. Math. So only by tapping into that mathematical pattern of the universe can man achieve salvation."

Selene looked to their resident nun for confirmation.

"It's an unorthodox interpretation," Maryam said stiffly. "But it's not wrong."

Selene grinned. "Good. So if Theo's right, and the Music of the Spheres is the most important manifestation of this divine pattern, then *that's* the melody that opens the portal."

Gabi scrubbed her face with uncharacteristic weariness.

"Okay, stop, stop. All very interesting, but since the universe isn't geocentric, and there's no such thing as celestial spheres, this is all useless. There *is* no Music of the Spheres. Right?"

Theo froze. He slumped into a chair and squeezed the bridge of his nose beneath his glasses.

"Right?" repeated Gabi, looking at Minh.

The astronomer gave her lover a smile of pure glee. "Wrong. The heavens *are* singing." She bent over her computer. "Pythagoras was wrong about the spheres, but he was right that music created the universe."

Theo scooted his chair closer, barely restraining himself from looming over her shoulder to see better.

Minh typed away for a moment, then sat back while the twang of a science fiction laser gun issued from her speakers. The sound dropped slowly in pitch, like an airplane crossing the sky, then settled into a low roar before climbing once more into a bright hiss, growing louder and louder until it stopped abruptly.

"That," Minh said with a satisfied smirk, "is the tune sung by the Big Bang."

Gabi leaned over to plant a kiss on her cheek. "Did I mention to y'all that my fiancée is a genius?"

"Many times, no doubt." Minh gave a self-deprecating snort. "But a colleague of mine over at the University of Virginia deserves the credit. Of course, it's been transposed fifty octaves upward and sped up by a factor of three trillion. The real sound would be far too deep for human hearing."

"Um." Theo felt like an idiot for questioning her, but that was, after all, a scholar's job. "I thought there was no sound in space."

"Not anymore, that's true. But when the universe began, it was full of a superbright fog of gas, dense enough for sound waves to travel through. Remember, I said the sound *created* the universe. It's not just some fun by-product."

"Explain," demanded Selene.

Minh took a deep breath. "Okay. The universe starts as a hot, dense fog of gas, right? Well, over time the universe expands. As it thins, it also cools, leaving us with the cold, black space we know today. But remember, when astronomers look through telescopes, they're not just looking into the distance; they're also looking into the *past*, because it takes so long for the light from the stars to reach us. When you look at something a distance of thirteen billion light-years away, you're seeing what it looked like thirteen billion *years ago*. So, with certain telescopes, we can actually look all the way back to the fog of the universe at the very beginning of time."

"Khaos," Selene said softly. "You're seeing *khaos.*"

"Uh, yes, sort of. It's not something you *see* exactly, because it travels to us as microwaves, not visible light. When we look at the sky, the closest things we can observe beyond our solar system are the individual stars here in our galaxy. Then whole other galaxies hurtling away from us. Then fainter and fainter galaxies until finally you *see*, so to speak, a bank of crackling static, like a TV tuned to an empty channel. We call it the cosmic microwave background." She stood and picked up a marker. "Starting in the 1990s, astronomers discovered that the CMB contains patches of low and high density."

Gabi winked at Theo. "I love when she uses the whiteboard."

Minh rolled her eyes, but Theo caught her smiling. She sketched a long, sinusoidal wave across the board. "Those differences in density in the CMB—in the fog of the primordial universe—are actually the peaks and troughs of *sound waves* left over from the original Big Bang. Sound moves like a slinky: It pushes some molecules together, then pulls others farther apart. When I talk—or sing—the air molecules from my mouth push together other air molecules to get the sound to your ear. If there hadn't been any sound waves in the Big Bang, all the matter in the universe would be spread out evenly—just an enormous, thin cloud of dust. But instead, the sound waves pushed some of the matter together, creating dense patches. Remember how the sound I played for you got louder and louder? That's because over millions of years, the differences in density got more extreme."

She drew another wave over the first, this one with higher peaks and lower troughs. "Eventually, the dense peaks collapsed under the weight of their own gravity to form matter—stars— and the troughs excavated to become the spaces between stars." She turned back to her listeners and capped her marker triumphantly. "Voila. Music forms the cosmos."

Theo jumped up from his chair and cracked his neck in both directions, as if warming up for a gymnastics competition. "Okay, okay." He cracked his knuckles, too, for good measure. "So Zeus and Scooter, along with a little involuntary help from the God of Time and some unintentional assistance from yours truly, re-created the sound waves of the Big Bang—the *Logos* of creation—and brought a new universe into being. To do it right, they needed an incredibly big instrument—a whole mountain— as a pipe organ to produce sounds far below the range of human hearing. But I *did* hear something. Not just a hiss, like what you played on your computer, but music."

Minh tapped a few more keys. This time, the sound came out as a major chord, bending and stretching into a higher-pitched minor and then back again. An eerie, ghostly melody.

The sound sent shivers of recognition across Theo's skin. "Yeah, that's it."

"It's the same sound I played before," Minh said, "just with the fundamental notes pulled out and modulated into a pentatonic scale." She glanced down at her screen and gave a short, dry laugh. "The other word for a pentatonic scale is, get this: Pythagorean."

Theo blew out a slow breath. Everything was moving very fast. "Okay. We know the right notes. Now we just need the right instrument to play them."

Gabi cocked her head. "I don't know of any mountain-sized pipe organs in Manhattan, do you?"

"*Hermes* preferred the pipes..." Selene said, her cheeks flushed. "But Apollo played the lyre."

Maryam nodded, a slow smile brightening her stern features. "The bridge between worlds hangs on lyre strings."

Theo looked from one to the other, not quite following their train of thought. "Where are we going to find a string instrument the size of a mountain?"

Selene grinned at him. "The *bridge* between worlds, Theo. We have five string instruments ready-made. Right now, they're connecting Manhattan to New Jersey, Brooklyn, and Queens. But with a little luck, they'll connect us to another universe instead."

Chapter 52

PONTIFEX MAXIMUS

"You need to watch your footwork," Selene commented, watching Maryam run through a series of lunges and parries with her spear in the living room.

Maryam ignored her and continued her exercises.

"Really, if you were in fighting shape, you could've stolen your aegis back from Father," Selene went on. "It protects the wearer from all harm, right? That'd be useful right about now. You're going to need to work much harder if we're going to face him again at his full strength."

Maryam spun her weapon in a tight arc and then brought it before her in a guard position. "Perhaps I'd be in better condition if the noise hadn't kept me up all night."

"You're not used to Manhattan traffic," Selene said with a shrug. Then, at Maryam's pointed stare, she felt her cheeks heat. *Were Theo and I really that loud?* It had been the first night they'd spent in a bed—rather than an airplane—since Mount Olympus, and they'd made the most of it. She could feel the rasp of his stubbled cheek against her breast even now. The first time they'd made love, six months before, it had been on a cold granite boulder with the frigid wind of the Hudson River at their backs. Last night, the air conditioner in her window had dripped and groaned in its effort to keep up with them. For so long, she'd lived with only dreams of him—she felt a warm flush as she remembered how the reality had exceeded her fantasies. She considered herself a woman of action, the Swiftly Bounding One; Theo had shown her how to move slowly. She'd returned the favor, stalking him, sniffing him, searching his body like a lioness with her prey. Then she'd given up on restraint and devoured him with all the greedy—

Maryam clacked her spear against the ground in a downward thrust, yanking Selene back to the present. Her gray eyes bored into her sister knowingly.

"Watch my hardwood floor," Selene snapped for lack of a better response. She retreated to the kitchen, needing sustenance for what promised to be a very long day.

She had her head buried in the refrigerator when Theo finally padded down the stairs in a gaping bathrobe, his hair a tousled mess.

He folded his arms around her and rested his chin on her shoulder to look into the fridge. He smelled like her. The heat of his skin poured through the thin fabric of his robe.

"What's for breakfast?" he asked drowsily.

"You tell me," she said with a scowl. "There's a disturbing lack of bacon. Ruth cleared everything out except the ketchup and . . . what is this . . . pickles?"

"Sounds like we're ordering delivery from the diner. Challah French toast for me, two orders of bacon and three breakfast sausages for you?"

"That sounds . . . amazing."

"Welcome home." He kissed her, light and lingering, on the neck. A reminder. An invitation.

Selene gently freed herself. "Maryam's in the living room."

Theo held up his hands guiltily and stepped back. "Right."

"And we have a big day."

He nodded. "Turn the bridges of Manhattan into a ginormous lyre to open a passage to another dimension. Got it. Very serious."

"Then why are you smiling?" she asked, although she already knew the answer. Despite the dangers they faced, she couldn't repress an answering grin.

"Because this morning I feel like we can do anything. Parallel universe? *Pshaw.* Symphony on suspension bridges? Whatever. I mean, if I can make a *goddess* orgasm four—"

Selene threw a dish towel at his face as Maryam entered the kitchen, still holding her spear.

Theo was still laughing as Maryam unfolded a map of New York City across the kitchen table.

"Here." She pointed to the George Washington Bridge. "This is the biggest one. It'll have the most power."

Selene willed the blood to leave her cheeks and asked, "When did you have time to learn that?" After their meeting with Minh last night, they'd come right back to the house.

"As I said," Maryam said calmly, "I didn't get much sleep. I used the professor's laptop."

Which means the woman who's been holed up in a convent for centuries just taught herself to use the Internet in the course of one night, while I can still barely get my camera phone to work, Selene thought. *But that doesn't mean she knows more than I do about my own city.* "The GWB may be Manhattan's biggest suspension bridge, but it's not the best choice. Remember, location matters, not just size. We need somewhere with great spiritual power, somewhere that symbolizes the city itself, somewhere *ancient.* Or at least, as ancient as things get in New York." She laid a finger on the Brooklyn Bridge. "*Here* is where we make our stand."

———◇———

Choosing the Brooklyn Bridge was one thing. *Playing* it was quite another.

After his enormous breakfast, Theo spent the rest of the day at Columbia, searching for a physics professor who hadn't taken off for the summer. When he finally found one, she'd downloaded a suite of sound-engineering software to Theo's laptop, lent him a set of contact microphones, and wished him a very skeptical good luck.

Just after sunset, he took the subway downtown to the bridge's pedestrian entrance. Rush hour was over, but hordes of people still crossed the wooden path above the roadway. Whole families with strollers, whizzing bicyclists, meandering tour groups, besotted couples, all enjoying the spectacular views of the Hudson, the New York skyline, and the bridge itself. Theo hadn't walked across it since he'd made the tourist circuit when he first moved to New York nearly ten years earlier, and the sheer grandeur of it filled him with some of the same awe he'd felt watching the Olympians grow to their full divine glory on the other side of the portal. This wasn't the work of a god; this was a man-made miracle constructed over a century ago. A masterpiece of gothic stone archways and crisscrossing metal cables that had, when built, been the biggest suspension bridge in the world. Even now, it possessed such beauty that the other bridges spanning the river to the north and south all seemed like ugly stepsisters in comparison.

He spotted Selene and Maryam right away—six-foot-tall women had a tendency to stand out in a crowd. To his surprise, Gabriela and Minh stood beside them.

Watching Selene's frown of concentration as she examined the bridge's cables, Theo couldn't help remembering the heat of her smile that morning when he'd awoken beside her. Selene had been staring at him while he slept—he wasn't sure for how long. He'd rolled to face her, and her eyes drifted from his face to his chest. She reached over to trace the pale Mercury symbol on his sternum, the one branded into his flesh by Saturn six months earlier, and her smile faded into something solemn and sad. He touched the scar between her breasts in turn: a ragged white oval seared there by Zeus's lightning bolt the night they'd fought atop the Statue of Liberty.

"We both have our scars," he'd murmured. "The ones we can see—and the ones we can't. And they might not be our last." He kept his eyes locked on hers even as his hand trailed down her ribs. "I'm willing to take that chance."

She'd leaned closer in answer, resting her lips on his before pulling him into her arms.

Gabriela's disgruntled snort broke Theo from his reverie. She strolled across the walkway to join him.

"I didn't expect to see you here," he ventured.

"I know, I swore I wouldn't let Minh get involved. But the problem with falling for strong women is that they rarely listen to you." At Theo's wry grin, she added, "I'm preaching to the choir, huh?"

"And I'm shouting, 'Amen.'"

Minh remained with the goddesses, still busy with the cables. Using a protractor and weighted string, Maryam surveyed the thick wires that supported the bridge's roadway, stopping every few seconds to jot down notes. Then Selene struck one of the cables with a small mallet while the astronomer placed the diaphragm of a stethoscope against the metal, listening intently.

"How's it going over there?" Theo asked Gabi.

She looked like she'd just sucked too much lime after a shot of tequila. "Minh's having the time of her life."

Theo laughed. "Then why the face?"

"Because this stupid plan might actually *work*. They've already measured the length of each cable, as well as the relative pitch. Athena, big surprise, is scary smart. You think she's gay? Because she and Minh are bonding over integrating the curve to find the arc length, and I don't even know what that means."

Even though she was too far away to hear, Maryam shot a glance over at Gabi and Theo at the mention of her name.

Theo lowered his voice, knowing that Selene, at least, could hear everything they said if she bothered to listen. "I don't think you have to worry—you've definitely got her beat in the personality department. And try calling her Maryam. Or Gray-Eyed Goddess. Using her real name can draw her attention to you."

Gabi rolled her eyes. "All those years studying indigenous folklore and magic and then it shows up at my doorstep, and I just want it all to go away."

"And yet we're both still here."

"Love makes idiots of us all, *chico*."

"True. But it's more than that. I mean yes, I'm here for Selene. But aren't you *excited*, Gabi?"

"I'm scared shitless. I mean that literally. Ever since you got back, my ass has been clenched tighter than a billionaire's wallet."

Theo wrapped an arm around her shoulders. "I've missed you."

She gave him a sideways smirk. "I know."

"We're about to answer one of the great questions of the universe, and I'm glad I've got your potty humor to keep it all in perspective."

"What great question? Like who gets arrested first for trying to knock down the Brooklyn Bridge? I can answer that." She jabbed a thumb into her own chest. "The brown lady."

"Not exactly the question I had in mind."

"You mean more like, 'What happens after we die?' I thought you knew the answer to that now."

He winced. "Maybe, but the Underworld I visited was created by my own belief. By Orphic ritual. The other time I died, nothing happened. So I guess I know what *can* happen after we die—not what *does*."

"Awesome. Then what *are* we answering?"

"On top of Olympus, Dennis posed the question as 'How do we live a better life?' But I think it's more like 'How do we transcend our mortal lives? How do we see what's *beyond* us?' I've been thinking about that question ever since Dennis asked it. It seems to me our answer has evolved over time. Orion's Eleusinian cult reached back to prehistory for answers—to human sacrifice and barbarism. Saturn's Mithraists chose the modern religion of Christianity instead. *We* are using science."

Gabi sighed. "I'll tell you what matters, *querido*. Not getting sucked into a black hole by your little experiment." She punched him lightly on the arm before marching over to the cable.

Minh held out the stethoscope when Theo joined them. "Take a listen."

Selene hit the suspender cable with her hammer. A tympanic crash rolled through the stethoscope and into his brain, a resonant, reverberating boom like a giant's footstep. He was sure the cable was about to snap under Selene's blow, sending cars and pedestrians plummeting into the East River.

He ripped the stethoscope from his ears with a yelped curse.

Selene smiled. "Not bad, huh?"

"You're going to bring the bridge down! Or at least get us all arrested!"

She laughed. "For this?" She tapped the cable again. Theo could barely hear the flat, dull slap above the rumble of the traffic below. "See? The bridge only speaks if you listen closely. And, as you know, most mortals are very bad at that."

Maryam held out a hand for Theo's bag. "You brought the other instruments? We've done as much as we can with what we have. The stethoscope is rudimentary."

He pulled out the microphones and his laptop and relayed the physicist's instructions. The contact mics looked like electrodes from an electrocardiogram, and when Maryam affixed one to the suspender cable, green lines began to oscillate across his laptop screen. Theo had the distinct impression they were about to record the heartbeat of the city itself.

Maryam nodded to Selene. "Okay, give it a whack."

Once again, even Selene's mighty strength produced nothing more than a mild clank. But the lines on Theo's laptop danced wildly, and when he transposed the sounds into the audible range, what emerged from the computer speakers was not the tympanic roll they'd heard through the stethoscope, but the subsonic voice of the entire bridge. Three tones woven into one: a deep rushing like a god's breath through a pipe, the bass hum of a diesel engine, the high ringing of a bell.

They all stood in astonished awe for a moment. Then Minh took Theo's laptop and started typing away. "We're hearing the harmonics," she murmured distractedly. "But if we condense the broad sound waves into sharper peaks, we can pick out the fundamental note at the center." After a little more typing, she looked up with a broad grin. "That's a G."

"Now do we have to do the same thing to every other cable?" asked Theo.

Maryam shook her head. "I've already measured the height of each, and we know that longer cables produce deeper tones, just as they would on a lyre. We just need to listen to one more so we can confirm the exact effect of the length differential on the pitch. Then Minh can compute the note of each cable based on my data—assuming they all have the same mass density per unit length."

After they finished with the next cable, Minh settled on a nearby bench, with Theo's computer on her lap. Maryam looked over her shoulder; Gabi hovered on the other side.

This is going to work, he thought. *We will be the Pontifex Maximus.* The Romans had given their head priest—and their emperor—the title of "bridge builder." The Catholics had stolen the epithet for their pope. Theo felt a sudden pride that he was about to help a pair of pagan goddesses steal it back.

Minh looked up from the computer. "Remember how the sound of the Big Bang that I played for you all had been transposed upward by fifty octaves? I thought there was no way we'd be able to replicate the original sound. We'd need a piano the length of *seven* pianos. But it turns out there's a half step in pitch between every two of the 1,520 suspender cables. That means our bridge is a lyre with a range of—"

"Fifty-eight octaves," Maryam interjected before Minh could do the math.

Theo whistled. "Sounds like we've got our instrument, folks. Now who's going to play it?"

"We all have to." Minh showed them the musical notation from the web page of her colleague at UVA. "We need to play four separate chords in series, each one composed of eight notes spread across more than three octaves."

Maryam frowned. "The cables are several feet apart, which means no one person can hit more than one note at the same time. We're going to need three more people."

"You're going to need *five* more," Gabi said quickly. "Minh may be helping you figure out the notes and whatever, but when it comes time to open your 'dimensional portal' or 'wormhole'— or, as I like to call it, 'vortex to certain death'—we'll be visiting my aunt in the Bronx. No, screw that, we'll go all the way to my cousin's house in Jersey."

"Gabi—" Minh began with her usual eye roll.

"No! I will *not* lose you, Minh. Not after I spent my whole life looking for you!"

Minh's face crumpled. Then Gabi's did too. They fell into each other's arms, laughing and crying at the same time.

Theo looked for Selene and found her already looking at him.

Minh and Gabi moved off to huddle together at the edge of the walkway, their intense voices too hushed for Theo to hear.

Selene cocked her head in a listening pose, but Theo decided he didn't need to eavesdrop on his friends. Either they'd help or they wouldn't; he respected them enough to leave the decision to them.

Maryam pulled his attention back to the task at hand. "We have a bigger problem than finding enough people to strike the chord. We don't have Saturn to control where—or *when*—the portal will lead."

"Damn," Theo said. "We could wind up in Paleolithic Manhattan instead of classical Athens."

"I don't think so," Selene said slowly. "When we were leaving the Underworld, Apollo was drawn back to Delphi. Maybe because it was the place he loved best."

"That's not the same thing—" Maryam interjected.

"All of this is unknown territory," Selene said, talking over her. "There's no way *Saturn* had the scientific knowledge necessary to control space and time. Yet something beyond science, something tied to his role as Kronos, God of Time, let him do it anyway. Well, just like Apollo's love for Delphi drew him there, the link between the other Athanatoi and me transcends anything you can measure or quantify or run through your software programs. Hermes may be the Messenger of the Gods, but I'm the Huntress. I'll track them down, no matter what universe they're in."

Maryam looked dubious. "They didn't exactly leave scat along the trail for you to sniff out."

Selene's chin lifted in disdain. "That's not what I meant. My twin understood the power of music—his songs opened the door from Delphi and led Theo to us in the Underworld. Now, with Apollo gone, it falls to me to sing the hymns that will bring me to my family."

Theo thought Maryam might protest. The plan was anything but practical. But Selene spoke with such force that even the Goddess of Wisdom seemed convinced.

"Then let's assume we get to the right place," Maryam said after a moment. "How do we actually crack open Tartarus once we get back to the field? Father has taken Poseidon's trident, and we have no other weapon that can shake the earth as effectively. I've considered trying to bring modern construction equipment through. Perhaps get hold of Flint's drilling machines left on Olympus—"

"You forget that once we cross the portal, we'll truly be Athanatoi once more," Selene said impatiently. "Possessing impossible power and strength."

"Impossible," Maryam agreed. "But not unlimited. My spear won't crack the earth. Nor will your bow or the professor's sword."

Selene nodded grimly. "But Hephaestus's hammer will."

Chapter 53

HOLDER OF THE BOUNDS OF THE WORLD

Three days had passed since they'd heard the bridge's voice. Three days of planning, preparing, and—most of all—waiting.

Waiting for Saturday night, when the bridge would be closed for repairs. For Esme to make up her mind and bring them the hammer Flint had left with Philippe—or not. For Maryam to finish whatever she'd been banging away on in Selene's basement for fourteen hours a day.

Selene felt herself going slowly mad. Time, she was sure, passed differently on the other side of the portal, just as it had in Delphi. How long had her family endured the torments of Tartarus? Every time she fell asleep, she dreamed of them besieged by the monsters and giants they'd cast into the pit in the time before time. Hephaestus still had her necklace in his pocket. Since he'd given Philippe his hammer, the golden javelin would be his only weapon. Would that be enough to defend so many Olympians from their ancient enemies?

The nightmares would rip her from sleep, shouting with rage and fear, only to find herself safe and warm in Theo's arms. For all the solace of his touch, she couldn't help feeling guilty. How dare she enjoy such comforts while her family suffered? She longed for the waiting to end.

Yet when she hopped the construction barricades and walked to the center of the Brooklyn Bridge just before midnight on Saturday, she wished she had more time.

I am not prepared, she worried, even though she'd done nothing else for three days. Desperate for divine weapons, she'd brought her twin's three plague arrows, along with her last two unerring golden shafts, but they seemed paltry tools for opening a portal between worlds and facing her father on the other side. Her heart tripped; she could feel the pulse of the blood in her veins, even as the city loomed eerily calm around her.

The office buildings of downtown Manhattan crowded so thickly that she couldn't tell one from the other, their windows like mosaic tiles of light dumped across the sky. Only the Municipal Building remained distinct, a forty-story wedding cake topped with a round Roman temple of Corinthian columns, too lofty by far for any but the gods to enter. To the north, the spires of Midtown emerged like fairy-tale palaces: the Chrysler Building with its white and chrome crown, the Empire State piercing the clouds with a spire of red and gold, the Bank of America building's antenna a blue lance.

Surrounding the bridge, the black river glimmered with white, reflecting not the moon or stars, but the lights of construction sites and ferryboats. In the distance, the Statue of Liberty glowed on her island retreat, a grim reminder of the last time Selene had sought to battle another Athanatos in her city. *I barely survived. Theo barely survived.*

Ahead of her, the wooden walkway sloped gently up toward the Brooklyn Bridge's first stone tower. On either side, the suspension cables soared heavenward, crisscrossed by slanting cantilever wires to create a massive metal net. Selene felt like a fly walking into a spider's web.

"I don't believe it," Theo murmured at her side.

She turned to follow his gaze to where Esme stood at the far end of the bridge. "You didn't think she'd come?"

"I thought it was a long shot. Esme doesn't strike me as the altruistic type. What does she care if the husband she barely admits exists—or half her family, for that matter—is trapped in Tartarus?"

"The bonds between us all are old and deep, even when we try to forget them."

"Yeah..." Theo said skeptically. "Or Philippe just insisted."

The God of Love appeared beside his mother. He carried his stepfather's hammer in one hand and his own myrtle bow in the other. His usually spiky hair was plastered to his forehead with sweat, and his cupid's bow of a mouth was pressed in a flat line of pain. He walked stiffly, as if unable to bend his torso. But whatever medical attention Esme had found in Athens—along with the god's own undoubtedly excellent healing powers—had clearly worked.

"Speaking of old bonds," Theo went on, "I'm still uncomfortable with Gabi and Minh being here." He glanced over at his friends. For all of Gabi's protective bluster, Minh wasn't about to let a portal to another universe open without her. There'd been some very specific negotiations about how much Minh would be allowed to report to the scientific community when it was all over; Selene and Maryam didn't want mortals tampering with realms best left to gods, but they allowed that Minh's contribution gave her the right to continue pursuing her research.

"You said they could make their own choices. They'll be fine," she assured him, although their safety was far from guaranteed. The women had strict instructions to get off the bridge as soon as they struck their cables. If they were still in place when the portal opened, they'd likely find themselves in classical Athens—and they might never get out again.

Shoulders thrown back, chin high, Maryam strode forward to meet Philippe and Esme. *All sign of the diffident nun has been beaten out of her,* Selene noted. *Perhaps that's what she was hammering away on in the basement for the last three days.*

The Goddess of Justified War carried her spear in one hand and an enormous duffel bag over one shoulder. "You have come," she pronounced.

Philippe pursed his lips. "Of course. I'll make sure Papa's own hammer sets him free."

Gabi piped up. "What good will that do without Flint to swing it? No one else can tap into its divine mojo, right?"

Philippe's glance slid to Theo. "The Makarites can."

Gabi crossed her arms over her chest, glaring from the god to her friend. "That means Theo has to be inside the portal to crack open Tartarus, right? I thought you were getting to safety with the rest of us mere mortals."

Theo didn't answer her directly. "None of that's going to matter if we don't find another person. Eight notes, eight people."

Maryam lifted one long arm and pointed to the end of the bridge. A small figure, no more than a silhouette in the darkness, appeared. Theo squinted in that direction. But Selene's keen eyes had already identified the narrow shoulders and wispy hair of their new volunteer. Theo wasn't going to like this.

"Ruth?" he breathed as she stepped into the light of a lamppost. "What are you doing here?"

"Maryam asked me to come. As backup."

"And you...said yes?" He looked completely shocked.

"She said you were conducting an experiment, and you needed as many scientists as you could muster."

Theo rounded on Maryam. "Ruth's a biologist, not an astronomer or a physicist. You shouldn't be putting more of my friends in danger."

Maryam looked at him steadily. "From what I've read of her research, your friend is a very intelligent woman. Intelligent enough to choose for herself."

Theo threw up his hands. "She doesn't want any part of this."

"Yes, I do," Ruth said, her voice quiet but firm. "I'm already in it too deep. I've spent the last three days wondering what on earth you were planning. Gabriela told me about the portal—it does sound dangerous, but it also sounds like a miracle. As a scientist, we don't see a lot of those."

"So you're here to satisfy your intellectual curiosity?" he demanded.

"I'm here because you need me," she replied calmly. "And because I need you." She took a step closer to Theo and reached for his hands. Selene could see the tension in his shoulders and had to stop herself from intervening. Theo had stood by and let her deal with Flint in her own way. The least she could do was let him do the same with Ruth.

Ruth looked up at him, her eyes wide. "I know I can never be the only woman in your life. But we've been through too much to throw our friendship away now. Let me do this, Theo. For the love we share."

Selene felt a stab of jealousy—not because of the warmth in Theo's eyes as he looked down at his friend, but because of the loyalty in Ruth's. Flint had been so hurt by Selene's rejection that he'd walked into the unknown of the portal rather than staying with her and the rest of his family. If he couldn't have all of her, he didn't want any of her. So it had always been for Athanatoi, even ones as human as Flint. *Either catch the maiden and have your way, or turn her into a laurel tree. There's never been much gray in our black-and-white world.*

Theo wrapped his arms around Ruth, who pressed her cheek into his chest. He kissed the top of her head lightly.

Maryam opened her large duffel and passed out small mallets.

They looked like jeweler's tools compared to the massive hammer Philippe handed to Theo.

Unlike the intricately carved ornaments and weapons that the Smith usually made, his hammer was a practical tool. Millennia of use had polished the ash-wood shaft to a silken shine. The head, as big around as a coffee can and twice as long, was dark iron, its blunt front and tapered tail mirroring the meteorite from which it had been forged.

Next, Maryam drew out a stack of what looked like very thin manhole covers. In fact, Selene realized, noting the NYC SEWER faintly visible on the surface, they *were* manhole covers. Or at least they had been before the Goddess of Crafts hammered them into shields and coated them in gleaming metal.

"Where'd you get the bronze?" Selene asked.

"Tin from some cans in your basement. Copper from your country's inappropriately named nickels."

"That's a hell of a lot of nickels."

Maryam shrugged. "I supplemented with the copper tubing from your pipes."

"My *pipes*?"

Maryam looked at her sternly. "You have more bathrooms than you need."

Selene frowned, but she had to admire her half sister's resourcefulness. In three days of work, she'd turned the basement into her own personal forge and created a total of seven shields. She offered the first one to Gabriela, who held both hands up in protest.

"If you think I need that, this whole idea is *way* too dangerous."

"It's wiser to be safe, is it not?" Maryam asked, her brow furrowed. "My Father must know we'll try to rescue our family. He'll be prepared for us. We need to be prepared for him."

Gabriela opened her mouth to refuse, then shut it with a snap when she looked down at the front of the shield. "You made this...for me?" She sounded completely nonplussed for the first time since Selene had known her. The front of the shield, she saw now, was embossed with the geometric figure of a Navajo eagle.

Maryam's lips tightened, rather than smiled, but Selene could see she was pleased with herself. "Your mother was Navajo, no? I've given you the warrior's symbol of your people, to bring out the warrior within."

"I'm not a—" Gabriela stopped herself, her eyes still on the shield.

"You mortals do not have defining attributes, as we do. And perhaps that gives you more flexibility to craft your own identity. But sometimes, when you are lost, overwhelmed, confused, an attribute can also remind you of your most essential self."

Gabriela swallowed whatever she was about to say. She slipped the shield over her left arm.

Maryam passed the next shield to Minh. Overlapping starbursts of pressed tin covered its face. "I don't get a constellation?" Minh asked.

"The gods put the constellations in the heavens," Maryam answered. "Or perhaps men just gave the stars names and stories to make the heavens seem a little less vast. But you, Miss Loi, see the universe as it is—infinite, unknowable, full of mystery. You have no need of constellations."

A pair of wide, feathered wings adorned Philippe's shield. His eyes filled with tears when he took it, recognizing the wings that had once grown from his own back before he'd sliced them off in a fit of self-loathing long ago.

"I cannot give you your wings again," Maryam said, "but if you wear this shield on your back, perhaps it can protect you as they once did."

Selene wondered what Maryam had put on Esme's shield. Flowers? Doves? Hearts? Instead, she'd simply polished its face to a mirror-bright shine. Aphrodite's hand mirror had always been her defining attribute, but not much of a weapon.

"When you turn it on others," Maryam explained, "they will either be blinded by its light or see themselves more clearly than before. Such is the power of falling in love, is it not?"

Esme gazed at her own reflection as if she barely heard Maryam's words. She looked like a midcentury Hollywood action heroine: high-waisted shorts that just brushed the top of her thighs, a button-down shirt with its tails tied in a neat bow below her ribs, and strappy stiletto heels. She wore her golden hair in a loose chignon. Esme stared for a moment longer at the shield before bending down to remove her shoes. She flexed manicured toes against the wooden planks of the walkway, as if listening to the vibrations of the bridge through the soles of her feet.

Ruth's shield carried two fish circling each other in a graceful yin-yang. She studied such fish as part of her microbiology research, but Selene immediately knew they symbolized more than just her scientific interests. They were a perfect pair, a symbol of the balance that Ruth provided to the friends in her life. How Maryam had read the young woman so accurately after only having seen her once, Selene couldn't begin to know. Probably something to do with the Internet.

Theo's shield, on the other hand, was blank. Faint disappointment etched his brow. "I was hoping for a pair of spectacles under a raised sword or something."

"You carry a sword meant for the hunter Orion and a helm crafted for Hades. They are not your attributes, but theirs. I thought to give you Selene's animal on your shield, since she protects you and you protect her with the force of a wide-antlered stag. But you need an attribute of your own. I'm just not sure what it is yet."

Selene was surprised to hear her half sister confess her own limitations. But Athena had always been careful: She wouldn't act unless she knew it was right.

She had no shield for Selene.

"You have a bow and arrows to hold," Maryam said. "You can't also carry a shield."

"Uh-huh. What about that one?" Selene asked, pointing to the last saucer in the pile.

Maryam hefted it on her own arm in answer. It was a foot wider than the others, thicker too. It must have weighed at least fifty pounds. The wild snakes of a Gorgon's hair decorated the front—but no Medusa face. Maryam didn't need to explain the symbolism: Athena had turned Medusa into a monster. Now she cut the serpents from the woman's head and set her free. *That's Athena's defining attribute now,* Selene thought. *Mercy. Mercy for herself and for others. She learned that lesson as Mary, for all that I reviled her false piety.*

Maryam raised her spear, bracing the butt against the walkway so the tip gleamed a full foot above the black cap of her shorn hair. She held her shield over one arm. She wore no tactical armor this time, but rather a long white tank top and wide-legged white sweatpants raided from Selene's closet. In the dim light of the bridge, she looked like Athena once more, missing only her shining helm and tasseled aegis.

She's given herself another attribute as well, Selene realized, looking around at the others. *An army.* For the first time in millennia, the One Who Musters the People led a troop of soldiers bearing matching shields.

Theo passed out earpieces so they could all coordinate the music; they'd be standing too far apart on the bridge to communicate any other way.

Ruth, Minh, and Gabi took their positions beside the shortest cables, closest to the Manhattan side, where they could quickly retreat to safety. Maryam came next, standing before a much larger cable close to the first of the stone towers. Figuring that the portal would likely open in the middle of the bridge,

Maryam had chosen her spot to be able to shield the three mortal women most effectively.

Selene headed to her position just in front of the second tower, where the suspension cables stretched the longest. She had the easiest part in the orchestra: the A in each chord. All the rest of her attention would be focused on reaching out for her family, willing the portal to open into the right time and place to rescue them.

Theo stood in the direct center of the bridge, where the suspension wires shortened once more beneath the main cables' swoop. As Selene walked by, she put a hand on his arm. "Hit the C-sharp in the first three chords and then, for the fourth, you don't play anything when it modulates to the minor third," she reminded him.

His cocky smile didn't reach his eyes. "I got this."

"You'll be the first one through the portal. You swing that hammer, open the cleft to Tartarus, and get the hell out again," she insisted, grasping his arm hard now. "I'll run right in and get everyone out, but you just keep going, okay? Meet up with the other thanatoi on the Manhattan side."

He kissed her lightly. "Understood."

Esme and Philippe walked past them to the tall cables beyond the second tower, where they could strike two of the deeper notes. Maryam had already marked the correct wires for them with strips of glow-in-the-dark tape. With a little extra help from the Columbia physics department, they'd also secured extra contact mics, signal processors, and speakers, which they attached to each cable. This time, when they played the bridge, they'd all hear the music.

Selene nudged her earpiece a little tighter against her skull. The wind picked up, warm and moist, lifting the hair from her neck. She wrapped her hand around the thick cable beside her, feeling the faint vibrations as the bridge sang in response to the breeze. Only Maryam, as the conductor of their symphony, had a microphone, but Selene wished she could speak to Theo again. She hadn't forgotten Dennis's warning when they'd stood before the portal on Olympus. *Once you go in, you might not be able to get back out.* She'd chosen not to remind Theo of that. He, she felt certain, would have no trouble escaping, since he'd done it once before. She would try to do the same, but if she failed, it was a price she'd have to pay to release her family from their captivity.

I'm not lying to Theo, she told herself for the fifth time. *He knows the risks we take, and if I don't make it out, he'll know this time it wasn't from lack of trying or lack of love. He won't mourn me again—he'll know I live on with the rest of my family. It's not the future I'd choose, but it's one we'll both survive.*

Maryam's voice sounded in her ear. *"Prepare for the first note. On three."*

Selene raised her mallet. She watched Theo, standing in the center of the bridge, do the same with Flint's hammer.

"One. Two. Three."

Selene swung her mallet as hard as she could.

Eight notes resounded at once, the subsonic frequencies so deep they could travel through the earth itself. The transposed sound issued from the speakers in a ringing chord, higher-pitched than Selene had expected, but rich with overtones and undertones. This was the sound of a universe filled with brilliant, blinding light, as crimson hot as a million suns. The tones rang for a full thirty seconds—the universe cooled. The crimson light faded to orange, to yellow, to green—a primordial fog as rainbow hued as the waters that fed the Lake of Memory. Maryam started the count over.

"One. Two. Three."

Almost the same chord this time—only Maryam had shifted position, striking a half step up from her first note. And yet with that one tiny change, light became matter.

"One. Two. Three."

Now half the musicians stayed where they were; the other half scurried to nearby cables. The result was eerie, discordant, unpleasant. Pythagoras and his followers would've cringed at such a chord. Yet as with most things, the world was less perfect than mortals believed. It was with this sound that the fog began to clear, to separate, the peaks of sound waves condensing into galaxies, and the troughs expanding into empty blackness. The *kosmos* was born.

Selene watched Theo heft his shield on one arm, still carrying Flint's hammer in the other. He was ready.

She lifted her own mallet for the final note while the previous chord's discordant tones still rang in her ears. She tried to block it all out and hear a different song instead: the song that would take her to her family. She sang the ancient Orphic hymns aloud, reciting the gods' epithets in turn:

Strong-handed Hephaestus, all-taming artisan...
Royal Hera, blessed queen of majestic mien...
Blue-haired Poseidon, whose awful hand bears the brazen trident...
Persephone of budding fruits...
Revered Demeter, who dwells in Eleusis...
Hestia, mistress of unwearying flame...
Reveling Dionysus, who delights in blood and vines and sacred rage...

Maryam counted one last time. Selene knew that the three mortal women would already be running off the bridge, Philippe following them for protection. This chord needed only four notes.

She struck her cable one final time. The sound was softer, anticlimactic, unresolved, but her own song rose to drown it out. Now she sang not in homage to the Athanatoi trapped in Tartarus, but to her own twin. Somewhere, Apollo's spirit still resided in the Delphi of his own imagining; he could lend her strength now. The ancient hymn's lyrics were strangely apt, as if

Orpheus had known this night would come, a night when Artemis would call upon Apollo to start a world anew.

You hold the bounds
Of the whole world;
The beginning and the end to come are yours.
It is for this you have
The master seal of the entire kosmos.

As the last chord drifted into silence, Selene closed her eyes and reached for her family.

O blessed ones, hear the suppliant voice as I summon you.

She repeated the final line, a whispered chant now: *"Hear the suppliant voice as I summon you. I summon you. I summon you."*

Beneath her feet, the bridge lurched and swayed as if a sudden gale had loosed it from its moorings.

Selene's eyes snapped open, and she grabbed hold of the cable to steady herself. The signal processors cracked; the contact mics flew from the cables. All was silent but for the terrifying creak and groan of metal and wood. The walkway reverberated, waving with the violence of subsonic frequencies, but no breeze fluttered the American flag flying above the stone tower.

Maryam shouted over the earpiece: *"The bridge is playing the song back to us!"*

Selene's eyes flew to Theo, who'd planted his feet like a surfer. His face paled, but he held the hammer ready.

Before the next echoed note could shake the bridge, Maryam hurtled forward from the Manhattan side and Esme from the Brooklyn half.

The next wave hit. This time, Esme toppled to the ground and lay spread-eagled as the walkway lurched beneath her. Maryam grabbed onto the railing, just managing to stay upright.

When that tone subsided, Selene let go of her cable and rushed toward Theo, taking her place at his side. Esme struggled to her feet and joined them. Maryam sprinted forward, spear held horizontally before her like a tightrope walker seeking balance.

The four stood together, back-to-back, as the third subsonic chord rocked the bridge.

Selene could no longer see the walkway beneath her feet or the web of cables around her.

The lights of Manhattan disappeared.

Only her lover, her sister, and her cousin remained, suspended in a world of starless black. Selene unslung her bow and nocked a black-fletched arrow to the string.

She couldn't feel the bridge's final chord.

She smelled the ripe grain an instant before she felt it brushing her thighs an instant before she heard the buzz of the cicadas an instant before she felt the sunlight heat her face an instant before she saw the Acropolis in the distance an instant before she became a goddess again.

Chapter 54

MOTHER OF DESIRE

"NOW!"

Selene's voice rang in Theo's ears like the baying of hounds. She stood nearly twice her usual height, her skin glowing with a goddess's aura and the white streak in her hair once again as black as a midnight sky.

"Now!" she repeated, pointing urgently to the hammer in his hands.

He raised it overhead and slammed it through the sunbright barley and into the rich earth below. He'd used the hammer before to cave in the windows on the Statue of Liberty's crown. It had proved more powerful than any sledgehammer. But he still assumed it would take more than one blow to open a rift all the way to Tartarus.

Instead, a dozen wide cracks raced across the ground from the spot of the hammer's strike, like lightning forking across the sky. He jumped backward as the cracks expanded and the ground crumbled. No gentle wisp of divine *pneuma* emerged—great columns of gray vapor shot from the cleft to stain the brilliant blue above.

Selene grabbed his arm with a hand as big as his head. She took the hammer from him—no doubt Flint would need it to battle the giants in Tartarus.

"You did it," she shouted. "Now go!" With her other massive hand, she pointed to the rift in the world, where the Brooklyn Bridge's walkway and the glimmering Manhattan skyline hung suspended a foot above the ground.

"Not without you."

Her silver eyes flashed with anger as she raised her arm, lifting him three feet from the ground as if to fling him bodily back through the portal.

"Don't you dare!" he shouted at her. "We make our own choices. That's the deal, Selene."

Athena, standing even taller than her sister, spoke with a voice clarion bright and as resonant as a war drum. "We go now, or you'll have no choices at all. The portal won't stay open long."

Selene gave an exasperated growl and yanked Theo higher so they were eye to enormous eye. He stared into the mirror of her left pupil. *That's me,* he thought. *Glasses askew, looking just a tad terrified. No way I can convince a ten-foot-tall goddess to listen to me.* But Selene must've seen him differently, because she pulled him close and pressed her lips against his in a kiss that covered half his face.

"I'll be right back," she said, lowering him quickly to the ground.

Golden bow at the ready, a quiver of gleaming gold and silver arrows at her waist, she leapt into the gray cloud above Tartarus and disappeared from view. Athena, who had tied a rope around her waist and secured one end with a spike in the ground, followed suit more cautiously.

Esme—Aphrodite, now—stood with her hands on her hips, staring at the chasm before her. To Theo's shock, she'd removed her clothes sometime in the last three minutes, revealing ten feet of glowing, creamy flesh. Her body was softer, rounder than modern standards of beauty might prefer, but Theo still couldn't stop his blood from pumping harder when he looked at her. Her nipples were gilded with gold rather than rosy flesh. Unlike the male gods, whose penises the Greeks had sculpted in loving detail, Aphrodite's ancient statues usually depicted her covering herself with a robe or her own hand—at most, she displayed only a smooth, unbroken triangle of flesh. But the real Aphrodite clearly didn't care that the Latin *pudendum* meant "something to be ashamed of." Her lower lips swelled from her body, slightly parted in invitation. Her folds blushed a coral pink that matched the color of her upper lips with disturbing exactness.

She looked over at Theo and caught him staring. "It feels wrong to wear clothes here," she said glumly. "I rarely did during my time as a goddess. But this is all you see, isn't it?"

Theo didn't think it would do him much good to lie to her, so he simply kept his mouth shut.

"I've spent centuries learning other ways to seduce men, other ways to display my beauty. But here there's no need. I could have you right here in the field before your lover even returns."

Theo opened his mouth to protest, but she cut him off.

"Don't bother. You think you'd resist me, and you'd be wrong, but that's my point. You wouldn't love me at all. In fact, you'd be racked with guilt and self-loathing the whole time, and you'd have sex with me anyway. Because that's what happens when the Mother of Desire is standing next to you." Her face turned hard—or at least, as hard as it could when her features were supernaturally smooth and soft. She scooped up her pile of discarded clothes in one large hand and turned toward the portal. "I knew I shouldn't have come back." She strode toward the opening, raising one bare leg to step through into Manhattan.

She stopped short with a lurch. "Damn."

"What?"

"I can't. It's...blocked." She slammed a palm on what looked like open space, then wheeled back to Theo. "You got out the first time. Go on! Go through and then maybe you can pull me after."

He shook his head. "No can do."

Aphrodite marched toward him. He forced himself not to flinch, not to turn away. He didn't raise his sword, knowing her attack would come not through force but through gentler wiles. But he lifted the iron shield Athena had made for him, bracing himself. "I'm not going without Selene."

"*Love*, huh?" She snorted delicately. "I can't fight my own most precious attribute, can I?"

Theo lowered the shield. "Then help her so we can all get out of this place together."

The Laughter-Loving Goddess threw back her head and chortled. Throaty, sensuous, burbling with delight. "You're as good at getting your way as I am!"

Still laughing, she jumped feetfirst into Tartarus.

I hope she's right, he thought, casting a wary glance at the portal. The edges of the opening had already begun to waver.

— ◇ —

Tartarus, so the poets said, was as far below the earth as the sky was above it. A brazen anvil would drop for nine days and nine nights before it finally thudded against the bottom of the pit on the tenth. Selene didn't have that long.

Good thing the poets were wrong.

She fell through storm clouds so thick they clung to her limbs like a shroud. The darkest of them swirled like a giant snake, twisting and rolling through the air in great coils. *Typhoeus.* The winged Storm Giant with two serpents for his legs and a hundred more for his fingers, whom Zeus had cast into Tartarus for trying to steal the heavens from their rightful king. Now he guarded the pit, making sure that whomever else Zeus hurled into its depths would never emerge again.

One thing at a time, she thought. *First, find Hephaestus and the others. Then worry about getting out again.*

A breath later, her booted feet slammed into rock. She crouched to ease her landing, resting a hand upon the ground. The stone was slick to the touch, as if covered with a thin layer of wet moss. Perhaps it was, but Selene couldn't tell. Everything was black. Not like a moonless night or even her mother's womb, but something beyond dark. Even her own aura had been quenched. This, she remembered, was not just a prison for monsters. It was the home of Night itself. The birthplace of the River Styx. It was, in a word, *stygian.*

How will I find them if I can't see my hand in front of my face? she wondered. *And why the FUCK didn't I bring a flashlight?*

A thud beside her. Then a shower of sparks and a ringing clash as spear struck shield, announcing the arrival of the Giant Killer. In that brief flash of light, Selene saw her half sister, her flushed cheeks slick with vapor and her brilliant gray eyes gleaming ferociously.

Then the sound of rummaging. A flashlight clicked on, the beam pointed straight at Selene.

She shielded her eyes against the sudden glare. "Hey!"

Athena held out a second flashlight to her.

Selene grunted a thanks.

Even with the flashlights, they could see nothing beyond a wall of cloud on all sides, so dark that it seemed to suck away the light rather than reflect it back at them. Despite the swirling mists, no wind brushed their skin or rushed past their ears.

"Hephaestus!" Selene shouted into the silence. "Hestia! Demeter!"

They didn't appear. But Aphrodite did, landing lightly beside them, completely nude but for her mirror shield, her golden hair loosed by her fall to brush against her ankles like a superhero's cape.

"Where are they?" she asked immediately. "We don't have time to dawdle."

"I don't know," Athena snapped at her.

"You don't have a plan?" Aphrodite returned.

"Of course I do," the Goddess of Wisdom huffed. "A plan to get us *out*. I didn't think it'd be hard to find them in the first place."

"Demeter!" Selene called again.

"You really think they can hear us?" Aphrodite scoffed. "The fog swallows all sound down here."

A distant roar shook the air around them.

"What was it you said about swallowing all sounds?" Selene asked grimly.

Aphrodite blanched. "What *is* that?"

A piercing scream like the brakes on a New York subway train.

"The giants." Maryam readied her spear. "We need to hurry."

"I'm the Huntress—I'll go track them down." Selene stepped toward the blackness.

"We'll just lose you, too!" Aphrodite protested.

"Do you have a better idea?"

"Yes, actually." She tossed back her hair to reveal the full glory of her body.

"You've got to be kidding me. No one can see you!"

"Desire is about far more than looks, my dear. It's about every sense you can name and some you can't. The gods will come." She spread her feet a bit wider, opening herself shamelessly, and raised her arms to place them at the nape of her neck so her breasts lifted. The distinct tang of pheromones wafted through the air. She closed her eyes and cocked one knee. Despite the clammy chill, her skin flushed pink.

Selene and Athena, for once, were on exactly the same page.

"Do *not* tell me this is going to work," Selene groaned, just as Athena grumbled, "If she's right, I'm—"

Dionysus was the first to stumble out of the mists, still in the tight shorts and filthy T-shirt he'd worn on Olympus. He held his hands over his eyes, peering out between slitted fingers, blinded by their flashlights.

Selene was shocked by the change in his appearance. When he'd first walked through the portal, the damage that centuries of lassitude had wreaked on his body had fallen away, sloughing off the potbelly, the puffy eyes, the easy slouch. But Dionysus's stay in Tartarus had ravaged him in a way all his excesses never could. His immortal face remained unlined above his dark beard, but his eyes had sunk deep into his skull, horror etched upon his face.

Yet the moment he saw Aphrodite, he managed a feral smile. "Oh, man, you have no idea how grateful I am to see *you*." He ignored the other goddesses entirely. "I mean, sorry Dad caught you, but you have no idea the blue balls I've got after being stuck down here with no one but Persephone to chase after."

Aphrodite cocked her other hip. Taking that as an invitation, Dionysus reached for the fly of his shorts like a starving man grasping blindly for food. Athena struck her spear against her shield again, stopping him in his tracks.

He noticed the other women for the first time. "Oh, hello, ladies," he said with a strained attempt at his old insouciance. "The more the merrier, you know." He seemed to speak more out of habit than will, barely able to focus on the images in front of him. His eyes kept flicking back to Aphrodite. Yet he saw the items in Athena's hands and managed, "Wait, Dad let you keep your weapons? His storm ripped away my thyrsus on the way here."

"Father didn't cast us down," Athena said sharply. "We came here to get you out."

Selene nodded curtly, although the more she looked at the line of drool dripping through Dionysus's beard, the less she wanted to rescue him. The world might be a little better off without the God of Frenzy.

Dionysus looked from one goddess to the other. "Can you do that?" Selene had never heard him so desperate.

"We can," Athena said firmly. "Where are the others?"

"I don't know." The lust drained from his gaze, replaced with the same raw fear he'd shown when he emerged from the fog. "We...wander. In the dark. Sometimes we run into each other, but sometimes we run into the giants instead."

As if on cue, the ground shuddered with the drumming of massive footsteps. Selene aimed a hawk-fletched arrow toward the fog but didn't shoot, tracking the sound as it passed before them and then faded into the distance again. Dionysus clutched his arms across his chest, staring into the black. "We fight. With tooth and nail. Our ichor flows. We feel pain. But then we heal again. There is no end to it. And there is nothing else."

Selene thought of the Smith stumbling through this eternal night, battling for an existence that was nothing like a life. *Come to me, Hephaestus,* she prayed silently. *Come so I can take you back into the sunlight where you belong.*

Poseidon appeared instead, hands outstretched as he staggered toward Aphrodite's naked body. Athena caught him by the arm.

He lashed out wildly, but she ducked the blow. "Peace, Uncle! I am no giant!" She wrapped her arms around him. "I've come to release you."

The God of the Sea began to weep with relief at the sight of her spear and shield. Torrents of salt water coursed down his face like ocean swells.

Selene turned her flashlight back to the darkness, peering in vain for her aunts Demeter, Hestia, and Hera. For her cousin Persephone. Most of all, for Hephaestus.

"Hurry, Flint," she murmured. This was the man who had crafted the golden necklace for her over centuries, carving her story upon its links. Surely that sort of love would draw him to her even now.

Her light picked out a dim silhouette amid the swirling fog, and her heart leapt in response. But the figure was too narrow-shouldered to be the Smith, too angular to be a goddess.

Hermes.

He stood just inside the circle of the flashlight's beam, taking in the scene with a wary expression. He still wore his helmet, but the wings flopped limply to brush his shoulders.

Selene swung her bow in his direction. "*You* do not get to escape."

Dionysus rushed forward with his fist upraised. "I've been looking for you, douchebag!"

Athena stepped neatly in front of Hermes, raising her shield over him. "Stop! I will not have him harmed."

"It's his fault we're here!" Poseidon cried.

"Our uncle's right," Selene seethed. "He helped Father. He watched his own kin murdered and did *nothing*. The Trickster stays in Tartarus—where he belongs."

Hermes bowed his head, all his customary lightness gone. "I, too, was deceived. Father didn't tell me about making Saturn stronger at first—I swear it on the Styx. I only learned about his role after Hades and Mars and Apollo were already dead. I was angry with Father, but I thought if I went ahead with the plan and built the hydraulis, if I recovered the lightning bolt and convinced Theo to use it, it would make up for everything. The portal would save so many of us—the others would not have died in vain." He stared at his family, hands open and pleading. "You must believe me. I had no idea Father meant to—"

"Shut up, *Scooter*." Selene stopped him before he could spin any more lies. "The portal is closing. So unless you can see through this fog and find the others before we all become some giant's after-dinner snack, I don't want to hear anything you have to say."

He looked at her solemnly. "I don't have to see in the dark. I'm the Messenger once more. I can find any god I wish."

He turned and sprinted through the wall of mist.

Chapter 55

OMNIPOTENT

Like a paranoid bird, Theo swiveled his gaze from the wavering portal to the belching chasm and back again. He glanced at his watch, looking for answers he knew it couldn't provide. Ten minutes had passed and the portal to Manhattan was about half as wide as it'd been at the start. Did he have another ten minutes, or would the closing accelerate? He couldn't remember how it had worked on Mount Olympus.

I could jump down into Tartarus and try to speed things along, he considered, but he knew the gesture would be pointless. In this world, the goddesses' powers so far outstripped his own that he'd have little to offer. He'd just be one more body to haul back up again.

The thrill and terror of finding himself in ancient Athens was beginning to wear off. It was just a barley field like any other barley field, and so far there was no sign of Zeus. The Acropolis was far enough away that the blur of grand buildings on its summit left his curiosity piqued but unsatisfied.

When this is all done, I wonder if we could just open up the occasional portal for research purposes, he mused. *Take a little weekend away in the Classical Age. Of course, we'd be dodging Zeus all the way, but perhaps if we—*

A whispered "Theo!" broke his reverie.

He looked through the portal to see Ruth, Gabi, and Minh standing on the New York side, peering at him with a mix of trepidation and fascination.

"What're you guys doing? Get off the bridge!"

Gabi frowned at him. "Where are the big bad goddesses who are supposed to be protecting you in case Zeus shows up?"

He jerked a thumb at the smoking ravine. "Down there, doing what they said they would. I'm fine, okay? Just waiting for them to get back."

"What does it feel like in there?" Minh asked, taking out her phone to video the portal.

"Hey! Do you really need to film this?" he begged. "Look, it's hot, okay? Like Greece-in-summer hot, what do you expect?"

Philippe joined the women. He still looked unsteady on his feet. "Shouldn't Mama be back by now? Do you need me to come in and help?" The God of Love looked like he could barely stand, much less rescue anyone from Tartarus. Theo could imagine the fight he must've had with Esme before she even allowed him to come at all.

"No, it's fine. I just..." Theo began with a sigh, but he trailed off when he noticed the look of horror cross his friends' faces. "What?"

Ruth pointed mutely over his shoulder.

A forest of spearpoints bobbed above the barley stalks. The grain waved and shuddered as if a hundred, a *thousand*, soldiers ran through it.

"Maybe they're just doing some military training exercise..." he said weakly.

"Get out of there," Ruth demanded, reaching out her hand to help him through.

"Not without Selene," he insisted. "She can't get back without me."

He could hear the thunder of marching footsteps now, feel the vibrations beneath the soles of his sneakers. The *promakhoi*—the first rank of soldiers—appeared at the edge of the field, spreading out beside the smoking cleft. In their breastplates and greaves, with the long cheek and nose guards of their helms hiding their faces, they looked fearsome, inhuman. Yet Theo could hear them panting; he could see the sweat running down their oiled arms. They were men, just like him. Men in *very* good shape.

"Please," Theo murmured to his friends without looking behind him. "Go now."

Instead, he heard the clatter of metal as his own beloved *promakhoi* raised the shields Athena had given them.

He left his own shield at his side. He didn't draw his sword. Perhaps he could talk his way out of this.

He offered a *"Khairete!"* in greeting. Beyond that, he wasn't exactly sure what to say. He pointed at the smoking cleft and settled for, *"Phylassesthe to khasma." Mind the gap.*

To his shock, the soldiers fell to one knee and bowed their heads.

From behind him, Theo heard Philippe's smug chuckle. "I see they still know a god when they see one."

Theo glanced around, but Philippe remained on the New York side of the portal. Handsome and well dressed—but godly? Not exactly.

"Shall I come through and give them a taste of my full glory?" Philippe asked eagerly.

"No—you may not be able to get out," Theo replied quickly. "It looks like everything's under control for the moment, so—"

An eagle's cry split the air.

The soldiers shuffled apart to leave an aisle clear between their ranks.

A figure three times the height of a man strode through, his thunderbolt in one hand and a golden eagle perched on his shoulder.

The King of the Gods stepped up to the lip of the cleft and stared down into the smoke. Then he looked at Theo, his gaze as piercing as any raptor's talons.

"Where are they?" he demanded, his voice rolling like thunder. Theo forced himself not to cover his ears.

"*Tell me!*" Zeus commanded, louder this time. But his voice cracked like a desperate father's when he added, "Without the rest of my children, I am incomplete."

Theo's mind whirled. If he admitted that Selene and the others were in Tartarus, Zeus would surely close the rift above them, trapping them for eternity. "They sent me in here to open the chasm," he said, "but they're still out there." He jerked a thumb toward Manhattan.

Zeus's lightning-stare bored into Theo. "My daughters are no cowards. Why send a thanatos to confront me alone?"

Theo let himself tremble in fear—it wasn't hard. "It's a trap," he blurted. "They don't really intend to rescue the others; they just want you to chase them back through the portal. They figured once you crossed over, you'd lose all your power again, and they could defeat you."

A sly smile drifted across Zeus's lips. Theo's unease grew, but he plowed onward. "I told them it wouldn't work—you wouldn't be so stupid. But you know Athena and Artemis. They don't take advice from a mere mortal like me."

Zeus's eyes flew to the portal. Theo's friends stood steadfast behind their raised shields; he could hear Gabi's muttered Spanish curses.

"They're out there?" the King of the Gods asked.

"Yup," Theo said with a contrite shrug. "And since you can't pass through, I guess that's where they're going to stay."

Zeus stared down at Theo. "I thought you were a scholar. Do you not recognize me?"

"Uh…"

The god drew himself up even taller than his already impossible height. He seemed to swell; his glowing aura burned a little brighter. "I am the Almighty. The Majesty of the Heavens. Lord of the Sky. The Omnipotent. I am the Maker of Laws! Do you really think I must follow yours?"

Theo wasn't sure how to respond. Zeus just laughed, the sound a drumming roar. "I do not need to remain in the ancient world to be the King of the Gods," he boomed. "I can bring the ancient world with me."

He strode right past Theo and onto the Brooklyn Bridge.

The Athenian army marched through after him.

Chapter 56

GIANT KILLER

Mere seconds after he'd sprinted off, Hermes returned through the mists of Tartarus with Persephone, Demeter, and Hestia in tow.

Selene looked beyond them, searching desperately. "Where's the Smith?"

"Patience," her brother chided.

She felt Hephaestus come before she saw him step from the mist. She was there to meet him when he emerged, tall and glorious and alive, walking with no hint of a limp. He carried her golden javelin in his fist.

She couldn't resist clasping him in her arms for just an instant, the strong planes of his chest hard against her, the muscles of his back rippling beneath her hands. His breathing quickened.

"You came." His voice was the one unchanged part of him. It still rumbled deep enough to send a low thrum through his chest and into hers.

"Of course." She pushed away, unable to say more. Not here, among the shadows and dread. She simply handed her friend his hammer. "Philippe asked me to make sure you had this."

Hephaestus looked down at his familiar weapon, and something of Flint passed across his face. Not the bitter, angry man who'd turned away from the world, but the doting stepfather who had found room in his heart for his wife's bastard.

Hera—no longer the dowdy Aunt June—stood beside her son. A sheen of sweat coated her white arms; her inky hair hung lank around her regal face. "Please," she begged Selene. Her wide eyes were shadowed with unspeakable horrors. "Get us out of here."

"We're going." Selene nodded. "Before the giants sniff us out."

As if in response, a monster bugled from somewhere in the distance. Selene loosed her golden arrow, aiming into the darkness and trusting the supernatural weapon to find its mark. The bugling cut off an instant later. "That's one down, but there'll be more," she said, reaching for her quiver. "And I've only got one more hawk-feather arrow. So unless the giants are susceptible to plague..." Her fingertips brushed the fletching of one of her twin's silver arrows. To her surprise, music floated from the quiver, so sweet and lovely it could only be a tune composed by Apollo himself.

"They're not all plague arrows," Hephaestus said. "I made different arrows for Apollo's different attributes. Here in Tartarus, the shafts have their power back. That one sings."

Selene scowled. "Awesome. That's not going to be much help defeating a horde of giants. We need to leave. Right now."

Athena gave a solemn nod of assent. She untied the rope from around her waist and handed the dangling end to Demeter. "Climb. As fast as you can. I won't be able to hold off Typhoeus forever." She walked to the edge of the swirling dark and lifted her spear above her shield.

"What the hell are you doing?" Selene demanded.

"Calling Typhoeus and the other giants to me. I will fight them while you escape."

"*That's* your wise plan? You won't survive. Not alone."

Athena just lifted her chin a little higher—but she didn't disagree.

Demeter, still standing with the rope in one hand, gave a mournful sigh. "She's sacrificing herself."

"Not on my watch," Selene insisted angrily. "You're not Mary or Jesus or some other Christian martyr, Athena. You're the Destroyer of Giants, not their prey."

Athena rounded on her. "Do you have a better idea?"

Selene didn't. But she wasn't about to admit that. "We need to get up there *fast*. Before the Storm Giant even knows we're coming."

"Then we fly," Hermes offered.

Every god turned to stare at the Trickster.

"*We* don't do anything," Selene snarled. "I told you—you don't get to come."

Persephone stepped forward and slapped Hermes hard across the face. "That's for my husband. You still helped Father, even after you knew what he'd done."

Aphrodite charged forward next, ready to rip Hermes to shreds for what had happened to her lover Mars. Hermes didn't flinch, didn't try to defend himself. Once again, it was Athena who stepped in front. She looked at Aphrodite, then Selene.

"Are you without blame? What did you do when our kin were pulled into Tartarus?" She slammed a fist against her own chest, turning the accusation on herself. "What did *I* do? Nothing. June and Philippe tried to save Flint—June lost her freedom and Philippe nearly lost his life in the process." Hephaestus groaned at the news, his knuckles white on the haft of his hammer.

"Only one other dared try to help," Athena went on. "*Hermes*. The Messenger could've flown away. He could've escaped the maelstrom. Instead, he flew down to save Hephaestus and got sucked into Tartarus in the process. He was willing to take that risk. *We* were not."

This time, when Athena placed a hand on her younger brother's shoulder, no one protested.

"Your cap works?" she asked solemnly.

"Yes, but it's not much good when Typhoeus guards the way out."

"I'll take care of the Storm Giant," Selene interjected, sure now of her plan. She looked to Hermes. "As long as I can get up there."

Hermes opened his arms. He didn't smile or tease. With his eyes alone, he asked to be trusted.

I don't *trust him,* Selene decided. *But I trust Athena.*

Another bellow from the fog decided her. Better they face one giant in the air than a thousand on the ground. She stepped into Hermes' embrace. He wrapped one supernaturally strong arm around his sister's waist.

Athena lashed the extra flashlight to the top of Hermes' cap.

A thousand heavy footsteps drummed behind them—another thousand drummed in front.

Persephone whimpered, clutching her mother's arm.

Athena raised her spear and shield, turning in every direction to seek her enemies. Selene hesitated, unwilling to leave her family to face their ancient nemeses without her bow to guard them.

"If you're going, go now!" Athena shouted to her. "I'll climb first, so if you can't stop Typhoeus, I'll be the first one it attacks. At least I'll stop it from getting to anyone else."

Selene knew that even Athena wouldn't survive such a battle. They might have changed the plan, but the outcome would be the same.

Hephaestus stepped forward. "I'll go up last to hold off the other giants from below. You just open the way."

Athena gave him a grim nod, then grabbed hold of the rope and began to climb. The others started up after her.

Hephaestus stayed at the base, the golden javelin now a long whip in one hand, his hammer ready in the other. Already, the source of the first hundred footsteps emerged from the mist: a hekatonkheir—a Hundred-Handed One with as many legs to match. Persephone screeched and climbed faster. Hephaestus's hammer flashed forward, knocking the monster's head from its body in a single blow.

Another hekatonkheir emerged to take its place. The Smith slung the end of the whip around its throat, then caved in its lungs with his hammer.

A third giant strode from the darkness.

"That one's mine!" Selene cried out.

"Artemis," Hermes protested.

But Selene ignored him, quickly lashing another of Athena's ropes to her last hawk-fletched golden arrow and shooting it toward the new giant. The shaft flew around the monster in a swift circle, binding all hundred arms tight against its body. Selene held the tail of the rope tight in both hands.

"Fly!" she shouted to her younger brother.

Hermes shot through storm and cloud with a speed that sucked the air from her chest.

The weight of the giant on the end of her rope only slowed their flight for an instant. Selene felt the line slipping from her grip but wrapped it around her wrists and held on with a strength she hadn't possessed in over a thousand years.

Hermes rocketed upward with a new burst of speed. Selene couldn't see her captive through the clouds below them, only the rope hanging taut like a fishing line hooked on a whale. Her joints popped, her muscles tore, and she screamed aloud with the strain of holding the massive creature aloft.

Hermes slowed only when the mists above them began to coil into the shape of a monster overhead. "I've gotten this far before," he explained. "But any higher and the serpent's winds would tear me limb from limb with the force of a hundred hurricanes. Typhoeus is made of storm clouds—your arrows will pass right through it."

"That's why we have to distract it," Selene panted. "Not destroy it."

She began to swing the rope back and forth. Hermes bent to help her. Wider and wider they swung, until the Hundred-Handed

One began to bellow with fear and rage, its voice undulating in time to its oscillations.

Typhoeus's head loomed before them, a gaping maw of thunderheads with fangs of lightning and a tongue of ash.

"Now!" Selene shouted as the hekatonkheir reached the apex of its swing.

They let go, flinging the creature upward like a bowling ball aimed at the sky. It sailed into view above the clouds. Fifty of its arms had slipped from their bindings, flailing so fast Selene wondered if it would take flight like a helicopter and ruin her plan.

Typhoeus wasn't about to let that happen. The hekatonkheires had been its first prisoners. It would never allow one to escape. Its cry was thunder's drum, lightning's cymbal, and a hurricane's reedy roar. It reached out with countless cloud-snake fingers and wrapped them around each of the hekatonkheir's hundred arms, plucking them off like the petals of a daisy.

Hermes shot past Typhoeus's thick body as it writhed and swirled around its prey. Selene could see a spot of light above them now, no bigger than a candle flame, but growing wider and bluer by the second. She looked across to the rope—Athena and the others were climbing with a speed only gods could muster. They were almost to the top.

Selene didn't bother telling Hermes to hurry. His own instinct for self-preservation sent him hurtling upward.

She risked a glance below. Typhoeus's fiery, unblinking eyes stared back from less than a hundred yards away. It saw them. It was coming.

If Hermes drops me, he can go faster, she realized. She grabbed onto his arm where it clasped her waist. *But if he tries it, I'm going to take his damn arm with me.*

But Hermes didn't let go. He only clutched her tighter, bared his teeth, and closed his eyes, as if to send all his force of will into his cap. The wings droned like a biplane's propeller, the feathers a shining blur.

The fiery eyes grew larger. Larger. Lightning spit from its mouth like a serpent's tongue.

They weren't going to make it.

"We can't stop Typhoeus," Hermes gasped, his voice barely audible above the rush of the wind. "I'm sorry."

He was right. The only thing that could clear away such storm clouds was the will of Zeus, the Sky God. Or the warming rays of the Sun itself. And there was no Sun in Tartarus.

Then Hephaestus's words came back to her: *Different arrows for Apollo's different attributes.*

She thrust a hand into her quiver, scrabbling at her twin's silver arrows. One turned her stomach. The next played a barely audible hymn. The third burned her skin. She snatched it up by its crow-feather fletching and nocked the white-hot shaft to her string.

Apollo, Bright One, God of the Sun, she prayed. *Guide my arrow.*

The shaft flew like a shooting star into the swirling darkness of Typhoeus's head, leaving a brilliant streak of white behind it. The arrow didn't lodge in the giant's body—it exploded. The burst of light and heat tore through the clouds, burning away the storm. Typhoeus's roar became a whimper. Its limbs thinned, dissipated, evaporated.

Hermes shot into a brilliant blue sky.

Beneath them, what was left of the mighty giant spun away from the cleft and disappeared into the darkness of Tartarus.

The two Athanatoi fell from the air, slammed into the barley field, and rolled apart.

Selene granted herself three panting breaths to stare at the cloudless blue before she sat up and looked for Theo.

He was gone.

The portal still hovered in the air—no wider than a door-frame. She looked through, desperate to find him.

What she saw instead was a battle.

An army had invaded Manhattan.

Chapter 57

PROMAKHOS

Gabriela sprinted off to alert the construction workers on the Manhattan side as the Athenian army marched through the portal. The construction workers called the local police precinct. The police summoned the city's SWAT team.

Before the Greeks could get off the bridge, the people of New York had set up a barricade of bulldozers and backhoes manned by machine-gun-toting cops. Police helicopters hovered overhead, blaring warnings over their loudspeakers and panning their floodlights over the ancient army.

That should've done the trick. Spears and javelins were no match for automatic rifles.

But mortals were no match for the King of the Gods.

Zeus towered two stories high even in this godless modern world. He raised his massive palm over the East River. The water swelled, domed, like a mass of iron filaments pulled by a magnet's inexorable force.

Theo watched it all from his position in the barley field, terrified for his friends and his city, knowing that if he left now, he'd take with him Selene's only hope of ever coming home. But when the massive dome of water broke into a tsunami-sized wave and rushed toward the bridge, Theo couldn't stand by any longer. It was his fault Zeus had reentered the world to hunt down the rest of his family, and now New York would suffer. Selene would want Theo to defend her city, no matter the cost.

He leapt through the portal, shield and sword raised. Only divine weapons could bring down a divinity. The cops' bullets might work against the Athenian *promakhoi*, but they'd be useless against an immortal.

The wave crashed against the construction machines, washing the barricade off the bridge and into the river below. A dozen police officers went with it.

My friends are up there somewhere, Theo thought, staggering to a halt. *Philippe too. They could be in the water right now. Drowning. Dead.* He forced himself to keep moving. *No! Don't think of that. Just end it, before anyone else gets hurt.*

But even with his divinely inspired skill with the sword, Theo could never fight his way through the entire Athenian army in time to reach Zeus. *Fighting's not my strong suit anyway,* he decided, yanking on Hades' helm.

Invisible, he clambered onto the metal girder that bordered the walkway. He had none of Selene's easy grace, but he grabbed onto one suspension cable after the other and made his way down the bridge, unseen by the *promakhoi* who would stop him.

Overhead, the police helicopters opened fire on Zeus.

The bullets never even made it to his skin. They hit an invisible barrier that surrounded the god and clattered to the walkway like leaden hail.

Athena's aegis, Theo realized as he scurried the last few yards along the beam, drawing even with the god. *It protects its bearer like an impenetrable cloak. But it can't protect all his soldiers.*

Even now, the cops had turned their guns on the Athenians. The *promakhoi* might be innocents, drafted into service by a god they dared not disobey and forced into a world they could never comprehend, but Theo felt little sympathy. They were, knowingly or not, providing Zeus with his strength. By leading his own army of worshipers, the god brought with him the ancient world—and all the power it provided.

Rank after rank of *promakhoi* fell beneath the wall of bullets that sheered across the bridge—and right into Theo's path. He ducked behind his shield.

"Holy shit. I wish invisible meant invincible." The constant hammer of bullets on bronze drowned his words, the force of the strikes nearly knocking him off the railing.

Then the barrage stopped.

He peeked over the shield's rim. Another dark cliff of water rose above the bridge. It collapsed in a river of foam, washing the next row of police officers aside.

Zeus flicked his lightning bolt like a conductor's wand, and a gust of wind dashed the two helicopters into each other in a ball of fire. Theo could hear the officers up ahead, screaming desperately into walkie-talkies suddenly gone dead.

Theo finally understood. *God of Storms. Now God of the Sea like Poseidon. God of Messages like Hermes. Is there anything he can't do?* By trapping his family in Tartarus, Zeus had become omnipotent indeed. He'd usurped their domains without allowing their deaths to sap his own strength. *How long before he withers the crops in the fields with Demeter's power, or stops the spring from coming with Persephone's?*

No longer protected by the ranks of police, four figures huddled at the far end of the bridge with Athena's shields linked before them.

Thunderbird. Fish. Stars. Wings. Symbols that could do nothing to protect them.

Still invisible, Theo charged toward Zeus, stumbling over the fallen bodies of the *promakhoi*, pushing past those still standing. The Athenians cursed in Ancient Greek and shouted in alarm as the invisible force knocked them aside, swinging their spears wildly at empty air.

Theo dodged their blows and kept running. He skidded to a halt before Zeus's colossal sandaled foot. Raised his sword to slice the god's Achilles tendon. Swung with all his might.

The invisible blade struck the aegis's invisible wall and lodged there like an axe in green wood. Theo yanked on the handle, trying to free his blade. A flash of bronze drew his attention to the end of the bridge. *No, no, no,* he begged silently. But the fish shield rose despite his pleas. Ruth stepped out from its protection.

"What do you want from us?" she called up to the looming god. "You have your own world now. Why do you want ours?"

Zeus bent his glorious visage toward Theo's friend. She squinted in the light from his aura, and the skin of her cheeks reddened as if burnt by the glow—but she did not look away.

"I don't," the god said, his voice so deep it reverberated through the sword's grip and hummed against Theo's hands. "I need those you harbor. Give me Artemis. Eros. Aphrodite. Only then can my new universe be complete. Only then can *I* be complete."

Theo choked back a cry. If he told Zeus that he'd lied and that the Athanatoi were actually in Tartarus, this massacre would stop. Ruth, Gabi, and the whole city would be safe—and Selene would be trapped for eternity. He knew what decision his lover would demand of him, yet he couldn't bring himself to say the words. There had to be another choice.

With a grunt of effort, he finally wrenched his sword free of the aegis and sprinted across the drenched walkway toward his friends.

"Your bow, Philippe!" He ducked behind the shields and pulled off his helmet. "It always strikes the heart, right? No matter what? Even through the aegis's shield?"

The Athanatos looked terrified, but he nodded.

"Shoot for Zeus's chest!"

"It won't kill him," Philippe said. "He's too strong."

Theo pointed to the face of the Gorgon emblazoned across the center of Zeus's tasseled aegis. "But *Medusa* isn't."

Philippe swallowed and nocked a small dart to the string of his miniature bow. He stood up from behind the shield's cover.

Zeus stepped forward eagerly, each stride buckling the wooden walkway. The eagle on his shoulder ruffled its wings and shrieked at the sight of its prey. Zeus's hand extended toward Philippe as if to pluck him from the ground.

The God of Love took aim.

The dart shot right through the invisible barrier and struck the Gorgon's face. Medusa's eyes rolled back in her head. Theo wondered if Philippe's dart would somehow give the Gorgon a heart attack, as he'd seen it do before. Instead, her stony face melted back into flesh. She gasped like a woman just woken from a nightmare. Her eyes sought the God of Love. Her expression calmed, softened, her lips parted in a sigh of desire. Every snake on her snake-laden head suddenly turned toward Philippe; their tongues darted forth to taste his scent.

Zeus ignored Medusa's metamorphosis, taking another step toward the god who would let him rule men's hearts.

"If you love me," Philippe shouted to the Gorgon, "save me!"

As one, the snakes uncoiled. They darted backward beyond the aegis's hem, sinking their fangs into Zeus's neck, ribs, stomach.

He stumbled to a halt, tearing at the snakes, ripping them from the cloak by the handful. His eagle launched itself into the air, diving amid the snakes to snap their throats with its wicked beak. Medusa screamed in pain as her serpents died.

Zeus tore off the aegis and tossed it aside. His skin blistered and swelled beneath the snakebites, and he moaned his agony in low counterpoint to the eagle's high-pitched shrieks.

Theo turned back to the remaining policemen on the bridge. *"Now!"*

They opened fire. The bullets pocked Zeus's skin like mosquito bites. The god swatted them away. Already, Theo saw with a sinking heart, the skin around the snakebites had healed.

"The longer you resist," Zeus called, "the more damage I will do." He raised an arm and swept it toward Manhattan.

The trees at the base of the bridge instantly withered, their thick summer leaves tumbling to the ground in a shower of brown.

Another sweep of his hand and the policemen around Theo collapsed, their legs suddenly shrunken and too weak to hold them.

"How's he doing that?" Minh gasped, still crouched behind her shield.

"The other gods have left our world." Theo had to shout to be heard over the cops' tortured groans. "Zeus has become Demeter now—Hephaestus, too."

Gabi looked at her own legs. "And why aren't *we* crippled?"

Philippe tapped the back of his winged shield. "Athena."

Gabi clutched her own shield tighter in one hand and grabbed Minh with the other. "You think she can protect us from getting ripped apart by Zeus like those snakes?"

Theo shook his head. "It'll take more than shields to save us then. We need the Olympians. If they come through, the presence of the Athenians will keep them divine, too."

"Oh yeah? Then what the hell are they waiting for?" Gabi demanded.

"They can't just walk out like Zeus. They're trapped until I pull them through." He looked at the ranks of *promakhoi* standing between him and the portal and felt his limbs grow numb with fear. "The portal will be almost closed by now—I won't reach it in time."

Around him, the police officers continued to moan. The trees continued to wither. His city continued to die.

Philippe added his own desperate groan to the cacophony. "I wish I really did have wings. I'd fly you back."

Ruth poked her head out from behind her fish shield. "I've got a better idea."

Chapter 58

THE GREAT MOTHER

"THEO!" Selene screamed.

She could see his blank shield on the far end of the bridge. Her immortal father and a whole army of *promakhoi* stood between them. She would've happily battled every one if she could. She pounded her fist against the invisible barrier of the portal.

"It's okay," Hermes soothed. "With Father out there, we'll be safe in here. Everyone else is almost free." He was right. Athena crawled over the lip of the cleft and started reeling in the rope. Selene had little hope that Typhoeus was gone forever, but so far, he had not returned.

"Look!" urged her brother. "We can all stay here now. Together."

Selene pointed an angry finger at the ever-narrowing portal. "No, *you* look! Look what Father is doing to my friends, my love, my city. He's killing the trees, flooding the river, killing the people. You think I can just stay here dancing with my nymphs while New York crumbles and burns?"

A sharp, piercing scream tore from the chasm behind her. Selene spun toward the sound to see Athena, Dionysus, and

Demeter pulling up the rope with all their combined strength. One by one, the other gods clambered to safety, white-faced and shaking. Another shrill scream. A sound not of terror, but of command. The sound of a queen. *Hera.*

Selene rushed to the chasm's lip just in time to see Typhoeus, his whirling body reformed, roaring toward the end of the rope, his jaws gaping open to swallow the last dangling god.

"Flint!" Selene cried, reaching desperately for her quiver. She had only two silver arrows left. She fired both at the Storm Giant, but neither music nor plague had any effect.

Hera, who hung from the rope just above her son, screamed at the giant one more time, as if her voice alone could stop the unstoppable.

Selene grabbed the end of the rope to help the others haul, but she knew it was too late. She watched in horror as Typhoeus's jaws opened around Hephaestus's strong, perfect legs. Hera cast one desperate look back at her son.

Then she let go.

She dropped straight into the giant's waiting maw.

It spiraled away, tearing the Queen of the Gods apart.

Flint stopped climbing, just stared at the fountain of blood that gushed from the giant's jaws. Selene and the others kept pulling, dragging him to safety whether he wanted to or not.

He lay on the ground at the chasm's edge, his flawless body trembling in a way his crippled one never had. Aphrodite crouched beside her husband, wrapping him in her arms.

Selene wanted desperately to help, but the roar of bullets on the Brooklyn Bridge sent her running back to the portal. "Zeus is killing them," she gasped.

Athena came to stand beside her, her knuckles white on the haft of her spear. "And he's using *my* Athenians to do it."

Aphrodite, still holding Hephaestus, looked up in alarm. "Where's my son?" she begged.

Selene pointed. "There." Philippe had laid his myrtle bow on the ground beside his winged shield. He walked forward with both hands outstretched, palms up, offering himself to Zeus.

"No!" Aphrodite struggled to her feet. Hephaestus rose beside her, his tears subsumed by volcanic rage as he watched his beloved stepson walk into danger.

"Father doesn't want Eros dead," Athena assured them. "Just captive."

But it was hard not to worry when Zeus reached down and grabbed Philippe by the neck. The young man looked like a child in the god's mighty hand. Zeus held him at eye level for just a moment.

Then he hurled him like a javelin toward the portal.

Hephaestus grabbed Hermes. "You have to catch him!" he shouted. "He'll go right into Tartarus!"

Hermes leaped into the air just as Philippe came soaring through the rift—they slammed together with a bone-crushing thud. Hermes deposited him next to his parents with a grunt of effort. "You've been putting on weight."

Theo popped into view, pulling off Hades' helmet and releasing Philippe's waist. "Oh no, that's just me. Now who wants to go home?"

Selene bent to slam him into a kiss, ignoring his muffled protests.

Hephaestus rushed toward his wounded stepson and folded him in his arms with a surprisingly careful embrace. "You all right, Phil?"

But the mortal moniker no longer applied. Even as Hephaestus pulled away, Philippe became Eros. No longer a slender young man, but a twelve-year-old boy with a golden halo of curls.

"Nothing like a little renewed supernatural power to heal what ails you," he said, rolling his shoulders. The gesture unfurled the long wings that had sprung from his back. The feathers gleamed brilliant crimson at his shoulder blades then cascaded through every shade of the rainbow until they brushed the ground with an indigo as dark as the midnight sky.

The universe is born of light, Selene thought, *but also of Love.*

"You went after my mother when she tried to save me," Hephaestus said hoarsely, gripping Eros's arms tight. "You risked your life to help her."

"Where is Hera?" Eros peered worriedly over his stepfather's massive shoulder at the assembled gods.

"She's gone," Hephaestus choked. "I would've given up my legs again to save her. But she did it before I could stop her…" He bent his head, leaning his massive skull atop Eros's smaller golden one.

A bellow from the Brooklyn Bridge drew Selene's attention back once more to the battle.

"Selene," Theo warned. "Zeus won't wait. And neither will the portal. Whoever's coming with us, we have to go. Now."

"I'll come," Hermes said quickly. "I helped Father regain his power. I will help take it back from him."

Dionysus, who'd been so eager to rejoin the ancient world, shrugged. "Yeah, Tartarus sort of took the joy out of antiquity for me."

Theo held out his hand to his old roommate. Dionysus held out his to Hermes. Hermes to Athena. To Aphrodite. Eros. Selene slipped her hand into his soft, small one.

The portal contracted another inch.

The other Athanatoi remained where they were.

Selene couldn't begrudge Persephone and the older gods the chance to be strong when they were so close to death in the other world. But Hephaestus…

The Smith looked not at her, nor at his wife or stepson, but at his hammer. "It couldn't save my mother," he said softly. "But it once made beauty because I had none of my own. If I am strong, and whole, then I am no longer the Smith." He turned to Eros. "I will fashion you a new pair of wings. For when you go back through the portal and lose them again. For when *we* go back through."

Selene held out her hand to the glorious god who had once been Flint. And would be again.

Theo led the way. The others followed like links on a chain.

They stood arrayed across the bridge, ready for battle. The Athenian *promakhoi* whose presence granted Zeus his strength did the same for Selene and the rest of her kin. The Olympians towered over Theo and the other mortals, their skin glowing in the night. Inhuman, immortal, divine. Selene motioned for her lover to stand behind her. This was a fight for Athanatoi alone.

Athena clanged her spear against her shield.

Zeus turned toward the sound. One great black brow rose above eyes that matched his daughters' for ferocity. His eagle launched into the air, talons extended.

"There you are," the Lightning Bringer rumbled as he scanned the line of Olympians. "So strong, I see, that even Tartarus could not hold you." Something that might have been pride gleamed in his eyes. "I created a mighty race. Next time, I will find stronger chains."

He slashed the air with his hand. The ranks of *promakhoi* with their bristling spears turned to face the line of Olympians.

Athena raised her own spear high. *"O Athenaioi!"* she bellowed, hailing her Athenians. Her voice clamored like a war trumpet, and the soldiers bent their heads before her in awe.

"Hark to the goddess to whom you owe obedience," she continued in the ancient tongue. "Once you asked a gift of me. I struck the rocks of the Acropolis with my spear, and an olive tree sprouted forth." She thrust her shaft against the walkway, shaking the bridge with her blow.

Even as Selene watched, a sapling sprang from the wooden planks, its branches spreading, thickening, and bursting into leaf in the span of a breath. "Did I not shelter you beneath its boughs? Feed you with its fruits? Light your way with its oil?

You are *my* people, not my father's," she roared. "You will listen to *my* commands."

The soldiers murmured among themselves, their spears wavering. They could not disobey their patron goddess—but to thwart the will of Zeus meant certain death.

"It is as the ancient prophecy foretold!" Zeus boomed, raising his thunderbolt. "You would challenge me, daughter! You would seize my throne for yourself. I cannot let that happen." A single thread of current shot across the bridge from his thunderbolt. The olive tree burst into flame.

Zeus turned to his other children. "I still control the storm! The sea! The seasons! The sky itself. You will come back to the land that birthed you, where my temples still stand and cities offer a hundred bulls in sacrifice to me! Where my glory expands with each plume of smoke, each spurt of blood."

Selene remembered the bull in the Phrygianum beneath Vatican City. The shower of blood had imbued her with the spirit of the Magna Mater—but none of her power. But that was Selene Neomenia who stood bound and captured, forced to participate in a rite stolen from the Great Mother and perverted by men. Selene Neomenia who lost the connection to her ancient grandmother when Saturn burned her alive.

This is not Selene, she thought, looking down at her golden bow and her impossibly long limbs. *This is ARTEMIS.*

Zeus followed her gaze. "I taught you how to use that bow— you think it can hurt me now?" He pointed his lightning bolt at Athena. "Or *your* spear? Who are you to stand against my will?"

"I am the Huntress you made me," Selene called to her father. "But I am also the Artemis dreamed of by the Ephesians. I carry my temple on my head and all the beasts of the world on my gown. I am Phrygian and Greek and Roman—and American too. I was made by those who worshiped me, those who loved me, and by myself most of all. I have always been and always will be." She put down her bow—and reached for Athena and Aphrodite's hands.

"Together, we are more than Olympians. We are the Great Mother herself. Protectress of Cities, Mother of Desire, Mistress of Beasts. We are Cybele, Ops, *Rhea*. We are our grandmother's granddaughter."

Zeus's face darkened. The sky above his head clouded in concert. "The Magna Mater never challenged me."

"Because her strength was divided among us. And we were too blind to see. We need no ritual or ceremony to make her part of us—she was always within each of us, waiting to reclaim her place as Queen. We are healers. We make the crops grow and the beasts roar. We give life and shepherd toward death."

The other goddesses held tight to her hands. Selene—*Artemis*—felt power surge between them. When she spoke again, the others spoke with her.

They were one Goddess now, ancient and powerful.

Long ago, She had gladly surrendered Her rule to Her son, the Sky God.

Now She wanted it back.

"The Earth herself is My mother, and I am the Mother of All."

The Magna Mater reached out Her hand toward the police officers still writhing in agony with their ruined legs. She made them whole again and brought them to their feet. On the banks of the river, the trees straightened, their branches sprouting new leaves of citron green.

She raised Her spear high. The bridge's floodlights struck the blade, lighting it like a torch.

"Go now, warriors," She cried to the Athenian army. "The Frontline Solider summons you home!"

She swung Her weapon toward far-off Athens, where the spearpoint's mirror image winked atop the Acropolis. The soldiers stared at their distant bronze *Promakhos* with eyes full of longing. "Go back to your mothers!" She commanded. "Your daughters, your sisters, your wives. *Go home.*"

Footsteps thundering as loud as a hekatonkheir's, the army of Athenians began to march toward the ever-narrowing portal.

Sparks flew from Zeus's thunderbolt. "You give me no choice but to kill you!" Tears brightened his eyes even as he raised the bolt high, ready to incinerate the Goddess before him. But a new cloud darkened the sky—one not summoned by He Who Marshals Thunderheads.

Thousands upon thousands of Aphrodite's pigeon doves rose from the city's streets and descended in a swirling mass upon the Father of the Gods. Their beaks pecked his eyes; their feet tangled in his beard. The golden eagle dove upon the flock, screeching in rage. Pigeon feathers fell like gray snow.

Artemis's hawks, summoned from the highest trees of Central Park, darted into the fray, tearing the Father's eagle apart with bloodied talons. Two of Athena's owls swooped across the river from Long Island on silent wings, ripping Zeus's thunderbolt from his hands before he even noticed their approach.

The bolt clutched tight between their talons, the owls flapped heavy wings to speed their escape from Zeus's desperate grasp. They soared back over the river. There, right between Manhattan and Brooklyn, their talons opened. The bolt plummeted into the water, its light forever swallowed by the dark.

The Goddess raised Her own spear once more. "Metis crafted My armor inside your mind. With every stroke, she told her daughter that it was She who would be the Savior. She who would fulfill the prophecy to throw you from your throne. You thought yourself safe when no son emerged. *You were a fool.*"

The words of the Pythia returned. "The Wise Woman's seat is *right here*, in the city where She stands tall. And Her spear alone can conquer our greatest foe."

Single file, the Athenian *promakhoi* passed through the portal.

With every one that vanished, the Goddess felt Herself weaken, Her three parts unravel.

But so did Zeus.

He fled toward the rift, growing shorter and more haggard with every step. His hair grayed, his limbs bent, his flashing eyes dimmed. The cloud of birds streamed in his wake like a dark cloak.

The Tetractys blocked his way.

Scooter Joveson wrapped his arms around his frail, stooped father. He clutched him tightly for an instant as the ancient world squeezed shut just inches away.

In the center of the Brooklyn Bridge, on a sultry summer night, with his exhausted siblings looking on, the Messenger sent his final message to the King.

The old man's neck snapped with a loud pop.

The stars did not fall from the heavens with his death. No thunder drummed across the sky. The world mourned the passing of its former ruler with tears instead.

Only the gentle patter of rain on the Brooklyn Bridge broke the silence.

Chapter 59

EPILOGUS

One year later.

The baby in Selene's arms had hair as black as midnight and eyes as green as new-sprung leaves.

Sibyl, they called her, in honor of Cybele, the Great Mother who'd saved New York from the hand of Zeus. Sibyl Jimenez-Loi.

Her parents had decided it was a fitting name for a baby girl with multiple mothers.

Sibyl screwed up her brow, and for just an instant, Selene wondered what it would be like to see her own expression on a child's face. *Would she scowl all the time?* The thought made her laugh.

"She's trying to poop," Gabriela said, holding out her arms to take back her child.

Selene relinquished the baby happily enough, averting her eyes as Gabriela dealt with the diaper.

Theo flashed her a grin. "That's the problem with having preternatural senses, right? The whole baby crap thing is that much worse."

Minh made an exhausted effort at a smile. "Selene never has to change a diaper if she doesn't want to." The astronomer had taken on responsibility for explaining the mayhem on the Brooklyn

Bridge to a bewildered city. So far, a description of Einstein's space-time theories and a claim of mass hysterical hallucinations had done the trick—anything seemed more plausible than Greek gods still wandering the earth. Between working on her latest journal article and caring for a newborn, Minh wasn't getting a lot of sleep. But she turned to Theo with more humor than weariness.

"You, on the other hand, Spunkle Theo, don't get that option. Just because Sibyl lives with us doesn't mean you don't have to help when you're around."

"Right, right," Theo said, going to help Gabi with what Selene considered a totally unjustifiable amount of cheer.

With everyone's attention on Sybil, Selene pulled out her baby gift and slipped it onto the coffee table. She wasn't sure exactly how Gabi and Minh would react to the present; she figured Theo would be better at explaining it to them.

She left the all-too-domestic scene in her living room and went out to her tiny backyard. Ruth and Maryam were working in the garden; Hippo lay on the ground, watching contentedly.

The two women bent over a sapling, discussing something about the interaction between rhizobium microorganisms and soil salinity.

"You really think you're going to get an olive tree to grow in Manhattan?" Selene asked.

Maryam looked up and gave her a baleful stare. "I can get olive trees to grow anywhere."

Selene raised her hands in submission. "Okay, okay, sorry. You're not the Great Mother anymore, but give it shot."

"Speaking of great mothers," Ruth said, rolling her eyes. "Please don't make me go back in there. I can't keep talking about poop."

"Huh." Selene couldn't help prodding. "You and Steve Atwood aren't..."

Ruth flushed to the roots of her hair. "He's very nice," she said stiffly. "But he's a classicist. I think I've had enough classicists for a while. No offense."

"None taken." Selene settled on the ground beside Hippo, who rolled over to lay her head in Selene's lap.

The dog looked up with big brown eyes that seemed to say, *Don't believe Ruth for a second. She thinks Steve's dreamy.* Selene stifled a chortle. She'd let Ruth figure it out in her own time. Since Philippe and Esme had returned to Paris months before, they were all free to find their own way, safe from love darts. Flint had gone with them. The three of them made an odd sort of family, but no stranger than the one Selene had constructed for herself on Manhattan's Upper West Side.

Ruth stood up from the garden and brushed her hands on the seat of her jeans. "I'll bring some rhizobacteria tomorrow to try, all right?" she said to Maryam. Then, turning to Selene, she added, "If that's okay?"

Selene shrugged. "It's Maryam's house, too. Or, her garden apartment in the basement of my house, I guess. So don't ask me."

Ruth gave Maryam a quick hug, uncomfortably returned, and an even quicker one to Selene, then darted back inside.

Maryam, dirt on her hands and smeared across her forehead, looked pensive. "As a goddess, they served me. As a nun, I served them. This…"

"Friendship?" Selene filled in.

"Yes. Friendship. It's…different."

"But not bad."

"No," Maryam agreed. She turned back to her spindly olive tree before murmuring, "Not bad."

Maryam had become a strange sort of Queen of the Gods. She'd taken on the mantle as her mother Metis had always intended. With Hera dead and Demeter and Hestia gone, they had all agreed Athena deserved the title.

"Selene!" Theo called from inside. "Your phone's buzzing!"

Selene snapped her fingers for Hippo to follow and went inside. Theo stood in the narrow hallway, holding out her phone. "I think it's the same woman who called a few days ago. The one with the boyfriend who keeps threatening her. She just texted you. It looks like she's finally ready to accept our help."

Selene reached for the phone, but Theo held it back for just a moment. "Gabi and Minh left, by the way. You should've seen their faces when they found the bear-fur onesie you made for Sibyl. I thought Gabi was going to report you to one of her animal rights activist friends right then. But I told them it meant Sibyl would always have your protection—just like the little girls in ancient Brauron. Minh convinced her it was sweet. I left out the part about the obligatory ecstatic naked dancing in homage to Artemis."

"Probably for the best." She gestured again for the phone. He pressed it against his chest.

"I've got to head over tomorrow around noon to drop off that new crib Maryam made, but besides that I'm free."

"Are you saying that if I'm about to hunt down a bad guy, you want in on the chase?"

"Uh-huh." He took a step closer to her, his eyes full of mischief. On the wall beside him hung a round shield. It was no longer blank. A suspension bridge gleamed across its surface, the attribute of a man who spanned two worlds. Who bent in the wind rather than broke. Who played the song that sang in her heart.

She laid a finger in the dimple on his chin. Flint's necklace, now looped twice around her wrist, glinted in the light. "You just like watching me work."

"I like tracking down bad guys and keeping our city safe, especially when those bad guys are in no way supernatural," he said defensively. "If I get to watch you work at the same time... hey, that's just a bonus." He rested his lips on hers, just long enough to remind her that for all the pain and violence and heartbreak this world still held, the love and joy were more than enough to make up for it.

She took the phone and called her client.

"This is Selene. How can I help?"

AUTHOR'S NOTE

While the myth of Orpheus, the musician whose song could overcome death itself, is well-known, the details of the cult that bore his name remain a mystery. Two major relics remain from this esoteric religion: the Orphic Hymns, including paeans to more than eighty different gods; and a collection of small gold pendants, many of them leaf-shaped, found on the corpses of the cult's initiates. The words Theo recites in the Underworld are based on actual translations of these "Orphic gold tablets," which were inscribed with instructions for the afterlife and passwords that would allow initiates to proceed past the guardians at the Lake of Memory. For the best modern version of the poetry that both Theo and Selene recite in rough fragments throughout the book, see *The Orphic Hymns*, translated by Apostolos N. Athanassakis and Benjamin M. Wolkow.

In the Classical period, Orphism bore a close relation to the cult of Dionysus, the God of Wine. The god's epithet "Releaser"—assumed by many to refer to drunken revelry—may have meant something different to Orphic initiates, who believed Dionysus could release them from the miseries of the afterlife. The exact connection between the two cults remains unclear; I've attempted to explain it through the oft-told myth of the rescue of Dionysus's mother from the Underworld. The sacred eating of raw meat, a famously Dionysian practice, was disdained by early Christians, but some scholars believe it may have influenced their conception of the Eucharist nonetheless.

Orphism's relationship to Mithraism also eludes easy description. Statues of a lion-headed god have been found in several mithraea, and many of his attributes mirror those of the Orphic Protogonos, sometimes known as Aion. Professor David Ulansey, whose work inspired the astronomical components of *Winter of the Gods*, has written extensively on the possible meanings of this Mithraic lion-headed figure. For more, see his website, mysterium.com.

Followers of the ancient mathematician Pythagoras, possibly influenced by Orphic concepts of the afterlife, believed mankind could transcend mortality by uncovering the mathematical patterns that underlie the universe. The discovery of the tetractys and the harmonic ratios, as Theo explains in Chapter Two, were essential to this Pythagorean philosophy, and still influence our vision of the world today.

We will never know the true extent of Christianity's relationship to Mithraism. Scholars who believe that Christianity borrowed heavily from Mithraism point to the origins of Saint Paul, the man most often credited with first teaching that Jesus was no mere prophet, but rather the divine son of God. Paul—originally named Saul—hailed from Tarsus, a city widely considered a key conduit for Mithraism's spread from Persia to Rome. Paul's prior knowledge of Mithras, one of the earliest gods concerned with man's individual salvation, may have influenced the apostle's belief in a divine Jesus as the one true path to heaven.

The Magna Mater's Phrygianum, the site of the bloody taurobolium rituals, once stood in what is today Vatican City. My description of its interior, however, is completely fictional—no remnants of the building remain beyond a few ancient inscriptions mentioning its existence. The meridian line and the necropolis beneath Saint Peter's Basilica are real, but the secret passages and the underground mithraeum, sadly, are not. If you're interested in seeing the excavated necropolis, however (including its Jesus-as-Sol-Invictus mosaic), check out the virtual tour on the Vatican's website, vatican.va.

Statues of Ephesian Artemis, complete with her temple crown and necklace of bull's testicles, exist in museums throughout the world, but my favorites reside in the museum at the Ephesus archeological site. To my eyes, they bear a striking resemblance to the statues of Jesus's mother in the nearby House of the Virgin Mary. The ancient city of Ephesus, where the Church declared Mary divine in the fifth century, is remarkably well-preserved, although the great Temple of Artemis is now little more than a single column surrounded by marshland. Still, it is fully worth traveling all the way to Turkey to walk through the city that once worshiped Artemis above all other goddesses. For photos of Ephesus, Brauron, Rome, Delphi, Athens, the cave in Crete, an ancient hydraulis, and more, visit my website, jordannamaxbrodsky.com.

Minh Loi's explanation of the music of the Big Bang is based on the work of several scientists, most notably Mark Whittle from the University of Virginia. His excellent and very readable website, Big Bang Acoustics: Sounds from the Newborn Universe, served as the inspiration for much of this book's climax and includes audio files of the sounds themselves. It does not, however, recommend playing the music on the cables of the Brooklyn Bridge. But lest you think such a thing impossible, watch Di Mainstone's astounding musical performance project at humanharp.org.

As for Mount Olympus, the hike to the summit takes most people two days. The journey up begins with gentle wildflowers and ends with a brutally steep climb across a barren scree field to a final near-vertical ascent. The clouds roll in nearly every afternoon, bringing thunderstorms and bitter chill even when the valley below remains swelteringly hot. It's easy to see why the ancients imagined Olympus as the home of Zeus, lord of storms and sky. While sprinting down from the summit, thunder rolling off the mountaintop, hail pounding my skull, and fierce winds tearing at my emergency poncho, I fully believed it myself.

Jordanna Max Brodsky
April 2017
New York, New York

APPENDIX

Olympians and Other Immortals

Roman names follow the Greek, where applicable. Relevant information from the Olympus Bound series appears in italics.

Aion: A minor Mithraic divinity associated with the proto-god of Orphism (see "Protogonos"). Sometimes portrayed as a snake-twined, lion-headed man with wings.

Aphrodite/Venus: Goddess of Erotic Love and Beauty. One of the Twelve Olympians. Born of sea foam after Kronos castrates his father, Ouranos, and throws his genitals into the ocean. Wife of Hephaestus and lover of Ares/Mars. Mother of Eros. Called Laughter-Loving, She Who Turns to Love, Mother of Desire. Attributes: dove, scallop shell, mirror. Modern alias: Esme Amata.

Apollo/Apollo: God of Light, Music, Healing, Prophecy, Poetry, Archery, Civilization, Plague, and the Sun. One of the Twelve Olympians. Leader of the Muses. Twin brother of Artemis. Son of Leto and Zeus. Born on the island of Delos, but counts Delphi, site of the famous Pythian oracle, as his most sacred precinct. Called Phoebus (Bright One), Delphic Diviner, Pythian God, God of the Golden Lyre. Attributes: silver bow and arrows, crow, laurel wreath, lyre. Modern alias: Paul Solson. *(Killed by Saturn's Mithraists in the modern day.)*

Ares/Mars: God of War, Bloodlust, and Manly Courage. One of the Twelve Olympians. Son of Zeus and Hera. Lover of Aphrodite. Brother to Hephaestus. Often considered the father of Eros. Called Man-Slayer, Battle-Insatiate. Attributes: armor, spear, poisonous serpent. Modern alias: Martin Bell. *(Killed by Saturn's Mithraists in the modern day.)*

Artemis/Diana: Goddess of the Wilderness, the Hunt, Virginity, Wild Animals, Hounds, Young Children, Childbirth, and the Moon. One of the Twelve Olympians. Twin sister of Apollo. Daughter of Leto and Zeus. Born on the island of Delos. Worshiped in Ephesus and other cities of Asia Minor (modern Turkey) as an aspect of the Great Mother, robed and crowned with animals, rather than as a virgin huntress. Her many epithets include Huntress, She Who Loves the Chase, Far Shooter, Protector of the Innocent, Lady of Clamors, She Who Helps One Climb Out, the Face of Death, and more. Attributes: golden bow and arrows, hounds, deer, bears, hawks. Modern aliases: Phoebe Hautman, Dianne Delia, Cynthia Forrester, Selene DiSilva, Selene Neomenia, and more.

Asclepius: Hero-God of Medicine. Son of Apollo and the mortal princess Coronis. Worshiped in the Eleusinian Mysteries and many other cults. Called He Who Soothes. Attribute: snake-twined staff.

Athena/Minerva: Goddess of Wisdom, Crafts, and Justified War. One of the Twelve Olympians. Virgin. Daughter of Zeus and Metis. Called Gray-Eyed, Protectress of Cities, Savior, Promakhos (frontline soldier). Patron goddess of Athens, to whom she gifted the olive tree. Attributes: helmet, spear, owl, shield or aegis with Gorgon's head. Modern alias: Maryam.

Cautes: Minor Mithraic divinity. A torchbearer who symbolizes Birth and Day. Attributes: upright torch, rooster.

Cautopates: Minor Mithraic divinity. A torchbearer who symbolizes Death and Night. Attributes: downward torch, owl.

Cybele/Magna Mater: The Great Mother, originally a primal nature deity from Asia Minor, later incorporated into the Greco-Roman pantheon. Sometimes associated with the Titan goddess Rhea. Mother of all gods, humans, and animals. Attributes: tall crown, lions, pine tree.

Demeter/Ceres: Goddess of Grain and Agriculture. One of the Twelve Olympians. Daughter of Kronos and Rhea. Sister of Zeus. Mother of Persephone. Called Bountiful, Bringer of Seasons. Attributes: wheat sheaves, torch.

Dionysus/Bacchus: God of Wine, Wild Plants, Festivity, Theater. One of the Twelve Olympians. Son of Zeus and Semele, a mortal. Called Phallic, Releaser, He of the Wild Revels. Attributes: grapevine, ivy, thyrsus (a pinecone-tipped staff), leopard. Modern alias: Dennis Boivin.

Eos/Aurora: Goddess and embodiment of the Dawn. After falling in love with Tithonus, she asked Zeus to grant him immortality—but forgot to ask for eternal youth, as well. Tithonus grew so old and shriveled that he turned into a grasshopper.

Eros/Cupid: God of Love. Son of Aphrodite and Ares. Commonly portrayed as a winged infant, although sometimes as a youth. Attributes: wings, myrtle bow. Modern alias: Philippe Amata.

Gaia: Primeval Earth Divinity. Mother to all. Consort of Ouranos the Sky.

Hades/Pluto: God of the Underworld, Death, Wealth. Son of Kronos and Rhea. Brother of Zeus. Husband of Persephone. Called Receiver of Many, Lord of the Dead, Hidden One. Attributes: helm of invisibility, bird-tipped scepter. Modern alias: Aiden McKelvey. *(Killed by Saturn's Mithraists in the modern day.)*

Hekatonkheires: The Hundred-Handed Ones. Giants cast into Tartarus by Zeus during the Gigantomachy.

Helios/Sol/Sol Invictus: God and embodiment of the Sun. Also identified with Apollo, who has dominion over the Sun. The Romans revered him as Sol Invictus, the "Invincible Sun," and celebrated his birthday on December 25. "Sol Invictus" was also a common epithet for Mithras. Attributes: seven-rayed crown.

Hephaestus/Vulcan: God of the Forge, Fire, and Volcanoes. One of the Twelve Olympians. Son of Hera, born parthenogenically. Husband of Aphrodite. Lamed when thrown off Olympus by Zeus, walks with a crutch. Called the Smith, the Sooty God, He of Many Arts and Skills, Lame One. Attributes: hammer, tongs. Modern alias: Flint Hamernik.

Hera/Juno: Queen of the Gods. Goddess of Women, Marriage, and the Heavens. One of the Twelve Olympians. Daughter of Kronos and Rhea. Sister and jealous wife of Zeus. Mother of Ares/Mars and Hephaestus. Known as "white-armed." Attributes: crown, peacock, lotus-tipped staff. Modern alias: June Ferarra.

Hermes/Mercury: God of Messengers, Thieves, Liars, Travel, Communication, Hospitality, Eloquence, and Athletics. One of the Twelve Olympians. Son of Zeus and a nymph, Maia. Herald to the gods. Called Messenger, Giver of Good Things, Trickster, Many-Turning. Attributes: caduceus (staff twined with snakes), winged sandals, winged cap. Modern aliases: Dash Mercer, Scooter Joveson.

Hestia/Vesta: Goddess of the Hearth and Home. Eldest daughter of Kronos and Rhea. Sister of Zeus. Virgin. Once part of the Twelve Olympians, she gave up her throne to Dionysus. She tended the sacred fire at the center of Mount Olympus. Attributes: veil, kettle.

Khaos: Primeval embodiment of Chaos. From the same root as "chasm," the name means the void from which all other primeval divinities sprang.

Kronos/Saturn: A Titan. With the help of his mother, Gaia (the Earth), he overthrew his father, Ouranos (the Sky), to become King of the Gods. Swallowed his children to prevent them from taking his crown until overthrown by Zeus, his youngest son. Father/grandfather of the Olympians. Also identified as the God of Time. Called "the Wily." Attributes: sickle. *(Also the Father— or "Pater"—of the Host, a secret order dedicated to Mithras.)*

Leto/Latona: Goddess of Motherhood and Modesty. Daughter of the Titans Phoibe and Koios. Lover of Zeus. Mother of Artemis and Apollo. Called "neat-ankled," Gentle Goddess, Mother of Twins. Attributes: veil, date palm. Modern alias: Leticia Delos. *(Dead of natural causes in the modern day.)*

Magna Mater: See "Cybele."

Medusa: One of the snake-haired Gorgons, whose gaze turns men to stone. Some stories identify her as a virgin priestess of Athena, raped by Poseidon.

Metis: Goddess and personification of Wisdom. After receiving a prophecy that Metis's child would overthrow him, Zeus swallowed the goddess after impregnating her. Later, Metis's daughter, Athena, emerged fully armed from Zeus's skull.

Mithras: God worshiped by a Mystery Cult during the late Roman era, especially popular with soldiers in the Roman legion, who believed Mithras moved the celestial spheres and shifted the equinoxes, allowing for the world's passage from one Age to another. He also provided a means of individual salvation for his followers. Epithets include Sol Invictus. Attributes: Phrygian cap, bull, and the other symbols of the tauroctony. *(Also the primary deity worshiped by the Host, a secret order that associates Mithras directly with Jesus.)*

Mnemosyne: Titan goddess and personification of Memory. Often identified as the mother of the Muses.

Muses: Nine minor goddesses of art, knowledge, and inspiration, each presiding over her own field: Calliope, epic poetry; Clio, history; Urania, astronomy; Thalia, comedy; Melpomene, tragedy; Polyhymnia, religious hymns; Erato, erotic poetry; Euterpe, lyric poetry; and Terpsichore, choral song and dance.

Orion: Son of Poseidon and a mortal woman. Artemis's only male hunting companion. Some tales describe him as blinded and exiled after raping Merope, a king's daughter. Other myths say he raped one of Artemis's nymphs. He was killed either by a scorpion or by Artemis's arrows, then placed as a constellation in the sky. Called the Hunter. Modern alias: Everett Halloran. *(Killed by Selene DiSilva after attempting to re-create the Eleusinian Mysteries through human sacrifice.)*

Orpheus: Legendary musician of the ancient world. When Eurydice, his wife, was killed, he journeyed to the Underworld to win her freedom through the power of his song. He is also credited with introducing the ancient world to the Orphic Mysteries, a cult that believed in reincarnation.

Ouranos/Uranus: Primeval Sky Divinity. Father of the Titans. Original ruler of the world until castrated by his son Kronos/Saturn.

Persephone/Proserpina: Goddess of Spring and the Underworld. Daughter of Demeter and Zeus. Wife of Hades. Called Kore ("Maiden"), Discreet, Lovely. Attributes: wheat sheaves, torch. Modern alias: Cora McKelvey.

Poseidon/Neptune: God of the Sea, Earthquakes, and Horses. One of the Twelve Olympians. Son of Kronos and Rhea. Brother of Zeus. Father of Orion, Theseus, and other heroes. Called "blue-haired," Earth Shaker, Horse Tender. Attributes: trident.

Prometheus: A Titan. After molding humans from clay and granting them life, he gave them fire—despite Zeus's prohibition. As punishment, the Olympians chained him to a rock and sent an eagle to eat his liver every day for eternity. Called Fire Bringer, Chained One. Attribute: fennel stalk of fire. *(Killed by Saturn's Mithraists in the modern day.)*

Protogonos: A proto-god worshiped by followers of Orphism. Usually portrayed as a winged, snake-twined young man standing on an eggshell, holding a torch. In some mythologies, he created the world from a primordial egg. (See "Aion.")

Rhea/Ops: A Titan. Goddess of Female Fertility. Queen of the Gods in the Age of Titans. Helped Zeus, her youngest son, overthrow his father, Kronos. Mother and grandmother to the Olympians. Sometimes associated with Cybele/the Magna Mater. Attribute: royal scepter.

Saturn: See "Kronos."

Typhoeus: Storm Giant cast into Tartarus by Zeus in the battle between gods and giants. Now Tartarus's guardian.

Zeus/Jupiter: King and Father of the Gods. God of the Sky, Lightning, Weather, Law, and Fate. One of the Twelve Olympians. Youngest son of Kronos and Rhea. After Kronos swallowed his first five children, Rhea hid baby Zeus in the Cave of Psychro. After reaching manhood, Zeus cut his siblings from his father's gullet, defeated the Titans in the Gigantomachy, and began the reign of the Olympians. He divided the world with his two brothers, taking the Sky for himself. Husband (and brother) of Hera, but lover of many. Father of untold gods, goddesses, and heroes, including Artemis, Apollo, Hermes, Ares, Dionysus, and Athena. Called Lightning Bringer, He Who Marshals Thunderheads, Raging One, Omnipotent, and more. Attributes: lightning bolt, eagle, royal scepter.

GLOSSARY OF GREEK AND LATIN TERMS

Aegis: Athena's goatskin cloak, used as a shield in battle, decorated with a Gorgon's head

Athanatos (pl. Athanatoi): "One Who Does Not Die" (an immortal)

Caduceus: a snake-twined herald's staff, the symbol of Hermes/Mercury

Gigantomachy: a great battle between gods and giants at the beginning of the world

Gorgon: a monstrous woman with snakes for hair whose gaze turns men to stone

Heliodromus: "the Sun-Runner," the penultimate rank in the Mithraic Mysteries

Khairete: a common greeting in both Ancient and Modern Greek

Leo: "a lion," a rank in the Mithraic Mysteries

Lethe: the River of Forgetfulness in the Underworld

Makarites (pl. Makaritai): "Blessed One"

Maenad: a female follower of Dionysus, often partaking in frenzied rites

Miles: "a soldier," a rank in the Mithraic Mysteries

Mithraeum (pl. mithraea): a sanctuary dedicated to Mithras

Mnemosyne: "Memory," also the name of a lake in the Underworld

Omphalos: navel

Parthenona: virgin or young woman

Parthenon: the temple atop the Athenian Acropolis, dedicated to Athena the Virgin

Pater Patrum: Father of Fathers, the leader of the Mithraic Mysteries

Phrygia: a region of ancient Asia Minor, now in modern Turkey

Pneuma: breath, air, or spirit

Promakhos (pl. promakhoi): Frontline soldier (also an epithet of Athena)

Pythia: title given to the prophetess at Delphi, named for the dragon-like Python who once guarded the oracle, later slain by Apollo

Satyr: a drunken, lustful woodland demigod, often portrayed with goat's horns or hooves and commonly associated with Dionysian revelry

Styx: the river that borders the Underworld. Swearing upon it is the most solemn vow a god can make.

Syndexios (pl. syndexioi): an initiate in the Mithraic Mysteries. Literally, "a joining of the right hands" (one who knows the secret handshake)

Tartarus: a pit far below the Underworld where the Olympians imprison their greatest foes

Tauroctony: "bull killing," the central image of the Mithraic Mysteries

Taurobolium: "bull sacrifice," a major ritual in the Magna Mater's cult

Tetractys: a triangular figure first discovered by the ancients, consisting of ten total dots arranged in four rows, creating an equilateral triangle with four dots on each side. Considered by followers of Pythagoras to be the "perfect number."

Thanatos (pl. thanatoi): "one who dies" (a mortal)

ACKNOWLEDGMENTS

A book that touches on so many different aspects of myth, mathematics, classics, and archeology requires the input of many different experts. My great thanks to Mine Gezen, my incomparable guide to Ephesus, who made Artemis's sacred city truly come alive. A special thank-you as well to the magnificent staff at the Cella Boutique Hotel in Selçuk, without whom my adventures in Ephesus might have ended abruptly in a busted rental car on a Turkish beach. Ian Caldwell volunteered his research on the site of the Phrygianum beneath Vatican City. Steve Anderson and Ben Arons assisted my understanding of Big Bang acoustics. Erika Schluntz lent her archeologist's eye to the entire text and provided invaluable help with Greek and Latin pronunciation. Kathy Seaman generously volunteered her exceptional proofreading skills. As always, my efforts at translating ancient languages would be impossible without the assistance of Dr. Anne Shaw and Dr. Michael Shaw, classicists extraordinaire. If errata remain, I alone am to blame.

Tegan Tigani, to whom this book is dedicated, has traveled with me into the worlds of our imagination since we first built gnome homes together on the shores of Narragansett Bay in 1986. My appreciation for her editorial and publishing advice is equaled only by my gratitude for her unfailing enthusiasm and friendship. Proving myself worthy of her love has been one of the great projects of my life.

To my other indefatigable readers, Helen Shaw and John Wray: This book would not be half as good without you. Your honesty—and your unstinting generosity of both spirit and time—made every chapter, every scene, better. Emily Shooltz and Sharon Green lent their much-needed fresh eyes at the last minute. Thanks as well to my agent, Jennifer Joel, my very own Protector of the Innocent Novelist.

My family—the Brodskys, Millses, and my New York family of friends—have not only shared this adventure with me; they've made it possible through their love and support.

Lindsey Hall, my editor at Orbit Books, took on *Olympus Bound* with enthusiasm and dedication. My great thanks to her for her excellent editorial suggestions, heartfelt encouragement, and hard work. And to the rest of the staff at Orbit and Hachette— Tim Holman, Ellen Wright, Laura Fitzgerald, Tommy Harron, Alex Lencicki, Kirk Benshoff, and so many others—I could not imagine a more supportive and joyful community than the one at Hachette Book Group. I'm honored you've made me a part of it.

And finally, to the man who held my hand and pulled me to the top of Mount Olympus while carrying every ounce of our supplies on his back, who happily trekked through Greece and Turkey hunting every possible Artemis reference, whose insights never failed to improve this book even after his third read, who inspired me with his love of both math and action movies, and who has been the love of my life for the past twenty years: Thank you, Jason. You are, and always will be, my Perfect Number.

extras

www.orbitbooks.net

about the author

Jordanna Max Brodsky hails from Virginia, where she spent four years at a science and technology high school pretending it was a theatre conservatory. She holds a degree in history and literature from Harvard University. When she's not wandering the forests of Maine, she lives in Manhattan with her husband. She often sees goddesses in Central Park and wishes she were one.

Find out more about Jordanna Max Brodsky and other Orbit authors by registering for the free monthly newsletter at www.orbitbooks.net.

if you enjoyed
OLYMPUS BOUND

look out for

STRANGE PRACTICE

by

Vivian Shaw

Meet Greta Helsing, doctor to the undead.

After inheriting a highly specialised, and highly peculiar, medical practice, Dr Helsing spends her days treating London's undead for a host of ills: vocal strain in banshees, arthritis in barrow-wights and entropy in mummies. Although barely making ends meet, this is just the quiet, supernatural-adjacent life Greta's dreamed of since childhood.

But when a sect of murderous monks emerges, killing human undead and alike, Greta must use all her unusual skills to keep her supernatural clients – and the rest of London – safe.

CHAPTER I

The sky was fading to ultramarine in the east over the Victoria Embankment when a battered Mini pulled in to the curb, not far from Blackfriars Bridge. Here and there in the maples lining the riverside walk, the morning's first sparrows had begun to sing.

A woman got out of the car and shut the door, swore, put down her bags, and shut the door again with more applied force; some fellow motorist had bashed into the panel at some time in the past and bent it sufficiently to make this a production every damn time. The Mini really needed to be replaced, but even with her inherited Harley Street consulting rooms Greta Helsing was not exactly drowning in cash.

She glowered at the car and then at the world in general, glancing around to make sure no one was watching her from the shadows. Satisfied, she picked up her black working bag and the shapeless oversize monster that was her current handbag and went to ring the doorbell. It was time to replace the handbag, too. The leather on this one was holding up but the lining was beginning to go, and Greta had limited patience regarding the retrieval of items from the mysterious dimension behind the lining itself.

The house to which she had been summoned was one of a row of magnificent old buildings separating Temple Gardens from the Embankment, mostly taken over by lawyers and publishing firms these days. It was a testament to this particular homeowner's rather special powers of persuasion that nobody had succeeded in buying the house out from under him and turning it into offices for overpriced attorneys, she thought, and then had to smile at the idea of anybody dislodging Edmund Ruthven from the lair he'd inhabited these two hundred years or more. He was as much a fixture of London as Lord Nelson on his pillar, albeit less encrusted with birdlime.

"Greta," said the fixture, opening the door. "Thanks for coming out on a Sunday. I know it's late."

She was just about as tall as he was, five foot five and a bit, which made it easy to look right into his eyes and be struck every single time by the fact that they were very large, so pale a grey they looked silver-white except for the dark ring at the edge of the iris, and fringed with heavy soot-black lashes of the sort you saw in advertisements for mascara. He looked tired, she thought. Tired, and older than the fortyish he usually appeared. The extreme pallor was normal, vivid against the pure slicked-back black of his hair, but the worried line between his eyebrows was not.

"It's not Sunday night, it's Monday morning," she said. "No worries, Ruthven. Tell me everything; I know you didn't go into lots of detail on the phone."

"Of course." He offered to take her coat. "I'll make you some coffee."

The entryway of the Embankment house was floored in black-and-white-checkered marble, and a large bronze ibis stood on a little side table where the mail and car keys and shopping lists were to be found. The mirror behind this reflected Greta dimly and greenly, like a woman underwater; she peered into it, making a face at herself, and tucked back her hair. It was pale Scandinavian blonde and cut like Liszt's in an off-the-shoulder bob, fine enough to slither free of whatever she used to pull it back; today it was in the process of escaping from a thoroughly childish headband. She kept meaning to have it all chopped off and be done with it but never seemed to find the time.

Greta Helsing was thirty-four, unmarried, and had taken over her late father's specialized medical practice after a brief stint as an internist at King's College Hospital. For the past five years she had run a bare-bones clinic out of Wilfert Helsing's old rooms in Harley Street, treating a patient base that to the majority of the population did not, technically, when you got right down to it, exist. It was a family thing.

There had never been much doubt which subspecialty of medicine she would pursue, once she began her training: treating the differently alive was not only more interesting than catering to the ordinary human population, it was in many ways a great deal more rewarding. She took a lot of satisfaction in being able to provide help to particularly underserved clients.

Greta's patients could largely be classified under the heading of *monstrous*—in its descriptive, rather than pejorative, sense: vampires, were-creatures, mummies, banshees, ghouls, bogeymen, the occasional arthritic barrow-wight. She herself was solidly and entirely human, with no noticeable eldritch qualities or powers whatsoever, not even a flicker of metaphysical sensitivity. Some of her patients found it difficult to trust a human physician at first, but Greta had built up an extremely good reputation over the five years she had been practicing supernatural medicine, largely by word of mouth: *Go to Helsing, she's reliable.*

And *discreet*. That was the first and fundamental tenet, after all. Keeping her patients safe meant keeping them secret, and Greta was good with secrets. She made sure the magical wards around her doorway in Harley Street were kept up properly, protecting anyone who approached from prying eyes.

Ruthven appeared in the kitchen doorway, outlined by light spilling warm over the black-and-white marble. "Greta?" he said, and she straightened up, realizing she'd been staring into the mirror without really seeing it for several minutes now. It really *was* late. Fatigue lapped heavily at the pilings of her mind.

"Sorry," she said, coming to join him, and a little of that

heaviness lifted as they passed through into the familiar warmth and brightness of the kitchen. It was all blue tile and blond wood, the cheerful rose-gold of polished copper pots and pans balancing the sleek chill of stainless steel, and right now it was also full of the scent of really *good* coffee. Ruthven's espresso machine was a La Cimbali, and it was serious business.

He handed her a large pottery mug. She recognized it as one of the set he generally used for blood, and had to smile a little, looking down at the contents—and then abruptly had to clamp down on a wave of thoroughly inconvenient emotion. There was no reason that Ruthven doing goddamn *latte art* for her at half-past four in the morning should make her want to cry.

He was *good* at it, too, which was a little infuriating; then again she supposed that with as much free time on her hands as he had on his, and as much disposable income, she might find herself learning and polishing new skills simply to stave off the encroaching spectre of boredom. Ruthven didn't go in for your standard-variety vampire angst, which was refreshing, but Greta knew very well he had bouts of something not unlike depression—especially in the winter—and he needed things to *do*.

She, however, *had* things to do, Greta reminded herself, taking a sip of the latte and closing her eyes for a moment. This was coffee that actually tasted as good as, if not better than, it smelled. *Focus,* she thought. This was not a social call. The lack of urgency in Ruthven's manner led her to believe that the situation was not immediately dire, but she was nonetheless here to do her job.

Greta licked coffee foam from her upper lip. "So," she said. "Tell me what happened."

"I was—" Ruthven sighed, leaning against the counter with his arms folded. "To be honest I was sitting around twiddling my thumbs and writing nasty letters to the *Times* about how much I loathe these execrable skyscrapers somebody keeps allowing vandals to build all over the city. I'd got to a particularly cutting phrase about the one that sets people's cars on fire, when somebody knocked on the door."

The passive-aggressive-letter stage tended to indicate that his levels of ennui were reaching critical intensity. Greta just nodded, watching him.

"I don't know if you've ever read an ancient penny-dreadful called *Varney the Vampyre, or The Feast of Blood*," he went on.

"Ages ago," she said. She'd read practically all the horror classics, well-known and otherwise, for research purposes rather than to enjoy their literary merit. Most of them were to some extent entertainingly wrong about the individuals they claimed to depict. "It was quite a lot funnier than your unofficial biography, but I'm not sure it was *meant* to be."

Ruthven made a face. John Polidori's *The Vampyre* was, he insisted, mostly libel—the very mention of the book was sufficient to bring on indignant protestations that he and the Lord Ruthven featured in the narrative shared little more than a name. "At least the authors got the spelling right, unlike bloody Polidori," he said. "I think probably *Feast of Blood* is about as historically accurate as *The Vampyre*, which is to say *not very*, but it does have the taxonomy right. Varney, unlike me, *is* a vampyre with a *y*."

"A lunar sensitive? I haven't actually met one before," she said, clinical interest surfacing through the fatigue. The vampires she knew were all classic draculines, like Ruthven himself and the handful of others in London. Lunar sensitives were rarer than the draculine vampires for a couple of reasons, chief among which was the fact that they were violently—and inconveniently—allergic to the blood of anyone but virgins. They did have the handy characteristic of being resurrected by moonlight every time they got themselves killed, which presumably came as some small comfort in the process of succumbing to violent throes of gastric distress brought on by dietary indiscretion.

"Well," Ruthven said, "now's your chance. He showed up on my doorstep, completely unannounced, looking like thirty kinds of warmed-over hell, and collapsed in the hallway. He is at the moment sleeping on the drawing room sofa, and I want you to look at him for me. I don't *think* there's any real danger, but he's been hurt—some maniacs apparently attacked him with a knife—and I'd feel better if you had a look."

Ruthven had lit a fire, despite the relative mildness of the evening, and the creature lying on the sofa was covered with two blankets. Greta glanced from him to Ruthven, who shrugged a little, that line of worry between his eyebrows very visible.

According to him, Sir Francis Varney, title and all, had come out of his faint quite quickly and perked up after some first aid and the administration of a nice hot mug of suitable and brandy-laced blood. Ruthven kept a selection of the stuff in his expensive fridge and freezer, stocked by Greta via fairly illegal supply chain management—she knew someone who knew someone who worked in a blood bank and was not above rescuing rejected units from the biohazard incinerator.

Sir Francis had drunk the whole of the mug's contents with every evidence of satisfaction and promptly gone to sleep as soon as Ruthven let him, whereupon Ruthven had called Greta and requested a house call. "I don't really like the look of him," he said now, standing in the doorway with uncharacteristic awkwardness. "He was bleeding a little—the wound's in his left shoulder. I cleaned it up and put a dressing on, but it was still sort of oozing. Which isn't like us."

"No," Greta agreed, "it's not. It's possible that lunar sensitives and draculines respond differently to tissue trauma, but even so, I would have expected him to have mostly finished healing already. You were right to call me."

"Do you need anything?" he asked, still standing in the doorway as Greta pulled over a chair and sat down beside the sofa.

"Possibly more coffee. Go on, Ruthven. I've got this; go and finish your unkind letter to the editor."

When he had gone she tucked back her hair and leaned over to examine her patient. He took up the entire length of the sofa, head pillowed on one armrest and one narrow foot resting on the other, half-exposed where the blankets had fallen away. She did a bit of rough calculation and guessed he must be at least six inches taller than Ruthven, possibly more.

His hair was tangled, streaky-grey, worn dramatically long— that was aging-rock-frontman hair if Greta had ever seen it, but nothing *else* about him seemed to fit with the Jagger aesthetic. An old-fashioned face, almost Puritan: long, narrow nose, deeply hooded eyes under intense eyebrows, thin mouth bracketed with habitual lines of disapproval.

Or pain, she thought. *That could be pain.*

The shifting of a log in the fireplace behind Greta made her jump a little, and she regathered the wandering edges of her concentration. With a nasty little flicker of surprise she noticed that there was a faint sheen of sweat on Varney's visible skin. That *really* wasn't right.

"Sir Francis?" she said, gently, and leaned over to touch his shoulder through the blankets—and a moment later had retreated halfway across the room, heart racing: Varney had gone from uneasy sleep to *sitting up and snarling viciously* in less than a second.

It was not unheard-of for Greta's patients to threaten her, especially when they were in considerable pain, and on the whole she probably should have thought this out a little better. She'd only got a glimpse before her own instincts had kicked in and got her the hell out of range of those teeth, but it would be a while before she could forget that pattern of dentition, or those mad tin-colored eyes.

He covered his face with his hands, shoulders slumping, and instead of menace was now giving off an air of intense embarrassment.

Greta came back over to the sofa. "I'm sorry," she said, tentatively, "I didn't mean to startle you—"

"I most devoutly apologize," he said, without taking his hands away. "I do *try* not to do that, but I am not quite at my best just now—forgive me, I don't believe we have been introduced."

He was looking at her from behind his fingers, and the eyes really *were* metallic. Even partly hidden she could see the room's reflection in his irises. She wondered if that was a peculiarity of his species, or an individual phenomenon.

"It's all right," she said, and sat down on the edge of the sofa, judging that he wasn't actually about to tear her throat out just at the moment. "My name's Greta. I'm a doctor; Ruthven called me to come and take a look at you."

When Varney finally took his hands away from his face, pushing the damp silvering hair back, his color was frankly terrible. He *was* sweating. That was not something she'd ever seen in sanguivores under any circumstance.

"A doctor?" he asked, blinking at her. "Are you sure?"

She was spared having to answer that. A moment later he squeezed his eyes shut, very faint color coming and going high on each cheek. "I really am sorry," he said. "What a remarkably stupid question. It's just—I tend to think of doctors as looking rather different than you."

"I left my pinstripe trousers and pocket-watch at home," she said drily. "But I've got my black bag, if that helps. Ruthven said you'd been hurt—attacked by somebody with a knife. May I take a look?"

He glanced up at her and then away again, and nodded once, leaning back against the sofa cushions, and Greta reached into her bag for the exam gloves.

The wound was in his left shoulder, as Ruthven had said, about two and a half inches south of the collarbone. It wasn't large—she had seen much nastier injuries from street fights, although in rather different species—but it was undoubtedly the *strangest* wound she'd ever come across.

"What made this?" she asked, looking closer, her gloved

fingers careful on his skin. Varney hissed and turned his face away, and she could feel a thrumming tension under her touch. "I've never seen anything like it. The wound is . . . *cross*-shaped."

It was. Instead of just the narrow entry mark of a knife, or the bruised puncture of something clumsier, Varney's wound appeared to have been made by something flanged. Not just two but four sharp edges, leaving a hole shaped like an X—or a cross.

"It was a spike," he said, between his teeth. "I didn't get a very good look at it. They had—broken into my flat, with garlic. Garlic was everywhere. Smeared on the walls, scattered all over the floor. I was—taken by surprise, and the fumes—I could hardly see or breathe."

"I'm not surprised," said Greta, sitting up. "It's extremely nasty stuff. Are you having any chest pain or trouble breathing now?"

A lot of the organic compounds in *Allium sativum* triggered a severe allergic response in vampires, varying in intensity based on amount and type of exposure. This wasn't garlic shock, or not *just* garlic shock, though. He was definitely running a fever, and the hole in his shoulder should have healed to a shiny pink memory within an hour or so after it happened. Right now it was purple-black and . . . oozing.

"No," Varney said, "just—the wound is, ah, really rather painful." He sounded apologetic. "As I said, I didn't get a close look at the spike, but it was short and pointed like a rondel dagger, with a round pommel. There were three people there, I don't know if they all had knives, but . . . well, as it turned out, all they needed was one."

This was so very much not her division. "Did—do you have any idea why they attacked you?" Or why they'd broken into his flat and poisoned it with garlic. That was a pretty specialized tactic, after all. Greta shivered in sudden unease.

"They were chanting, or . . . reciting something," he said, his odd eyes drifting shut. "I couldn't make out much of it, just that it sounded sort of ecclesiastical."

He had a remarkably beautiful voice, she noticed. The rest of him wasn't tremendously prepossessing, particularly those eyes, but his voice was *lovely*: sweet and warm and clear. It contrasted oddly with the actual content of what he was saying. "Something about…*unclean*," he continued, "*unclean* and wicked, *wickedness*, foulness, and…*demons*. Creatures of darkness."

He still had his eyes half-closed, and Greta frowned and bent over him again. "Sir Francis?"

"Hurts," he murmured, sounding very far away. "They were dressed…strangely."

She rested two fingers against the pulse in his throat: much too fast, and he couldn't have spiked *that* much in the minutes she had been with him, but he felt noticeably warmer to her touch. She reached into the bag for her thermometer and the BP cuff. "Strangely how?"

"Like…monks," he said, and blinked up at her, hazy and confused. "In…brown robes. With crosses round their necks. Like *monks*."

His eyes rolled back slightly, slipping closed, and he gave a little terrible sigh; when Greta took him by the shoulders and gave him a shake he did not rouse at all, head rolling limp against the cushions. *What the hell,* she thought, *what the actual hell is going on here, there's no way a wound like this should be affecting him so badly, this is—it looks like systemic inflammatory response but the garlic should have worn off by now, there's nothing to* cause *it, unless—*

Unless there had been something on the blade. Something *left behind*.

That flicker of visceral unease was much stronger now. She leaned closer, gently drawing apart the edges of the wound—the tissue was swollen, red, warmer than the surrounding skin—and was surprised to notice a faint but present smell. Not the characteristic smell of infection, but something sharper, almost metallic, with a sulfurous edge on it like silver tarnish. It was strangely familiar, but she couldn't seem to place it.

Greta was rather glad he was unconscious just at the moment, because what she was about to do would be quite remarkably painful. She stretched the wound open a little wider, wishing she had her penlight to get a better view, and he shifted a little, his breath catching; as he moved she caught a glimpse of something reflective half-obscured by dark blood. There *was* something still in there. Something that needed to come out right now.

"Ruthven," she called, sitting up. "Ruthven, I need you."

He emerged from the kitchen, looking anxious. "What is it?

"Get the green leather instrument case out of my bag," she said, "and put a pan of water on to boil. There's a foreign body in here I need to extract."

Without a word Ruthven took the instrument case and disappeared again. Greta turned her attention back to her patient, noticing for the first time that the pale skin of his chest was crisscrossed by old scarring—*very* old, she thought, looking at the silvery laddered marks of long-healed injuries. She had seen Ruthven without his shirt on, and he had a pretty good collection of scars from four centuries' worth of misadventure, but Varney put him to shame. *A lot of duels,* she thought. *A lot of . . . lost duels.*

Greta wondered how much of *Feast of Blood* was actually based on historical events. He had died at least once in the part of it that she remembered, and had spent a lot of time running away from various pitchfork-wielding mobs. None of *them* had been dressed up in monastic drag, as far as she knew, but they had certainly demonstrated the same intent as whoever had hurt Varney tonight.

A cold flicker of something close to fear slipped down her spine, and she turned abruptly to look over her shoulder at the empty room, pushing away a sudden and irrational sensation of being watched.

Don't be ridiculous, she told herself, *and do your damn job.* She was a little grateful for the business of wrapping the BP cuff around his arm, and less pleased by what it told her. Not critical, but certainly a long way from what she considered normal for sanguivores. She didn't know what was going on in there, but she didn't like it one bit.

When Ruthven returned carrying a tea tray, she felt irrationally relieved to see him—and then had to raise an eyebrow at the contents of the tray. Her probes and forceps and retractors lay on a metal dish Greta recognized after a moment as the one that normally went under the toast rack, dish and instruments steaming gently from the boiling water—and beside them was an empty basin with a clean tea towel draped over it. Everything was very, very neat, as if he had done it many times before. As if he'd had practice.

"Since when are *you* a scrub nurse?" she asked, nodding for him to set the tray down. "I mean—thank you, this is exactly what I need, I appreciate it, and if you could hold the light for me I'd appreciate that even more."

"*De rien*," said Ruthven, and went to fetch her penlight.

A few minutes later, Greta held her breath as she carefully, carefully withdrew her forceps from Varney's shoulder. Held between the steel tips was a piece of something hard and angular, about the size of a pea. That metallic, sharp smell was much stronger now, much more noticeable.

She turned to the tray on the table beside her, dropped the thing into the china basin with a little *rat-tat* sound, and straightened up. The wound was bleeding again; she pressed a gauze pad over it. The blood looked *brighter* now, somehow, which made no sense at all.

Ruthven clicked off the penlight, swallowing hard, and Greta looked up at him. "What *is* that thing?" he asked, nodding to the basin.

"I've no idea," she told him. "I'll have a look at it after I'm happier with him. He's pushing eighty-five degrees and his pulse rate is approaching low human baseline—"

Greta cut herself off and felt the vein in Varney's throat again. "That's strange," she said. "That's *very* strange. It's already coming down."

The beat was noticeably slower. She had another look at his blood pressure; this time the reading was much more reasonable. "I'll be damned. In a human I'd be seriously alarmed at that rapid a transient, but all bets are off with regard to hemodynamic stability in sanguivores. It's as if that thing, whatever it is, was directly responsible for the acute inflammatory reaction."

"And now that it's gone, he's starting to recover?"

"Something like that. *Don't* touch it," Greta said sharply, as Ruthven reached for the basin. "Don't even go near it. I have no idea what it would do to you, and I don't want to have two patients on my hands."

Ruthven backed away a few steps. "You're quite right," he said. "Greta, something about this smells peculiar."

"In more than one sense," she said, checking the gauze. The bleeding had almost stopped. "Did he tell you how it happened?"

"Not really. Just that he'd been jumped by several people armed with a strange kind of knife."

"Mm. A very strange kind of knife. I've never seen anything like this wound. He didn't mention that these people were dressed up like monks, or that they were reciting something about unclean creatures of darkness?"

"No," said Ruthven, flopping into a chair. "He neglected to share that tidbit with me. Monks?"

"So he said," Greta told him. "Robes and hoods, big crosses round their necks, the whole bit. Monks. And some kind of stabby weapon. Remind you of anything?"

"The Ripper," said Ruthven, slowly. "You think this has something to do with the murders?"

"I think it's one hell of a coincidence if it *doesn't*," Greta said. That feeling of unease hadn't gone away with Varney's physical improvement. It really was impossible to ignore. She'd been too busy with the immediate work at hand to consider the similarities before, but now she couldn't help thinking about it.

There had been a series of unsolved murders in London over

the past month and a half. Eight people dead, all apparently the work of the same individual, all stabbed to death, all *found with a cheap plastic rosary stuffed into their mouths*. Six of the victims had been prostitutes. The killer had, inevitably, been nicknamed the Rosary Ripper.

The MO didn't exactly match how Varney had described his attack—multiple assailants, a strange-shaped knife—but it was way the hell too close for Greta's taste. "Unless whoever got Varney was a copycat," she said. "Or maybe there isn't just one Ripper. Maybe it's a group of people running around stabbing unsuspecting citizens."

"There was nothing on the news about the murders that mentioned weird-shaped wounds," Ruthven said. "Although I suppose the police might be keeping that to themselves."

The police had not apparently been able to do much of *anything* about the murders, and as one victim followed another with no end in sight the general confidence in Scotland Yard— never tremendously high—was plummeting. The entire city was both angry and frightened. Conspiracy theories abounded on the Internet, some less believable than others. This, however, was the first time Greta had heard anything about the Ripper branching out into *supernatural* victims. The garlic on the walls of Varney's flat bothered her a great deal.

Varney shifted a little, with a faint moan, and Greta returned her attention to her patient. There was visible improvement; his vitals were stabilizing, much more satisfactory than they had been before the extraction.

"He's beginning to come around," she said. "We should get him into a proper bed, but I think he's over the worst of this."

Ruthven didn't reply at once, and she looked over to see him tapping his fingers on the arm of his chair with a thoughtful expression. "What?" she asked.

"Nothing. Well, *maybe* nothing. I think I'll call Cranswell at the Museum, see if he can look a few things up for me. I will, however, wait until the morning is a little further advanced, because I am a kind man."

"What time *is* it?" Greta asked, stripping off her gloves.

"Getting on for six, I'm afraid."

"Jesus. I need to call in—there's no way I'm going to be able to do clinic hours today. Hopefully Anna or Nadezhda can take an extra shift if I do a bit of groveling."

"I have faith in your ability to grovel convincingly," Ruthven said. "Shall I go and make some more coffee?"

"Yes," she said. Both of them knew this wasn't over. "Yes, do precisely that thing, and you will earn my everlasting fealty."

"I earned your everlasting fealty last time I drove you to the airport," Ruthven said. "Or was it when I made you tiramisu a few weeks ago? I can't keep track."

He smiled, despite the line of worry still between his eyebrows, and Greta found herself smiling wearily in return.

CHAPTER 2

Neither Ruthven nor Greta noticed when something that had been watching them through the drawing room window for some time retreated, slipping away before the full light of dawn could discover it; nor were there any passersby there to watch as it crossed the road to the river and disappeared down the water stairs by the Submariners' Memorial.

In the early hours of that same Monday morning, the owner of a little corner grocery shop in Whitechapel came down to unlock the steel security grates over his display window and start preparing for the day. He had just rolled the grates up when he saw something in the street that at first he thought to be a stolen department store mannequin; on closer examination it turned out to be the body of a naked woman, her eyes nothing but raw red holes, with something pale spilling from her gaping mouth. He didn't look closely enough to make out that this was a cheap plastic rosary: as soon as he'd finished being sick, he stumbled back inside and rang the police. By the time most people were awake, it was plastered all over the newsfeeds: RIPPER STRIKES AGAIN! DEATH TOLL RISES TO NINE.

A few streets away from the grocer's shop and his unpleasant early morning discovery was the tiny office sign of Loders & Lethbridge (Chartered Accountants), one floor up from Akbar Kebab and an establishment offering money transfer and check-cashing services. The Whitechapel Road accounting firm pre-dated its neighbors by approximately forty years, but times were tight all over, and it had been deemed wise to move the offices upstairs and let the ground-floor space to other businesses. This meant that the entire atmosphere of the firm was permanently permeated with the smell of kebabs.

Fastitocalon, who had worked as a clerk for the firm for almost as long as it had been around, didn't really mind the grease and spice in the air, but he did object to taking it home with him in his clothes. He'd made the best of it by demanding of old Lethbridge that he be allowed to smoke in his office. This Lethbridge had grudgingly permitted, mostly because he enjoyed the occasional cigar himself—and perhaps on an unconscious level because he'd found that keeping "Mr. Frederick Vasse" more or less content seemed to be correlated with fewer boils on the back of his, Lethbridge's, neck.

Lethbridge was actually one of the more accommodating employers Fastitocalon had known in his time. It wasn't all that easy to find someone willing to hire a middle-aged and unprepossessing person with an oddly greyish complexion and a chronic cough, even if reassured that he wasn't actually contagious. Lethbridge had overlooked the physical shortcomings and hired him because of his uncanny gift for numbers, which had worked out in everyone's favor.

As a general rule Fastitocalon did his best not to read people's minds, partly out of basic good manners and partly for his own sake—most people's thoughts were not only banal but *loud*—but he knew perfectly well what Lethbridge thought of him. When he thought of Frederick Vasse at all.

Right now, for example, Lethbridge was thinking very clearly *if he can't stop that goddamn racket I'm sending him home for the day*. Fastitocalon's cough never really went away, but there were times when it was better and times when it was worse. He had run out of his prescription antitussives and kept meaning to call his doctor to get more of them, but hadn't gotten around to it; the cough had been bad for several days now, a miserable hack that hurt deep in his chest no matter how many awful blue menthol lozenges he went through.

The thought of going home was really rather appealing, even if his flat was currently on the chilly side, and when Lethbridge came into his office a few minutes later scowling intently he argued against it—but didn't argue very long.

Ruthven moved through the empty drawing room, picking up the debris of first aid supplies scattered on the floor around the sofa, the discarded gauze-pad and alcohol-wipe packaging looking oddly tawdry in the light of day. He was very much aware of the fact that he had not actually been *bored* for coming up on ten or eleven straight hours now, and that this was a profound relief.

It had become increasingly apparent to him over the past weeks that he had, yet again, run out of things to *do*, which was a perilous state of affairs. He had staved off ennui for a while this time by first renovating his house again and then by restoring an old Jaguar E-type, but the kitchen was as improved as it was going to get and the Jag was running better than new, and he had felt the soft, inexorable tides of boredom rolling in. It was November, the grey end of the year, and November always made him feel his age.

He had considered going up to Scotland, moping about a bit in more appropriate scenery. Going back to his roots. There were several extremely good reasons *not* to do this, but faced with the spectre of serious boredom Ruthven had begun to let himself imagine the muted melancholy colors of heather and gorse, the coolness of mist on his face, the somewhat excruciatingly romantic ruins of his ancestral pile. And sheep. There would be sheep, which went some way toward mitigating the Gothic atmosphere.

Technically Edmund St. James Ruthven was an earl, not a count, and he only sort of owned a ruined castle. There had been a great deal of unpleasantness at the beginning of the seventeenth century that had done funny things to the clan succession, and in any case he was also technically dead, which complicated matters. So: ruined castle, to which his claim was debatable, almost certainly featuring bats, but no wolves. Two out of three wasn't bad, even if the castle didn't overlook the Argeş.

Ruthven wasn't much of a traditionalist. He didn't even *own* a coffin, let alone sleep in one; there simply wasn't room to roll over, even in the newer, wider models, and anyway the mattresses were a complete joke and played merry hell with one's back.

He took the crumpled wrappers into the kitchen and disposed of them. Having seen Varney properly installed in one of the guest bedrooms, and been reassured that his condition—while serious—was stable, Ruthven had spent a couple of hours looking through his own not inconsiderable library. The peculiar nature of the weapon Varney had described didn't fit with anything that immediately came to mind, but something about the *idea* of it was familiar.

Now, having killed a few hours, he judged it late enough in the morning to call August Cranswell at the British Museum, hoping to catch him in the office rather than somewhere in the complicated warren of the conservation department. He was rather more relieved than he would have liked to admit when Cranswell picked up on the third ring, sounding distracted. "Hello?"

"August," Ruthven said. "Am I interrupting something?"

"No, no, no—well, yes, but it's okay. What's up?"

"I need your help with a bit of research. As usual."

"At your service, lordship," said Cranswell, a smile in his voice. "Also as usual. What's the topic this time?"

"Ceremonial daggers. To be more exact, ceremonial daggers dipped in something poisonous." Ruthven leaned against the kitchen counter, looking at the draining board by the sink: Greta's surgical instruments lay side by side on the stainless steel, once more boiled clean. It had been a long time since he'd been called upon to sterilize operating tools, not since the Second World War, in fact—but the memory was still vivid in his mind seventy-odd years later.

Cranswell's voice sharpened. "What kind of poison?"

"We don't know yet. But the dagger itself is extremely peculiar."

"You are not being even slightly reassuring," Cranswell said. "What happened?"

Ruthven sighed, removing his gaze from the probes and tweezers and directing it at the decorative tile work on the walls instead. He sketched out the events of the past night and morning as briefly as he could, feeling obscurely as if the details ought to be communicated in person, as if the phone line itself was vulnerable. "Varney is stable, at least," he concluded, "and all the...foreign material... has been removed and taken for proper analysis. Greta says he should recover, but nobody knows quite how long it'll take, and she pointed out the rather obvious similarities between this business and the Ripper cases. But the dagger is why I'm calling you."

"Wow," said Cranswell, sounding somewhat overwhelmed, and then rallied: "Tell me everything you can. I don't have our catalog of arms and armor memorized, but I can go and look."

"Varney didn't get a good look at it—he described it as a spike, or a short weapon like a rondel dagger. But the blade itself was cross-shaped. Like two individual blades intersecting at right angles. I have no idea how one would go about making such a thing."

"I've seen something like that, but it wasn't a knife," Cranswell told him. "Lawn sprinklers have spikes like that to anchor them in the ground. I'm guessing your friend didn't encounter a ritual lawn sprinkler stake, however."

"The likelihood is slim. But if you could look through the daggers you've got hidden away and see if anything even close to this exists in your catalog, I'd appreciate it—but mostly I want you to check the manuscript collection."

"Manuscripts," Cranswell repeated. "You think this thing might show up in one of them?"

"It's the monk costumes. I can't get the medieval warrior-monk orders out of my mind, you know, taking up arms in the service of some flavor or other of god. Varney said they went on a bit about unclean creatures of darkness and purification and so on, which is difficult to credit in the modern age, but then again this whole wretched business is somewhat unbelievable."

"I'll have a look," said Cranswell. "If we have anything it'll be in storage; none of the manuscripts on display are likely to have anything useful to offer, but I'll check."

"Thank you. I . . . do know you're busy," Ruthven said, wryly. "I appreciate it."

"I could kind of use a break right now, actually. I'll call you this afternoon if I find anything, okay?"

"Splendid," he said. "If you aren't doing anything tonight and feel like being social, come over. I'll make you dinner in partial recompense for your time."

Cranswell chuckled. "Done," he said. "Any opportunity to avoid eating my own cooking, you know. Okay, I'll go see what we've got."

"Thank you," Ruthven said again, meaning it. He set the phone back in its cradle, feeling somewhat guilty at having dragged another person into this business but mostly relieved to have Cranswell's assistance and his access to a staggering number of primary sources.

Greta rubbed at the hollows of her temples, leaning against the lab bench and watching her ex-boyfriend twiddle knobs on his microscope. "Well?" she said.

"Well what?" Twiddle, twiddle. "How do you expect me to do any sort of analysis if you keep interrupting me to say 'well'? In fact I can't make out anything useful in this. Just looks like a sharp piece of silvery metal to me. I'll have to run it through the GC–MS." Harry sounded interested.

She came forward; after a moment he moved to let her have a look down the scope. As he'd said, it wasn't much use: a triangular fragment of white metal, presumably the tip of some kind of blade, with a weird greyish coating on bits of it. The coating was what worried Greta. Other than metal and blood, it had smelled sulfur-sharp and *familiar*, as if she'd been around that scent some time before, but she couldn't place it. And Varney's reaction to whatever it was had indicated a fairly complicated inflammatory response.

"*Can* you?" she asked. "Last time I had to get some spectrometry done I had to wait ages for my samples to be processed, there was a queue of several labs ahead of me, and anyway it must cost something awful."

"Maybe at King's College you'd have to wait, but this is the Royal London," Harry told her with a smirk. "As it happens we don't have a queue for the mass spec just at the moment and this is weird enough to be interesting, so I'm willing to take it on."

"You're magnificent," said Greta, straightening up. "Completely *magnifique*."

Harry laughed. "You didn't get any sleep at all, did you? I can tell. Go away and let me get on with my work. I'll ring you as soon as I get any results out of this mess."

She nodded, stifling another yawn, and collected her vast and untidy handbag. "Right. I'll be in touch, Harry, and thanks. I really do appreciate it."

He was already packing up the sample to prepare it for the gas chromatograph–mass spectrometer, and just nodded—the same annoyingly distracted little nod she remembered without love from the time they'd spent together. Greta shoved her hands into her pockets and headed out of the laboratory, making a conscious effort to think about something—anything—else.

Greta's personal life was practically nonexistent, given the demands of her career, and in any case it had been a losing proposition trying to date someone completely outside the world she worked in. She had had a handful of relationships in her adult life, none of them lasting more than a few months and all of them largely unsatisfactory. It was difficult to keep coming up with new and inventive cover stories for her day job, for one thing, and while she defaulted to *I run a private clinic for special-needs patients* and relied on doctor-patient confidentiality to avoid having to discuss what it was she actually did, Greta found the effort of it exhausting. She had allowed Harry to think that the nature of her clinic tended toward the discreet treatment of diseases one simply did not talk about, but dinner-table *how was your day* conversations had been a daily minefield to negotiate, and the benefits of being involved with someone had simply not measured up.

He was a useful acquaintance, however, and Greta had from time to time presumed on that acquaintance to get some lab work done—and been very, very glad that Harry didn't ask questions, particularly those starting with "why."

She made her way out of the lab building without paying much attention to her surroundings until she was outside again, looking up at the façade.

The original structure of the Royal London Hospital wasn't a particularly prepossessing building, made out of yellow-brown brick with some cursory pilasters stuck on the front in a stab at classical gravitas. Over the years new bits had been built on here and there, including a vast series of rectangular additions clad in blue glass that contrasted very oddly with the Georgian design of the original building. It was ugly but it was also clearly thriving, busy, and not relying on optimism and duct tape to keep going.

Her own clinic in Harley Street was about as spartan as you could get, and the only reason she was located in that particular hallowed realm at all was that her father had owned the property outright and left it entirely to her on his death, along with just about enough to pay the taxes. These days her neighbors were mostly other specialist clinics rather than the personal offices of famous and/or knighted medical men, but she was still very conscious of her own comparative unimportance. Premises in London's historic medical VIP area were a bit exhausting to live up to, especially when she couldn't afford to keep the place looking quite as glossy as the rest of the street, despite the protective illusion wards on the door. What money she could spare after expenses and upkeep went toward helping her more disadvantaged patients with necessities.

Greta let herself entertain a thoroughly idiotic fancy of building some modern blue glass boxes on the roof of the property to create a solarium for her mummy patients, and shook her head. Harry was right. She needed sleep.

She had called her friend Nadezhda Serenskaya early that morning to see if she could possibly take Greta's office hours for the day; Nadezhda, who was a witch and thus well acquainted with London's supernatural community, and Anna Volkov, a part-rusalka nurse practitioner, regularly stepped in to help Greta out, but generally with more notice. Now she took out her phone again and dialed the clinic.

It rang three times before Nadezhda came on the line, and Greta knew it would have gone to voice mail if she was with a patient, but there was still a stab of guilt at having to make her friends do the receptionist part of her job as well as the actual doctoring.

"Greta," Nadezhda said, sounding unruffled. "What's up?"

"Hey, Dez. At the moment, not a lot." She couldn't suppress a yawn. "Thanks again for stepping in on zero notice. How's it been so far?"

"Hush, you know I *like* the work, I'm glad to help. Pretty quiet, some walk-ins but mostly I'm amusing myself tidying up your sample cabinets and dusting your office, which is hilariously disorganized. Are you okay? What's going on?"

"I'm fine," she said. She could picture Dez bustling and had to smile. "I just didn't get any sleep last night—house call, and a bad one; it's something I've never seen before. I think we're out of the woods, but I'm waiting on test results."

"Which are going to take forever," said Nadezhda. "So you ought to go home and get some damn sleep while you can manage it. Don't worry about the clinic, everything's under control, and Anna says she can take tomorrow and the day after if you need them, I've called her already."

There was absolutely nothing in that statement that should make Greta want to cry, but much like Ruthven's latte art it tightened her throat nonetheless. She didn't *deserve* friends like these. "Thank you," she said, and was relieved to hear that her voice sounded entirely ordinary. "I'll...find something to eat, and then yeah, okay, I will go home for a little while. Thanks, Dez." What she really wanted to do was hurry back to Ruthven's to see how Varney was doing, but she knew perfectly well that Ruthven would call her if there was any change.

"No worries. You call me if you need anything, all right?"

"I will," she told the phone, and "Good-bye," and swallowed hard. This was fatigue and low blood sugar. Nadezhda was right: food first, and *then* rest.

With a sigh Greta turned and started off along Whitechapel Road. There was a fairly decent pub just a block away, the Blind Beggar, which ought to be able to provide her with some lunch; then perhaps she might actually have a chance to drive home and get some sleep.

It surprised her not in the slightest when this prospect became, once more, totally unattainable.

A familiar rattling cough from behind her made Greta stop and look back to see the grey figure of her most frequent patient: coatless, suit-jacket collar turned up and hat jammed over ears, trudging along glumly against the November wind. She said a few unladylike words and trotted back to Fastitocalon, nudging her way through midday shoppers.

"Fass, what the devil are you doing out in this weather without a coat? You sound dreadful."

"Thank you, I'm sure," he said, giving her a look. "What a nice surprise it is to see you, Dr. Helsing, as always you brighten up the day like a little ray of sunshine." Then he started to cough again, and whatever else he might have had to say was lost. It was an unpleasant sound, bronchial and sharp, almost like fabric being ripped.

Greta put her arm around him. "Right, enough of this, come with me." She propelled him briskly in the other direction, toward the nearest pharmacy, wishing to God she'd had another cup of coffee. He went biddably enough, although he did point out that people were staring at them. "I don't give a damn about staring," she said. "Look, sit down. I won't be long."